Baiting the Wolf

By A. P. Lawrence

To my wonderful family,
whose support has been unending.

The Known Lands of Bluewind

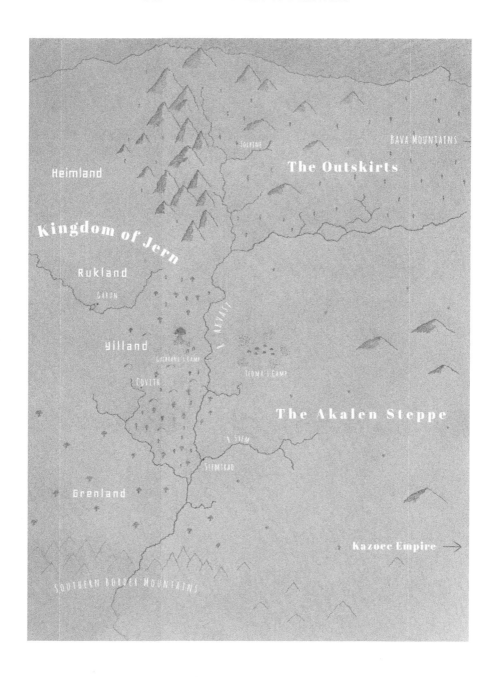

Chapter 1

Herleif crouched low to the ground, examining the tracks in the snow. They were thin and deep, made by the delicate ankle of a female.

Most importantly they were fresh.

He pressed three fingers into one of the tracks until he touched bare earth, frozen so hard it felt like rock. That was why she hadn't stopped, there was nothing to eat here.

Herleif stood up again, fur cloak hanging heavy over his broad shoulders. Being large for his age, hunting had not come easy, stealth was not his forte, but he now viewed that early handicap as a late advantage. Those that had taken to hunting more quickly didn't have to understand their craft to be proficient at it, but Herleif did. Every move had to be carefully planned, he had to know what his quarry was seeing, what it listened for, and how it thought. He'd fought hard for his skill, and now, at only sixteen winters old, was a better hunter than most.

He pushed a lock of dark hair out of his eyes and trudged on through the snow, shuffling in and out of the great red pines that stretched up into the sky around him. The tracks of his prey crossed over those of a boar, but they were old, the edges of the prints blunted by a now deceased wind.

A robin followed him as he walked, flitting down to investigate his own tracks now and again to see if he'd uncovered anything to eat under the snow, freezing whenever he turned to watch it. Its presence was a comfort, along with the noise of other birds arguing with one another overhead, high in the canopy. There wouldn't be that sort of activity if there was a Demon nearby. Silence was what he had to look out for.

You had to walk a long way from the village to find game, but that was the cost of permanent homes. Around his village the forest was stunted and empty, and aside from crows and rooks, most animals knew to stay away. He'd had to walk all morning to find these tracks, and only now, at the edge of the day, had begun to catch up with his quarry. Much longer and he would've had to abandon her, for the forest was no place to be after dark.

Abruptly he stopped. There she was, downhill from him and less than sixty feet away. He kept his eyes on her as he knocked an arrow to his bow.

She was a beautiful creature, one of the deep forest deer. Covered in thick fur, pale as the snow that surrounded her but for the flecks of brown hair running down her spine, ending at the tip of a long tail. She had her head down and was using small spiked horns scratch away the surface layer of snow. The delicate tools atop her head were not designed for that though, and she kept straightening up to survey her surroundings, before returning to the laborious task.

Herleif made sure not to move unless she had her head down, for those big brown eyes were tuned to movement. He was a hunter though, he knew how to be patient.

Wind flicked the hair away from his face, exposing his own eyes which were the blue grey of river ice. That meant she couldn't smell him either. He waited until her head was buried in the snow before pulling back on the string of his bow, loosing an arrow into the air a moment later. It thumped into her side and she wobbled off her feet into the cold, her legs suddenly failing her.

He sprinted over to her wheezing body, shouldering his bow and drawing his knife as he did so. Dropping down onto his knees, his blade found the tender spot between her forelegs, and a few moments later she was gone. He allowed himself to whisper a thanks to the forest, an old tradition, but one that comforted him.

He was unsure how long he'd be able to hold onto this prize for, the other boys at camp usually managed to steal any big game that he returned with, so he cut out the pieces he could eat raw and held a skin to the wound in her side to catch the blood. Once he began to eat, his hunger caught up with him, and now that he'd stopped walking the cold began to seep through his clothes. He finished what he could before tying her legs together and slinging the kill over his shoulder.

It had begun snowing now, and the wind had picked up, making the trees groan high above him, warning him home.

Snowflakes matted his hair as he walked, before melting and cooling his head. He knew he shouldn't have stayed out so long, but it had been weeks since he or Fin had eaten a meal comprised of anything other than old rations of mutton, or rabbit, and there was rarely enough to fill either of their bellies.

The trek back to the village wasn't as long as he'd expected, he'd forgotten how slowly he moved when following prey. Taking in every detail of the landscape, constantly assessing how close the prey was and trying to stay silent were all factors that slowed the pace. Even walking with a carcass on his back he was twice as fast as his stalking speed.

It wasn't long before the familiar signs of his home returned. The trees were smaller and sparser, the birds were quieter, and it smelt worse. He was reminded again that these were not really his people. These people were farmers, unclean, and disrespectful.

He was so deep in thought, head down, marching along, that he almost walked into right into Fin.

"You're back late," his brother quipped, smiling broadly at the deer on Herleifs' back.

Fin was three winters younger than Herleif, and his opposite in build. Where Herleif was broad and tall, Fin was wiry and small. Like Herleif, he had long hair, but where Herleif wore his in a shaggy mess below the shoulder, Fin's hair was tied at the back of his head and braided neatly down his spine.

The joke had caught Herleif at the wrong time. "You try carrying it then," he said as he lumped it over at Fin, who had no choice but to catch the deer in his arms, almost toppling over to steady himself.

"Anyway, why are you out here and not at the hut, thought I'd be getting back to a stew?" Herleif said, now noticing a red mark under his brother's eye.

Fin bit the inside of his mouth, "Hok came over and took the rabbit I caught earlier, so I came out here to see if I could find anything else."

There was a hint of shame in Fins voice but Hok had taken food from them many times before, it no longer came as a surprise.

Herleif took a deep breath. Hok's father was one of the village leaders, not a reasonable man in the least, and Herleif knew better than to go picking fights with his son. A lost rabbit wasn't worth a week's food. He tried to ignore the mark Hok had put on his brother's face.

"Well they've lost out. You try and catch something else in case they get suspicious and we'll try and keep this one secret," he said, taking the deer back from a stumbling Fin and lifting it easily onto his own shoulders. His brother gave him a look of gratitude and stalked away to find some food.

Keeping his prize safe shouldn't have been difficult, for their hut was on the outskirts of Tolpine, their village, and beyond where the only road tracked in. They'd been living there for nearly ten winters and Herleif still hated it.

Located on the side of a shallow valley, it overlooked a small river that connected to the Runner many miles to the south. In the north, low, rough mountains cut into the sky, keen to blanket them in shadow during winter. The village was close enough to the Kingdom of Jern to fall under its rule, and far enough away that it afforded them next to no protection. They called this area the Outskirts, a frontier on which no progress could be made.

Herleif ducked through a small break in the outer wooden wall, an awkward move for most with a deer on their back, but his legs were strong, and he made it look almost easy. That dilapidated barrier, covered with ancient, swirling runes of protection, was the only reason he stayed. Beyond these walls, he wouldn't last a week. Demons prowled the forest, and too

10

many outlaws eked a living off lone traders and unguarded caravans. The village was not his ideal home, but at least it was safe.

Quickly he moved to his own hut, glancing about to make sure no one could see him and doing his best not to slip in the icy mud which covered the ground. He pushed through the door, and shouldered the deer onto the workbench. It was bright inside, and crucially, warm. Fin had probably put too much wood on the fire, but Herleif was in no mood to complain.

Shaking off his cloak he turned to warm his hands against the fire. Abruptly he was aware of movement outside his hut. The footsteps were too heavy for Fin, and he wouldn't be back so soon anyway. Herleif stayed very still until he heard a voice call out to him.

"Get out here, I know you're in there."

Herleif clenched his jaw.

It was Hok. He straightened up and turned to the door. As he wandered outside, as slowly and calmly as possible, he noticed Hok's reluctance to actually enter his dwelling. The knowledge that this pig of a boy was at least a little scared of him was enough to bring a smile to his face.

"What's got you in such a good mood?" Hok asked, narrowing his eyes. He was the only other boy in the village of a size similar to Herleif, but he was always hesitant to confront him without any friends about. His father's responsibilities meant he was often absent from his home, and the lack of attention seemed to have made an otherwise irritating character completely without morals. He had a handsome square face, short close-cropped hair, and currently four other boys milling around behind him.

"What do you want?" Herleif snapped, ignoring the question as the smile died on his face.

Hok did an involuntary glance to his left, checking his friends were still there, then lifted his head and smiled.

"Good weather for hunting isn't it?"

Herleif cringed.

I thought I'd been careful?

"It's awful weather for hunting. Tracks fill right up with snow," he said, keeping a calm face but feeling his cheeks flush with anger.

"Well, you must be pretty good at it then, seeing as you caught a whole deer." Hok said, taking another glance at his cronies, who were paying full attention to the conversation now that the topic of food had been brought up.

"Yes, I'm good," Herleif replied slowly, his hands balling into fists.

Hok wasn't quite brave enough to laugh yet but his smile was growing wider every second.

"You know what we want," he gestured to his friends around him, still keeping an eye on Herleif as he did so. "And we don't want to give your brother another beating, so just hand it over. You two don't need that much food anyway."

Herleif stared at the boy in front of him, ready to fight. He'd already planned what to do with every part of that deer. If he was careful with it he could make some of the meat last for months, and the hide could go toward mending some of Fin's clothes. There was no way he was giving that up to this boy.

"I think you're well enough fed. I caught this deer, so I'm the one keeping it," he snarled, almost shaking with anger now.

Just as Herleif finished speaking he caught sight of Fin, ducking through the same gap in the wall. He was returning with a rabbit, but had slowed down now, and was looking at his brother for instruction. Herleif shot him a glance that warned him to stay away, and luckily Hok didn't notice.

"I wasn't asking, Nomad," said Hok, his face a picture of smugness.

Herleif glanced over at Fin again, the mark under his eye was darker now, visible even from here. Hok must have been watching his eyes because he picked that exact moment to strike.

He smacked Herleif across the side of his head, causing him to stumble awkwardly, before attempting to follow up with a punch to the gut. Herleif was better in a brawl than Hok though, and he caught his arm, twisting it violently inwards as he knocked the other boy off balance and sent him sprawling into the mud, his rage lending him even more strength.

He'd made Hok look like a fool. That was a win.

Stop now.

He knew he should, but his anger had taken him.

As the other boy attempted to return to his feet Herleif kicked him hard in the ribs.

"Get off him, he's down!" came a shout from one of Hok's gang, but Herleif ignored him, looming over the other boy.

"My brother is half your size you coward," he spat, as he knelt and grabbed a fistful of Hok's tunic. There were warning bells going off in his head now, but he ignored them.

If I'd gone down, he wouldn't care. Why should I?

He twisted his fist into the material, lifting the other boy off the ground, knuckles butted up against his chin.

Then he used Hok's tunic as leverage to hit him in the face.

The other boy yelped in pain, blood immediately pouring from his nose. In panic he grabbed at Herleifs neck, but Herleif easily swiped his hand away and hit him again, harder than the first time.

Now the other boys were shouting, moving toward him, but he couldn't hear them. He wasn't really listening, he was focused on the enemy in front of him.

He cocked his fist back for another punch, staring into the other boy's terrified eyes.

Abruptly, Herleif felt a blow across his head, and his vision blurred.

Then he was tasting earth.

There was another blow, a kick, hard to his stomach, hard enough to make him retch. Another kick to his side and he felt a rib crack.

He couldn't tell which way was up.

Someone grabbed his hair, wrenching his head up, before smacking him across the face. Then his head was forced down into the slurry. Mouth, nose, eyes, all were enveloped by the freezing mud. Sharp cold bit his cheeks as he tried to buck, and muscle his way out, acting now from pure panic.

But there were more holding him down now. Hands on his head, his neck, across his back. There were too many holding him down.

He tried to breathe, but mud filled his mouth.

Cold continued to burn his face, and his limbs began to fail as he felt his strength fade.

***

Consciousness brought with it only pain.

Herleif wondered if it might have been a dream, but when he tried to open his eyes they felt raw, and his cheeks stung with every movement of his face.

He was in his hut, he could tell that from the hard bed, but it was colder than usual, and he seemed to be alone. Suddenly he thought of Fin and tried to sit up, but pain blossomed from his body as he did, forcing him back down.

"Don't move," came Fins voice. He'd been sat in the shadows of the room, but now he moved over to Herleif.

"Stay still. You aren't ready to get up just yet." Herleif recognised the worry in his brothers voice and wondered what had happened.

"Why isn't the fire lit?" he rasped, shivering under the thin covers of his bed. Speaking hurt his throat. In the gloom he could barely see Fin's face, but he could tell his brother was uncomfortable in the way he moved.

"After they beat you, Hok came in to take the deer. When he saw the fire, he filled it with snow. His friends threw our wood stores out into the slush. It's all soaked now..." his voice trailed off.

Herleif felt Fin look down at him, "I tried to stop them, I really did, but-"

"It's okay," he cut in. "There were too many of them. Wouldn't have done you any good if you had stopped them." he sighed.

They sat there in the dark for some time not speaking. Herleif thought about how much longer he would have to endure this sort of treatment. *How long* can *I endure it?*

"You should have walked away when you'd won," Fin said quietly, an undertone of anger in his voice. "His father gave him a beating after I'd dragged you inside; called him pathetic for losing to you. He's not going to forget what you did you know."

Fin paused, "He was down and you kept hitting him. If you'd just-"

"Walked away?" Herleif interrupted, feeling his anger rising once more. "I'm not going to roll over like a damn dog anytime someone wants something we have," He leant up despite the pain, grimacing. "If I didn't fight on our behalf, you wouldn't even be alive today!"

He tried to shout but his voice was weak, even so Fin flinched in the gloom.

Maybe he'd gone too far. He knew that wasn't fair, but before he could apologise Fin was up and walking out of the hut.

"I'll find some more firewood," he said in a quiet tone. Fin was out the door in a moment but Herleif still felt the cold rush in from outside, and shivered again.

Chapter 2

Herleif awoke earlier than usual.

It was freezing, and the fire had almost died, so he decided to get some firewood, going out alone and leaving Fin to sleep a little longer. The past few days he had returned to work, mucking out the few animals kept by the village and beginning work on fertilizing the fields. It was unpleasant, hard labour, but he had returned to full health quickly and most of the bruises he had sustained were now healed.

He didn't mind being alone, it gave him time to clear muddled thoughts, and as he pulled on his boot's he wondered about how different his life would have been if his father were still with them.

He pictured the man's face, bathed in the warm glow of fire, in a forest that had seemed friendly to a child's eyes. But it hadn't been friendly, at least not in Herleif's lifetime. Since The Akalen War, a great conflict between the Kingdom of Jern and the Akalens, the forest had been filled with the scattered spirits of lost warriors, stripped of their burial rights and consigned to roam through the trees, alone and dishonoured. Those that did happen upon the living tried to share their bodies, and in doing so warped their flesh into hideous forms. That was how Demons were born, and the Nomadic Lands were bursting with them.

No wonder his father had left them here. Unless you had an armed militia, walls were the only protection from Demons, and only children were allowed in, young enough that they could still assimilate into the culture of the Kingdom. Adults were left to the wilds.

Herleif wondered about the war, an event he had never seen, and had no part of, but which had moulded his life so drastically. If not for the Akalens perhaps he would be living comfortably in the heart of this great wilderness with his family. He pushed the dreams away and stepped out into the morning chill.

It was a clear day, the sun itself not yet visible, but the sky was painted a deep orange for its arrival. Hok hadn't bothered them since the day he stole the deer and Herleif hoped that would be the end of their fighting, but in truth it just made him more nervous.

As he fetched his felling axe from the heavy chest he kept outside, Herleif noticed there was some commotion coming from the main square. He didn't usually venture up there because as a Nomad it was better to stay scarce. But his interest was piqued, and he trudged up through the muddy road toward the Inn to see what was happening. Before he got there, he heard the distinct sounds of horses, which was strange as there were none stationed here.

He stopped at the corner of the smithy and peered round into the square, which was really just a muddy patch of open ground surrounded by the ramshackle buildings that made up the centre of the village.

Standing in the square, in front of the Inn, were a group of soldiers, all next to horses which had been hitched to a few flimsy wooden posts. The soldiers wore long, dark green surcoats that fell below their knees, over what Herleif recognised as gambesons, thick coats of cloth worn as armour. All of them carried spears, most had axes or long knives at their hips, and all had shields slung over their backs. Pale faces and light hair were a trait they shared with the villagers, quite different from Herleifs more coppery skin. Off to the side was a heavy wagon with two huge horses tied into it, presumably theirs as well.

What were they doing here? The Outskirts almost never saw officers from the Kingdom that ruled them, Jern was more preoccupied with expansion in the south than with a barren wasteland at the fringes of their rule.

He seemed to be the only one interested, for almost no one else was around. Usually strangers were mobbed out of curiosity, but the square was dead.

Standing a little way off in the shadows of the buildings Herleif decided to watch them for a while. He realised they were all younger than he had first thought, most looked a similar age to himself, or only a little older, and the way they handled themselves was strange as well. Despite the dress none of them looked quite as disciplined as he would expect.

Suddenly they all straightened up, as an angry figure left the Inn. This one was older than the others by a few years, a young man, and judging by their reactions, their senior. He was slightly taller than them but moved with the grace of a man half his size. Long pale hair was tied similarly to Fins, plaited neatly behind his back, but his most interesting trait was the runes tattooed on his neck and cheeks, for even at this distance Herleif could make them out relatively clearly.

"Another village unwilling to contribute anything," he sighed to a stocky soldier, who was holding himself more confidently than the others.

"My Lord, you told them it's Olvaldr himself asking?" the soldier replied.

What was a Lord doing way out here?

"Yes I did, it doesn't mean anything to them," the man said, waving his hand dismissively. "And why should it really? To say this place is under his protection is an insult to him and the Kingdom."

The soldier paused for a moment, "Are we heading home now then?"

The young Lord looked at the ground scratching his chin for a few seconds, like he hadn't heard him. Then he straightened up and smiled warmly.

"Yes, Gulbrand won't be happy but I suppose we've done our best. Let's get some supplies loaded into the wagon and head home."

They're recruiters.

Herleif wondered what had happened in the Kingdom to force a Lord into sifting through the Outskirts for soldiers. He also wondered why the village leaders hadn't asked anyone if they wanted to join up.

For a moment the world outside Herleif's village beckoned to him. He'd never left except when he was a child, and he'd all but forgotten those early days. Perhaps he and Fin could sign up, then once they'd served they could move out and live somewhere within the Kingdom. But what conflict would they be signing up for? There would be no guarantee they would survive their service.

His thoughts were interrupted by a punch in the ribs before a bag was pulled over his head, his arms suddenly restrained. He tried to struggle away, but was hit hard in the side of the face, dizzying him. Someone began to bind his wrists, and by the time he realised it was happening it was too late.

It was Hok. It had to be, there to finish the job. He tried to shout out, but someone stuffed and handful of snow up under the bag and into his face.

He didn't feel the blow that knocked him out.

***

Herleif drifted back into consciousness, head pounding, his body feeling raw and bruised again. He was sure they'd opened up his old wounds.

"Has he woken up?" the voice belonged to Hok, as Herleif had guessed, but he sounded nervous. Hok was never unsure of himself, he was one of the cockiest people Herleif had ever met. Nervousness worried him.

He opened his eyes to see the other boy pacing over to him. He realised they had tied him upright to a tree, tight enough that he couldn't move.

Hoks face was unsmiling. He looked somewhat deranged and was covered in marks that were not made by Herleif.

"Oh yes he is awake," Hok said, licking his lower lip, which had been split. "I was worried they'd beaten you to death, but now you've woken up you're looking very…" he paused, losing his trail of thought.

"Let me out of here now," Herleif cut in. They were in the forest, a dark part of it where the trees seemed to loom over them. Herleif didn't recognise the place but it was near silent, and he couldn't hear any sounds of the village. Something else was off about the situation but he couldn't pin down what exactly it was, his head was still swimming from the ambush. Only two of Hok's friends were visible now, but he guessed the others were either behind him, or on watch.

They all looked nervous..

"No, I'm not going to do that," the boy hissed. He still had a black eye from where Herleif had hit him the other day, and Hok caught him looking.

"You made me look like a fool last time I saw you, do you remember? Throwing that cheap shot whilst I wasn't looking."

Herleif tensed against the rope, clenching his jaw. Everyone knew that wasn't what had happened, but Hok's gang murmured their agreement anyway. There wasn't much point arguing, but Herleif couldn't help it.

"That wasn't what happened," he growled.

Hok slapped him across the face. The blow wasn't particularly powerful, but it caught Herleif by surprise and he winced, feeling it begin to sting in the cold.

"Just get on with it," one of the other boys snapped. He was a skinny creature, a winter or so younger than Herleif with a crooked face and thin red hair. Herleif recognised him as a regular but of Hok's jokes, and he looked exceptionally scared out here in the forest. He was facing the trees, his head cocking and twitching like a sparrow. Something was still off, but Herleif was so angry he was struggling to concentrate.

"No, no," Hok replied. "We're going to make him apologise for what he did to me first."

As Herleif watched, he pulled out a knife from under his winter coat, an oversized thing, it looked more ceremonial than practical, but it was wickedly sharp and he was in no position to defend himself.

"We need to get out of here, someone's coming I know it," said the boy with red hair.

This time Hok rounded on him angrily, "Don't interrupt me again," he said, pointing his knife at the boy. "Or you'll be next!"

The words fell flat in the silence that followed.

The red haired boy looked at Hok with more surprise than fear, and Herleif sensed the others withdraw from him as well. Only when all eyes were off him did Herleif realise what had been bothering him.

It was silent. And not the usual calm of the forest, but a dead, lifeless absence.

He began to panic. This had happened to him a few times before when he was out hunting but he'd always been able to move, to follow the creatures that fled, weave his way back to the village. Here he suddenly felt a lot more helpless.

"I know we have our quarrels Hok," Herleif tried to reason, forcibly controlling his voice so as not to let his anger show. "But we need to get out of here, now. Cut me down, challenge me to a Kala'Tam when we get back, whatever you want, but there's something coming."

Hok turned his head slowly, looking at Herleif with utter contempt.

"I agree with the Nomad," said another boy.

Hok turned around, "I decide what we do, and we aren't leaving yet! Not until this scum apologises to me and we bleed him dry!" he screamed the words at his gang, a picture of madness as spittle flew from his mouth. He really had lost it, and the other boys sensed it too. Herleif realised his power was slipping within the group, none of them seemed keen on murder, especially if they were caught by whatever was with them in the forest.

"Cut me down now!" Herleif shouted, the veins on his forehead standing out as he strained against his bonds. He was shaking not from anger now but from panic, he could feel the presence of something dark.

"Shut up!" screamed Hok. "In fact, I'm going to permanently shut you up," he said and with that he marched over to Herleif gripping his dagger with white knuckles.

Herleif glanced at the other boys, desperately searching for some sign of empathy. They all looked uncomfortable, but he realised that none of them were going to stand up to their leader.

Hok grabbed Herleif's throat and held the knife level with his mouth, the other boy's face so close to Herleif's own that he could smell his breath. The blade pressed against the skin of his cheek.

Someone screamed.

It was only for a moment, but it was the sort of noise that brought on gooseflesh and made the spine tingle. It was ended so abruptly Herleif wondered for a moment if he had imagined it.

There was silence, and then a howl. When Hok turned to look behind him Herleif wished he hadn't.

The red haired boy was lying in a crooked mess in the snow, eyes wide open, but with nothing behind them.

Something hideous towered over his corpse.

The air seemed darker around the creature, as if even the light wanted to avoid its deformed body. Standing on four legs it was easily of a height with Herleif, taller if you included its bony crest. It looked as though it may once have resembled a great Boar, and he guessed that's what the original host was, but it had been changed. Where once its body would have been sleek and smooth, its hair was now tattered, exposing chunks of raw skin that oozed puss and blood. Herleif knew this was the curse of confining two souls to one body, unmatched strength, but with it a deep rotting of the core, and a turmoil of the mind.

A Demon.

As Herleif watched, it charged at another boy with its tusks lowered, a foul, heavy saliva falling from its maw as it did. The boy was still frozen in shock, and the Demon gored him with its tusk, flailing its head around madly until he went quiet.

It walked with an unnatural jarring gait, its body shivering violently as though every movement was painful and fought for, and slowly, it opened its mouth, revealing massive square teeth, which then crushed the boys limp body.

Herleif thought he was going to be sick.

Suddenly the ropes around him loosened. Hok still had a hand on Herleifs shoulder but he didn't notice, he was watching in horror as his friend was devoured by the monster. Once Herleif had shrugged off enough of the rope he swiped Hok's hand away from his shoulder and punched him in the gut, sending Hok to the floor gasping.

A boy appeared in front of him, glancing at Hok only for a moment as Herleif hurriedly untangled the rest of the rope.

"We let you free, now help us!" the boy whispered urgently, wide eyes boring into Herleif's own as two other boys, previously out of earshot, appeared next to him. Only then did he realise why they had helped him.

They think I can do something about this.

Part of him wanted to laugh, but he was too afraid.

"Run, that's all you can do," he said, and sprinted into the trees, instinctually following the tracks the boys had left when they'd captured him.

He was alone in his flight, and as he ran the boys cursed him, before yelling at one another, split between helping their friends and saving themselves. They joined him in his retreat too late, and more screams followed him as he ran.

He felt sympathy for some of them, caught up in a bully's petty squabble, but he was not about to risk his life for theirs. Against a demon he had no weapons. He ignored the terrible noises that dogged his steps and focused on the ground ahead. His back was slick with sweat despite the chill in the air, and tears ran down his face. From fear or pity he didn't know, he just kept running.

Another cry forced him to look around. He regretted it immediately.

Far off he could see the virgin snow stained scarlet with the blood of his captors. The demon had injured most of the boys mortally and was now methodically following the survivors, sniffing them out and squealing loudly as it finished them off, using its massive jaws to crush them into silence.

Herleif watched one boy who was unable to walk, put up a hand in a final pathetic effort to stop the monster. He screamed as his hand was devoured, the bones cracking loudly in the jaws of the beast. Herleif looked away before it moved on to the rest of him, but that wasn't who had yelled out.

He noticed movement. Between him and the Demon, was Hok.

He was in a sorry state. Staggering toward Herleif, one arm hung limply by his side, the fingers dripping blood from an unseen wound. He had a gash on the side of his head and his limp was testament to another injury.

"Please, get help," he pleaded.

The demon seemed to hear and raised its head slowly, a stuttering, mechanical motion, the eyes searching the forest for the boy. Herleif saw its eyes, pools of black centred with white. He could see pain, but also a sadness that unsettled him, for it was so human.

He stared at Hok for a moment.

The other boy was much closer to the Demon than Herleif, and it had definitely seen him now.

Slowly Herleif shook his head.

Hok's eyes widened and he began screaming, drawing the creature like a moth to a flame.

Herleif ignored him, turned, and ran.

Chapter 3

Herleif sprinted back to camp, heart hammering in his chest.

He ducked through the wall and headed for his hut, mud spraying up against his boots as he ran. When he got there he barely slowed, barging through the door panting as his eyes frantically assessed the room.

The day was still early but Fin wasn't in, he was probably out collecting firewood. Herleif would find him soon, first he had to move.

Sweeping away the thick rushes covering the floor he exposed a little hollow which he opened, exposing a meagre collection of coins and some blustone spearheads that had belonged to his father. He gathered them up and stuffed them into a pack along with some other items he owned and a few of Fins belongings he knew his brother couldn't do without, like a collection of fishhooks that had been used only a handful of times.

You left him to die, a voice in Herleif's head suddenly accused him.

It had to be ignored. What could he have done anyway? There was no fighting that creature.

Despite his innocence he had to fight off tears.

After he'd filled one bag, he went outside to collect up some of his tools from the chest he kept there. He was so focused on his task that he didn't notice Fin watching him.

"What are you doing?" his brother said in a wary tone, making Herleif jump.

He couldn't meet his brothers eyes, "We have to leave," he said, grabbing his spare axe. He wasn't sure what had happened to his other one, the boys must have taken it when he was attacked. They might have kept it, but he would not be going back to check.

"What? Why?" Fin said, suddenly glancing around nervously.

"We have to leave now, I'll explain everything when we're on the road, we might be too late as it is."

Herleif didn't have time to explain, all he knew was that the blame was on him. Almost half the young men had disappeared into the woods, all of them had been killed and the only tracks leading out belonged to Herleif, the only survivor. It would look like murder to the villagers, and he was a Nomad, that would be reason enough. Hok's father was sure to have known what his son had been planning, he may even have suggested it to him. Once he realised what had happened Herleif would likely be killed on sight. A trial was out of the question.

You did leave him to die.

Herleif pushed those thoughts away for the second time, he could wallow in his pity later, but that luxury was not one he could afford just yet. He had to get away, if only for Fins sake. He'd already let him down enough.

"Are we coming back?" Fin said, his face a mask.

Herleif shook his head, studying his brothers face for a reaction.

Fin nodded, giving nothing away.

They both went inside, and Fin began helping Herleif pack their things. He gave him a few sideways glances but to his credit, asked no more questions. Once they had packed, they moved out into the village.

It was still early, but people were moving about now, drawn out by the rising sun. Together the two boys walked quickly through the square and onto the main road, a muddy track used more by wildlife than people. Herleif would have liked to have left without witnesses, but it didn't make any difference, when people realised they were gone the outcome would be the same.

When the village was out of sight Herleif began giving Fin details about what had happened. He left out the part about leaving Hok behind.

Still, by the time he was done, they were both running.

Lord Brynjar was happy to be going home.

He hadn't enjoyed his time on the fringes of the Kingdom, scouring the Outskirts, searching for willing recruits to help defend a border so far from home.

Few had joined up. It annoyed him, but he understood. He probably would have done the same in their position. And it was hardly the threat of the century, a village destroyed, some innocents killed yes, but that was nothing new for a frontier region like Yilland, and certainly nothing new for the Akalens. The Kingdom had been there less than three generations, and borders took a while to consolidate.

He himself wouldn't have answered Lord Gulbrand's call to arms if it wasn't for his father, Alvard, the Lord of Rukland, who had been keen for him to go. It was good experience in leadership, and an opportunity to see some action without too much risk. His father had always been keen that he keep up with the goings on of the other territories, and this affair would certainly keep him up to date.

At first the idea had appealed to him, but he hadn't been in Yilland for more than a week before he was sent out on a mission.

King Olvaldr had not thought the Akalen threat serious enough to call his banners, and indeed neither had Brynjar's father, who, despite having the largest count of men to call upon in the entire Kingdom, had not offered aid in any form other than his son. That meant the only region Gulbrand had to call upon to boost his force was The Outskirts, a place with no Lord.

The task of recruiting was up to Brynjar. After two months of dragging his men through this dangerous, frozen area of the world, two of his soldiers had been killed by raiders and he'd managed to recruit a total of eighty-four men to the cause, along with over double that number in malnourished boys pretending to be old enough to sign up. He'd taken them on without losing much sleep, their prospects as soldiers in a minor border dispute were significantly better than their future in this cursed place.

Brynjar did worry about the state of the army Gulbrand was raising however, there were scarce men of proper fighting age and almost none with experience. A smile came to his lips as he realised that included himself.

At each village he had armed the recruits, put a few of his own men in charge of them, and sent them back south to Yilland, Gulbrands country. The village he was leaving behind him had been the last one on his list, and now Brynjar had only a few weeks of travel before he would be back in his preferred, warmer climate.

He shivered and patted his horse. She was a large thing, mostly white but spotted with blotches of black, with long hair about her hooves. She was not built for speed, but she could endure the worst weather the Outskirts could throw at them, and he had grown fond of her over the months they'd been trekking together.

Most of his men were trailing behind him, next to the supply wagon, as they ambled their way along the narrow muddy track. He had two riding up ahead, scouting for any one of the many dangers in this forest. He'd grown more cautious since the bandit attack, for it had been his first taste of losing men under his command, and he had not enjoyed it.

"Sir we've got some people trying to chase us down," his squire Ojak said, interrupting his thoughts.

Abruptly Brynjar was on alert, his hand instinctually going to the hilt of his sword as he turned to study the trees around them, wary of a trap. He wasn't wearing any gloves and the mail of his hauberk was cold against his wrists.

"Ready yourselves," he barked, "I'll find out what they want, you lot keep an eye on the trees."

He kicked his horse back the way he'd come and turned her, so they were side on to the pursuers. She was so big she almost blocked the track the whole way across.

Brynjar watched two figures, a man and a boy, running toward him along the track, large bags bouncing against their backs as they did. His guard was still up and he called out to them.

"Stop there or I'll draw," he shouted, in his most authoritative tone. The figures stopped, both of their hands held open at their sides to show they were unarmed.

"Come over here, slowly," Brynjar said.

"We aren't bandits, or raiders," the larger one said, for Brynjar now realised that he was not yet a man.

"Then why are you following us?"

As the boys drew closer he began to relax. Their faces were young, and he recognised from their tanned skin they were Nomads, or descendants of. Both looked panicked and red faced, and the smaller one kept checking behind him.

"We want to sign up," the larger boy said, swallowing. He might have just passed for a man, but his companion was clearly too young. Still, they intrigued him.

"What are your names?" Brynjar said. He didn't have to shout anymore as they were now only a few feet away.

"I'm Herleif, and this is my brother Fin."

Neither of those were Nomad names, but he wasn't surprised, many Nomads had given their children names from the Kingdom to help them better merge with the culture that had eclipsed them.

"Why didn't you sign up earlier?" Brynjar said, probing. At this point he didn't feel in danger, but he could tell they were in trouble, and he wanted to find out exactly what sort.

"Well…" the larger boy said, faltering for a moment. "We, didn't realise you would be leaving so soon."

It was a blatant lie, and Brynjar saw through it easily.

"Have you stolen anything?" he said, staring at the boy.

"No."

He wasn't lying.

"Have you killed anyone?"

There was a twitch in the boy's face, he looked away for a moment, and there was a small pause.

"No."

Brynjar drew his sword.

Immediately Herleif was in front of his brother, moving back from Brynjar's blade, terrified but still hesitant to leave. Brynjar stared hard at the boy. He saw desperation above all else.

"Tell me the truth," he commanded, making the alternative clear with the glint of his weapon.

The boy stared at Brynjar's sword and then took a deep breath.

"I didn't kill anyone, but that doesn't matter to them," he gestured behind him at the village. "They'll say I did." He paused, "My brother won't last here without me."

Brynjar noticed the smaller boy shift uncomfortably, obviously ashamed, but he didn't correct him.

He realised that once again Herleif was telling the truth. Whatever had happened, it sounded like it wasn't up to him, and it wasn't hard to believe that two Nomad children would receive unfair treatment out here. Their history with the Kingdom was complicated at best.

"Tell me."

Herleif shifted uncomfortably, looking at the ground, "I got into a fight with the son of a village leader a while back, and I beat him. In revenge he and his friends ambushed me. They were going to kill me."

The boy paused, remembering something unpleasant.

"There was a Demon," he said. "It, killed them, but I escaped. I was the only one." When he looked up his eyes were bloodshot and angry.

Brynjar pondered that for a moment, letting his sword hang by his side. He noted the way Herleif stood, right in front of his brother, ready to absorb any punishment either might receive. Brynjar had felt that care before, he'd had a brother once.

By all rights these boys should have been handed back to their village for due punishment. These hostile territories had a right to their own council, and the Nomad may well have been lying. But Brynjar didn't think he was, and he didn't believe the judgement these boys would receive was likely to be fair. There was an odd kind of responsibility he felt for them, he was their lifeline after all, and sending them back would be the same as killing them himself.

He sheathed his blade and saw Herleif relax somewhat.

For all the mystery surrounding them, something about the pair made the young Lord smile. It might have been their boldness, or how much he was reminded of his own kin. In truth he didn't know.

"Am I the last resort then?" he said, a little amused.

Herleif looked wary.

"Our father fought in the war against the Akalens, we would be honoured to do the same," he said, dodging the question neatly.

Brynjar turned around and called to his men.

"Lads, we've just picked up two new recruits."

Chapter 4

A week of trekking was beginning to take its toll on Fin. He'd never spent so much time on the road, and never with so many people.

He adjusted himself on his mount. Riding was chafing his legs again.

They'd woken early to the usual bitter cold. Off the road snow still covered the ground, but it was steadily getting warmer the further south they went. The days seemed longer, and the sun was more hesitant to vanish than in the north.

Brynjar was at the head of the group, as was usual, but this time Herleif, and Ojak, Brynjars second in command, had been sent ahead to scout. Fin was at the back of the group as usual, and, though it wasn't out of choice, he did like being there. From the rear he could listen to the other boys talking and joking with one another, but didn't have to speak himself. That was better for him, he had little experience with people his own age.

They'd been allowed to ride the two horses of soldiers who had been killed in a bandit attack, and, though he was grateful of that fact, he'd never been on horseback before.

To his brother, like so many things, it had come easily. He'd been able to control the animal almost immediately and was already a passable rider. Fin however, could barely get his horse to keep pace with the rest of the group without it diving off to one side to investigate a smell, or take a bite from the soggy brown grass that sprouted at the sides of the road.

He'd tried kicking it on like he'd been shown, but the animal barely noticed. The only thing that seemed to work with any kind of reliability was speaking to it very softly and feeding it carrots, but even then, half the time it would ignore him, and Herleif would have to get involved, much to Fin's embarrassment.

Being uprooted from home had not bothered him nearly as much as the daily reminders of his brothers' superiority. Herleif was already taller, stronger, and more confident, now he was also shown to be a better rider, better at making friends and more competent at the tests they had been asked to carry out.

On the second night after they'd joined Brynjar's group, the young Lord had wanted to see how competent they were at fighting, and Fin and Herleif had been forced to wrestle a few of the other soldiers.

They were all close to Herleif in age, and he'd done well, besting his opponents with only a few struggles. But Fin, smaller and not as strong as the older boys, had lost to every opponent he'd faced. At the end of the ordeal he was covered in bruises, though that pain was overshadowed by his embarrassment.

That was nearly five days ago, but the wound to Fins pride hadn't healed. Today, like all other days, he'd woken up even further from the only lands he knew, with people he wasn't sure he understood. He found himself looking behind him a lot, along the winding dirt tracks back toward the village. Even though it was long out of sight, part of him was still expecting to see angry villagers chasing him and his brother down. That image frightened him almost as much as the Demon's did.

That had yet to happen, and if it did he hoped Brynjar would speak for them, though he wasn't sure what exactly the young Lord had got him to sign up to. The parts of the conflict he'd heard from Brynjar and the other soldiers had been vague, and worryingly none of them seemed to know very much about what exactly was happening on the border.

He watched a Pixie Drakin buzz past, its slim, scaly body humming lazily through the air on gossamer wings. It was no bigger than one of Fin's fingers, and would be searching for the few insects that could survive the cold.

Abruptly the tiny creature caught sight of a beetle and seemed to wake up. With a burst of speed, it knocked the insect off its perch on a branch and began prizing open its armour with tiny claws. Funny that a creature so small could one day grow to be larger than his horse.

Fin sighed enviously. He hadn't even been able to go hunting, which was the one activity he was better at than Herleif. Though once his brother was strong enough to pull on the heavier bows, Fin had been overshadowed even in that. His own bow didn't have enough draw weight to punch arrows through the thick hides of the bigger creatures that dwelt the deep forest.

Still, he could track better than his brother, and that alone would calm him. He would relish being allowed to wander in the forest, in the quiet, with only his thoughts to keep him company. More and more he found himself envious of Herleif, and frustrated with his apparent disregard for his own abilities.

Given that strength, he'd be twice the hunter his brother was.

Abruptly his horse changed direction, pulling him from his thoughts as it veered off the muddy track they were following, down a small bank and into a clumpy bush, where it lowered its head and began grazing.

"What are you doing you stupid creature," Fin muttered, his cheeks reddening as he looked around to make sure no one was watching him.

"I didn't think horses even ate leaves."

Despite his worries no one had even noticed what had happened, and they were continuing up the track in front of him.

"Come on, lets go," he said, pulling gently on the reigns.

As the soldiers got further away he began to notice the quiet. All around him was a thick, dark forest, and thoughts of Herleif's Demon began to play on his mind.

Ahead of him a shadow moved through the trees.

He pulled on the reins again, trying to get his horse to budge. She didn't move an inch, continuing to feed.

Fin gave her a gentle kick in the flank, "Come on girl."

He fetched another carrot out of his saddlebag and leant forward to put it in front of her face, "Please can we go, I'll give you as many carrots as you want?"

With a whinny she lowered her head, pulling Fin forward by the reigns, and then flicked back up, headbutting him.

For a moment white dots flitted in front of his eyes, and he let go of the reigns, rubbing his head.

"You stupid animal."

He glanced back at the road, head still swimming. There was no sign of anyone, even the soldiers' laughs couldn't be heard now, the only thing punctuating the silence was the munching of his horse.

"Oh hells," he muttered, aware now of how easily he could be left behind. Again, he gave a gentle pull on the reigns, and again she lowered her head, though this time he was clever enough to let go when she did.

Desperation was setting in, and that led to anger, he didn't know these lands, or what was in them. Again a shadow moved in the trees ahead of him. It might have been a deer but the forest was so dimly lit he couldn't tell.

His breathing quickened.

He sat up straight, dropped the carrot and grabbed the reigns hard speaking loudly to his horse, "Stop eating or we'll be left behind!"

The horse slowly raised its head and turned away from the bush. Fin almost flinched with surprise.

Had it understood him?

"Can you understand me?" he asked tentatively.

Nothing happened.

Was I expecting it to answer back?

He felt like an idiot. Even so, maybe he was on to something.

"We're going back up to the road," he said with authority, kicking her on a little harder.

Slowly, the horse turned, and began to walk back toward the road.

If it would only listen to authority, Fin would speak with authority.

"Right, let's catch up with the others," he said sharply once they were up on the road, and gave her another kick.

Gently, she began to move, the slow plod he was used to. They were a long way behind now though, so he tried another command.

"Come on," he snapped. "Faster!"

Immediately she was at a gallop, Fin almost falling off her back with the sudden change of speed, but he held on tight. The sensation of galloping was terrifying, but he drank it in, a smile growing on his face as he flew past the trees.

Together they turned a corner, and Fin had only a moment to take in the scene before she skidded to a halt, throwing him from her back. He landed well, managing to absorb most of the impact in a half roll, but still skidded a little way, landing on his side and facing the way he'd just come. Behind him the horse had turned hard to its right and he could hear it galloping into the forest.

"Fin get off the road!" a voice cried out.

It sounded like Herleif's.

He couldn't tell where it came from, but he had bigger things to worry about.

Slowly, he propped himself up on one arm, and turned, his eyes on the road ahead.

He couldn't see any of the soldiers, but in the middle of the muddy track was an auroch corpse. A bull, and so fresh it had not yet been turned stiff by the cold.

Steam drifted from its open mouth, and standing over it, holding the corpse up by the throat, was a Khutaen Drakin.

Fin froze.

It was the size of a bison, but moved like a tiger, its body sleek and powerful, with thick shoulders and a rounded reptilian jaw. Its skin was covered with dappled white feathers that ran all the way down to a long tail, a tail which flicked curiously as it watched him.

This was the first time he had ever seen one, they were notoriously rare. Drakins seldom lasted long enough to reach that stage of development. Only a handful of Pixie Drakins would ever become Drakinhawks, and even fewer of those would become Khutaen. Once they had however, nothing dared oppose them, not even the Spoken Races.

Fin eyed its kill. The dead auroch was massive, with horns bigger than the span of a man's arms. Khutaen were fearless hunters, but auroch were huge, nothing in the forest matched them in size or strength. For one Khutaen to take it down was an immense feat.

Fin cursed his horse silently. He'd been doing so well with her up until that point.

Raising himself slowly into a crouch he began to back away.

The Khutaen stared at him with large, inquisitive eyes, and as Fin watched, a set of blue feathers, which he'd missed until now, began to flex on its back like the hairs of a cat.

It was an impressive display, and one that meant it felt threatened. Fin was aware of that and stopped again.

The feathers stayed upright.

Slowly, eyes never leaving Fin's, the Khutaen lowered its head and let the auroch drop to the ground.

"Just ru-" came the shout from one of the soldiers, the words disappearing into a muffle. At least one of his comrades had the sense to shut him up.

This time Fin realised where they were, hiding at the side of the road, behind thick trees and mossy boulders. He could see now the crumpled ferns where they had tracked off the road and into the forest. Brynjar and the others must have seen the Khutaen and been in the process of moving past it when Fin had come around the corner.

His looked back at the Drakin, knowing that if he turned to flee it would chase him down.

Its lips curled back, showing huge white teeth.

Fin once again tried to back away, but as he did so the creature began to growl. It was a deep noise, almost like a hum, but loud. He could feel the vibrations through his chest.

The Khutaen had not stopped looking at him, and now it placed one massive paw forward, starting toward Fin.

Immediately he went cold.

There was nothing he could do.

Even if all of Brynjar's soldiers were crazy enough to attack the Khutaen together, their odds of fighting it off were not high.

He kept eye contact as it stalked over. It was not afraid of him, but somehow, he sensed a hesitation there. A caution of some kind. Why a creature like that felt the need for any degree of caution toward him was a mystery, but its movements were slow and deliberate.

"What do you want?" Fin whispered.

The growl was loud enough now that Fin could feel it through the ground. The Khutaen was only ten feet away, but still it came closer. He could feel blood pounding behind his eyes.

He tried to take a breath, and couldn't.

Fear had gripped him with an iron fist. His lungs felt hot and empty.

It was five feet away now, the creature's eyes still boring into his own. It really was massive, he could feel the power radiating off the beast.

Three feet.

Two.

Without thinking Fin reached forward and placed a hand on the Khutaen's massive head.

For the briefest moment his world was transformed.

Warmth seeped into his bones, and the dark winter forest was splashed in colours that were more vivid than summer itself. He could see traces of life in every corner of the world, and he felt no fear. The effect was a bustling world of activity and life.

He *felt* different as well, for though the forest was soaked in colour it was dominated by smell, and feel, and gesture.

Something crashed into the trees ahead of him and abruptly the world was gone. He realised his eyes had been closed.

The Khutaen sprinted back toward the auroch, snatching up the kill between its jaws and dragging it away into the trees.

Fin sat back heavily on the road, stunned, trying to find his breath.

Once again he was cold, but now he felt blind and deaf as well.

Shakily he got to his feet.

"Are you alright?" Herleif asked, appearing in front of him and grabbing his shoulders tight. Fin could see the worry on his brother's face.

"I'm fine, just I felt odd for a moment," Fin said, brushing away his brother's hands. Herleif stared at him, then gave a relieved laugh.

"I thought you were finished there."

"Me too for a moment. What was that noise?" Fin said, rubbing his temple. His head was throbbing, and he felt weak from the encounter.

"Your brother. He saved you," came Brynjars voice as he walked out from the trees leading his horse, soldiers in tow. "You were lucky lad, if your brother hadn't of thrown that rock and distracted it, I think you would have been…" he paused, and then smiled. "Well it wouldn't have been good."

Fin nodded, feeling his cheeks redden. Once again he was playing the damsel in distress, and once again his brother had stepped in.

"Thank you," he said curtly. "I'm not sure I was in trouble though."

"I'm sure you would have been fine," laughed Ojak, walking forward and clapping him on the shoulder as he handed over the reigns to his horse. "Maybe try and keep up next time though?"

Fin nodded and took the reins.

"I will," he said. "But I didn't feel afraid, when it touched me something happened, the forest changed." He found himself struggling to explain what had happened.

"Drakins are an ancient race, we don't know everything about them," Ojak admitted, scratching his chin and staring down, looking very much like

Brynjar. "But I do know if your brother hadn't been here, you'd be dead."

Fin bit his tongue.

"Yes, maybe," he replied quietly, but Ojak didn't hear him, Brynjar had begun yelling at them to mount up before the Drakin returned.

Fin hopped up onto his horses back. She stood still, watching the others move off. "Come on girl," Fin said, giving her a kick.

She began to follow the group.

There was a lot of travel ahead of them, but Fin had a lot to think about.

Chapter 5

Dagtok tossed another log onto his fire.

The flames warmed his cheeks only a little, for it was bitterly cold.

Around him the trees danced with their puppet shadows, mocking his failure and his shame.

Pulling his cloak tighter around his neck, he managed to block some of the chill. He was a large man, good looking with a square face and a solid jaw. It had been several days since he'd shaved, and the beginnings of a rough beard were showing on his cheeks. He looked tired.

He was alone now, a dangerous thing out here, for Demons were almost impossible to hear at night. In the day, the absence of a vibrant forest was a glaring indicator of a Demon's presence, but at night everything slept. A monster could blend into the silence of a world abandoned by the sun.

Dagtok glanced behind him.

Nothing, as there had been every other time he checked. There was no crunch of snow and nothing moved. Only shadow.

He looked back into the fire, transfixed by faces he didn't want to see.

Closing his eyes earned him little respite. In his mind the gruesome corpses looked as clear as the first time he had seen them. Boys on the cusp of manhood, torn apart and left to freeze in the cold. The face of his son was vivid.

The fire cracked, and his eyelids snapped open. Dagtok would have flinched, but there was little left to fear in this life, he had been numbed by loss. His leg was aching now, an old injury that refused to heal and tormented him for walking. Massaging his thigh gave him a measure of relief, and he dug his knuckles into the taught muscle of his leg.

He closed his eyes again, remembering how his wife had cried when they burnt the body. She had soaked his chest with tears, squeezed his hands until they went white, and all the while he had stood, silent, watching the body of his son as it was consumed by the flames.

Hok was to be his legacy, and now he was ash.

The smell of burning flesh still lingered in his nose. He could still taste that acrid smoke. The dogs had whined and barked in anticipation of a meal, so sweet an aroma for them and such a bitter stench for himself. He had killed them out of anger, splitting their skulls with his axe, but even that had not satisfied him. It was then that he realised nothing other than the death of his son's killer would allow him peace. And so he had left, for vengeance.

A Demon had ended the lives of those boys, and of his son, that was for sure. Nothing else could have torn them open with such fury, but blaming a Demon for killing was like blaming the river for flowing. The Demon was not what he sought. Who had led Hok there, who had lured the boys into the depths of the forest where they knew Demons roamed? Only someone born of the forest.

Dagtok opened his eyes, looking up to the heavens.

The sky was black, and so was everything around him. The fire was the centre of his world. He still had firewood, but he was too tired to keep his little fire alive.

As the flames faded, the trees slowed their dance and the shadows closed in on him.

He stared into the embers, seeing the footprints again, clearly. One set of large prints, from a large boy, moving fast. They led away from the corpse of his son, back toward his village.

Back toward the empty house of the Nomads.

There would be no mercy for those who had stolen his legacy.

He sat there in silence until the fire had died, letting darkness engulf him.

42

***

Kiakra was uncomfortable.

She yawned and looked away from the fugitive's camp for a moment. She'd been lying in the dirt since midday, and now the sun was beginning to dip into the earth.

Twisting onto her back she stretched out, rolling her shoulders and feeling her bones cracking as they moved back into place. She yawned again and rolled onto her stomach, propping herself up on her elbows and feeling the familiar contours of earth that had been warmed by her body.

Ahead, vast, barren hills flowed across the landscape, covered in the dry yellow-green grass, which was almost the only thing that grew here. In the distance she could see the peaks of ancient mountains, worn down by time, but still just able to break the horizon, cutting into the orange sky. She couldn't name them, and they were too far off to be clear, but they had a lingering, eerie presence. In the north, dust had been thrown up by a large herd of game and now it drifted slowly across to the east, taken up by a gentle wind.

The Akalen Steppe was a harsh, empty place, but Kiakra could appreciate its beauty.

She shared many traits with this most ancient region of the world. Her warm, friendly face hid a ruthlessness that her actions did not, and her hands were slim, but worn and rough from heavy usage. The skin on her face and arms had been tanned dark by the sun, the result of a lifetime sleeping in the wild, and she had short, sand coloured hair which she tied in a neat bun on the top of her head. Her ears stuck out slightly, and that had earned her the nickname of 'Pixie' from her absent father, though it was a name no one else used.

A scar that ran from the left side of her jaw all the way down to her collarbone, and a nick out the top of her left ear were the only indicators of her difficult life. At only nineteen years old, she had already seen a lot.

She'd been lying in wait for a long time covered by her wolf skin cloak, watching the activities of the criminals below her. They'd chosen to camp against a crumbling dirt cliff, which was held up by a few gnarled old trees and gave them some meagre protection from the elements. It had also given Kiakra a perfect position to watch them from. Neither had shown themselves yet though, and she was getting impatient.

Just as she was about to ask for Tiko to take over the watch, a man came out of the hide tent. He was human, and fat, but in a slabby way that suggested he possessed a measure of strength.

Lax, target number one.

Kiakra dropped down onto her belly and peered at him through the grass.

She was glad she hadn't let Tiko take over, Kiakra was much smaller, and better at remaining unseen.

Reaching carefully to her side with a callused hand, she checked her bow for the hundredth time.

It was a small recurve design made from horn, and was brilliant both on horseback and for travel due to its small size. Slowly she picked it up, rolled onto her back and knocked a blunt arrow. She pulled back on the string awkwardly and loosed it off away from the camp.

Quickly she flipped over and checked Lax was still there. He seemed to be rooting around for something in his horse's saddlebags.

Kiakra heard shuffling coming toward her from behind.

"You want to be more careful where you're shooting that thing," said Aldrid, in a whisper that was barely below a shout.

Kiakra clenched her jaw and stuck a finger to her lips.

She'd forgotten it was Aldrid helping on this job.

"Sorry," he said, at a more tolerable volume, "What's happened?"

"Well," Kiakra said in an actual whisper, pointing down at the tent below them, "There are meant to be two of them down there, but so far I've only seen one."

Aldrid frowned, "The human or the Bavagai?"

Kiakra blinked and bit her lip, gesturing to the human man searching the saddlebags.

"Oh okay, so where's the big one?" Aldrid replied.

"I'm guessing still in the tent," Kiakra said. "He might have snuck off, but I think that's unlikely."

"I see," said Aldrid.

"Do you want to get into position then?" Kiakra asked, raising her eyebrows.

Aldrid nodded his head knowingly.

He had already forgotten their discussion.

"Oh for…" Kiakra clenched her jaw, trying not to swear at him.

Aldrid was a good man. He was more than twice her age, with a round open face and thick eyebrows. He was the sort of man who knew a little about everything, but not much about anything. A thick waist was the by-product of loving both food and drink, and he was good at finding the group jobs and looking after their finances. Kiakra liked him, but recently he'd been very vocal about his issues with not being a real Hunter. Finally, she had given in and let him accompany her on this job, but already she was regretting it.

She took a deep breath, "Aldrid, shall I remind you of the plan?"

"Ah yes that would be helpful," he said, furrowing his brows seriously.

"You go down on the left and take a shot at the human. I'll track around to the right, so if you miss, I can get him. Once he's dealt with, we do the same for the big guy. We just don't want to take them on at the same time, okay?"

"Right, got it," he said slinging a crossbow onto his shoulder and getting up to leave.

Kiakra dragged him back into the grass before he ruined their cover.

"Stay low," she growled, "And remember nothing lethal, we want them alive."

Aldrid nodded again, and then awkwardly crawled away.

Kiakra waited for a little while, watching the man Lax as he pulled out a loaf of bread. He tore off a piece and shoved it all in his mouth, not bothering to keep it closed as he chewed. Then he picked up a small axe and wandered over to sit on a nearby rock. As he began to sharpen it, Kiakra slunk off to the right.

The grass was as tough as the earth and it scratched at her face as she crawled. She squinted instinctually. It was cooling off now but Kiakra felt warm, and though she was calm on the outside her heart was pounding in her chest, readying her for what was to come.

She always felt like this before a job, fear and anticipation mixed together so potently it made her want to laugh.

Her fingers ached for her bowstring.

The cliff went a long way around to the right, ending in a gentle slope where the few trees faded, giving way to the sea of tall grass around her. When she was this far she moved into a crouch, turning back toward the camp to help backup Aldrid.

Down here the grass had not been so buffeted by the elements, and so was able to grow longer. Standing, it was almost up to her shoulders in height.

She weaved through the brush, less worried about being seen and more concerned with how much noise she was making. A lack of wind meant that down here it was near silent.

A little further on and she spotted her quarry. He was still sat on his rock, sharpening his axe and oblivious to the trap closing in around him. The sky had turned blood red now, the sun was nearly gone.

Kiakra pulled an arrow from her quiver and knocked it to her bow. She couldn't see Aldrid, but if he was doing his job correctly then that was a good thing.

There was movement from the tent.

Kiakra tensed.

The opening flaps were thrown aside and out came the second man, the Bavagai, rolling his heavy head from side to side as several goats followed him into the evening air.

He was not the biggest Kiakra had ever seen, but even smaller Bavagai were not to be underestimated, for they were the largest of all the Spoken Races, and this man still looked to be over seven feet in size.

Jutai.

His body was thick and stout, made to look more so by the shaggy dreadlocked hair that covered his entire frame. He had legs like tree trunks, and wide, heavy shoulders. A solid line of horn ran from his brow, all the way to the back of his neck, it was a trait all Bavagai shared, a remnant of their ancient ancestry with the mountains. Needless to say, a headbutt from one of them was usually fatal.

The fat man on the rock rolled his eyes, "Do those filthy things have to come inside with us?" he moaned, "They don't half stink the place up."

Kutai crouched down and took the animals face in his huge hands, grinning like a child. The only thing he was wearing were dark green striped trousers, held up by a thick belt that was covered in bronze.

"But they're family," he said in a deep voice as the goat tried to bite his face.

In the corner of Kiakra's vision she saw Aldrid's head emerge from the grass.

Oh please no.

As the two men spoke to one another Aldrid stood up a little more, his crossbow pointed in their direction.

Kiakra tried to stop Aldrid with her eyes, but he wasn't looking for her. His focus was solely on the two men.

"At least take out the human," she whispered to herself, pleading, but he was aiming a bolt at the Bavagai.

Not now.

Aldrid loosed, and everything seemed to slow.

The bolt flew through the air and buried itself in the giant mans' back.

He roared.

Goats scattered as the Bavagai flailed around trying to dislodge the bolt from his ribs.

Kiakra jumped up and aimed at the human, who had reacted remarkably fast and was running toward Aldrid's position with his axe raised above his head.

Aldrid fumbled with his bow, dropping bolts as he tried to reload and take a shot at the man who was running him down, now only a few feet away, and closing the distance fast.

Kiakra loosed an arrow toward him.

It found it's mark, biting into the meat on the back of his leg. The man screamed and plummeted into the dirt only seconds before he would have reached Aldrid.

Jutai meanwhile had managed to break the haft of the arrow embedded in his back, and had spotted Kiakra.

He roared again, and ran at her.

There was no weapon in his hands, but Kiakra knew he didn't need one to kill her, he'd rip her apart like a child pulling legs from a spider.

Breathing fast she knocked another arrow to her bow and loosed it at the Bavagai. This one hit him full in the chest, making him cough but barely slowing him.

Kiakra walked backwards, reaching for another arrow. The grass had covered her approach, but now it hindered her retreat, pulling at her legs, threatening to trip her.

He was close now, and barrelling toward her with all the force of a bison.

She got another arrow to her bow, raised it, and loosed.

This one hit him in the throat, stunning him, but doing nothing to kill his momentum. He lunged at her, carried by the last strength in his legs and the weight still driving his body forward.

Kiakra stumbled back but his shoulder smashed into her ribs and knocked her to the ground, sharp pain emanating from her midsection as her lungs were forcefully emptied.

He'd fallen partly on top of her, and though the Bavagai's strength was failing he managed to get a hand to her throat. She scratched and kicked at his face, trying to get him off, desperately trying to prize his fingers from her throat, feeling his warm blood seeping into her clothes.

Suddenly she remembered her knife and twisted to try and pull it from its sheath. But it was under her thigh, which was now pinned to the earth by the man's massive bulk.

As soon as she let go of Jutai's hand around her throat he began to squeeze. Immediately her vision began to spot with dark shapes.

Blood pounded in her skull.

Her fingers found the handle of her knife, but her hands were covered in sweat and blood, and she couldn't get a grip.

She tried to cough but nothing happened.

A tear ran down her cheek, but she couldn't feel it, panic had set in.

Then abruptly his hand let off pressure for a moment, and her vision cleared enough for her to see the angry bloodshot eyes of the Bavagai.

No, not angry. Sad.

"Why?" Jutai choked, spitting blood into her face as he spoke.

Kiakra didn't bother to reply, he'd let up enough for her to get a good grip on the knife, and with a burst of power she finally pulled it free. A fraction of a moment was wasted on hesitation, and then she pushed the blade hard into the space between his collar bone and his neck.

His eyes opened wide in shock, and then winced in pain as she used the last of her strength to twist the knife further into the sinew of his throat.

The hand around her own neck went limp, and the face of Jutai relaxed into an open, lifeless stare.

Coughing violently, she grabbed his arm and hefted it to one side. She crawled out from under him and collapsed onto her back. Chest heaving, she drank in fresh air. Sweat and blood dried on her face and she felt herself begin to shiver in the cool evening air. A giggle escaped her lips, and before she knew what was happening she was laughing like a madman.

She was alive.

Tears of laughter turned to tears of pain as she began to feel the effects of having such a head on collision with a Bavagai. Gently she pulled up her tunic, seeing dark splotches of colour beginning to form on her ribs. They were likely broken but she wasn't going to dwell on it, her head was still pounding.

She got to her feet with more than a little effort and saw Aldrid running toward her.

"Are you okay?" he said, worry etched onto his face as he slowed down, frantically looking her over.

Kiakra waited for him to get close, then punched him in the gut.

"A little better now," she rasped, as he sunk to the floor groaning.

***

Sometime later the guilt had set in.

Kiakra was sat cross legged on her sleeping mat, looking up at the clear night sky. It was cold, and the moon was absent, but all around her stars spotted the heavens. She wondered if they were watching her, as she watched them. She imagined they could hear her thoughts, and she felt very small under their gaze.

She shuffled closer to the fire.

Jutai hadn't needed to die, it was Aldrids fault for shooting him.

The fire crackled and spat at her.

And it was your fault for letting him.

She shivered and pulled a thick bearskin cloak around her a little tighter, until only her head was poking through the fur. It was comfortable and warm, and that made her feel safe, but she knew she didn't deserve it after what she had done. She pushed it from her shoulders and let the chill of the night steal her breath. Cold was all that Jutai would feel in his huge grave, and so she would suffer with him.

The other criminal had survived the ordeal, he was with Cypher now, having his leg taken care of.

He hadn't spoken since he'd found out his friend had been killed. Cypher was a talented healer, but she could not bring back the dead any more than she could make the flowers bloom.

After the disastrous ambush Kiakra had made it clear that Aldrid would not be taking part in hunts ever again. He was a talented treasurer, and that was what he would continue doing. He'd not argued, and Kiakra sensed that however gormless he seemed at times, he felt bad about what had happened.

He was asleep now, as was everyone else. Tiko had stayed by the fire with her for some time, but she had little empathy for Kiakra and her guilt, and once she realised there was no good conversation to be had she had moved away to set up her sleeping sack. Tiko wasn't interested enough to pry, and never slept near the rest of the group.

"So how much did we lose then?" came Rat's voice from beyond the fire.

Kiakra hadn't realised he was still awake.

She took a deep breath, "Only about fifty, our contractor would have preferred them both alive, but as long as they're stopped he doesn't mind much."

"Hmm, that is a shame," Rat said, his voice drifting away. He shuffled a little closer to the fire. He was an outcast of the Kazoec empire in the south, an exile still not used to the colder weather of the plains.

"Sounded like Aldrid was pretty useless?" he said, holding his hands out toward the fire.

At only five feet tall he was a short even by the standards of the Kaz. His skin was leathery, dotted with tough plates of scale, and his round head was supported by a thick neck. Despite his small frame he was remarkably strong and moved with a smooth grace that was not achievable for most humans.

Usually a deep green, the firelight had turned his skin the colour of wine, and though Kiakra had known him for many years she still found his look deceptively animalistic.

"He was an idiot," she said, "But I should have known he was going to be like that, it's not his craft."

Rat chuckled, an odd noise, "You're getting soft in your old age, you would have ignored the fool any other time."

Kiakra frowned, "I should have ignored him, we'd be up fifty Olvir's if I had, and that big bastard wouldn't have gotten blood all over my damn tunic."

And he'd still be alive.

"Next time I'm sticking with you, or Tiko."

Rat chuckled again, and then was interrupted by Cypher coming out of her tent with a stoic looking man behind her.

To any onlooker it would have seemed strange, the small girl leading a six-foot-tall, broad chested criminal, but he was bound at his hands and feet, so he could only waddle. His wounds were gone, only the ripped material of his legging showing any sign of attack.

Rat stood, quicker than Kiakra. He walked over to Cypher and grabbed the criminal by the shoulder, pulling him away.

"Come on," said Rat, leading him off into the dark. Kiakra stared at the man, but he wouldn't meet her eyes, and as he disappeared off into the gloom she felt another pang of guilt. It was quickly replaced by annoyance.

"Ungrateful idiot, should have killed him too," she muttered as she stood up slowly, and with great effort.

"You ought to have seen me first," said Cypher, ignoring her comment but noticing how difficult it had been for her to stand.

"I'm not too bad, he was worse," she replied, trying to hide some of her pain.

The other girl nodded her head in agreement but missed nothing.

"You're right there, he almost bled to death while I was working on him."

Kiakra knew that was not the only injury she had inflicted.

"Come inside," Cypher sighed, moving back into her tent, "You look freezing."

It was not a traditional tent, closer to the Akalen 'Ovook' which were heavy hides and skins wound around a latticework of wooden structure. This was smaller, only able to fit two or three people at the most. Inside, there was another fire, and it was so warm and smoky that Kiakra's eyes began to water.

Despite that, she liked it in here. The walls and floor were covered in furs, and it had a strong earthy smell from the types of wood and herbs that were burnt. Kiakra found the warmth very welcome, undeserved as it was.

She had known Cypher for longer than any of her other companions, having found her shortly after her own father left. She'd been lucky, even at a young age Cypher had been a powerful healer and had Kiakra not taken the young girl under her wing, she was unsure what would have happened. Healers were valuable commodities for many groups, good and bad.

She was only sixteen, but strong willed and fiercely loyal. She had dark hair that she tied up similarly to Kiakra, and a petite, delicate frame, quite unlike Kiakra's wiry, muscled body. Her face was freckled and her features were plain, but only a fool could miss her beauty.

"Undress," Cypher said as she grabbed at a root and began chewing it, looking around for her knife.

Kiakra did, removing her long tunic and pulling off her boots and trousers. It was a lot of effort, and she had to bite her tongue to stop from crying out.

Her ribs were purple, her neck was red and raw, and she had a long gash down one leg, presumably caused by the Bavagai falling on her. Cyphers face betrayed little as she turned around and surveyed Kiakra's beat up frame.

"He didn't go down easy then," Cypher muttered, more to herself than anyone else.

"Lie down."

Kiakra had a love-hate relationship with the healing process, but she did as Cypher commanded. In here, she was in charge.

"How do you feel?"

Kiakra tried to laugh, but it turned into grunt of pain, "How do you think?"

"I don't mean physically, where's your head at? A man died today."

Kiakra tensed up.

"He went for me, now he's dead. I'm fine," Kiakra lied.

Cypher shook her head and sighed, "You aren't meant for this business Ki. You look half dead and you've barely spoken all evening, I know you're not alright."

"I'm tired, and I'm aching, that's all," Kiakra muttered.

Cypher sighed again, "I can only help you so much," she said softly.

She put two hands on Kiakra's body, one on her head, and the other on her stomach. Heat poured through her, a couple of her joints popped and cracked as Cypher closed her eyes.

"The ligaments in your knee are torn, I don't know how you're still walking," the girl said scornfully.

"You've completely broken several ribs, got severe bruising around your throat, and a host of torn muscle throughout your entire body."

Kiakra wanted to cut in but she felt dizzy and numb, as if her soul was looking down on her, no longer connected to her physical element.

"This is going to be a lot of effort," Cypher said, furrowing her brows.

She let go of Kiakra, and then made several incisions at different points on her body, one on her leg, another on her stomach, and one on her shoulder. Kiakra felt nothing and lay there passively.

Then the girl made an incision on her own hand, gritting her teeth as she did. She pressed it against the incision on Kiakra's knee, touching the two wounds together, and for a moment nothing happened. Gradually Cyphers palms began to glow red. Starting off as a dim light, it grew, brighter and brighter until eventually it was competing with the fire, illuminating the tent with an otherworldly light.

Suddenly Kiakra was back in her body, feeling the tissue in her knee twisting and binding together as Cypher's energy poured through her flesh. The sensation was not pain, but a deep ache, as her body rearranged itself according to the designs of her healer. Consciousness began to slip away as a numbness took over, defending her body from the foreign forces at work beneath her skin.

And then she was gone, passing into sleep as Cypher continued her task.

Chapter 6

Herleif was enjoying himself.

He raised his sword high and brought it down on his opponent's shield, though the impact did little other than deafen him. Then he danced back out of his adversaries reach, easily avoiding a stab aimed at his stomach.

He was shirtless and covered in mud, as was the boy opposite him, though Herleif was not nearly as red in the face.

The other boy made a clumsy swipe at his shoulder. It was a slow, high to low, arc that was telegraphed so severely Herleif blocked the move almost before his opponent made it. As the practice swords snapped together Herleif hooked one of the boy's feet with his own, before punching him hard with his shield, knocking the boy off balance and down into the mud. His opponent gasped, winded, and Herleif cringed a little, as the mud was obviously not so a soft landing as he'd expected.

He grabbed his partner by the wrist and hauled him up to his feet.

"Switch!" came a yell from the Sergeant, an older man who seemed to do very little other than shout and pace.

The boy Herleif had been matched against stalked off without a backwards glance, muttering insults, pride obviously bruised. Herleif spat in his general direction and then wandered over to his waterskin. There was an uneven amount of boys training in their group, and so Herleif was allowed a brief break, to catch his breath and take a drink.

"And fight!" the Sergeant yelled, the boys immediately clashing together as Herleif drank deeply from his skin. The water was so cold it hurt his teeth.

They'd arrived in Gulbrand's camp several days ago with Lord Brynjar, and since then he had been questioning whether it'd been the right choice to leave his home.

The northern camp was apparently the largest of any camp set up by Gulbrand in his country, though Herleif had only Brynjar's word to go off. Situated in the open land west of the Akvast, it was close enough to defend the river and far enough away that his force could still manoeuvre if it needed to. Stakes had been erected and pits had been dug to defend the camp from all angles, and there were guards on watch both day and night.

Inside the camp it was a flat sprawling mass of men and boys and tents, all clustered so close together that you couldn't blink without someone hearing. It stank of excrement, both human and animal, for the only creatures here other than men were livestock used occasionally to feed the troops.

The whole place made him feel trapped, nervous and on guard almost perpetually, it was exhausting. He enjoyed training purely because of the location, which was the only patch of open ground he had come across inside the camp.

Beyond the stakes and ditches a colossal tree stretched into the clouds, dwarfing the terrain around it as its branches creeped across the sky. That was the Yilland Oak, where Gulbrand himself resided, and Herleif could understand why. It was a powerful place, a soft border between this world and the beyond. Even far away Herleif could feel its presence. As a child father had told him stories of such monstrous structures, but still, it had not prerpared him for the sight of it up close.

Beyond the great tree Herleif could see forests and green rolling hills. He wished he was there instead, he craved the wilds. Here everything was stagnant and motionless, save for the people. But he was sick of people, and he felt as though he hadn't taken a breath of fresh air since he'd been here.

For a moment he wondered if that was why he hadn't been sleeping well recently, but in asking the question he was lying to himself.

He knew exactly why he couldn't sleep.

At night he saw the faces of those he'd abandoned to the monster and, more than once, he had awoken to screams that no living soul had made.

He dragged his mind from those thoughts, no point dwelling on them in the day, they would haunt him enough in the night. Instead he put his waterskin down and watched his brother locked in battle on the other side of the training field. Fin was doing well against his opponent. Despite being smaller and weaker than most of the boys, he was taking to the sword very well.

Even so, Fin had been worrying him. Most of the time he didn't speak, and when he did, he had little to say.

"Switch!" yelled the Sergeant again, and Herleif watched his brother break away from his opponent and dip his head in respect. Perhaps he shouldn't worry.

"So scared he won't even look at me," came a voice from behind him.

Herleif turned and smiled, it was Ojak.

"Ready for some more bruises?" the other boy smirked.

Ojak was a little shorter than Herleif, with choppy dark hair and an open face. He was built to be a soldier, stocky and strong, and he was the only one of the new recruits that could give him a decent fight.

"No thanks," Herleif said. He'd lost almost every encounter he'd had before with Ojak. This time would be different.

He wasn't good at making friends, but he had been drawn to the boy. As Lord Brynjar's squire, Ojak had been slightly outcast from the other soldiers in a similar way to Herleif, the difference being he was outcast due to respect, whereas Herleif was not.

Maybe that was why he liked him. He wasn't quite sure if they were friends, but he'd enjoyed the boy's company during the journey south.

However, it wouldn't stop him trying to deliver some bruises.

"And Fight!" the Sergeant screamed.

Spring had arrived, and the ground wasn't as solid as it had been.

Instead the mud was thick and sticky, dragging at Herleif's feet as he lunged forward, trying to close the distance in order to use his superior size. But Ojak was shorter, and better balanced on this ground. As Herleif thrust forward, Ojak twisted, letting the blunt blade skitter off his shield as he followed up with his own attack.

Herleif only just managed to defend, remembering to get his shield in the way at the last second as the force of Ojak's thrust knocked him back.

The other boy followed up with a flurry of strikes at Herleif's shield. He knew they were not designed to connect, but to force him to cover up and blind himself.

It worked.

As Herleif raised his shield to block the strikes aimed at his head, suddenly he felt a crack across his thigh. His leg went numb and he fell into the mud.

Ojak laughed, and grabbed Herleif by the wrist, helping him up.

"I almost had you," said Herleif, lying and wiping mud from his leggings.

Ojak laughed, "You were nowhere near me!"

Herleif shook his head, "You move so much better than me on this ground."

"It's nothing to do with the ground," Ojak said, turning serious for a moment. "You always put too much into your attack, then when it fails, you have nothing to fall back on."

Herleif nodded. Ojak was a much more experienced fighter, having trained extensively with the young Lord Brynjar.

Herleif was happy to take advice from him.

"Okay, so less attacking then?"

"Not "less attacking", just don't always commit quite so much," Ojak said, "Gotta keep your options open."

Herleif nodded again, "Alright, give me another try."

Suddenly a horn blasted in the distance, interrupting their practise.

The Sergeant immediately began shouting at the boys who had stopped to look toward it, but almost all of them had. Beyond the training area the camp was single minded, everyone rushing toward the horn to investigate.

Herleif shivered, "What's that?"

Ojak's face was stoic.

"More people have come."

***

Brynjar looked down on the camp from up high. It was dark now, but still he could see the hunched shapes of villagers as they shambled into the camp.

The horn still rung in his ears.

"I don't enjoy calling them away from their homes," Gulbrand sighed, "But at least here they will be safe."

Brynjar hoped that was true.

He was standing on one of the roots of the Great Oak next to the Lord of Yilland. The root was big enough that both men could comfortably stand side by side on top of it, wider than most tree trunks and covered in a thick green moss that felt like padding under Brynjar's boots, it gave them a perfect view out over the camp.

Branches above them were extensive enough to hide the stars overhead, and at over eight hundred feet in height it dominated the landscape of Yilland.

Gulbrand had chosen a sheltered area amongst its large twisting roots to set up his pavilion, away from the main camp. After pouring over maps and debating with the numerous generals for what seemed like an age, they had come out here to take a break from their work.

"You seem tired Brynjar?" Gulbrand said, smiling sadly.

He was a large, heavy man, a little taller than Brynjar, with a dark round beard and long hair tied behind his head in a simple ponytail. His face was square, and his nose angled. Big hands and broad shoulders made him look like a born warrior of the Kingdom, but his face was rarely without a smile.

"I'm sorry my Lord," Brynjar said, blinking hard against his weariness. The evening air was still, and the tree was silent. It wasn't helping him stay awake.

Gulbrand turned, the movement exaggerated by his bulk and the thick bearskin cloak he wore about his shoulders, "What's troubling you lad?"

Brynjar couldn't look at him.

"I lost a couple of men whilst I was out recruiting."

"Ah," Gulbrand said, turning back to look at the camp again. The fires were lit, illuminating the soldiers gathered around them, little black shapes against the light.

"Were those the first you've lost?"

"Yes sir," Brynjar said.

Gulbrand paused for a moment, "It's a tricky thing, losing men, but you have to remember that it's part of a bigger picture that isn't always so easy to see."

Brynjar had heard it before, "But, with all due respect sir, it was my fault. I led them-"

"Did you kill them yourself?" Gulbrand said, cutting him off with sudden intensity.

"Not with my own blade but-"

"Then they died doing their job," he said sharply. He stared at Brynjar for a moment longer, and then sighed, "Our soldiers defend our lands from harm, and that puts them directly in harm's way."

He turned back to Brynjar, "Did you stop whatever, or whoever it was that killed them?"

Brynjar thought back to the sleeping men he'd killed all those weeks ago. They were raiders, criminals, but they had faces that visited him at night, and eyes that would never open. He understood their desperation, the Outskirts were a difficult place to live, but they had killed his men, and would have killed more had he not stopped them.

"Yes sir."

"Then you have avenged them. Mistakes will be made, you have to learn from them and know how to move on, you won't do your men any favours if you lose confidence."

"I know sir," Brynjar said, taking a deep breath.

Gulbrand glanced at him and then looked back down at the refugees.

Suddenly he felt a fool, bringing up his meagre losses in the face of Gulbrand's crisis. This man was on the brink of war, and he was complaining about two men.

He's lost entire villages.

"What do you think about my decision?" Gulbrand said hesitantly.

It occurred then to Brynjar that this man, like any man of power, probably had very few people with whom he could speak openly.

He rubbed his eyes.

The Akalen Warlord Teoma, the Pale Wolf of the Steppe, had set up camp only a few miles from Gulbrands borders. Since then, two villages in Yilland had been destroyed, and neither time were there any survivors. In response, Gulbrand had asked that every person in Yilland muster at the Great Oak, in order that he could protect them until the threat was destroyed.

"The messengers you sent to speak with the Akalens, have any returned?" Brynjar asked, though he could guess at the answer.

The big man shook his head.

Brynjar sighed. It was a complicated topic, and one that he was currently too tired to speak about in any great length. He smacked a mosquito trying to land on his hand, and then gave the easy answer.

"I think it was the right thing to do my Lord. With all your people in one place you can better protect them."

Gulbrand laughed, startling him somewhat, "You can speak freely lad."

His faced turned serious. Brynjar knew this was the man exposing himself to criticism, the usual guard of smiles and haughty jokes were now gone, and his look was far from confident. Few people would ever see that side of him.

Brynjar took a moment to gather what he wanted to say.

"My worries are that those who do not answer your call will be left alone, and that it sends a message to the people that you are unable to defend them from these foreign invaders. Your country cannot thrive without people farming the land, which they cannot do if they are here."

Gulbrand furrowed his brows, and for a moment Brynjar wondered if he should have stayed silent.

"I had the same concerns," he said finally, "What would you do in my place?"

Brynjar wasn't sure.

"I would want to ride out with your forces and meet them head on, have one battle between warriors and let that be the end of it." He clenched the pommel of his sword in frustration, "But there are not enough men for that."

"There are not," Gulbrand agreed sadly, "King Olvaldr still refuses to send aid, but that would be something wouldn't it?" he turned and smiled at Brynjar.

"Anyway, get some rest, I may have work for you tomorrow," and with that his guard was up again, the world shut out.

Gulbrand turned and walked away, heading for the ornate steps that were carved into the tree, leading down to his pavilion.

"Are you coming?" he said, turning back to Brynjar with an open face.

"I'll make my way back to my tent in a little while my Lord," Brynjar said.

Gulbrand nodded, and descended out of view, leaving Brynjar alone in the dark.

The stars were bright now, and the roots of the tree were glowing dimly. The spirits tethered to this place trying to outshine their kin in the heavens.

Brynjar closed his eyes and soaked up the quiet.

Chapter 7

The earth was cool beneath his fingers, the grass soft.

He breathed deeply, the open air cleansing him as he stood and moved on.

Out here was the only quiet he could find, the camp was too busy for him, even at night. Guards patrolled through the sleeping quarters and officers staggered about drunk, noisily searching for fights. Even those that slept were too disturbing for Fin.

Everyone breathed so loudly.

He'd tried to forget about what happened with the Drakin, but the more he tried to forget, the more it stuck in his mind. Something within him had awoken, and now he couldn't rid himself of it. The space he needed to study his thoughts was not going to be found within the camp, and so he had snuck out, dodging the patrols easily and slipping through the breaks in the camp's defences.

Away from the bright torches and churned earth, the gloom now embraced him. Around him it was almost pitch black, with only the faint glow of the Yilland Oak ahead, and the dim lights from the camp behind, though they cast no shadows out here. It was open and, despite the lack of forest, he felt oddly safe.

He walked on.

At first he was without purpose, the simple joy of being free kept him walking. But gradually something began to pull.

His pace increased, legs carrying him toward a place he hadn't been. The feeling was like hunger. Powerful, instinctual.

Without realising why, he dropped down again, hands pawing at the ground. The pull was stronger now, he reckoned he could still fight it if he wanted to, but it commanded his attention.

He was in a crouch, kneading his hands into the earth, searching for something. What he searched for he didn't know. He'd missed the feeling of dirt between his fingers, and the smell of wounded grass.

Pulling up a clump of earth he began to dig. He scratched at the ground with his hands, dirt collecting under his fingernails as he felt the pull from below.

What are you doing?

He carried on, not knowing the answer but unable to stop himself.

A rock came away in his hand, and suddenly his face was illuminated by a dull green light. He recoiled hastily, whipping his hand away, almost crying out in surprise.

It was a root from the Great Oak, twisted and pale, much brighter than the tree itself. Why that had frightened him, he did not know, but he reached out and grabbed it, entwining his fingers with those of the root. It was tough and flexible, like overcooked meat.

Abruptly he was blind.

Panicking, he tried to pull his hand away, but found he no longer had control of his body.

And then he was moving. Pulled along the twisting road so fast he didn't know which way was up. It wound its way through the earth, dodging the rocks submerged by dirt as the grass clawed at his face. Rabbits bolted from their holes, worms danced around him blindly and all the while he was moving toward something massive.

His body abandoned him, and the panic dissipated. There was nothing he could do anyway.

And then he stopped.

His vision returned to him, distinct, but malleable, like a memory. He was looking down on the camp from an impossible height, birds clutching at his unmoving arms, seeking shelter from the cold night, as moss clung to every corner of his body, using him as a platform for their growth.

Water, earth, sky, he felt them all, and was part of them all.

Despite the confusion and utter helplessness, for a long moment he found himself at peace.

And then he was aware of a presence with him. At first he thought it was the Oak itself, for that was what he must be linked with. But that was somehow above him, too great to notice.

This was different, alive in the same way he was. It was organic, real, and excited.

It moved toward him, trying to go unseen, predatory in its stealth. It was powerful, its spirit large, much larger than him.

Fin tried to move away, to sever his link with the Oak. He began back the way he had come, finding there was no longer any current dragging him.

The thing began to follow. Slowly, at first, but keeping pace with him, speeding up as he began to flee. Panic took over, and though he didn't know how he was moving, he moved as fast as he could, sheer effort driving him on.

But *it* was faster. Suddenly it was with him, scratching at his substance, trying to get a hold on his spirit.

For the briefest moment the two of them touched, he felt it ravage through his mind, searching for something.

Abruptly he was cut off.

He fell backwards and hit the earth. Shaking and panting, he was covered in sweat, shivering in the cold night. Whatever that thing was, it knew where to find him now. It had learnt something about him when they made contact, and Fin had learnt nothing. All he had felt was hot breath, claws and strength.

So much strength.

A horse snickered, and Fin's eyes flicked open.

Around him were soldiers, looking down with a mixture of fear and concern. Every one of them was in full mail armour, armed, and most had hands wrapped around the hilt of their sword. Though none had drawn on him yet, some were pointing spears at him.

You idiot.

"What the hell were you doing?" one of the men said. He sounded more frightened than angry.

Fin had no idea how to answer.

"Leave him with me for a moment," said someone with a deep voice. It had come from behind Fin, and as he turned, a large man dismounted from his horse and walked over.

"Are you sure that's wise my Lord?" said the first man, still eyeing Fin warily from his horse.

It was then that he noticed the soldier had the Yilland Oak on his surcoat. Even in the dark the golden emblem of the tree stood out clearly.

"I am," said the big man, "Now leave us."

The Guards were obviously uncomfortable but kicked their horses away obediently.

Their leader was large, and had presence, but he was not threatening. He didn't seem in a hurry to speak, and in their shared silence Fin noticed the grass around him beginning to spot with light.

Strikers, hundreds of them, all over the field around him, the little bugs that emitted a dim white light from their bodies, and if you squeezed them they'd kick out a spark in defence. It was as though the ground mirrored the sky, insects dotting the expanse of darkness instead of stars, steadily wandering through the night.

"Beautiful, aren't they?" said the big man, smiling warmly.

Fin nodded, unsure what to say.

"What's your name lad?"

"Fin, sir."

"Do you know who I am?"

"I don't, sir" Fin said, adding "sir," onto the end quickly, almost forgetting.

The big man snorted, amused, "I suppose that makes sense, I've not spent very long in camp yet. I'm Gulbrand."

Fin dropped into a bow immediately, turning pink at his cheeks.

"I'm sorry my Lord, I didn't know."

He didn't know the disposition of Gulbrand, what he did know was that this man could have him killed for being out here. All he needed was to call the guards back. Fin glanced up at him, and then realised that, in fact, he probably wouldn't need them.

Gulbrand laughed, "Stand up, there's need for that. I just want to talk."

Fin slowly rose from his bow.

"I'm sorry my Lord, it's just," he paused, aware he was speaking without permission, but Gulbrand gestured for him to continue, still smiling. "Well, I'm from the outskirts, I just came out here to get some fresh air."

He didn't say how much he hated the camp.

"Who is your commanding officer?" Gulbrand said, squinting at him. Somehow, he commanded respect without asking for it, and Fin understood why he was the Lord of Yilland.

"Lord Brynjar, my Lord"

"Ah yes, he's a good man."

"He's treated us well," Fin said, nodding.

"Did you come from the Outskirts?" Gulbrand asked.

"Yes, my Lord."

"Your parents were Nomads?" Gulbrand said slowly. It was more of a statement than a question, but he was still looking for an answer.

Fin was taken off guard, somehow in only a matter of weeks he had forgotten his heritage of difference. He was unsure how to answer, the Kingdom's treatment of Nomads varied greatly from place to place.

"They were," he said finally, reasoning that the Lord probably had already guessed.

Gulbrand nodded, "I fought alongside your people in the war, they were fierce warriors."

"Thank you," Fin said, and despite himself he meant it. Pride welled up from somewhere he hadn't known existed, and he stood a little taller.

Gulbrand turned and looked out over the expanse of flat ground, and Fin followed his gaze, eyes catching on every wriggling spot of light cast by the tiny creatures.

"You know they only shine when there is no moon to compete with," Gulbrand said, his smile turning sorrowful. He glanced at the hole Fin had dug. Fin held his breath, but Gulbrand just nodded, as if noting something for himself.

"The Great Oak has made many men do strange things, I wonder what it wanted with you?" he said.

For a moment his look was unreadable, and Fin felt fear flush onto his cheeks, but then the big man's face split into a smile, and he turned away, back to his horse.

"Get back to camp," Gulbrand said as he mounted up. "There will be work to do tomorrow, and you'll need to be well rested."

"Work my Lord?" Fin asked hesitantly.

"Yes."

Before Fin could ask any more questions Gulbrand had ridden away, back toward his guards. When he reached the group they peeled off to join him, and together they thundered toward the camp.

For a moment Fin felt part of what was happening here.

Then he remembered the creature that had grabbed him, and looked around shivering, suddenly feeling cold again.

Far away in the treeline, two spots of light shone out at him, like glowing eyes.

Just more strikers.

He turned and began walking back toward the fires of the camp.

When next he looked, those two spots of light had disappeared, and his walk turned into a run.

***

The next day Fin was back at practise.

He slipped forward and thrust with his sword, narrowly missing before he jumped out the way of his opponent's counter.

They were still using the sword and shield, a fighting style he had so far preferred from the heavy spears they had used earlier. He felt like he could utilise his speed more effectively with the sword, and had more control over the smaller weapon than he did with the spear.

Another frustrated swing came his way and he danced off to the left. His opponent had overcommitted, giving Fin time to jump forward and rap him on the shoulder. The boy yelped and recoiled, laughing in pain as he dropped his sword and clutched at his shoulder.

"Damn, you're a quick bugger," he said smiling and breathing hard. Only a little older than Fin, and very lean, the boy was a good match for him.

"Oh, you too," Fin replied. He never knew what to say to the other boys, even when they were nice to him.

"Well not fast enough," the boy said, laughing again.

They both circled around one another and reset at opposite ends of their practice area.

The areas were just a series of muddy circles drawn into the ground, but it served its purpose. The soldiers training had long since killed the grass, and the mud was growing thicker by the day.

Fin set himself up facing the sun. It wasn't ideal, but they swapped sides each time, and so far it had not cost him more than a couple of losses.

Fin heard a thwack, and a boy shouted. He looked over to his right.

Herleif was standing over a boy of similar size who had obviously not won their bout. Both were red faced and breathing heavily, but as Herleif reached a hand out to help his opponent up, it was smacked away violently.

"Don't touch me," the other boy snapped, getting to his feet quickly.

His eyes flicked around, gauging which of his companions had seen his defeat. He had a large chest and thick arms covered in tattooed symbols Fin didn't recognise. His head was shaved, apart from a long tail of light hair coming from his crown.

Fin saw the muscles in Herleif's jaw tense up.

Don't do anything stupid.

He was in a sensible mood however, and Herleif turned on his heel to reset himself back at the other end of the circle.

"Switch!" came the Sergeants yell.

Fin's opponent walked past, giving him a clap on the shoulder and smiling broadly, "Next time."

Fin smiled awkwardly, "Yes, maybe."

He watched him walk away, then turned to see Herleif's former opponent standing at the other end of his practice ring. For a moment the boy's eyes narrowed, and he shot a glance at Herleif, who had been watching out of the corner of his eye. Amusement flickered across his face and he rolled his shoulders, looking back toward Fin.

Fin raised his shield, knowing this was going to be bad.

"And fight!" the sergeant yelled.

The other boy was much bigger than him, Herleif's size, and he didn't look like he would go easy on him if he won.

He advanced quickly and Fin walked forward to meet him. As his opponent swung, Fin blocked with his shield, a poor move, for the impact still jarred his arm. He ducked away, avoiding the follow up blow altogether.

He saw a flicker of frustration in his opponents face. Those strikes had obviously meant to end the fight then and there.

The boy attacked again, thrusting at Fins shield. He was quick, and the strike landed solidly, the force knocking Fin backwards, almost tripping him in the mud. But again he managed to avoid the follow up, staying out of range.

The boy was gritting his teeth now, this fight was meant to have finished quickly, and Fin was making him look a fool.

Fin saw him wind up for another powerful thrust, his anger making him predictable. Fin held his ground, and as the thrust came in he caught the wooden blade on his shield again, this time twisting, allowing it to slide past and opening his opponent up.

Seeing an open target, Fin hit him with a swift jab to his ribs and the boy flinched back with a yell.

Fin stopped, he'd won.

The boy was trying to straighten up awkwardly, but the jab had obviously hurt more than Fin had meant.

"I'm sorry, I didn't mean to-" he was cut off as the boy rushed at him. He tried to twist away but the attack was so fast he didn't have time to react. A shoulder impacted with his midsection and he was thrown onto his side, the wind knocked out of him.

He tried to take a breath, but as he gasped, a fist crashed into his cheek, the force of the blow almost knocking him out.

Instinctively Fin tried to cover his head, but the other boy was much stronger, and prized his hands from his face.

Another fist connected with his ribs, and as he gasped again he caught sight of his opponents face. It was red and angry, his teeth bared. He pulled Fin's arms away and pinned them above his head, before grabbing a fistful of mud and forcing it into Fin's face, making him splutter.

The boy's knee was driving into his chest the whole time, pinning him to the floor. Fin could feel him shaking with anger.

"See, I win the real fight!" he hissed, eyes red.

Sucking in through his nose, he readied himself to spit.

Suddenly a knee smashed into the boy's face and his weight was no longer on Fin's chest.

The boy toppled backwards and Herleif was there, pushing him into the mud, the positions reversed as he now knelt on the other boy.

Fin spat out dirt and scrambled to his feet, his head still not clear from the blow he had taken. He watched dumbstruck as Herleif hit the boy, again, and again. He tried to squirm away but Herleif was stronger than him, and had already dealt a colossal blow.

The boy tried to defend, but his arms were getting slower. He wasn't shying from Herleif's punches as much now.

Fin could see the expression on his brothers face, unforgiving, uncontrollable anger. Fin shivered, part of him afraid of his brother.

Herleif still hadn't let up his attack, elbows and fists crashing down on the boy, blind rage dictating his attacks. Emotion lending him strength.

Fin walked over to Herleif, paused for a moment, and then grabbed his shoulder gently.

Herleif's head spun round, and for a moment Fin wondered if he was going to attack him. He stood and grabbed Fins shoulders, making him flinch. His eyes were nervous, and he was breathing hard.

"Are you okay?" he said quickly, genuine worry on his face.

"I'm fine," said Fin quietly. His cheek ached where he'd been hit, but he gestured to the groaning boy in front of them.

It was only then Herleif seemed to realise what he'd done, seeing the black welts on the boy's ribs and the blood running from his brow.

"I'm sorry," said Herleif, though Fin wasn't sure who he was talking to.

"Let me fight my own battles," Fin said, pushing his brother's hands away. "You always make things worse."

"But you were-"

"Yes I know!" Fin cut in, suddenly shouting, the mixture of frustration, jealousy and fear finally flooding over.

He took a breath, "You don't learn, you're the reason we had to come here," he gestured at the boy in the mud, lying unconscious and barely breathing. "That's the reason we had to come here!"

He was panting, shaking with his own rage, "I can look after myself. I don't need you to kill someone every time I get in a scrap!"

"I'm sorry," Herleif said again, hurt etched onto his face.

"No, you aren't, otherwise you wouldn't have done it," Fin snapped.

Immediately he saw Herleif withdraw from him.

"Fight your own battle's then, I won't help you any more," he said bluntly, standing and walking away from the training grounds.

Fin realised his fingers were balled up into fists. He was still shaking.

He hadn't even noticed the crowd of boys that had gathered around them, but now they began to disperse, helped on by the Sergeant who shouted for a few of them to take the beaten boy off to find a healer, though he didn't seem to care too much about the fight.

A hand landed on Fin's shoulder.

"Times like these, it pays to have family close by," said a voice behind him.

It was Brynjar, wearing his full mail armour and a long purple surcoat, so dark it almost looked black. The young Lord look concerned, but there was something behind it, nervousness perhaps. The hand not on Fin's shoulder was resting easily on the pommel of his sword.

Fin nodded, "I know my Lord. I'm sorry about that."

"I saw what happened, and we'll deal with that another time. For now get him back, and then get some rest. We have work to do this evening," Brynjar said.

"Work my Lord?" Fin replied. His thoughts immediately turned to the evening previously with Gulbrand.

"Yes, the worst kind," Brynjar said. His eyes flicked across the boys training and he nodded, looking almost afraid.

"What are we doing my Lord?"

Brynjar took a deep breath.

"Meeting our enemy."

Chapter 8

Brynjar's heart hammered in his chest. This was his first trip east of the great Akvast river.

It was dark now, the only light cast from distant stars, and a curved slice of the pale moon. Ahead of him was an Akalen camp.

Lying still on his belly he mapped out the terrain in his head.

Most of the Steppe was grassy and barren, but here, so close to the river, there was more vegetation. Few trees grew, but bracken and heather covered the ground, and the shrubs that managed to grow were good eating for livestock. Maybe that was why the Akalens had come so close to Yilland's borders.

Brynjar doubted it, they were perfectly suited to living out on the steppe, which was hardly a densely populated place.

He watched a sentry plod along in the dark on the outskirts of the camp, only his long frame, and hefty spear visible. The round ovook huts, in which the Akalens lived, sat stoic in the gloom, smoking gently from the fires inside.

Scouting was not work for a Lord, but he had been too excited to allow his men to go ahead without him, and had taken the job of one of the younger lads for himself, checking the western side of the camp.

There didn't seem to be much in the way of defence, and the layout was simple because Brynjar knew the traditional way in which the Akalens set up. The ovook were arranged in a circular pattern around the centre of the camp, which wasn't visible from here, with the most respected warriors and chieftains setting up in the centre, the safest part, while the warriors with lower social standing would be forced to set themselves further from the middle. The lowest ranked members would make up the very edges of camp, and act as sentries. It wasn't a large camp for a war party, and he guessed only a few hundred warriors were living there.

They'd chosen to set themselves up in a shallow, grassy bowl, open only from the south-west, where the soft ridges surrounding them sloped away, and the rough lines of a track into the camp could be seen.

He watched the sentry stop, turn, and then walk back the way he had come. The man was big, like all Akalens, but his posture was stooped, and his steps were slow. A good sign.

Brynjar shuffled his way back from the hill he was peering from. He had seen as much as he could in this gloom and would now have to commit the layout of this place to memory.

Once he was down from the crest of the hill he stood, and walked quickly back to his horse. Mail armour usually felt a little cumbersome to him, but tonight the strength of the metal had seeped into his bones. He was ready for a fight.

He stepped a foot up into the stirrup and easily swung himself onto his horses back, kicking him on toward his waiting soldiers.

Gulbrand had given him fifty men for this operation. The purpose was to bloody the Akalens in the hopes of provoking a reaction. Perhaps that was the only way to get the Pale Wolf, Teoma, to take notice.

The darkness was cool, the moon sucking any residual warmth from the air, and as Brynjar rode the wind began to pick up. Hair flicked in front of his face as he continued to ride, and a smile began to creep onto his mouth. Exhaustion had been one of his biggest worries about carrying out a night mission, for a tired mind was seldom wise, but now he had the opposite problem. He was buzzing with energy.

He clenched his jaw. Now was not the time to get excited, he had to speak with his men before he went ahead with anything.

He hadn't received any specific orders from Gulbrand, but he meant to take prisoners. There were questions that needed answering, and he would speak to the Akalens one way or another, even if Teoma wouldn't speak with him. What motivated the enemy was his biggest question. The raids carried out in Yilland had left no survivors, and were seemingly random, having no specific targets and making no attempt to hold land. Brynjar was prepared to believe these were the actions of a few extremists, but if that was the case, why hadn't Teoma opened up a dialogue with Gulbrand? Why had none of his messengers returned?

Brynjar intended to get some answers this night.

Staying off the ridges of the hills in case unfriendly eyes were watching, Brynjar wound his way west until he reached the camp of his own men.

It was far better hidden and far more alert than the Akalen dwelling.

He'd left them on a treeline, horses hidden in the forest and his men sleeping only in sacks, with oiled hides to keep off the rain. There were no fires, lest they attract attention, and several sentries were hidden around the camp. Looking on it now, even knowing it was there, he could see no signs of disturbance.

As Brynjar slowed his horse a man popped up in front of him, holding a bow low in front of him.

"State your name," the man said, his words ringing out clearly, even against the growing wind.

"Lord Brynjar, at ease," Brynjar said, happy his guards were still awake.

"Sorry my Lord," the man replied.

"Have the others returned yet?" he asked, looking around.

"Yes sir, they'll be glad to see you back safe," the man replied, shifting his weight uncomfortably. He was likely aware that with every passing moment his position was more exposed.

"Good to hear, I'll let you return to your watch," Brynjar said. He could just make out the man nod at him, and then he sunk back down into cover. In the dark it looked as if he had been swallowed up by the ground.

Brynjar trotted toward the camp, now able to pick out dark shapes in the grass, which were his men sleeping. He didn't think trampling them would inspire confidence in his leadership, so he dismounted a little way off, and walked over on foot.

An older thin man ran over to him, from the shadows.

"My Lord, you're back," he said, relief evident on his face, even in the low light of the moon. He was one of the higher-ranking scouts, a sergeant.

"Did you see anything we might have missed?" he said. It was a question asked out of respect, rather than concern. If there had been anything there, this man would have seen it.

Brynjar rolled his shoulders, "I saw their huts and a single sentry, the defences seemed negligible, what about you?"

The man shook his head, "I was looking from the east, so I went the whole way around the camp. There were no extra defences that I could see."

"Good," Brynjar nodded. He was struggling to stay calm, for all the signs were good that they should move in. "Wake the men up and call back all but two of our sentries, we'll discuss our angle of attack and then move out."

The sergeant in front of him smiled and bowed, "Yes my Lord," he said, before disappearing to wake up the others.

Brynjar paced away from the camp to gather his thoughts and calm his nerves.

The wind was still picking up. Now it swayed the bracken, and drew patterns in the heather, it seemed the spirits themselves felt what was to come. He knew they would favour him; his cause was justice.

He watched the night moving for some time before he heard someone walk up behind him.

"My Lord, the men are assembled," came the voice of Ojak. Brynjar had almost forgotten he was with them.

"Thank you," Brynjar said. He closed his eyes for a moment, letting the wind chill his skin, giving himself over to the cold. Then he turned and walked back toward his men, clapping Ojak on the shoulder as he did so.

They were in a rough semicircle facing him, most with horses by their sides ready to mount up. Many faces were still dreary from sleep, some were shivering, and most were very young. Brynjar wondered how many were actually men yet. He caught a glimpse of the boy Herleif, standing next to his brother. He smiled at them, noting how small Fin looked and reminding himself that this was a raid, not a battle. If he had to command children, he would not march them to their deaths.

Despite their youth, many faces looked ready for a fight, unbothered by the wind that whipped their hair. All had spears at their sides and shields hanging from their arms.

"Lads," Brynjar said, demanding everyone's attention. "We have a simple task tonight, to make ourselves known to our enemy."

There were grumbles of agreement. Many of these men had known the villages that had been destroyed, and were afraid for their own families.

"They have minimal defences," continued Brynjar, "And I think as long as we do not linger, our chances of returning home unscathed are high." He thought for a moment about the men he had lost in the Outskirts, and his confidence wavered, though nothing in his face gave it away. He straightened up, determined not spread his doubts to his men.

"I do not mean to lose any of you today," he said, pausing to look several of his men in the eye. "We attack like the river eagle, we go in fast and fierce, and we get out quickly. If you linger after I make the call to withdraw, then you *will* be left behind. Is that clear?"

"Yes, sir," came the confident reply from the group.

They are ready for this, as much as I am.

"Good," Brynjar said. "We will attack from the North and exit along the south-west road. Do not stop to loot, that is not our job today, understand?"

"Yes, sir," came the reply, surprisingly no less enthusiastic.

Brynjar lowered his voice, "These *creatures* have bloodied us, in our own lands. I suggest we return the favour."

The men looked at him with a smouldering anger and a fire that reflected Brynjar's own feelings. Reports of villages left lifeless by this unseen foe had left Brynjar with a strong desire to meet his enemy.

"Mount up!" He shouted, for the wind was strong enough now that his words would not carry far.

As one they climbed up onto their mounts. Brynjar walked over to his own horse, picked up his spear and shield, and jumped onto the creatures back. The heavy mare he had used in the Outskirts was not suited for war, so tonight he rode a great black stallion, an angry beast, dark as the sky and as ready for a fight as Brynjar himself.

He kicked the animal on to a gallop, turning to see that his men followed before heading north.

This time he took the higher ground, using it to make sure no enemy parties were waiting for an ambush. They were more visible up here, but their attack was imminent so it mattered little.

Dark clouds rolled across a darker sky, rumbling with discontent as they obscured the stars.

The wind grew in power as they came closer to the enemy camp, hiding the footfalls of the horses and pushing Brynjar back in his saddle. As he crested the ridge he stopped, looking down on the quiet camp. His men followed suit, stopping at the top of the hill and lining up alongside him.

If any Akalens were watching, the sight would have been nightmarish. Fifty mounted soldiers, armed to the teeth, illuminated on the hill by the moon at their backs. At least that's what they would look like in the gloom.

Several of his men lit torches, the fires catching quickly as the powerful breeze encouraged the flames. Restless horses bucked, knowing something was about to happen, and Brynjar could feel the energy of the men by his side.

A spot of rain hit his face. His entire body turned to gooseflesh, the feeling of fear and excitement washing down his spine. He was electrified.

Now was the time.

"Charge!" he screamed, kicking his horse down the hill.

The voices of his men rang out, rising in volume and overtaking Brynjar's own cry as he hurtled down, his screaming soldiers on his heels. He heard warning cries, no doubt from the Akalen sentries on watch, but they were too late to do anything now.

He and his men flooded into the camp as a swarm, immediately fires were lit and the ovook began to burn, illuminating the night in an orange glow. At the same time, the rain fell harder, smoking the fires but doing nothing to stop them. It was a storm of flame, and water and smoke, twisted together by the wind.

Brynjar saw the outline of an Akalen and charged into it, levelling his spear out in front of him. The point sunk into something soft and heavy, and there was a scream. He felt the flex of his spear and Brynjar had to pull the weapon away before the shaft snapped.

He carried on stabbing at the shapes in the dark, the elements daring him to go on as the rain soaked his skin. There were flashes of eyes and teeth, and he stabbed at another warrior, feeling the point punch into flesh once again. Shapes lurked in the gloom, and it was so dark down here in the camp that Brynjar had to slow his horse to avoid crashing into the round huts.

He broke away from the fight and headed for the centre of the camp. Alone now, for his men had gotten caught up in their rage, burning the warrior's homes and indulging their anger upon the enemy. His own blood was up, his instincts taking over, but he rose above them. He would not lose control of himself. Then he would be no better than those he fought.

Weaving in and out of the huts he tried to move faster. It was a dangerous thing to do in the dark atop a warhorse. He only needed to take a wrong turn, or for his mount to throw him, and he would be at the mercy of his foe. But he was determined to send a message to the leaders of his enemy.

He thundered past another ovook and abruptly was out in the open.

This wasn't right.

Pulling on the reigns he came to a stop, looking around at where the huts of the Akalen leaders should have been. Instead he could make out only a weaved fence, and inside it, livestock. Yaks, goats, sheep and horses, that was all. They were noisy, snorting and bleating, obviously scared of the spreading fire and angry shouts. Beyond it were more ovook, for this was the centre of the camp.

Something was wrong. Small military camps like this did not bring any animals other than horses with them when they fought, the bigger camps further from the fighting would provide them with food. They certainly wouldn't keep livestock in the middle of the camp where the chiefs and respected warriors should have been.

Brynjar's felt his hands go weak, his lungs were hot and suddenly the sweat on his brow turned cold.

A nightmarish possibility entered his mind. Maybe these people were not warriors. There were no defences, because they weren't expecting a fight. He couldn't find the warrior chiefs, because they weren't here.

Wind battered his face, berating him for the mistake. He had misread the signs, the wind, the rain, they were warnings. Cold seeped into his bones, drawing away his strength and replacing it with doubt, and pain.

This camp would not be made up of warriors, but of families. The screams began to sound different to Brynjar, and the flames, which only a moment ago were a signal of his victory, now provoked a feeling of horror.

Blood from his spear seeped onto his hand, making him flinch. He was no longer sure it was from his enemy.

Tears mixed with the rain on his cheeks, as he kicked his horse back to the fight.

He screamed for his men to withdraw, but the damage had already been done.

Chapter 9

Herleif galloped through the dark, desperately searching for his brother.

Stay with me, he had said, over and over. But once they charged, Fin had been deaf to his warnings, and was swept along by the anger of their fellow soldiers.

Or perhaps his own.

Now Herleif was riding alone, praying his brother was safe, though it was difficult to imagine anyone was safe. The burning ovook scarred his eyes, rendering him night blind, and the screams of Akalens filled the night, making his skin draw into gooseflesh.

Please be okay.

Something spooked his horse and before he could react, he had been thrown, landing heavily on his side. He pushed himself to his feet and tried to catch the reigns, but he slipped on the slick ground, and in a moment the horse was gone. Swearing, he snatched up his spear and continued on foot.

There were shouts coming from behind another line of ovook, and he guessed that was where the bulk of the soldiers had regrouped. He sprinted through the dark, gripping his spear like a frightened child clutches his mother's hand. His breathing was fast, and his bloodshot eyes were constantly moving, darting to every flicker of movement. He didn't want to go on, but nor could he stay. Fear had gripped him, pushing through it was like fighting through a forest of hawthorn, but he had to keep moving.

A soldier loomed out of the darkness, rushing at him on horseback, aiming his spear at Herleif, not able to tell friend from foe. At the last moment he recognised his mistake, lifting his weapon away and cursing his horse as he thundered past, kicking up mud and water into Herleifs face as he did.

Under his gambeson his body was soaked with sweat, and he could feel it cooling his skin. There were bodies by some of the ovook. Some were human, some weren't, and some were very small. He did not want to see.

What has happened?

He continued running, there would be time to ask questions later.

Turning a corner, he saw two tall black figures jogging away from him, both holding spears. Neither were human.

He ignored them and ran on.

Now the shouts were clearer, and he could make out Brynjar calling to withdraw. Another wave of panic surged through him, time was running out. He needed to find Fin, and a horse, otherwise they were both dead. Harsh words had been spoken, but Fin was family. His only family.

As he moved further into the camp, wails of pain and the screams of animals filled the air. There was an atmosphere of suffering from which he could not escape. The smell of blood and panic filled his nose, a hot, bitter scent. Still he did not stop, unable to veer from his task.

Stopping to catch his breath, his eyes caught on an ovook that had been engulfed in fire, lighting the ground around it. And there, standing with his back to the flames, was Fin.

Two Akalen men were advancing on him. They were both long limbed, wiry and very tall, at least six and half feet. Short, dark hair covered their bodies and shone in the light of the flames, giving them a sleek, powerful look. The only clothes they wore were long, patterned trousers.

They had their backs to him. He couldn't see their faces, but one of the men was holding a smooth, blustone club, and the other a pointed flint knife. The only thing that had stopped them using their weapons was Fin's spear, which he was flailing around wildly.

Herleif forgot he was out of breath and sprinted toward them, yelling at the top of his lungs. Neither of the Akalens seemed to notice, but Fin caught his eye, relief washing over his face.

As Herleif drew closer his yell faded, and he made up the last few feet in silence.

Everything happened very quickly.

With his spear extended, he barrelled into the man with the knife, stabbing him through the back. He felt the blade glance off bone, and then continue through something softer. The man was dead in an instant, but it was a poor choice of attack, for the spear had gone so deep that most of the haft was embedded in the Akalen, and as his legs gave way, the weapon was ripped from Herleif's hand. That left him without a weapon as the second man swung at Herleif with the stone club.

He saw a flash of white teeth and bright pained eyes, and tried to dodge, but the ground betrayed him, and his foot slipped. The club connected with Herleif's ribcage, caving in his bones as if they were eggshell. Bright lightning cut through his vision, and the air was forced from his lungs. He fell to the floor, unable to breathe.

Mud soaked his gambeson as he writhed on the ground, eyes squeezed shut, trying to suck in air. Drowning in the rain. He could feel chaos around him, but he was pinned to the floor by pain, unable to focus on anything other than breathing. A moment later he felt Fin's hands on his shoulders and heard his brother.

"Herleif, you have to get up, there are more coming," Fin said. There were tears in his voice.

Suddenly Herleif could breathe, and he gasped uncontrollably, a new pain shooting through his lungs. With each breath he took, he felt his ribs crackling under the skin.

Rain fell on his face, cooling his boiling skin. He opened his eyes. Fin was pulling him to his feet. He saw that the second Akalen man was lying in a heap, with Fin's spear embedded in his chest.

"We… we need to…" Herleif managed, the words unbearably painful.

Fin glanced at his wound, and he caught a glimpse of the terror in his brothers face before he managed to compose himself again.

"Don't speak, let's just get out of here," Fin said, smiling, though his voice was rough with emotion.

Herleif staggered away from the burning ovook and the two dead men, leaning heavily on Fin, who was struggling to stay on his feet. He pressed a hand to his wound. It felt like there was porridge under the skin.

This was bad.

They trudged away from the camp, fighting their way back up the hill. It was quieter now, he couldn't hear Brynjar shouting any more, only the rain, and the uneven slap of his boots against the wet ground.

Stars were visible in the sky again, and the wind had died down, letting the rain take over. It was beautiful out here, away from the noise of the camp. Herleif closed his eyes and leant a little more of his weight on Fin's shoulder. His brother was saying something again, but it sounded distant.

Herleif needed rest, he was too cold to keep walking.

Something smacked him across the face and his eyes snapped open.

"Get on the damn horse!" Fin screamed at him, rain streaming down his cheeks from puffy, bloodshot eyes.

A large brown horse with a white face stood in front of him, and big dark eyes stared into Herleif's own. Behind them, down the hill, Herleif could see a group of Akalens that were beginning to organise themselves on horseback. There were not many, only a dozen or so, but in his state that was more than enough.

"You should go alone... be faster..." Herleif managed, but Fin was shaking his head before he'd even finished.

"You aren't going to die because of me," his brother said sternly, though it sounded more like he was talking to himself.

Herleif attempted to step up onto the horse, and with monumental effort he managed to get a leg onto its back, but still almost fell off. Luckily Fin was there, and pushed him onto the creature, before jumping up himself.

Herleif lay on the horse's neck, twisting his fingers into it's mane so that he didn't fall. He tried to grip with his thighs but one of his legs had gone numb.

"Don't fall," said Fin, turning the horse. "I'm going to try and catch up with Brynjar. Hang on."

Herleif got the impression Fin was still talking to himself.

Every step the horse took made him wince. He closed his eyes again, his side throbbing and burned. Every jolt of impact from the horses stride brought him closer to tears.

For a while he lay there, trying to fight the pain, but eventually it became too much, and he slipped away.

***

Fin was riding not only for his life, but for the life of his brother too.

Light was starting to show in the east, turning the black sky to blue, and the blue to pink. Grass turned golden in the prevailing light, and the gloom was fading, making room for the day. To the west was the Akvast, the powerful water carving away the landscape in its rush south. Fin mirrored its route, staying close to its banks and praying to the great river for help as he fled.

So far it had not answered.

At first he had tried to follow Brynjar, heading for the northern crossing, but the Akalen's had headed him off, forcing him to flee south on the wrong side of the river. They followed him and Herleif like a pack of wild dogs, keeping them moving, pushing the pace and forcing them to tire. Three always stayed close behind as the others rode further back, switching in and out when the energy of their horses began to wane, taking turns exhausting their quarry. They were in no rush to kill Fin and Herleif however, for they'd been riding all through the night.

Once the panic had worn off, Fin's fatigue had begun to show. His eyes were heavy now as they rode on, the energy of fear long used up, and his mount was slowing considerably.

"Faster girl!" he snapped at her, leaning awkwardly over Herleif, who had barely moved since they'd begun riding. Earlier Fin's words had driven her on, but now she didn't have anything left to give, and her pace remained steady.

A steep bank covered in trees rose up on his right, obscuring his view of the river and forcing him away east onto the grassy steppe. As his course changed, he could feel eyes boring into his back.

He looked behind him.

They were the eyes of hunters, hungry and pained. He knew then that the Akalens would not give up until he was dead.

Behind he could see more had joined the chase, there seemed to be more than ten now, all holding weapons. Some had long spears with strips of cloth tied to the ends, which snapped in the wind as they rode, others held clubs of blustone low by their sides, but all were armed. The ones who had joined the chase late were easily recognised by their face paint, the ones chasing Fin initially hadn't time to dress themselves for battle.

Suddenly his horse whinnied and stopped, almost throwing Herleif from her back. Fin whipped his head around to look in front of him.

His heart sank.

Ahead the grass crumbled away from a bank held up only by roots and weeds. Beyond that was the Akvast, flowing directly across their path. The river had cut through the land in a large crescent, around a flood plain on which Fin now stood. Water hemmed him in on both sides, and behind him were the Akalens.

He thought about jumping in the river, but quickly decided against it. The water had come down from the mountains in the north, it would be cold enough to kill, and besides it was moving so fast that getting out would be next to impossible.

Fin was so very tired. The horse was exhausted too, her sides dripping with sweat and heaving from the effort of breathing. Now she had stopped he knew she wouldn't start again.

Herleif stirred from his sleep, his face white, the veins a vivid blue around his mouth and eyes. He looked drained, but Fin was happy he was still even breathing.

"We've... stopped?" he managed, his tone questioning.

Fin turned the horse to face the Akalens.

"Yes, we have, we'll be safe soon," he said, but Herleif, even this state, could see the warriors riding toward them.

They'd spread out, encircling the curve of land, cutting off any escape that Fin might have dashed for. They didn't need to bother, he was too tired to try anything like that now.

He slid off the horse and drew his sword, the action more ceremonial than practical, for he was too tired to use it with any sort of skill. It felt so heavy in his hand.

"Let me fight my own battles."

Fin trembled at those stupid words he had spoken to his brother, but he kept his head up, he would not defeat himself.

The wind was gone, there was perfect stillness here. He could hear the birds singing, calling out for the morning, and the air smelt fresh and sweet. He decided it wasn't the worst place to die.

You wouldn't have to die if you'd stayed with him.

Dew that had formed on the grass overnight now made his boots wet as he walked towards the Akalens. They were lined up, facing him, but in no hurry to deliver the death blow. All stayed on their horses. None spoke.

Fin would force them to acknowledge him before his death.

"Are you going to kill us then? Two boys?" he shouted. It took a massive amount of energy to even speak, and his voice was rough and throaty.

An Akalen man stepped off his horse. He stroked the animals nose affectionately and then turned to face Fin.

He wore beautifully patterned, red, baggy trousers, and an ornate gilded cloth that covered his groin and fell to mid-thigh. An impressive headdress made of dark yellow hair cascaded down his shoulders and back. It was crested with two massive stag horns, so big Fin wondered how the man kept his head up. His wrists were covered in bracelets of gold, and he carried a spear that was a foot taller than his head.

As ornate as his clothes were, it was not what Fin fixated on. He had only seen Akalen faces in the gloom before, but now, in the light before the dawn, this man's features were clear, and Fin struggled to look away.

The face was dark and hairless, but ringed with grey fur that crept onto his cheeks. Large, dark eyes were centred with hazel, and his nose was long down his face, but not protruding. The features were alien to Fin, yet utterly familiar.

"You killed our children," he said. Fin had almost expected a growl, for he had never talked to another of the Spoken Races before. He was surprised how little difference there were between accents.

The Akalen continued, "Your people attack us when all we have offered is peace. Have you not had enough war?"

Despite the words, his tone was more remorseful than accusing.

Fin faltered, he knew little history.

"Your people started the last war," he said, ignoring the accusation of slaughter. There was little weight behind his words, but even so some of the other Akalens stirred.

"We are not proud of that, but it ended decades ago, and none of us here now fought then," the man said, and it seemed to settle the others.

"So, you will kill us?" Fin said, more to clarify the Akalen's intent than anything else. He didn't have the energy left to talk himself out of this.

"I am Chief Aska, from the Warband of Teoma, the Pale Wolf of the Steppe," he said. That must have been where the other Akalens came from, he looked more formidable than the first men that had been chasing them.

"She would not approve of killing someone so young as yourself," he continued. Some of the more plainly dressed men from the camp snapped their heads around, staring at Aska, obviously unhappy that vengeance would not be enacted upon Fin. One of the men started to challenge his decision but was silenced by a raised hand. He cursed, but did not press the matter.

"So we will be spared?" said Fin, a spark of hope lending him strength.

"Teoma will want to question you," Aska said. "After that, your fate will be decided by her."

Fin nodded, feeling an odd mixture of fear and relief.

"My brother needs a healer," he said quickly, stepping forward. "If you can help him, we will come with you."

He rushed the words out, even though he knew his resistance would be nothing more than a mild annoyance to the Chief.

The Akalen looked over at Herleif, who was lying on the horse watching the situation. "He is no child," Aska snapped. "We have healers who use blood magic, but they would not join with him knowing he has taken the lives of our own. He will be killed, and offered to the river."

Fin heard the words but didn't properly take them in until another Akalen man, at a nod from Aska, moved forward on his horse, brandishing a long blustone knife.

"No, please, he is my brother," Fin managed to get out, seeing the situation turn on him again. Herleif was watching them with stoic eyes. On the brink of death his gaze was somehow still imposing. The Akalen paused.

"He will suffer less this way," Aska said softly, as if that were some great comfort for Fin. The man with the knife began to move forward again.

"I will fight you for his life," Fin blurted out, thinking of nothing else to say.

Everyone, stopped.

"Yes, I-I challenge you to a Kala'Tam," Fin said again.

A Kala'Tam was a part of Nomad culture, a fight to settle differences. It could be used to allow two parties to let off steam, to settle an argument between families, or, as a fight to the death. He knew it was used on the plains as well, but nothing past that basic fact.

Aska's face saddened, "You dishonour me," he said. "My judgement was fair, and you are not my equal."

For a moment Fin was worried. He didn't know whether it could be turned down or not. Aska stared at Fin for a long moment, and then turned to remove his headdress, leaning his spear on his horses flank.

Fin breathed a sigh of relief, before remembering what was about to happen.

You have won nothing yet, only a chance.

"We wear no armour in a Kala'Tam," one of the other Akalens spat, pointing at Fin's padded gambeson. He was more plainly dressed, one of the warriors from the camp who no doubt wanted to see Fin's blood spilt.

"I'm half his size," Fin said, looking to Aska, who still had his back turned and was removing the gold bracelets around his wrists.

"It is a Kala'Tam, we will treat it as such," Aska said, looking over his shoulder at the ground. His tone left no room for argument.

Fin, considered pressing the matter, but he knew he was lucky to have gotten this much. He turned and walked back over to Herleif.

His brother looked awful still, and Fin could hear his ragged breaths from a long way away. When he got closer he patted the horses neck.

"Just… go with them," Herleif rasped as Fin began to undo the sword belt around his waist. Obviously, he'd heard enough of their conversation to know what was happening.

"I can't back out, otherwise they'll kill you," Fin said, not making eye contact with him. He unbuttoned his padded armour and then pulled his shirt over his head. The morning chill scratched at his skin, but the cold also gave him strength.

"I'm not… going to make it anyway," Herleif said. His speech was slow, and he had to break between his sentences to breathe.

Fin didn't want to think about that.

He looked down at the river behind them, the water pulling at the bank. Lying down he reached his hands into the current. The water was freezing, and he flinched as he splashed it into his face, using the pain to wake himself up. Clear and cool as the water was, he could not see the riverbed, it must have been very deep.

"I have to try," he said, getting back to his feet and beginning to walk back to Aska.

"Please…" Herleif said, desperation in his broken voice.

Fin would have replied, but he was afraid he would break into tears. He continued his walk toward the Chieftain in silence.

It was almost dawn now. The sky was a bright, clear blue, and the sun was sitting just below the hills to the east, wanting no part of the fight to come.

Aska was in the open waiting for him, pacing slowly from side to side. He looked smaller without his headdress on, but streamlined, like a viper. He was now sporting white paint under his lips and dotted on his forehead, vivid against his black fur and skin.

All the Akalens here were long and lean, and Aska was no different. There was no excess bulk to him, and the muscles in his arms and torso showed clearly even through his short fur.

Fin knew how fragile he looked in comparison and flicked his sword with his wrist in an attempt to show some measure of strength. The action felt slow, only serving to highlight what he thought was already obvious.

Aska's dark eyes flicked down to Fin's weapon, then back up to his face.

"Let the Sky hold up the honoured," he said slowly.

"And let the Earth pull down the wretched," Fin finished. The words were sacred, but he had never said them before. Remembering them in his exhausted state was a small victory in itself.

"The Sky watches," said the Akalen warrior with the knife, signalling the start of the fight.

Aska moved first, advancing over to Fin quickly, his footsteps almost silent. He held his spear low and as he got closer he began to bounce into his stride, so he was going at a half run. Fin had never seen someone move like that in a fight and raised his sword overhead defensively.

Aska moved around him in his weird, hopping run. He ran side on to him, staying completely out of range. Fin followed the Akalen's movements, taking slow, deliberate steps to keep the man to his front.

Suddenly Aska dived forward, spear aimed directly at Fins stomach. Fin whipped his sword down and knocked the attack away, stepping forward to follow up. But Aska had already bounced out of range, and his sword met nothing but air as the chief began to circle him again.

Fin raised his sword back up above his head, he was already breathing heavily, with nerves as much as effort. That attack was much faster than he had expected, and he had barely gotten his sword down in time.

Aska moved forward again. It was exactly the same attack but somehow Fin had not been expecting it. He whipped his sword down a moment too late, and the spearhead grazed his ribs before he knocked it off to the side. Pain blossomed from his bones and he grimaced. This time he was unable even to begin his follow up before Aska was gone.

This was going badly. Fin knew he was completely outclassed. The chief was bigger, faster, more experienced, and had far more energy.

Frustrated, he advanced on Aska, running forward to try and pressure his opponent.

Aska's face was calm and he retreated easily, moving back as Fin came forward, matching him step for step.

Fin wanted to yell out in anger, but the fight would be done on Aska's terms, he had the range and the speed, Fin would be resigned to counters.

As he watched, the Akalen twirled his spear around skilfully, so the blunt end was now facing toward him.

Abruptly he bounced in with a thrust to Fins chest. Fin pulled his sword down to block, but Aska had feigned, holding his attack for a moment longer than expected, using the full length of his stride and arm to time his strike.

Fin tried to right his mistake, but the momentum of his own swing pulled his arms down, allowing Aska thrust his spear into Fin's chest.

It was only the blunt end of the weapon, but even so Fin was knocked off his feet from the impact of the strike. His lungs were empty as he tried to scramble back up, his chest burning with pain.

A sharp spearhead pressed into his throat, forcing him to stay down.

"It is over," said Aska, a calm pity in his eyes.

You lost.

Fin tried to object but no words came from his mouth. He looked over to Herleif, his heart pounding in his chest.

You failed.

Herleif was sat up on the horse, looking drunkenly at the Akalen's facing him. One man with a bow was knocking an arrow to it.

Fin opened his mouth, but no words came out.

The Akalen pulled back on the string of his bow and aimed it at Herleif.

Fin stared at his brother, but Herleif wasn't looking at him, his eyes were fixed on the arrow.

In a few quick moments the arrow had been loosed, zipping through the air and hitting Herleif square in the chest, knocking him backwards. The horse whinnied, rearing up, and Herleif slid off its back, crashing into the water behind him.

And then it was over, before Fin could even process what was happening.

He stared numbly at the space where his brother had been, as men hurried over to him.

He put up no struggle, and they bound him in silence as the sun spilt over the horizon.

Chapter 10

The sun beat down on the landscape.

It was warm now, and growing warmer, even as Kiakra and her band headed north. The sky was clear and blue, but despite the powerful rays of light, the chill still lingered in the shadows, and at night the ground was like ice.

Wearing only a linin tunic and hide leggings she was stood up on a boulder checking the way north. She'd taken her boots off to relieve her boiling feet, and it was too hot for a cloak. They still had a few days of travel before they reached Stemrad, but the route seemed clear enough, nothing but long hills and green grass cut short by herds of bison and other grazers. To the west was the Akvast, wide and powerful, leading the way.

They'd stopped at the top of a small hill dotted with sand coloured rocks to take a break. Aldrid had passed out immediately, taking a nap with the large black Yaks they used to carry their supplies, but they hadn't seemed to mind his company and were all sleeping together in a tight bundle in the sun. Cypher had disappeared to forage, as was her way, Tiko had gone to spot game in the east, and Rat was up on one of the boulders sharpening a beautiful greenstone knife, keeping half an eye on their captive.

Other than the basic facts of Lax's crimes, Kiakra knew very little about their captive, and she intended to keep it that way. There was no reason for her to know anything about him other than that he was wanted for thieving and murder, and that was what the Weasel Pack dealt with. That was the name of her odd band of hunters, and she found it fitting. They weren't the biggest, or the strongest, but they were cunning and lethal all the same.

She climbed off her perch on the boulder and began to walk down the hill toward the river.

"Oi, where you going?" shouted Rat from his rock. He had paused sharpening his knife and was looking at her with a mischievous grin. He was bare chested and the smooth plates of scale on his back were glinting in the sunlight.

Kiakra smirked, "Just for a walk," she said, and continued down the hill.

The earth was hard beneath her feet as she walked, and the grass was cool, still slightly damp from the morning dew. She'd been on horseback since dawn and her legs were enjoying getting some use.

It wasn't far to the river, but down here was much cooler. A large willow reached out over the water, it's lower tendrils getting caught in the flow, and at the river's edge the earth gave way to silt and sand, leading into clear rocky water. Upriver was a huge fallen trunk which had created an eddy, which had then in turn formed this small beach.

Kiakra walked straight in, feeling the icy water flowing gently past her feet, cooling her sore toes. She sighed, relieved.

Across the river she noticed a family of wild boar coming down for a drink. They were followed by a bold little robin, which she knew from experience would follow the broken earth left by the mother to pick out worms. None seemed bothered by Kiakra's presence, and they had no reason to, for the mother was a huge beast with a thick neck and short wiry hair. Her eyes flicked over to Kiakra for a moment, letting her know she had been seen, and then she lowered her head to the water, her piglets copying her. Obviously Kiakra posed no threat to them.

She looked back down into the water. The rocks glinted like diamonds, but she knew from experience that, were you to pick them up out of the water, they would turn brown and drab. She rolled up her sleeves and cupped some water up into her palms, splashing it into her face to wash away the dirt of travel.

Out here the Akvast was the mother of all life. It felt good to be a part of that again.

She smiled, turned and waded out of the water. A wagtail was flitting from the riverbank to some rocks in the slower flowing patches of river, its yellow underside flashing in the sun. She watched it searching the shallows for the insects, bobbing and dipping as it moved. As she watched it hopping up the river, something caught in the corner of her eye.

Upstream, lying on another patch of beach, was a man.

He wasn't moving.

Instinctively she looked around, checking for an ambush, and for a moment she regretted not bringing her sword with her. A few moments later she decided it wasn't an ambush, the boar were completely relaxed, there was little cover in which to hide, and the man looked to be dead, washed up on the shore.

Kiakra wandered over to have a look at him, out of curiosity more than concern.

When she drew closer she realised that he was a lot younger than she'd first thought, he couldn't be much older than her.

He was lying on his back, his legs still in the water, and there was the haft of an arrow sticking out of his chest. The end had snapped off, but the wood was soaked through, he must have been in the water a long time.

She knelt next to him, examining his face.

From his appearance Kiakra knew he was undoubtedly Nomadic. The features were distinct and familiar, his skin was the same tanned colour as her own.

My kin.

He was not dressed like a Nomad though, his clothes were from the Kingdom. He wore a scabbard, with no sword, and a thick, soaking gambeson. A soldier by the looks of it.

For a moment she felt some pity for him, he looked healthy, apart from his wounds, and too young to be caught up in any sort of fighting. Maybe if the Kingdom let women fight, she would have ended up here instead of him, a soldier instead of a hunter.

You can't mourn every passing.

Kiakra looked over him once again, this time putting a hand on his shoulder, and whispering a quiet prayer.

"Let him find his way home," she asked of the Akvast in a whisper.

"What have you found?" came a voice from behind her.

Immediately Kiakra was on her feet, cursing herself for letting her guard down, but it was only Cypher, wandering toward her with her tunic turned up in a pouch. It was full of roots and berries, no doubt with various medicinal uses, and she had been smiling, but as she noticed the body her face dropped.

Kiakra straightened up, "He's dead, I was just seeing if he had anything useful on him."

"You don't know if he's dead, there's no rot on his body," Cypher said, dumping out the contents of her tunic and hurrying over. She knelt and placed a hand gently on his throat.

"There is some life in him," she said quietly, sounding surprised. The she looked back up at Kiakra, "I would have expected better of you" she said, scorn in her voice.

Kiakra grit her teeth, she hated when Cypher spoke like that.

"Pass me those roots," Cypher said, pointing behind her at the food she had dumped on the floor.

Kiakra took a firmer stance, "There's no point, he's not going to make it and we don't know what to do with him even if he does."

The words were said with authority, but Cypher didn't move, she simply turned her head and looked up at Kiakra.

"But we can't just leave him here if he's still alive?" she said. Her eyes were wounded as she spoke, and that was Cyphers flaw, she cared too much about people, even when they didn't deserve it. It came with being a healer.

"I said no, I'm not letting you kill yourself trying to bring back some soldier on the brink of death," Kiakra said firmly. "It'll drain you, and we can't look after him anyway."

"We could just take him to Stemtrad and drop him off there?" Cypher said, completely ignoring Kiakra's firm tone, "We could even charge him for our trouble!"

It was a blatant afterthought to appease her.

Kiakra rubbed her face in frustration and spoke slowly, "He doesn't have any money on him."

"Well I'm not leaving him, he *can* be saved, and so he *should* be saved." Cypher said. She kept her voice low, but nonetheless there was power behind the words. She was breathing heavily and crouching over the boy defensively.

"This was me once," she said, gesturing at him. "I couldn't look after myself, and you took me in, even though I was useless and close to death."

Kiakra was reminded vividly of the thin little girl she had first come across all those years ago, so weak she could barely talk. She'd had to steal twice as much food to feed her, and had been beaten more than once because of it.

"You were a healer though, there was some benefit to saving you," Kiakra said. "He's just another mouth that'll cost us to feed."

Cypher was looking at her with fire in her eyes, "So you wouldn't have helped me if I didn't serve some purpose?"

"You know what I mean," Kiakra said, slightly frustrated at how poorly she was making her argument. "Once I'd helped you, you could at least hold your own."

Cypher shook her head, "You're starting to think like a hunter, and I don't think that's a good thing."

"Alright, alright," Kiakra said, rubbing her face in frustration. The girl had a habit of highlighting problems she wasn't yet ready to admit to. "We'll make sure he doesn't die, but after Stemtrad he's gone."

Cypher nodded, her smile barely contained. Then she remembered the boys state and her face was serious again. "Can you-"

"Yes," Kiakra sighed, walking over to pick up the dumped food. There was no one else in her Pack that could speak to Kiakra like that, but Cypher was different. She knew that the girl's actions came from a selfless place that she herself could no longer access. That innocence and trust, and the moral rigidity that came along with it, were traits Kiakra had long ago abandoned in herself, she'd had to. But she was somehow unable to destroy them in Cypher. The girl was an idealist, and sometimes she got caught up in that.

She gathered up the food and scooped it into her own tunic. "Is this enough for his injuries?" she said, reservation in her voice. "He has got an arrow in his chest."

Cypher pulled a knife from somewhere, "Yes I think so, the arrow has actually barely punctured his skin, the gambeson has protected him quite well, and the cold water might have helped preserve him."

Kiakra frowned as she walked back with the food, "Then why is he in such a poor state? Did he drown?"

Cypher cut open the padded armour, revealing a huge black welt across the boy's ribs. She gently touched a hand to the wound, "I think it might be this," she said, as her finger sunk into the skin. There was no resistance to her touch.

"That's going to take a lot of energy," said Kiakra, handing Cypher a nasty looking brown root. "Are you really sure you want to do this?"

"Yes, I'll be a little weaker for the rest of today, but I won't get hurt." Her eyes did not meet Kiakra's own.

"Can you promise me that?" said Kiakra, grabbing the girl's arm and forcing eye contact. Cypher looked at her and nodded, confident as she could manage, then she bit off half the brown root and began chewing. It smelt better than it looked.

"You don't need to get him conscious yet, just stop him from dying and we can sort him out properly when you're strong again," Kiakra said, switching from sounding like a hunter, to a fussing mother.

Cypher just nodded, it was nothing she didn't know already.

She shoved a handful of berries into her mouth and then made two incisions either side of the boys wound. After she'd done that, she swallowed the food and made similar cuts on her own hands.

Kiakra always hated seeing Cypher use blood magic.

As she watched, the girl took a deep breath and then placed her palms over the incisions she had made on the boy's body, touching their wounds together. Making the connection.

Nothing happened for many moments, but then, gradually, Cyphers hands began to glow as her blood flowed under the boy's skin. It was a faint light, fainter than usual, his spirit must have been close to leaving him.

Kiakra looked up from the boy and saw the effort in Cyphers face, sweat already beginning to bead on her forehead. Something thick and black oozed out from under her palms, but before Kiakra could say anything Cypher spoke.

"Don't worry, it's just the old blood escaping."

Kiakra nodded, not wanting to distract her any further.

Something cracked loudly, and Kiakra winced, screwing her face up and turning away. She couldn't watch any more. Something else made a squelching, sucking noise, and she imagined flesh knitting itself together at Cyphers will.

She was fine with blood and injuries, Kiakra was in no way squeamish, but there was something about this process that made her skin crawl.

For a long while they stayed like that. Kiakra sat close behind Cypher, watching the hills and listening to the river flow past, silent and protective as the smaller girl worked.

Birds grew accustomed to their presence, and a few of the more curious ones flitted down to investigate before zipping back off into the branches as more cracking bones scared them away.

Kiakra looked back up at the hill to see if the others were missing them yet, but she could still see the dark outlines of the Yaks, led out in sprawling heaps in the sun. Aldrid was likely still asleep with them, so she didn't worry.

She could also see the herd of goats milling about near the rocks where Rat had been perched. Since Kiakra had killed Jutai the Bavagai, the animals had been following them on the road, unable to function without a master, but still weary of the group they followed.

Kiakra didn't want them around, they ate everything and the bells they wore about their necks made so much noise. She'd tried to scare them off but so far nothing had worked, and though killing them would have been easier, Rat and Aldrid had pointed out they could be sold back to the contractor if they continued to follow.

After some time, the noises of binding sinew and bone began to fade, along with the red glow. Kiakra looked behind her.

Cypher removed her hands from the boy. He still had the shallow cut in his chest, but his ribs were solid and pink, as if there had never been an injury there and he had just been slapped.

Cypher, however, looked like death.

"I told you not to go on for so long," Kiakra said, twisting quickly to support the girl as she drifted backwards. She was so light she felt hollow.

"I, didn't... mean to," Cypher replied, as her eyes began to close. Her hands were still bleeding, she was pale, and her skin looked paper thin. Her head lolled back onto Kiakra's shoulder as she went unconscious.

"Stupid bloody girl," Kiakra muttered.

Keeping Cypher supported, Kiakra stood and then hefted her up onto her shoulders, leaving the boy by the river and hurrying back up the hill toward the others.

***

She was greeted by bleating goats nipping at her knees as she arrived. She kicked them away, growling. Rat saw her and scrambled down his rock, running over to meet them. He'd been picking at his skin, which involved peeling the dead layer off, much like a snake sheds itself, and one arm was a much brighter green than the other.

"What happened?" he said, helping Kiakra as she lowered Cypher from her back onto a bed of soft grass next to the yaks.

"We found someone who looked dead down by the river," Kiakra said, feeling Cypher's head, which was very cold. The sleeping yaks didn't wake as she rummaged through their bags to fish out her own bearskin cloak.

"This one decided to try and heal him up," she continued, gesturing at Cypher before heaving out her cloak and using it to wrap up the unconscious girl.

"How's the one down by the river?" Rat said, looking at Cypher with concern. "He must have been in a bad way to do this to her."

Kiakra looked back down to where she'd left the boy, she couldn't see him from here, but she knew where he was. "He's better than he was, but still out of it. Like how Aldrid was when he slipped off that cliff in Aslund?"

Rat made a whistling noise, "No wonder she's down," he said. Then he looked at Kiakra sideways, "Why did you let her? She hasn't had time to recover from the last heal she did on you and Lax."

Kiakra bit her tongue, "She'd already started when I got there, and it seemed a waste if she didn't revive him," she lied. It seemed better than admitting her lack of control over the girl.

Rat nodded slowly, unconvinced, "And how can we afford to look after this lad?"

Kiakra met his gaze, which had turned very serious, and reminded her of his motivations.

"I'm not far from being able to pay off my exile, I don't need any more setbacks," he said. That hope of buying back into his empire was what drove him on in this harsh profession, and she doubted he would show much sympathy to anyone getting in the way of that goal.

"We're just going to drop him off in Stemtrad," she said, looking down.

Kiakra led the group, but she didn't own them. Her authority was far from supreme and occasionally it showed.

"Stemtrad is another week's travel away, it'll cost us to look after him until then," Rat said. There was an edge to his voice.

"Don't worry, we'll hunt more to minimise the cost of food, and whatever it does cost to get him there, we will charge him for."

"What if he can't pay?"

"It won't be coming out of your share," she said firmly, silencing him with a look.

He nodded and took a breath, dismissive of his own worries.

"Just making sure," he said. He smiled, but it didn't reach his eyes.

Another goat started sniffing at Cypher's face, and he pushed it away firmly. "Do we need to go and get him then?" he asked in a more neutral tone.

Kiakra rubbed her face, "Suppose we do really."

"Who is he?" Rat said, his mischievous grin returning.

"A soldier," Kiakra replied.

"From up North?"

"Looks that way."

Rat laughed, "Tiko isn't going to be happy if we bring him back up, you know that? Her family have been involved in that mess for months now."

"I know that," Kiakra said quietly.

"Should have just stopped Cypher from healing him, would have been easier," Rat sighed.

She knew that, but there was something in the boys' face that spoke to her, and despite her best efforts to ignore them, Cyphers words had cut deep.

She was like a sister to her, and she didn't know where she'd be if they hadn't met. Maybe this boy would turn out to be the same.

Probably not.

A vulture appeared overhead, drifting in lazy circles high above the boy, and for a moment the answer to her problem seemed so simple.

Another goat wandered over, trying to nibble at Cyphers ear. Kiakra kicked the animal away, but several others were hanging around.

Turning to face the yaks she cupped two hands to her mouth, "Oi Aldrid, wake up!"

The animals barely moved as the older man sat up quickly, alarm on his sleepy face.

"Cypher is down, look after her whilst we're gone," she shouted. She heard some mutterings and an irritated reply which sounded positive. It was more enthusiasm than she had for fetching the soldier.

"Come on then, we better go get him," she said, walking down the hill.

Rat chuckled, following her, "I do not want to be around when Tiko gets back."

"I don't blame you," she said, as the vulture continued to circle, mocking her.

Chapter 11

Brynjar had barely slept since his raid.

He slogged through the camp, his boots sinking into deep mud with every step.

It was a dark day. Black clouds sat above him, growling. The rain that fell was heavy and cold, and there was no wind. It gave the camp a dead feel, despite the amount of people now occupying it. The birds were the only ones enjoying the weather, crows and rooks swooping down from tent poles to pick out worms from the soil, bouncing back up to their perches when disturbed.

Brynjar barely noticed any of it.

He had lost six of his own in his attack. One had died during the raid, another three had lost their lives afterwards from injuries sustained during the fighting, and the two boys he had picked up in the Outskirts were missing.

A couple of stooping soldiers straightened up as he marched through the camp, aware of his recent mistakes and the temper that had come with it. Past them an elderly couple crouched under a rotting hide cover, both soaked through and shivering. Despite his best efforts, it was becoming increasingly obvious that Gulbrand was unable to look after the sheer volume of displaced villagers now in camp. Soon it would not be the Akalens that these people would lose their lives to, but negligence.

Brynjar wanted to help them, but he knew bringing them here was not a tactic that could work long term. Soon the food supplies would run out, and with no land being cultivated they would have to lean on the other regions to keep themselves fed. The problem had to be dealt with now, and that was what he intended to propose. He was headed to Gulbrand's pavilion.

He walked past huddling families that found shelter where they could, and stoic men clutching spears, their gambesons heavy and wet. His own clothes were soaked, his cloak swaying just shy of the ground with the weight of the rain, and his uncovered braid hanging down from his head like the tail of a leopard.

He passed through the gate at the edge of the camp with only a nod from the guards stationed there, crossed the crude wooden bridge that forded the waterlogged ditches, and headed towards Gulbrand.

Ahead of him was clear ground, and beyond that the Yilland Oak, blocking out much of the sky. Moss on its roots had been saturated by the rain and was a deep, nourished green, whilst its upper branches twisted through the sky like serpents. Brynjar could see why it was a beacon that the people of Yilland flocked to. He felt its presence in his core, and he had no ties to this place. Under its branches was darker, but it felt safe, as though the surroundings were hugging him.

The pavilion shone out brightly from between the massive roots of the tree, and Brynjar headed toward it, aware of how strange he looked, alone, on this open field.

When he got closer he saw Gulbrand's guard, standing to attention outside. They were older men, large, veterans of Yilland who had likely served under the Lord their entire life. Their mail armour was covered by dark green surcoats that had the golden Oak emblazoned on the chest, another symbol of their loyalty to the region, and the man who ruled it. Bad weather had done little to dampen their spirits, and they were still bolt upright, alert and standing tall against the rain that filtered its way through the great tree's branches. They saw Brynjar long before he got to the pavilion and had ample time to identify him. When he arrived they simply nodded their heads and let him enter.

He pushed through the opening to Gulbrand's tent slowly, so as not to disturb the man. The guards would not have let him enter if the Lord was not in a state to take guests, but barging in would set a poor precedent for the type of delicate conversation he wished to have.

Inside the rain was even louder, as it pattered against the roof, but it was warm and a little smoky. There was a small fire burning, and Gulbrand was sat reading at a heavy wooden table covered in maps and letters. He wore a dark blue tunic, tied at the waist with a thick gold studded belt, and was pouring over a particularly detailed map of Yilland. He looked up quickly as Brynjar entered.

"Oh, my lad," he said, his face dropping. "I am sorry."

Brynjar lifted his chin, "You don't need to apologise my Lord, it was my own fault."

Gulbrand shook his head and waved Brynjar's words away, "Our information was off, you can't blame yourself," he said, leaning back in his chair and rubbing his temples. "I should have made sure our spies were certain before sending you out to do anything."

"I checked it myself, and I still didn't realise," Brynjar said. "The camp was big and close to our border." He shrugged, defeated, "I thought that meant there'd be a military force there."

Gulbrand sighed, "And while I was sending you out there to attack the innocent, Captain Egil has returned with news that more blood has soaked our own soil."

Brynjar clenched his jaw at the word innocent. He knew Gulbrand had not meant to offend him, but he needed no more mention of his mistakes. The dead were only too keen to remind him of those.

"Did the Captain manage to get eyes on the Akalens? See if they flew any banners?" Brynjar said, trying to move past his error.

Gulbrand shook his head, "No he didn't. No survivors or witnesses either, just bodies, again."

The Lord leant forward staring at the map in front of him. It was a detailed representation of Yilland and the beginning of the steppe to the east. There were three little black x's drawn to show where they had been attacked, two to the north and one freshly drawn on in the south.

"Is there any way to increase Yilland's defences, any bottlenecks we can take advantage of?" Brynjar asked, staring down at the map.

Gulbrand shook his head, "Our defences are as good as they can be, I don't know how the enemy is getting past us, but they are. We need to destroy the threat from its source."

The man looked exhausted, and Brynjar could understand why. Those small black symbols were a stain on the man's pride, a clear mark of his inability to protect his own people from harm.

He leant back in his chair and pulled an ornate blue bottle from a draw, before pouring some out into a glass.

There was a pause as he looked up at Brynjar, "You want some? All the way from the Southern Empire apparently."

Brynjar shook his head, "I'm fine."

Gulbrand nodded, "I understand. It tastes like pig crap, but it is at least very strong. Apparently, all they know how to do down there is poison you." Even so he took a long drink from his glass before wincing.

Brynjar looked back at the map.

"Are all your men loyal to you?" he said carefully, "Perhaps someone has been letting our enemies through."

Gulbrand furrowed his brow, "You know, as well as I, that many of our recruits are young," he shook his head, "But I can't imagine they would yield to the Akalens."

Brynjar nodded. It was unlikely there were traitors among them, for though they were not as disciplined as Gulbrand's elite, many had families they were trying to protect.

"We don't have enough men to guard Yilland, if Teoma decides to focus an attack anywhere on the border she will smash our defences," Gulbrand said, oddly calm. "Grenland is still establishing itself, and Brunland has even fewer resources than we do. We need Lord Alvard. He has men assembled on our western border in case we are overrun, but your father still refuses to join us in defending the east."

Brynjar felt somewhat embarrassed. Surely three villages would have been enough to sway his father? At least he had mustered his forces, but keeping them back on his own borders seemed an odd move for Alvard, as though he was acknowledging the risk, but still choosing not to help.

"I will send a message, maybe the new circumstances will sway him," Brynjar said, puzzled. "In the meantime I wanted to ask you something."

Gulbrand straightened up a little, "Go on."

Brynjar drew his shoulders back and stood up as tall as he could manage, "I lost six of my own in the raid, I am sure you know this."

Gulbrand nodded solemnly.

"Well two of them were not killed, they were separated from us," he continued. "I ask your permission to ride out and attempt a rescue. I also wish to try and take their captors as our own prisoners, in order to question them on the intentions of the Pale Wolf, Teoma."

Gulbrand was already shaking his head regretfully, "We do not have the manpower to risk braving enemy territory in a search for two soldiers who are, with all due respect, probably already dead."

Not soldiers, boys.

He sometimes wondered if Gulbrand was even aware of the people that made up his army. Many were certainly not old enough to be soldiers, but who's fault was that? Who had been the one to let them sign up?

He shook his head and took a deep breath, "Sir they were only boys, and would have been lighter on a horse than the warriors that were chasing-"

"I understand how you feel about losing men," Gulbrand said, cutting him off with a gentle voice. "But that is war, and to risk the lives of more men hunting for corpses is simply not something we can do." His face was full of sympathy as he spoke.

"They might not be dead," Brynjar said, looking into the older man's eyes. "And even if they are, I cannot sleep knowing two brothers I recruited will die without burials, far from their homes." He lowered his voice, "I do not know how the people of the Steppe bury their dead, and Fin and Herleif do not deserve to become Demons."

Recognition flickered across Gulbrand's face.

"How old were they?" he said slowly, his eyes narrowing.

"Herleif was fifteen or sixteen, and Fin was a few years younger than that," Brynjar said, keeping the hope from his voice so as not to harm his chances.

Gulbrand shook his head, "That *is* too young," he muttered, and just those words reassured Brynjar. Perhaps he did know the people he commanded.

Gulbrand stood and began to pace the room, the exhaustion from earlier had dissipated, now he seemed deep in thought.

"Do you know them sir?" Brynjar asked quickly, perhaps he could persuade him that way.

Gulbrand nodded, crossing his arms and raising a hand to scratch his beard, "I've met Fin, only briefly, but there was something about him."

He turned and looked at Brynjar, "The Oak wanted him."

Brynjar was not easily swayed by omens, as many other Lords of the Kingdom were, but those four words made him aware of the huge weight around him. He was sandwiched in the tree. Its crown loomed over his head, and the roots made up the ground on which he stood. He knew a spirit as great as this, which occupied both the earth and the sky, was not to be ignored.

He shivered, and then, feeling the change in Gulbrand, ventured another ask, "Will you let me search for them? And try to work out what Teoma wants?"

Gulbrand rubbed his temple, "I will give you a week, and fifty men. You are to bring Captain Egil with you. He fought with me in the war, he knows our enemy well," he nodded, then looked back at Brynjar. "You find the boys, catch your prisoners for questioning, and then return here. Understood?" he spoke now with the authority Brynjar was used to.

"Yes, and thank you my Lord, if it's alright with you I will leave now," he said, surprised at his own luck and not wanting to test it.

Gulbrand walked over and clapped a big hand on Brynjar's shoulder, "Go, bring them back, let's find some good amongst all this bad." He smiled warmly, and Brynjar nodded, turning to leave.

Outside the rain continued to fall, but now, Brynjar could feel it.

***

It was cold. The rain had stopped in the late afternoon, but the evening light had done little to dry Fin's clothes, and so now he was lying in the dark, shaking. He wasn't sure if that was because of the cold, or his head.

His hands were bound, and so were his feet, tight enough to make the skin around his wrists blistered and raw. Moving hurt, and so did thinking.

Everything hurts.

He concentrated on trying to get fed, Herleif wouldn't have wanted him to starve.

It was a clear, still night out on the steppe. Not even the Akvast could be heard, for they had begun to head east. Chief Aska had left in the morning, riding on ahead with his warriors to report back to Teoma. He'd left just one of his warriors to lead the remaining men and make sure Fin got to Teoma alive.

Since Aska had left, Fin's treatment had gotten worse. He'd received a beating only moments after the Chief was out of sight, splitting his lip and closing up one of his eyes. The offending Akalen had been pulled off him, but nothing more. He hadn't been fed either. The first night he hadn't been able to sleep because of his brother. This night, hunger was keeping him awake too.

They'd lit a couple of fires, but Fin was too far away to benefit from any of the warmth.

He thought back to nights in the village with his brother, only weeks ago, eating warm rabbit stew and cracking jokes with one another. The shack had been small, but it was insulated better than some of the others, and Herleif had done a good job of keeping the wood stores well stocked so the fire was always warm.

Herleif had been good at everything. All Fin wanted, was to be able to look after them as well as his brother had. Now his brother was dead, and on his second night alone, Fin was freezing and starving, a prisoner of war with an uncertain future.

I am so sorry.

His thoughts turned to the charge, and his brothers voice. That was the last time he had heard it clearly, yelling words of warning that he had ignored out of spite. Those words haunted him, reminding him of his part in Herleif's death. The anger he had felt towards his brother had stagnated in his chest, rotting him from the inside.

The events played over and over in his head. If only he had stayed with him. If only he had fought harder… no, Fin was not meant for that. By the time he had to fight it was too late. Herleif was the strong one, the protector, not him. He was the weak one, the fool who should have died.

Useless.

Only now could he appreciate his brother's intentions. Herleif had tried to take care of him the best way he could, and that love had gotten him killed in the end.

You got him killed.

"Ay," one of the men shouted to Fin, snapping him out of his thoughts. He realised his feet were numb and there were tears on his cheeks.

"You want some food?" the man said. It was the leader, the man Aska had left in charge. Fin thought his name was Yatu, but he wasn't sure. He recognised reluctance on the Akalen's face, and knew he wouldn't ask twice.

If he was stronger, he would have spat at him, cursed, refused the hospitality of those who had killed his kin. But he didn't, his mouth watered, and his stomach was sick with hunger. He nodded, gently.

Coward.

Some of the other Akalens laughed, and a few of them muttered, but Yatu quieted them with a hand before standing and moving over to Fin. He sat down in front of him, long legs folding up beneath himself as he did. The man had a drawn, dark face, and his eyes could barely be seen by the dim light from the fires. He grabbed Fin by the back of his shirt and lifted him, so they were facing one another.

The group had gone quiet, and Fin felt the gaze of every Akalen.

Yatu placed a bowl down in front of him, his face unreadable.

Vegetables, cooked meat, and sweet cheese, these were the smells that drifted up to Fin's nose, making his mouth water. Tentatively he reached down and slid the bowl a little closer to himself. The portion was tiny, but it was enough to keep himself going for another night.

Yatu watched him as he reached out a shaky hand, picked up a morsel of food and stuffed it in his mouth. Flavour exploded on his tongue, the taste was so rich it was almost painful. He chewed only a few times before swallowing and reaching for more. He hadn't realised how hungry he truly was.

The stares of angry men still clung to him as he ate, and the warrior sat only a foot away, watching him carefully, the bands of silver around his wrists and throat glinting in the fireflight.

Fin wanted to exercise caution, but he was ravenous, and before long the portion was gone. He shamelessly licked the last juices of taste from his fingers, his stomach rumbling for more. He couldn't thank the warrior, so he simply nodded.

"Ach," one of the other men said, waving a hand and standing up in front of the fire. "You feed him from our fire after what he's done?" There were murmurs of agreement as the man spat on the ground.

The warrior's eyes stayed on Fin. He picked up the bowl, uncrossed his legs, and stood. Only then did Yatu look back at the group.

"Aska, asked me to try and keep this one alive," he said slowly. He looked at them collectively as he spoke, demonstrating his confidence as he did so. Behind his gaze Fin could sense a challenge to them all. None returned his stare. "You have had your vengeance, and I have no love for the Humans, I do not care if he dies," he said, gesturing at Fin, "But he is a boy, and I will not be the cause of his death."

There were murmurs of agreement, and then Yatu returned to the fire. The man who had spoken earlier did not sit, instead he cursed and stalked off into the dark.

Fin shivered again. After having eaten, his body now had enough energy to inform him how much pain he should have been feeling. The bruises on his ribs ached, and the cuts on his face stung. He regretted taking the food, it was undeserved.

Then a scream rocked the night.

In an instant, every man was on his feet, the calmness of the evening gone as the Akalens scrambled to pick up their weapons. Yatu looked over to Fin, making sure he was still there, and not the cause of the commotion.

Fin saw emotion then in the warrior's face, it was fear.

Horses whinnied, and away from the fire he heard the creatures thunder away. The fire was abandoned as each man ran off into the dark to catch his mount before it fled into the night.

For a moment Fin was utterly alone, sitting back from the light of the fire in a not so empty gloom. Then something moved at the edges of the light, on the other side of the dull flames. It was too big to be a horse, its gait heavy and wide.

Fin felt himself sweat, waves of fear shooting down his spine. There was nothing he could do. He had no horse, no weapons, he couldn't even move.

Pulling at the bonds around his wrists, he twisted on the floor like a snake, the pain of the sores ignored as he tried to free himself.

But the ropes were thick and unyielding. He managed to twist himself up onto his knees, and then, with great effort, his feet. But his ankles were tied together and he immediately fell back onto his side.

A horse and rider charged back into the light of the fire, both wild eyed with terror. Fin flinched, but then recognised Yatu. He rushed at Fin, and for a moment he thought the man would trample him, but on the final stride the Akalen twisted and leaped down from the creatures back, keeping a hand on its reigns as he pulled out a knife.

Something moved behind them, away from the fire.

The horse bucked wildly, the warrior barely able to hold on. He threw the knife down by Fin.

"Good luck," he said, jumping onto his mount, which by this point was trying to gallop away, even against the pull of the reigns.

In a moment the warrior was off, unable to control his horse as together they tore away into the night. Fin looked around him. There was nothing except the distant rumbling of hooves and the crackling of the remaining fire.

Frantically, shuffling on his belly, he moved to the knife, only a few feet away. He picked it up with sweaty hands. It was a short choppy thing, made of rusted iron, but it cut through the binding at his wrists well enough.

As the sound of hooves faded, the noise of iron wheezing through the rope became deafening and Fin could barely keep his hands steady. The fire died down as he cut through, reducing the hot yellow flames to dark red embers.

He allowed himself to hope that the creature had gone.

Finally he snapped though the rope and pulled his hands apart. But his feet were still tied. He was about to begin cutting through when he heard breathing.

He stopped, frozen by instinct.

Glowing dimly above the embers of the fire, were two spots of light. They were eyes, the same eyes he had seen peering at him from the great Oak.

Slowly, a paw the size of Fin's chest stepped over one side of the fire, followed by another on the other side. Filthy, dreadlocked hair matted the creature's legs.

Its breathing was slow and deep, like bellows blowing through a furnace. Despite its size, Fin knew it would not be slow.

He couldn't move. He was pinned to the spot by fear.

Slowly, the rest of its body passed over the dim light, and it moved towards him.

He could see little of its face, but he made out a huge muscular head, connected to a limp low hanging jaw, from which a long string of saliva hung, the embers of the fire turning it to liquid gold in the darkness.

Now he could see the eyes clearly, and they weren't white, but a brilliant grey, metallic and old.

Hot breath touched his face as it moved closer, and he could smell blood in its fur.

His mouth went dry and he gripped the knife with white fingers.

It had found him.

Chapter 12

"I don't care, just leave him."

Herleif didn't know who was speaking, the voice sounded alien to him, and he was too tired to open his eyes. The air was cool, but he could hear the crackle of a fire somewhere nearby. Strong animal smells filled his nose, though none of the aromas were offensive.

"Cypher is barely able to walk," said another voice, calmer than the first. "It'd be a pointless waste of all that energy."

He had no idea what they were talking about, or who they were, but his body ached all over.

"Don't worry," someone whispered into his ear. "You were hurt very badly, you'll still be feeling the effects of the bone manipulation, especially if it was your first time."

A female voice, friendly, though Herleif still didn't know who was speaking to him. He struggled to open his eyes, but when he did it was a pleasant sight.

It was dark, and above him was a very thin girl, pretty, with hair tied above her head. Despite her comforting tone she looked tired. She was very pale, and though she was wrapped up in a thick bison hide, she was shivering slightly. He noticed bandages on her hands.

She had a kind face, and Herleif managed a little smile before closing his eyes again.

"Cypher, is he awake?" came the angry voice.

"Yes, he's very weak though," said the girl next to him, presumably Cypher. Herleif felt oddly safe with her watching over him, but he decided it might be best to stay awake. The other person sounded outright hostile.

"See, we can't leave him now, that'd be akin to murder." It was the one with the calm voice, another girl.

"He's a soldier!" said the angry one. "How many of my people do you think he killed? It looks like he got what he deserved, and now we're *helping* him?"

Herleif was becoming more aware that he might well be in danger. With great effort he opened his eyes again and looked over in the direction the voices were coming from.

There was a hard faced girl sat up on a rock, also with a thick cloak wrapped around her. Behind her was a clear sky, bustling with stars, and to her side was a small ovook. The ground around them was covered in sleeping goats, who had piled together in little clusters, presumably to keep warm away from the fire, which was in the centre of the camp. Over the flames a large hunk of meat was being cooked on a spit.

Standing next to the fire, dark and tall, was an Akalen.

Suddenly everything returned to Herleif. The arrow hitting his chest, the hot wound in his side, the freezing water that stung his face. And Fin.

You failed him, again.

Had he been stronger he would have stood to face her, but as it was he simply hitched himself up onto his elbows. That's when he realised the only thing covering him was a woollen blanket. He was naked underneath, and that coupled with his drowsiness and confusion made him feel incredibly vulnerable.

"Oh, he is awake," said the Akalen, striding over to him on long limbs.

Herleif then realised then that she was a woman. Her features seemed softer than the Akalen men, more rounded and smooth, and though her height was no different to those he had encountered, her voice was not quite the same. She wore the same style of trousers that Aska had but was sporting more jewellery around her neck and wrists. She wore nothing on her upper half except a long dark cloak which came down to her ankles.

"Stay away from me," Herleif croaked. He'd meant it as a threat, but it ended up sounding more like a plea.

Unexpectedly the Akalen stopped and glared at him, "Were you serving under Gulbrand?" she asked, venom in her voice.

He nodded slowly, his head not clear enough to think up any lies.

The Akalen woman bared her white teeth and balled her fists. She looked terrifying in the light of the fire.

Turning around she addressed the girl on the rock, "He's killed my people, doesn't that mean anything to you?"

"Tiko, calm down," said the girl. "It looks like he may have come off worse than whoever he was fighting." She looked past the Akalen woman, Tiko, to Herleif, "Did you kill any Akalens?" she said bluntly.

Herleif readjusted himself, wincing as he did so, "Who are you, and where-"

"Answer the question," the girl on the rock cut in sharply.

Herleif took a deep breath, this was a lot to wake up to, "Yes, one."

Tiko, snarled.

Uncertainty flickered across the other girl's face. She covered it up quickly but he saw it, and it was enough to worry him.

"Tell us what happened," she said.

Herleif did his best to collect himself, "He was trying to kill my brother, so I stabbed him."

The Akalen woman advanced on him again, making him immediately regret his honesty. Next to him Cypher grabbed his arm with an iron grip.

"Tiko stop!" the girl on the rock said in a commanding tone. Surprisingly the woman halted a couple of paces away, but he could feel the anger radiating off her. He sensed the authority this girl had over the Akalen, though impressive, was far from absolute.

The girl on the rock spoke again, "He killed in defence of his kin, that is not something you can argue with, even if it was against your people."

"But..." Tiko started, and then grit her teeth. "Argh!" she shouted, and stomped back to the fire, slumping down onto crossed legs. "My people are dying and I'm looking after the enemy!" she snapped, throwing her arms in the air.

The girl on the rock jumped down, keeping her cloak wrapped tightly around her. "Tiko, the fighting is not here, it's north, between your Pale Wolf and Gulbrand. And anyway, he's just a soldier," she said, gesturing at Herleif. "You think he makes any of the decisions? He was probably forced to join up."

Herleif was surprised at her rationality.

"I know," Tiko said, glancing over to him. "That's the only reason I haven't killed him yet."

He stirred a little, but he was far from strong enough to defend himself if she decided to go for him again. Looking at the way she moved he questioned how well he would come off even if he wasn't injured.

Checking his ego, he addressed the girl who'd been on the rock, the one that seemed to be in charge, "Who are you and, where am I?"

"No, no," she said, walking toward him. "You first. I'm not looking after anyone I don't know."

A few different lies came to mind, but he was too tired to think of anything convincing. The truth had worked so far.

He sighed, "My name is Herleif. Lord Gulbrand was recruiting men from the Outskirts, me and my brother joined up to escape our village."

Tiko made a noise, but the girl gave her a sharp look and gestured for Herleif to continue. He, glanced at Tiko and then at the meat cooking on the spit, "We wanted nothing to do with the fighting, we didn't even know about it, but we didn't have anywhere else to go."

"Why did you have to *escape* your village?" the girl asked, crouching down to his level and cocking her head to one side suspiciously.

Herleif shifted, meeting her eyes for a moment, "The Outskirts are not kind to Nomads," he said slowly, weighing up how much to tell them. He decided that they might interpret the truth differently to him, and this was an easy lie to tell.

"They thought I had stolen some belongings that I had not. My brother overhead them planning to put me on trial, and, so I left," he said, feeling the weight of her gaze.

"If you were innocent then you wouldn't have been scared of a trial," Tiko growled from beside the fire, not looking at him. He flushed red and paused, kicking himself for not having quicker wits. But oddly, the other girl came to his rescue.

"You don't understand how Nomads are treated within the Kingdom," she said, turning to face the Akalen woman. Tiko snorted, and the girl turned back to him, "And how did you end up in the river?"

He decided the truth would be easier here.

"We had only been in camp for a few days when we were sent out on a raid," Herleif said, taking a deep breath, remembering the night. "My brother and I were separated in the attack, when I found him he was cut off two by Akalen men."

Suddenly he remembered the extent of his wounds, and confusion swept across his face, "I was hurt, badly," he said, patting his side with his hands and looking down.

"We healed you," said Cypher who was still sat next to him smiling.

"Yes, you can thank Cypher for that, she risked a lot for you," the other girl said.

Herleif wasn't sure what that meant.

"Kiakra, don't. I'm fine now, I wasn't in any danger," Cypher replied, blushing in the firelight.

"But how," Herleif said. "My side was…" he stopped suddenly, as panic set in. "How long have I been out?" he said looking back and forth between the two girls.

"Kiakra found you today, lying on the riverbank," said Cypher.

Kiakra looked away, "You're lucky she was with me otherwise you'd still be there."

Cypher scowled at her.

Herleif ignored her comment and relaxed a little. He still had time, Fin wouldn't have gotten far in only one day. The Akalens would need to stop and rest, they'd been riding all night same as he and Fin.

"Thank you for your help," he said, thinking about standing, but then remembering his exhaustion and nakedness. "But I need to find my brother, where are we now?"

"East of Grenland, just a little north of the border mountains," Kiakra said. "We're headed to Stemtrad so we'll take you that far, but after that you're on your own."

Her voice didn't suggest any flexibility in the plan.

Herleif didn't know this country. He would need a guide to get back up to Yilland. From there he was sure he could convince Brynjar to help him find his brother. It was a long shot, but there was a chance it could work if he was quick enough. Little had stuck in his memory, but he had remembered the Akalens clearly stating that they would not kill children.

"Can you take me back to Yilland?" he asked, aiming the question at everyone, but mostly Kiakra.

Cypher looked down awkwardly, and he heard Tiko laugh from the fire, "You're lucky Kiakra is willing to take you as far as we will, Yilland is a long way from Stemtrad."

Herleif looked from Tiko to Kiakra.

She shrugged, "We're the Weasel Pack, Hunters. We don't do jobs for free, and you don't even have clothes, let alone any money."

That makes sense.

He'd heard of Hunters before. Groups that would track down criminals in exchange for payment, but that was not their only work, and many struggled to stay distinct from the criminals they tracked. A few had passed through his village in the Outskirts once, offering protection. They had been turned down by the elders, and then a few weeks later had been put on trial for raiding other nearby villages. Often it seemed that morals would not get in the way of them making money.

"I do have money!" he blurted. "Not with me, but we get paid by Gulbrand."

He knew that was right. He'd never even asked about a wage, he'd been too preoccupied with escaping and learning to fight, but the other lads had spoken about it many times.

"I don't know how much, but anything me and my brother have earned, you can have it."

Kiakra seemed to ponder that for a moment.

"We're heading north anyway, why not?" Cypher said hopefully.

Kiakra scratched at a small scar on her chin and looked behind her at Tiko, "What do you think?"

The Akalen woman stared at the meat on the spit, "I don't want him with us," she said bluntly.

"You sure?" Kiakra said. "Sounds to me like it'd be easy money."

Tiko spat into the fire, watching her saliva bubble and evaporate in the flames. "I don't want him anywhere near me," she said quietly. "And make damn sure he doesn't speak to me."

"Sound's good to me," Kiakra said nonchalantly, turning back to Herleif. "Guess that's settled then. We'll take you to Yilland in exchange for everything you're worth."

She showed him a white toothed smile that reminded him of a predatory animal, and presented her hand to him. Herleif shook it with as much vigour as he could muster.

There was hope now. Fin was a long way off, and he may have to wait, but Herleif would get to him eventually. He told himself that the situation could have been much worse, and that he had no real need for money anyway. Fin would just have to look after himself for a while, he could do that. He told himself these things, but deep down he could feel a great well of worry churning in his gut.

Kiakra released his hand and wandered over to the fire. She crouched down next to Tiko and placed a hand on her shoulder. Even from here Herleif could see it was a reassuring gesture, not accidental.

"That looks about done wouldn't you say?" Tiko said, looking at the meat and acting as though their conversation had never happened.

"I think so." Kiakra replied. She pulled out a knife and began to cut off a large slice, "Can you pass me that bowl?"

Tiko leaned behind her and picked up a wooden bowl, handing it to Kiakra, who lumped the meat into it. Then she stood up and walked over to Cypher, handing it to the slim girl.

"Eat that, get your strength back."

The lump of meat was bigger than the girls arm, but she tore off a few slithers and stuffed them into her mouth ravenously. As Herleif watched, she picked the food apart and had demolished it in half the time it would take him to eat such a large amount.

"Ah, that's better," she sighed, closing her eyes and leaning back.

Suddenly Kiakra was in front of him holding another bowl, "Here take this," she said, passing it to him. "You can't pay us if you're dead."

Herleif smiled, but her face was serious. He took the bowl and thanked her, making a mental note that their kindness was dependant on the promise of payment.

"Cypher do you want some more?" Kiakra asked, seeing the girls empty bowl.

"Oh yes please, have Aldrid and rat had any yet though?" she replied, looking about the camp.

"No, but I'll call them over in a little while, they're out looking for mushrooms at the moment."

Cyphers face twisted to the side, "Now? But it's dark?"

"I don't know," said Kiakra exhaustedly. She went and brought Cypher another meal of similar proportion to the first, before clambering back up to her rock with her own bowl.

Herleif made a start on his meal, and hoped the other two members of the group were more welcoming than Tiko had been.

While he was eating, one of the sleeping goats stood up, stretched, and then dug itself into his side as it slumped back down to rest, leaning on him heavily. He tried pushing the animal away with his free hand, but its body was like lead, and it was already asleep again.

"You're making friends fast," Cypher said, distorting the words around the food in her mouth and smiling awkwardly.

Herleif sighed, "And an enemy," he said quietly, looking over to Tiko who had finished her food and was wandering off into the dark.

Cypher followed his gaze, "Ah, steer clear of her for this journey. She's been with a few Hunters before us, and she's not familiar with hospitality."

"Noted," he said, feeling like he had made another friend.

He was about to ask some more questions, but abruptly Cyphers hands began to glow. Colour came onto her face, and the gentle shiver that she'd had since he woke up, stopped. She smiled contentedly.

Herleif opened his mouth, realising finally what she could do.

"Was that blood magic?"

Cypher nodded, as she unwrapped the bandages around her hands, which were pink and undamaged. "Yes, that's how I healed you," she said plainly.

Herleif had heard stories of blood magic before but had never seen it performed. To see someone using it with such openness was rare, for those who had the ability were highly sought after.

"Thank you for helping me," he said, smiling sincerely and suddenly feeling a little guilty for her weak state just moments ago.

Cypher waved him away, "It's fine, it wouldn't have been right to just leave you."

The face of Hok flashed through his mind, and he nodded, his smile fading.

"I suppose you're right."

Something walked into Herleif's back, making him jump. It was another goat, settling itself down behind him. He looked at Cypher, who had stood up and was looking a completely different person now, stretching herself out and yawning.

"We usually leave at dawn, I'll see you then," she said, walking over to the ovook.

Herleif looked around him. He was still without any clothes, surrounded by goats out in the dark.

"Do you have my clothes?" he said sheepishly.

Cypher spun around and gestured over to the fire, "Yes, just there. Your gambeson was ruined but the rest is drying off." She smiled, "Night!" and disappeared into the ovook.

Herleif wondered how he had missed the clothes earlier, they were hanging on a rack right behind the flames, still soaking wet by the looks of it. Kiakra was still sat up on her rock, but now she was facing away from the camp, watching the stars as she ate. All he could see was her head poking out from her bearskin cloak, making her look much younger than she had seemed earlier. Still, knowing she was on watch put him at ease, and at least now there was a reason to keep him alive.

He sighed and leant back to sleep, his head falling onto the fur of another goat. He grumbled and tried to adjust himself, but it was lying on his blanket, and once again pushing the animal did nothing. It was not going to be moved.

Frustrated, he curled up into a ball and tried to get some rest.

Despite the awkward positioning and the unusual company, he was asleep in moments, the exertion of the last few days finally catching up with him.

Chapter 13

On the slopes of the steppe, he had found them.

It was late, and a fire burned, casting out light from gaps between the trees. Somehow a small wood had managed to grow in the most sheltered crevice of this otherwise barren valley. Around the fire he could hear men laughing and boasting, their voices clear, but not human. Pixie drakins buzzed between the trees, plucking mosquitoes and flies from the still air.

Brynjar's approach had been silent. He had scouted himself, on foot so as not to alert the his quarry.

The Akalens had set up camp in this little forest at the bottom of the valley, hidden from the wind, but easily surrounded. It was likely the weather had been their only concern when they'd set up, and Brynjar was hoping that, this deep in their own territory, he could catch them off guard.

He'd followed them from the site of his own raid. The ovook and the people that lived in them were all gone, packed up and moved, but the tracks remained. Retracing the boys chase he had followed the Akvast south, then turned east out onto the steppe, where they had found the body of an Akalen man, almost torn in half. The tracks split up for a while after that, and he had almost lost them. Luckily, he was working with highly skilled men, and one of the scouts had rediscovered the trail a few miles to the north.

Now he was close enough that he could see them.

From his hiding place he could make out that most were dressed plainly, which fitted with his expectations. They also seemed to be drunk.

"If we attack now then it will be to our advantage," said the man next to him. "They'll be night blind from staring into that fire."

Brynjar was kneeling behind a tree on the edge of the patch of forest. A long dark gambeson was his only armour, and his shield and spear were leant up against a big pine that he was using for cover. He had a sword at his hip, and standing beside him was Captain Egil.

Almost a decade Brynjar's senior, he was a tall man, with a narrow, weathered face and bright green eyes. He had broad shoulders and a strong, though slightly stiff, way of moving. Light hair was cut short, and he sported no tattoos, which was unusual for a man of the Kingdom. He wore a green surcoat over his mail, with the gold oak of Yilland covering his chest.

"If we wanted to kill them then that would be fine," Brynjar whispered, irritated. "But we don't. We want to capture them for questioning, so we can find the boys."

He hadn't seen Fin or Herleif here, but he was sure they weren't dead. None of his scouts had found their bodies during the hunt, and there were no fires large enough to have burned their bodies. He had to find out where they had been taken.

And there was another element to his mercy: guilt. He couldn't put these people through any more pain. Even if they were the enemy, he had attacked their homes, and their families.

"I keep telling you, it's too dangerous to try and take prisoners," the Captain said quietly, shaking his head. "You haven't seen what they can do."

He turned his gaze on Brynjar, green eyes glinting in the dim firelight with an intensity that made him uncomfortable.

"These creatures are dangerous, and I value the life of my men over theirs. Kill them, and be done with it."

Once again Brynjar found himself questioning how suitable Egil was for this undertaking. Part of him understood the Captain, after all the man had been following Akalens in Yilland for months, trying and failing to catch the raiders, and having to clean up after their attacks. But that must have eaten away at his morality, and now he was only a few hundred feet away from his enemy. In his shoes, would Brynjar make the same decisions?

"I am not discussing this again," he said sternly. He was about to go on, but he heard footfalls coming their way. Both he and the Captain went silent, their hands wrapped tightly around the hilts of their weapons as they sunk lower into the foliage around them.

Ojak popped into view, and Brynjar relaxed. The boy was slinking in and out of cover, sticking to bushes and staying low to the undergrowth. It was probably overkill, the Akalens were not very alert and far enough away for movement out here to be unseen, but Brynajr didn't mind. This deep into their territory, the more careful, the better.

Ojak weaved his way over to them and dropped down on one knee, panting, "My Lord. Sir," he said, bowing his head at Brynjar, and then Egil. He looked worried.

"Whats wrong Ojak?" Brynjar said, looking sideways back over to the fire.

"Well my Lord," he said, stopping to take a deep breath. "One of the sergeants has found the Akalen's horses tied up a little way off, he asked permission to cut them loose so that they can't escape?"

Brynjar spun around and almost yelled in his whisper, "And alert them to our presence? If we do that, we'll be guaranteed a fight. And these are Akalens, they'll just call their horses back and then scatter!"

The boy lowered his eyes and shrunk back. Ojak was not the person he should be directing his anger toward. The boy was merely acting messenger.

"I'm sorry, but that is not the plan," he smiled apologetically. Ojak returned the expression. "We want to take them with such speed, and such force, that they have no option but to surrender, anything else will mean unnecessary bloodshed."

"I did tell him that sir, but he was adamant that I ask you," Ojak said, and bowed again, "I will report back," and with that he slipped away into the trees.

Brynjar had worried this would happen. These were Egil's men, and like their commander it seemed they were keen for a fight. Unlike the last force Brynjar commanded, they were standing soldiers of Yilland, trained well and of fighting age, many older than himself.

Egil was shaking his head, "Apologies, my men are good at heart, but you see even they know a fight is inevitable." A drakin landed on his shoulder and he swiped it away aggressively, sending it sprawling off into the bracken. "Bloody creatures…"

Brynjar nodded dismissively, raising his hand for quiet. He could hear something.

The Akalens were singing.

The noise was fractured at first, several voices out of time with the main group, but as they continued, and the stragglers synced up, the effect was surreal. Deep and throaty, unlike any noise a human could make, the song was made up not of words, but of strange guttural notes that made the hairs on Brynjar's arm rise. It was the strangest sound he had ever heard, but quite beautiful. Despite the lack of speech, every emotion was clear in their voices, and when it died down the forest felt very empty.

Abruptly another noise could be heard, a deep rumble.

Horses, running.

No.

He squinted down at the camp. The Akalens had stood up and some were collecting their weapons, staggering around trying to find where the sound was coming from.

He scanned the trees, desperately trying to see if it was the horses, and instead saw Ojak waving frantically at him. The boy made enough hand gestures for him to understand that his suspicions were correct. Ojak hadn't got to the sergeant in time and the idiot had let the animals free, blowing their cover completely. This confusion would only last a moment, and then the Akalens would either set themselves up for a fight, or disappear again. Either way, Herleif and Fin would be lost, along with any information Brynjar could get about his enemy.

"Oh, those stupid…" the Captain said, and then swore loudly, before turning to Brynjar for instruction.

Brynjar had a split-second choice to make. He didn't want his men to come off badly if there was going to be a fight, and he couldn't lose the boys for a second time.

Idiot!

As he cursed the sergeant who'd let the horses free, more Akalens got to their feet, wandering off into the forest to investigate. Time was running out.

He grabbed his spear and whacked it against the round metal boss on his shield, the noise slicing through the dull thunder of hooves. Yelling out into the night, he started to walk down toward the clearing, the Captain immediately picking up his own weapon and joining him.

For a moment it was only the two of them, but then, from all around in the forest, noises of wood clanging into steel could be heard.

"Go now!" yelled Brynjar, continuing down toward the camp.

More than once he had instructed Egil and his men not to kill the Akalens. Their job was to take prisoners, but now it seemed that blood was sure to be shed, for most of the Akalens were on their feet with weapons in hand. They would still be somewhat blinded from the fire, and he hoped the grogginess from drink would slow their movements, but those advantages would fade.

As he drew closer, he began to pick up the pace, and saw more men emerging from the trees around him, spears smashing against their shields. Many had broken into a run, tearing toward the fight with dark faces and nervous, excited smiles.

There was a terrible familiarity to it.

Just ahead of him was Ojak, running toward the Akalens alongside the other men.

Brynjar yelled again, as the fastest of them broke into the camp.

Someone screamed as the two sides collided, the humans thrusting their spears at the enemy as the drunken Akalens tried to defend as best they could.

Panicked drakins whirled high into the air to avoid the clash, little spits of flame shooting out of their snouts and lighting up the sky as they did.

The impact was brutal. Egil's men swarmed the position from all sides, cutting off the Akalen retreat as they threw themselves into the fray. The Akalen's fought like wounded lions and his own men were as ravenous as hunting dogs. Brynjar watched a man so ready for battle that he ran onto the end of an enemy spear, the tip coming clear of his body by several feet. Another soldier managed to stab an Akalen in the leg, dropping him to his knees before another two men ran him through the chest, their faces bright with triumph.

The plan to capture, rather than kill, had been abandoned immediately. Even though they were heavily outnumbered, the Akalens were too big and too aggressive to take prisoner, and it seemed that drink had made them fearless. Brynjar also didn't imagine that any of Egils men wanted to take the enemy alive.

This shouldn't have happened again.

Brynjar tried to focus on the battle, but it seemed too surreal to threaten him.

An Akalen rushed him, and abruptly he was fighting for his life. Brynjar dodged, hours of practice taking control of his limbs as he brought his spear up to try and catch the man's shoulder. But his opponent twisted at the last moment, and Brynjars spear instead sunk into the flesh below the Akalen's chin. There was a gargled cough and his opponent dropped to the floor, the fur on his hands matted with blood as he tried to stop the bleeding. Before Brynjar could react, he was shoved to the side as more soldiers piled in.

"Prisoners!" he yelled desperately as the meagre Akalen force began to crumble, overwhelmed by his own vicious onslaught.

"Take prisoners!" said Egil from a few feet away. He was shouting too, but just as he did an Akalen thrust a spear at the Captain's throat. Egil swept the weapon aside with his sword, and then brought the blade down onto his opponent's shoulder, almost taking the arm off. The Akalen dropped to the floor screaming, and the Captain silenced him by thrusting his sword into the man's chest.

Brynjar realised that Egil's words were just that; words. There was a savagery to the man now, his eyes bright with vengeance as he stalked through the battle.

He's been waiting for a chance at revenge, and I've given it to him.

Ojak was the only one other than himself who was trying to take prisoners, and ahead Brynjar saw him jump onto the back of one of the enemy, trying to tackle him to the ground. This Akalen was dressed like a warrior, white tattoos matching the panicked white of his eyes, which were vivid against his dark cheeks. He threw Ojak to the ground, kicking away the boy's weapon before he stamped on his chest, pinning him to the floor with his weight. Brynjar lunged in with his spear, nicking the Akalen's thigh through his patterned trousers.

Yelling in pain the warrior turned to face Brynjar, letting his foot off Ojak. He bounced off to the side, almost overbalancing as he thrust at the young Lord with his own spear.

He'd been drinking, and Brynjar easily dodged the attack, following up with a thrust of his own, hitting low once again and cutting the Akalen at his navel. The warrior flinched and backed up, snarling.

The fight around them was dying down. The few remaining Akalens in camp had been surrounded, and were now being cut down. Others were injured, and had stumbled off into the trees, followed closely by Egil's men who were now drunk on victory. Several soldiers had now gathered behind the warrior to cut off his escape, but Brynjar was worried they might kill him.

"Surrender and you will be treated well," Brynjar yelled, panting, loud enough so his own soldiers could hear too.

The warrior was swaying gently as Brynjar spoke. He looked tired. Even from where Brynjar was stood, out of spears reach, it was clear the

Akalen's eyes were dulled from drink. He must know there was no way out of this if he fought.

Glancing around, he seemed to weigh up the situation. The clearing, previously peaceful, was now covered in bodies, both human and Akalen. Groans of dying men had replaced the drunken songs Brynjar had heard earlier.

More soldiers gathered around him, penning him in on all sides.

Please do not fight.

Eventually the Akalen dropped his weapon, sighing deeply and holding his head up high. He looked fearsome even in surrender, and Brynjar was glad he had not met the man on an even field.

"I am Yatu, and I yield," the Akalen said.

Brynjar lowered his own weapon, "You've made a good choice, you will be treated-"

He was cut off as a spear erupted from the Akalen's stomach, making Brynjar flinch.

Confusion swept across the face of the warrior as he looked down at the blood-soaked spearhead poking through his ribs. He tried to remove the weapon from his torso, his legs giving way as he fell to his knees, the haft of the spear not allowing him to fall backwards.

"Get away!" Brynjar shouted at the soldiers, dropping his own spear as he rushed over to the warrior.

Fear had replaced the confusion on the Akalen's face, and as Brynjar grabbed him, he began to plead with him.

"Please burn me," he coughed. "I do not want to become a Demon."

Brynjar nodded frantically, "Of course, but where are the two boys you chased?"

The Akalens eyelids fluttered, his vision dying. "I can't see," he said.

Brynjar shook the man, shouting, "Where are the boys!"

His eyes came alive again for a moment, "One... we killed, the other was taken by a Demon. Do not let me become one!" The warrior gripped

Brynjar's arm so hard it hurt, even through his gambeson.

I've have failed them.

Brynjar straightened up, now was not the time to show emotion.

"You have my word. Tell me one more thing and I will make your death quick, what does Warlord Teoma want?" He forced the words out as quickly as he could.

The Akalen's eyes had gone again but his face turned sad, "The Pale Wolf? She wants safety for her people," he said. He seemed puzzled by the question.

"Then why is she attacking us?" Brynjar said, trying to make sense of the warrior's words.

The Akalen furrowed his brows, despite his blindness, "She hasn't. No Akalen has set foot on your lands." His faced screwed up in pain as he tried to take a breath in, "I have told you what you wanted to know," he slurred, his ability to speak fading. "Please, let me die."

For a moment Brynjar considered leaving him, the man had admitted to killing one of the boys. But he did not want this conflict to consume him. Nodding, he pulled a knife from his belt and pushed it up under the warrior's chin, ending his life. Blood flowed onto his hands, and soaked into the dirt on which he knelt.

He whispered an apology to the still corpse.

Brynjar led the warriors great frame gently down on his side, and stood up. Around him the soldiers were staring, some relieved the fight was over, others looking concerned. Many were muttering in hushed voices.

He was no closer to any answers, if anything there were more questions now. And he had failed Fin and Herleif.

Brynjar's hand balled up into a fist.

"Who struck this man?" he said quietly.

There was a moment of quiet and then some movement from within the crowd. A man was pushed forward from the group. The circle of soldiers closed behind him, shutting him out.

"You did this?" he said gesturing at the man. The soldier was broad across the shoulders and a few years Brynjar's senior. He had an open face with short brown hair falling over his ears.

He nodded, trying to put on an illusion of confidence, his head held high.

The other soldiers leaned in, their attention solely on the two men. Everyone was silent now, and it was completely still. The drakins had fled and the groans of the wounded had stopped.

"Why?" Brynjar said, pulling his sword from its scabbard.

The man swallowed, eyes locked on Brynjar's blade. He was using every ounce of energy to keep himself from running, and Brynjar could tell.

"He looked like he was going to make a move," the man said twitching.

It was a lie. His blood had been up, he wanted a kill to boast of.

Brynjar extended his sword out toward the man, "He was unarmed. Tell me the truth."

The man looked around him, a nervous smile creeping onto his face, "I am telling the tru-"

Brynjar cleaved his sword into the man's neck, cutting him off. The soldier flinched, his face twisting in pain as his shoulders shrugged up, an instinctive response to protect himself. But it was too late, Brynjar had already cut into him and now he drew his sword back for another strike. Again and again he brought the blade down, hacking at the soldier's body until it stopped moving.

Around him, the other men shrank back, as if worried his anger would extend to them.

He was shaking when he finished, his arm tired.

"Bring me the sergeant who let the horses free."

Egil pushed his way to the front of the men, his surcoat stained dark with blood, "My Lord this is not the way to-"

"Shut, up!" Brynjar shouted, his hands still shaking as he turned to face Egil. "Bring him to me!"

For a moment the Captain held Brynjar's gaze, challenging the young Lord's decision. Brynjar did not look away, and after a while the Captain gave in, his mouth shutting tight into a scowl as he looked down nodding.

He waved his hand and another of the men was brought forward, this time not so voluntarily. He was thrown at Brynjars feet and only stopped struggling when he felt the blade at his throat.

This man was older, probably forty or so, and had a dark brown moustache that drooped to below his chin. He had a slimmer build than most and looked angry rather than afraid.

"Why did you release the horses?" Brynjar said, looking down at the sergeant.

"I thought it would help," he said, eyes never leaving Brynjar's own.

"You sent a messenger to ask me and then didn't even wait for him to return, why?"

The sergeant glanced over at Egil, who was glaring at him, and then looked back to Brynjar.

"I thought, I was helping," he said slowly, his gaze unyielding.

Every muscle in Brynjars body was tense, poised to kill the man, to once again feel the heavy resistance of flesh. But that gaze cautioned him, and doubt seeped into his mind.

He looked over at Egil and found that the Captain would not meet his eye. Brynjar looked back at the sergeant.

He was put up to this.

Around him the soldiers were holding their breath, waiting for the death blow as the fire cast yellow light across their faces and the drakins began to hum again, drawn down now that the fighting had stopped.

There was tension in the air. A bow had been drawn, people were waiting for the release.

"Bind this man," Brynjar said, turning to walk away, "And build a fire for the dead."

Soldiers rushed in to grab the sergeant, and dragged him off to be tied, though this time he did not struggle.

The soldiers in the circle surrounding Brynjar parted before him, fear on their faces. He ignored them and stalked off into the trees.

Night vision returned to him quickly once he was out of sight of the fire, and he navigated through the woods with ease. As always, the trees were silent in their judgement of him as he strode past, but they didn't need to speak for him to know their thoughts.

He heard the stream before he saw it. It was a small thing, only a hand wide, and barely deep enough for a fist. There were a few tiny fish in the water, glowing a faint green as a boast of how poisonous they were, to help dissuade anything from eating them. Brynjar ignored them and, following the stream uphill, he reached a small boulder covered in dry moss. That would do. He brushed off some leaves atop it and sat down to wash his hands.

It was only then that he began to weep. It started off with a few tears, but after a moment he was choking back sobs, holding his face in his dirtied hands. He would never usually allow himself this weakness, but now, after everything that had happened, he was broken.

Lowering his hands to the water he began to wash away the blood. It would never be enough, and even if he were to clean it all away, it would not bring back those he had killed. The pain was all he was trying to wash away, the scars of his actions would remain, the wound would linger. His wrongs could not be righted now.

He had failed in everything. The Akalens had seen nothing but injustice from him. Families killed, homes burned, and now he had wiped out the men from that village as well. He wasn't sure they were even to blame anymore.

"I hadn't meant for this to happen," he whispered to the trees around him as he sobbed.

That will not bring them back.

Fin and Herleif he had failed too. If that had been the only victory he had taken from this mess then he would have had something. But no, they were dead as well. All courtesy of his leadership.

Every decision I have made has ended in death.

No part of him wanted to return to Gulbrand to report on his further failings, and for a moment he thought about running, leaving his mistakes behind him. If he stayed, what more damage would he do?

In the centre of the forest a great fire began to rise, the work of his soldiers. There were so many bodies to burn.

The flames seemed to grant him back his rationality, and he saw that running was not an option. Those were the thoughts of a child. The knowledge that such cowardice existed within him made him made him a little disgusted, and he wiped his face with his sleeve. He had made mistakes, but that was why he needed to stay. He would be brave enough to face the consequences of his actions, and he would strive to right those wrongs he could.

His legacy would not be failure.

Someone came up behind him, shuffling through the bracken, "My Lord, shall we go?" said a worried voice in the dark.

It was Ojak.

Brynjar stared into the water, "Was I wrong to strike that man down?"

Ojak hesitated, "If I may speak frankly my Lord, I think both actions were regrettable."

Brynjar almost laughed. "I think you're right there," he said, scratching his neck. He paused, "You're a good man Ojak, you'll go far."

The boy shifted behind him, "For you to think of me as anything more than a servant is high praise, thank you," he replied. Despite the modest answer a smile could be heard in his words.

A moment passed and then Ojak spoke again, "The fire is getting very large now my Lord, shall we leave?"

Brynjar sighed, before splashing some water into his face to wake himself up. He had indulged in enough self loathing, now it was time to get to work again.

"Yes," he said, standing, "We have some questions that need answering."

Chapter 14

Sunlight warmed his cheeks. A gentle breeze stroked his hair, beckoning him back to the world.

Fin opened his eyes.

He was on his back, lying in tall, lush grass which had collapsed over him, forming a delicate net of green. A ladybird crawled along one of the soft blades, inching its way upward until it reached the tip. He watched it open its wings and fly away.

Slowly he sat up, brushing away the grass. His skin felt sore. To one side of him was a sparse wood, young, none of the trees older than a few decades. Little birds chirped loudly, flaunting their plumage and flitting down to land on piles of chopped wood that sat under some of the bigger trees. To the other side of him the green grass continued, blossoming meadows covered in dandelions and daisies that sloped up to a gentle ridge spotted with more woodland.

It felt like spring.

Fin looked around some more. There was no sign of a Demon.

The last thing he remembered were bright eyes, and a huge paw swiping at his head. As far as he could tell, he wasn't even on the steppe any more.

Am I dead?

He thought not, his head ached too much, and his back felt bruised and raw. Surely he wouldn't be as sore as this if he was dead, but in that case, where was he?

Standing, he rolled his shoulders and twisted, his back making a few satisfying cracks, thanking him for the movement. It was only then that he noticed the figures ahead of him. There was a yak, two boars and what looked like a woman standing in the middle of them.

Unsure if she was in trouble or not, he jogged over, slowing down as he got closer so as not to spook the animals into aggression. He realised she was digging, the creatures around her unbothered as they grazed.

"Are you alright?" Fin said loudly.

She had her back to him, and when he spoke she spun around with such speed he wondered if a pixie drakin had spat on her.

"Aha, you're finally awake!" she said smiling manically, showing crooked and yellowing teeth.

She was ancient, lines chiselled into her face from the decades of sun and snow which had weathered her tanned skin. Her frame was bony and slight, as if the wind could take her up into the sky if it blew hard enough. Wispy grey hair was tied back in an unkempt bun, and she wore a big furry shawl that came well past her knees.

Despite all the indicators of age her stance was strong and upright, her eyes alert like those of a child. They were light grey, and shone out at him defiantly.

"Means I won't have to keep dragging you around with me," she said, walking over and thrusting her spade into Fin's chest, making him stagger backwards.

"You finish that off, then we'll have some food." She proceeded to sit down between the animals and pull a long pipe from inside her shawl, into which she began stuffing a reddish weed.

The two boars next to her were spectacular things, huge white tusks curving back toward their eyes, shoulders the same height as Fin's, and with thick, wiry grey fur covering their solid, muscular bodies. They snorted at the woman, and then fell heavily onto their sides. Larger than both of them was the yak, eyes shrouded in tangled white hair, with long, polished horns. It followed the lead of the boars, lying down next to the old woman and chewing loudly.

Fin had no idea what was happening.

"Sorry, who are you?" he managed after a few moments.

"I'm Gatty, and you should be digging," she said, not looking up from her pipe.

Fin nodded, and reluctantly stepped down into the hole. He was starving, and he figured it was better to go along with her nonsense if he could get a meal out of it.

"You said you'd been dragging me around?" he said, probing as he began to dig. The dark earth was heavy with moisture, and though it was easy to cut through it with the spade, it was an effort to lift the dirt away.

"Yes, I did," said Gatty. "Sorry about your back by the way, it was too much effort to carry you when I got home, I see you've got some burns."

"You mean you actually dragged me?" Fin said stopping and looking at her. She was tiny, he couldn't imagine her carrying anything, even the spade had looked out of place in her frail hands. She smiled quickly and then used a striker to light her pipe, taking a deep pull from it.

"Keep digging lad," she muttered, exhaling a putrid wine-coloured smog. "But yes, I did. That's why I said it. Couldn't have you running off on me before I'd explained."

Fin started digging again, expecting her to continue. After a few moments it was clear she wasn't going to speak again.

"Explained what?" Fin asked, beginning to feel a little frustrated. It was hot out here, and the last few days had exhausted him.

"By the spirits, you ask a lot of questions don't you," she muttered, closing her eyes and turning her face to the sun. "I'll tell you when you've finished that hole."

Fin felt his jaw tighten, "What is this even for?"

One of the boars grunted and rolled onto its side.

"Deathweed," Gatty said.

146

"What's that?"

She sighed deeply and tapped her pipe.

Fin frowned, "Why is it called death weed?" Then he stopped and rubbed his face. That wasn't what he needed to know. He needed to know where he was and how to get back to… he wasn't even sure where he needed to go. Returning to the Outskirts was out of the question, there was nothing left for him there, and despite his sympathy with Gulbrand, that camp was not his home.

"Just finish the hole," Gatty said, interrupting his thoughts. "Another half a foot will do, then we'll get some food."

The thought of a meal drove him on, and he continued in silence, thinking over what exactly he needed to ask this woman.

It was not unpleasant work, and Fin found himself getting lost in the task. Birds continued chattering, and Gatty and the three animals next to her continued to bathe in the warm sun.

When Fin next looked up from his hole a small field mouse had climbed up a stalk of grass and was watching him intently as he worked. It was a strange sight, to see the creature almost level with his own eyes, and he dismissed it at first. But the next time he looked up, it was still there, perched high on its stalk, right out in the open. Oddly he found there was a part of him that began to worry. It was very exposed up there, and a hawk might get it.

With the intent of putting it somewhere safer, he reached out to pick the creature up. It was gone in a flash, scurrying away into the grass and leaving him feeling stupid.

He shook his head and carried on.

After a little while he stepped out of the pit, stabbing the spade into the earth, "Does that look alright?"

Gatty opened one of her eyes and looked at his work.

"Took you longer than expected," she said frowning. Fin bit his lip, but she didn't seem to notice his irritation. Elders were to be respected, he knew that, but she was making it very difficult.

"Yes, I suppose it looks deep enough, come on then," she said, and with that she was on her feet and walking back from where Fin had come, smoke billowing from her mouth like a chimney as her animals scrambled to follow her.

It was then that Fin saw the tracks of where she had dragged him, a long line of flattened grass. They followed the tracks uphill for quite a way until they reached a squat wooden house. It was a long way, she must have been stronger than she looked.

The house was made of wood and stone, with an overhanging thatch roof that reminded Fin of the yak's fringe. There were a few small windows, through which he could see the light of a fire. At the front, behind a low weaved fence, was a beautifully flowered garden, filled with herbs and vegetables. The building was situated between a well-used road, and a little river that ran past the back of the house and led into another wood, though this one looked much older, for the trees were huge and bright green with moss.

"Right, this is where you'll be staying," Gatty said, coming up to a heavy wooden door and pushing her way through it with considerable effort.

"Staying?" Fin asked, frowning as he followed her in.

Inside was unlike any place Fin had ever seen. The door opened into a spacious room with a low ceiling, at the back of which was a large red fire. Rickety wooden stairs set into the stone led up to a second floor, but, unlike most houses, the whole space was covered top to bottom in pelts. They covered the walls, the floor and even the ceiling. It was mostly game and domestic animals, deer, auroch, bison and yak, but there were bear and wolf furs here as well. Deep chairs and heavy wooden benches were set up next to the walls and windows and looked as though they had been used throughout the ages, polished from touch.

Ironically, the place felt friendly and alive, despite there being nothing living in the room, as if the spirits of those many creatures still lingered here.

Gatty wore no shoes, and as she walked in ahead of him she threw some logs on the fire, before crouching down to check on a big black cauldron. Again he noticed that she moved like a woman half her age.

"Don't worry," she said, looking around the room to address the pelts. "I'm not a trophy hunter like those damn Lords from the west," the words came out with some venom, "I use everything I kill, and I give my quarry the respect they deserve when they do pass, too many have forgotten that rule…" her voice trailed off sadly.

Fin realised she must be *very* old. Few people still alive said the sacred words on their hunts, the only other person he had ever seen do it was Herleif. He nodded solemnly.

"Anyway, I suppose you'll be wanting to know what's for lunch?" she said, standing and smiling at Fin.

He tilted his head, there was something that had been bothering him, "I was actually wondering where you found me? You said you were going to explain when we got here."

She frowned, "I found you on the steppe? Don't you remember?" Her eyes were searching his own for some recollection.

Confused, Fin stared back at her, back at those grey eyes.

Slowly, gently, the fear crept up on him. He realised he was afraid of her, this old lady who had apparently been dragging him around like a rag doll. He glanced around at the pelts, a collection that even a veteran hunter would have been in awe at. It would take a lifetime to catch that much game.

The room seemed to darken, become emptier, but she loomed closer. Still she stared at him with those piercing grey eyes. And then finally, he realised.

I have seen those eyes before.

They bored into him, shining out as though they were alive, and her face twisted into a thin smile. "Now you remember," she murmured in a soft tone.

"You're, the Demon…" Fin said. His body felt heavy as he paced back toward the door.

Gatty's smile turned into a scowl as she peered back at him with those grey eyes, so bright now they were like steel.

"I am no Demon," she whispered, and her body transformed.

***

The Weasel Pack and Herleif were coming to the end of their journey across the steppe, keeping the river to their left as they kept heading toward Stemtrad. With only a few miles left to go, they were all feeling restless, and it had brought them out of the silence the group had maintained for much of their journeying. The terrain was much the same as it had been the past few days, rolling hills of grass and flowers, though after some rain it had turned more green than yellow, and the land near the river town was richer than the higher plains, meaning some bushes grew, though only sparsely.

Tiko was up ahead scouting, and Kiakra was behind her, keeping an eye on the group, making sure they were heading the right way.

Herleif was glad he hadn't had much contact with Tiko, she seemed a loner even within the Weasel Pack, though he suspected that might be his doing. Often at camp she would stalk over to collect her food, shoot him an angry look, and then disappear to eat alone. Apparently, even though they had met only days ago, deep wounds ran between them. Herleif would not be the one to do any healing, he had done nothing to her. The rest of the group had been kind to him, but he sensed their unease at the friction he was causing, whether he could help it or not.

"They do what?" Herleif said, smiling wearily, realising he hadn't replied.

"Let you see at night," Aldrid repeated, his face deadly serious.

Cypher rode a little way in front of him and Aldrid, who were with the Yaks that carried their supplies, the trailing Yak carrying their sombre prisoner, Lax. Rat rode at the back of the group with the herd of goats that were still resolutely following them. They were moving up the side of a gentle ridge that connected two steep hills, chased by the sunlight warming their backs.

Rat trotted up next to them, "You're talking out your arse again Aldrid," he said smirking.

They were riding shoulder to shoulder, Herleif on a chestnut horse, Aldrid on one of the Yaks, and Rat on a long tailed deer from the south, a creature that was too small for the others to ride but as fast as the wind and as beautiful as any of the deep forest deer. She was sleek and feathered, a deep blue that looked black in most lights. Rat himself was wrapped up in a thick leopard skin fur, almost shivering against the gentle breeze.

He directed his speech toward Herleif now, "The night we picked you up we went and got some of these night vision mushrooms, had to be in the dark for its full effect," he shot a look at Aldrid, who was staring straight ahead, doing his best to ignore the Kazoec man. "Did nothing but make me dizzy."

Herleif chuckled, and Aldrid spun around on his Yak, "I could see almost as clearly as day, they probably didn't work on you because your digestive system is different," he said, swatting the air dismissively.

"You could see clearly because you were dreaming, you old fool. You passed out as soon as you ate them!" Rat replied, laughing. Herleif joined him and even Aldrid broke into a smile, despite his best efforts.

"Alright maybe I didn't pick the right ones, but they do exist…"

"Well if they did exist then I would have come across them back home," Rat said confidently. The home to which he was referring was the Empire down in the south, a place about which he knew very little.

"They don't have absolutely everything down there," Aldrid sighed.

Rat nodded, his eyes lighting up, "Mushrooms they do! Mostly grown there, but the ones that like the cold get imported from everywhere. The cooking vendors can do amazing things with them, and if memory serves, it's not even expensive." He looked into the distance with a dull gaze, "In the cities, even the beggars can eat like kings. I used to get food from them with my friends, and then we'd go eat under the great arch while we watched people dance in the square..." his voice trailed off, mind obviously far away.

Abruptly he seemed to realise he'd been talking out loud, and smiled awkwardly, giving his mount a pat on the side, "It's bloody cold again today. I wish we weren't heading north."

Herleif just smiled back, thinking of his own home and how different his views toward it were.

"Uh oh, trouble," Aldrid said, stopping.

Up ahead Cypher had come to a halt, and in front of her Kiakra was galloping back toward them, kicking her horse on furiously. She looked mad, her wolf-skin cloak billowing out behind her as she waved her hands and shouted.

"Stampede!" she yelled at them. "Head for high ground!" She pointed at the hill to their right and began trotting toward it, her arm pointing out toward it.

"Okay, let's move," Aldrid snapped.

Herleif sat bolt upright and pulled the reigns close, immediately out of the slump he'd been riding in. Rat was gone immediately, flying toward higher ground, whilst to Herleif's side Aldrid was smacking the rump of the lead Yak, trying to get it to turn from its course. The beast was slow, but obedient, and gradually it drifted the right way, following Rat's trail uphill.

Kiakra had turned as well now, seeing her warning take effect she had begun galloping toward the same ground Rat was, not looking back.

Herleif cantered alongside the older man, the Yaks were slow with their cargo but still fast enough to outrun the charge. The goats had been unable to stick with Rat and now jostled around the feet of the pack animals in fear.

"Herleif look!" Aldrid shouted, despite being only feet from him.

Up ahead Cypher had not turned, she was not even riding. Instead she was on foot, crouching next to her horse and doing something to its foreleg.

A pang of worry hit Herleif, and he glanced toward Kiakra and Rat, but they both had their backs to him, unaware of the danger their healer was in.

"What's she doing?" Herleif said, glancing at Aldrid, "She's right where the stampede is coming through."

Aldrid's face was desperate, and he kept looking from his yak, then to the girl and back again. He wasn't listening, he was weighing up if he had time to get to her and still be clear of the animals. He obviously didn't, the Yak's were far too slow.

There was a thunder in the air, quiet now, but growing. A gentle hum that made the spine tingle.

Herleif wasted another second deliberating and then wheeled his horse away from Aldrid. "I'll get her, keep going," he shouted, pointing to the safety of the ridge. Aldrid just stared and nodded at him as he rushed away.

Why are you doing this?

Any other member of the Pack he would have left behind. They were friendly, but he was a paying customer after all, and he wouldn't risk his life on the charms of strangers. Cypher was different though. Herleif certainly owed her his life, and maybe because of that, if he was lucky, the life of his brother too.

Deep bellows could now be heard, and as Herleif rushed toward Cypher, the stampede broke over the top of the hill.

It was mostly bison, but there were other creatures caught up in the rush as well. Terrabirds weaved in and out of the great lumbering animals, their golden plumes bobbing with every step as they kept pace, whilst the larger wirehogs made their own room, spiking anything that decided to rub shoulders with them.

Herleif jumped off his horse when he reached Cypher and grabbed the girl by her shoulders.

"What are you doing?" he yelled over the rumble of the stampede. She turned to him with panicked eyes, and then he saw. Her mount had put its foot in an owl burrow, almost up to its knee, and she had been trying desperately to pull it out. It was a miracle the creature hadn't broken its leg.

"I tried to free her but-" she stared down at its leg again. She glanced up at the stampede, and her face turned pale, that same shade Herleif had first seen her wear.

The ground was trembling now, shaking like the back of a horse trying to rid itself of flies.

Herleif gestured to his mount, "Get up there, I'll free her and catch up," he knelt down and grabbed at the other horse's leg, trying to ignore the anarchy that approached them.

Cypher didn't move. "I can't *leave* you," she said, barely audible over the din of the charge.

Herleif turned and yelled, "Go, I'll be fine." He forced a smile and she returned it, stepping up onto his horse reluctantly. Cypher lingered for a moment, watching him as he pulled at the horse's leg.

"Go!" he shouted again, his smile fading.

She nodded and kicked the horse uphill toward the others, finally crumbling to her terror.

Herleif looked back to his task. The hole that the horses leg in was curved, and the way the creature was leaning meant that when it pulled, the pressure on its limb was increased. The ground gripped it harder. He had to force its knee to relax so that he could thread it out.

Pushing gently against the back of its knee he whispered in it's ear, trying in vain to calm it down. But the horse was watching the stampede as well, it's leg as taught as a bowstring.

The horde of animals were only a few hundred feet away now, tearing down the slope in a frenzy of fear.

Herleif was running out of time. Either he freed it now or he was going to be trampled. He kicked the horse's knee, breaking its posture. For a moment the leg was limp, and in that moment he pulled it free, and relief washed over him.

Then the horse bolted.

It's instinct to run won out over any control Herleif might have had over it. He scrabbled at the reigns, but they were through his fingers in a flash. Disbelief, as well as fear, filled him as he watched it tear away.

The thundering in his ears increased, until he could hear nothing else. And then the storm was on him.

Several terrabird's whipped past at an impossible speed, their long legs carrying them effortlessly over this ground. Then bison were around him, rumbling past faster than creatures that big had any right to move. Before he knew what was happening he was running, sprinting with the torrent of flesh that surrounded him, knowing the only way to survive was to move with the charge, and not against it.

A huge male bison lumbered next to him and he grabbed it's shaggy mane, trying to find something to anchor himself to. The animal was so large it barely noticed, and it's fur so thick that his hands were likely not even touching its thick hide.

The roar of hooves deafened him as he was dragged along, his legs trailing in the dirt as he used every ounce of effort to keep hold of the beast.

Dust choked his eyes and mouth, blinding him as he was pulled along. Another bison shouldered into him, bumped against the other during the chaos. The impact was gentle in comparison to the other monumental forces at work, but it was still enough to smash the air from his lungs and rip his hands from the big male's fur. He bounced into the dirt, rolling, trying in vain to regain his feet as immediately another creature shouldered into him, sending him twisting off to the side. Missing horns or hooves had been a miracle, but the force had whipped his head back so fast his vision had blurred.

Staggering, he struggled to stay upright as he felt another animal crash into his shoulder. The air was hot and damp with the breath of a thousand terrified monsters, the ground churned up from their bulk.

Stay on your feet.

Suddenly a hand grabbed him, pulling him out of the chaos and up into clear air.

Herleif was above it now, the struggle just as ferocious but taking place somewhere else.

"Thank you," he groaned. There was no reply.

He bounced on the back of a horse, his strength used up and his dusty eyes glued shut.

Chapter 15

Herleif spent a long time in silence, slung over the horse's back like a corpse. He had tried to rub away the dirt in his eyes, but big hands combined with the movement of the mount caused more harm than good. The rider made no effort to speak to him, but he was too tired to worry about talking anyway. Blind from the dust in his face, and exhausted from the battering his body had taken, he was content to simply lie there and recover.

After some time he heard familiar voices.

"Well he isn't looking great," he heard Kiakra's distinct tone a few paces away. It was mingled with the sound of horses snorting and a strong smell of yak.

"I'm feeling better," Herleif said, before breaking into a coughing fit. He felt a few pairs of hands heave him off the horse.

"Lie down on your back," he heard Cypher say in a gentle tone. He obeyed, finding there was a mat beneath him.

Then someone threw water in his face.

Herleif spluttered and sat back up, rubbing his eyes again, managing finally to dislodge the dirt that had collected there. In front of him was Kiakra, smiling broadly with an empty wooden bucket in her hands.

"There, now you can see again," she said.

Cypher shot her an irritated look, "That wasn't really necessary."

"It's okay, thanks," Herleif wheezed. He was just glad he could see again.

Around him was the whole pack, Aldrid was looking the yaks over, making sure they hadn't lost any of their supplies, Kiakra and Cypher were looking over him, and Rat was talking to the rider that had saved him.

It was Tiko.

For a moment the Akalen caught his eye, and he saw an expression he could not read. Then she said something else to Rat, before pulling her massive horse off to the side and cantering away.

"Thank you," Herleif mumbled, looking back to Cypher, blinking hard.

"It should be me who is thanking you," Cypher said, lowering her voice. She seemed more shaken than he did.

"Don't worry about it, you've saved me, now I've returned the favour," Herleif said smiling.

"Oh, yes, suppose we're even then," Cypher said, her eyes dropping awkwardly. Suddenly Herleif regretted saying it. Blaming his actions on a mere contract of obligation.

You're my friend, that's why I saved you. But he couldn't quite bring himself to say it, especially not in front of the others.

"I may have to call on your aid again," he added quickly, apologetic. "I have sustained a few injuries."

He lifted his shirt revealing a few newly formed bruises.

Cypher's smile returned, "I'm glad I can help."

Kiakra gave a disproving look, but said nothing, and wandered off to speak with Tiko.

Cypher went through the same process as before, making small incisions on her hands and doing the same to Herleif, before pressing them together and using her energy to heal him. After the light-headedness had subsided Herleif felt reborn, though he noted with some guilt that Cypher had paid for it.

"You okay?" he asked. She looked as though she was going to faint.

Cypher nodded weakly, "I'm fine, just… I can't do that again, not for a while."

"No, you can't," Kiakra said, suddenly behind the girl. "Come on, lets get into Stemtrad. We can sort ourselves out once we get there." And with that she led Cypher back to her horse.

Watching her stumble away, Herleif decided that would be the last time he would rely on her abilities, it was too costly for her.

Despite the events that had just happened, the party was quick to get moving again and Herleif once again found himself riding in the easy company of Aldrid, though now everyone stayed much closer together and the conversation flowed between them all.

All of them except Tiko, who stayed out of sight, scouting ahead as usual, speaking only to Kiakra when she had anything to report.

They dropped down steeply onto a wide flat plain, before rising one last time over the ridge at the northern end of it.

Herleif reached the top of the hill alongside Aldrid and stopped to take in the view.

The sweeping hills of grass had finally ended, giving way to a long shallow valley, this one stretching off to the east, scarring the barren steppe with an abundance of life. Trees soared into the sky, jostling for position against the banks of the Stem river that ran down the middle of the valley. Reeds cluttered the shallows and would give cover for the hunting birds that lived here, and where there weren't trees there were small fields of crop, sparsely littered with farmers and their homes.

"Little oasis ain't it?" chuckled Rat as he slunk past on his deer, followed closely by the goats.

Herleif nodded slowly, transfixed by the beautiful valley, following it with his eyes, watching the flow of water from the Stem join up with the Great Akvast. And there, where the two rivers met, was Stemtrad.

From here he could see very little, only that the settlement was in two halves', one on the north and one on the south side of the Stem. He could make out a stone wall that surrounded it, but not much more than that.

It was only then that he realised how far he had travelled along the Akvast. He knew the power of the river, but days of travel and he was still yet to reach the place where he and Fin had been cornered.

The others had continued on without him, and he was about to join them when Tiko thundered over to him. She'd been waiting on the ridge, probably watching for them, and now she headed straight for him.

For a moment he was worried, but he caught Kiakra glance back at him and Tiko before carrying on. If there was anything to worry about then she wouldn't have left him.

I hope.

The horse Tiko rode was almost a full foot taller than Herleif's own, a speckled blonde thing with white streaks running along its side, and thick fur over its shins that hid the animal's hooves. The creature served to increase Tiko's presence that much more as she stopped next to him.

"I didn't get a chance to thank you," Herleif offered, his voice close to a shout in order to be heard over the wind up here. Tiko had set herself up at an angle to him, not a standoff, but she wasn't talking to a friend either.

"I don't want you to thank me," she said, her voice quieter than he'd expected. "I came to assure you my actions were not an attempt to befriend you."

Herleif felt his cheeks turn hot, "Then why did you save my life?" he questioned. "You owe me no debt."

"That is where you are wrong," Tiko said, expertly moving her horse over to Herleif so she was almost on top of him. She leant down from her mount and looked at him with her big brown eyes. "I hate you," she said, almost a whisper. "You are my enemy. My kin in the north have died because of people like you. I think there would be a divine justice if I left your body on our lands, killed by the very beasts we hunt."

Herleif was about to step in but she continued, "I think this mission to help you is pathetic. Kiakra is my friend but she is a fool in this, you are a soldier, one who kills without thought or remorse, and I hope with all my heart that when we have taken your money, the only prize you shall receive is your brothers corpse."

Herleif's hands clenched into fists, his body shaking.

"Then why help me?" he growled.

Tiko straightened up, taking herself out of range of any of the many attacks Herleif had considered attempting.

"You saved my friend." She turned to him, speaking loudly, "You are also a contract, and for the sake of business, I will stay my hand. And also, I suppose for the sake of Kiakra's wishes, I have vowed never to let my own feelings get in the way of those." Her lips turned up into a snarl, and her voice lowered again, "But believe me when that duty is fulfilled, money is given, and you are no longer bound to me, it shall be with a clear conscience that I take your life. There will be no unpaid debts to dishonour me. I will challenge you to a Kala'tam, and, well fed and strong, I will kill you."

Nothing more than to save face.

Herleif clenched his teeth and was on the verge of drawing his weapon when suddenly Tiko trotted away. He felt the anger inside him bubble, but with no outlet he just clenched his jaw until she moved away. This was his chance to find Fin, he couldn't afford to mess things up with the pack, not even for her.

Just as he thought the conversation was over she turned back to him from some distance, yelling over her shoulder, "None here are your friends. Despite how they may treat you. Remember, they are only after your coin."

And then she kicked her horse on to a canter and disappeared down the hill, leaving Herleif alone with his thoughts.

***

Kiakra had passed through Stemtrad many times over the years, and the place always smelled the same; sweat, excrement, blood, and strong, sweet alcohol. The smell told you as much about the settlement as anyone needed to know, it was the result of ambition, demanding work and shady dealings gone wrong.

The walls at the edges of the settlement were little more than show now, dilapidated stone structures surrounded some of the town, hinting at better days now passed. The walls were simply absent in other places, the materials taken for usage some place else. She'd noticed more than once how many of the buildings inside Stemtrad were made of that same stone, but no one seemed to care.

There were no gates, and the guardhouses were few and far between. The guards themselves were not expected to do much, being drunk more often than not, and they smiled, gormless, at the Weasel Pack as they made their way through the main gate.

Kiakra smiled back, she was happy to be here.

The town itself was nothing much to speak of, crude wooden shacks had been constructed wherever there was space, stifling the taller stone structures that seemed to make up the core of the place. Streets twisted sharply and bustled with traders and merchants, on the surface the town dealt mostly in fish, but it was a trading hub between all the Spoken Races and anything could be found if you looked for long enough.

Kiakra led, moving through the streets with confidence as she made her way toward her contractor's usual hiding place. She glanced back at Herleif a few times, making sure he hadn't been lured away from the Pack by any shady locals, but he didn't seem to be taking in much of his surroundings. She noted, with some relief, that Rat was riding close next to him, watching over the boy like a hawk.

She crossed over the main bridge and then followed the cobbled stone harbourside that ran along the edge of the river Stem. Looking upriver she could see the wetlands in the distance, beautiful in the afternoon light.

Soon, only another season, then we can stop all this.

"Ki, I think I'd like to get a boat as well," Cypher said, riding up next to her, still looking weary but with a playful smile on her face. The girl had obviously known what was on her mind.

Kiakra cocked her head to the side, "And how many extra contracts will we have to take to afford that as well as your land?"

Cypher made a show of thinking it over, scratching at a non-existent beard on her chin, "On second thought, maybe we can get Aldrid to make us one."

That made Kiakra laugh, "Yes we could, I've always wondered what it would feel like to drown and then get eaten by a mudgulp."

Cypher stifled a giggle and looked around to make sure Aldrid hadn't heard them. She turned back and was about to say more, but something caught her eye and the words were left unspoken. Kiakra followed her gaze. It was a solid wooden building, a tavern, with "Boars Tongue" written in gold lettering on a sign above the door.

"Ah, we're here," she muttered. "You'll feel better after some food?"

Cypher nodded, looking tired once again.

 Kiakra stopped outside the establishment and dismounted, stretching to get rid of the ache in her joints. A couple of wasters were sat outside on the edge of the harbour, horns of mead in hand as they dangled their legs over brown water, soaking up the last of the sun. Both nodded at her and raised their drinks.

The Pack stopped behind Kiakra, and Aldrid appeared, pulling Lax on a rope behind him. The man had seemed distant for most of the journey, but now he was looking far more alert, his bald head beginning to bead with sweat.

Aldrid looked at Kiakra, "Will Tovum want us to take this guy in?"

Kiakra sighed, "I have no idea," she said, scratching at the scar on her chin. "Better to keep him close though I think."

Lax suddenly began to speak, fast. "Please, I'm sorry I tried to attack you," he said gesturing at Aldrid, "It really wasn't personal, and I don't have much money, but I can pay your group in favours, I'm owed a lot of them around-"

Kiakra raised her hand, "I don't care, we don't break contracts, and certainly not contracts with Tovum."

"He's going to kill me," begged the big man, but Kiakra ignored him and addressed Rat.

"We won't be long, can you look after Herleif and the supplies?" she said.

Tiko had disappeared when they'd arrived, but Kiakra wasn't worried, the Akalen woman could look after herself.

Rat nodded agreeably, "I can do that, what about all these bloody animals though?" he said, gesturing at a billy goat that had just headbutted a drunkard into the harbour, and was now licking up his spilt mead from the cobbled ground.

"Look after them," she said, and pushed her way into the tavern before he had a chance to reply.

Inside it was dark, and there was a strong smell of deathweed and woodsmoke to greet her as she entered. It was warm and dry, full of heavy, dark wood furniture and warm fires that burned about the place. In the evenings the establishment would be full, traders and fisherman gathering to bicker and joke until they lost consciousness and were thrown back out into the street, where they would wake, and resume their work, only to repeat the process again the next night. Now however it was quiet, too early for most, and so the few that were here almost had a fireplace each.

Stemtrad was not part of any empire, and had no agenda other than making money, so it attracted all of the Spoken Races. This meant that finding someone here was usually difficult, and that made it a haven for those wishing not to be found.

There was no problem finding Tovum.

Kiakra spotted him in a dimly lit corner, sat at an angle to the biggest fire there was. She made her way across the dark floorboards up to the bar and bought three horns of mead, two were for her and Aldrid, the other was for Tovum. She handed one of the drinks to Aldrid, and then sauntered over to her contractor.

The Bavagai had his eyes closed when she got there, a real sign of confidence in a place like this, but Tovum was a man who had little to fear. His massive blustone armour was hung on the wall behind him, the links of stone so delicately interwoven that it was hard to imagine he had made it.

She sat down opposite him in a cushioned armchair and placed his drink on the table. Tovum's amber eyes flicked open, and a smile spread across his face.

"Kiakra," he said, with more than a little warmth as his voice rumbled through her chest. "It's been too long." He spoke slowly, as he always did.

The chair he was sat in was custom made to fit, for even amongst the Bavagai he was huge. He looked similar to the other member of his race they had come across, with thick limbs and shaggy hair covering all his body, except his face, which was friendly and open. The skin on his face was golden in colour and littered with tiny scars. One past injury stood out from the others however, going from above his eye and running all the way down his face, across his lips, before disappearing off his heavy jaw. His eyes were small but bright, he had two holes for his nostrils that were set above a wide mouth, and the ridge of bone on his head was notched with the same texture as the horns of a ram.

Tovum was a wealthy man, and he dressed like it. He wore a pair beautifully styled trousers, gilded, and made up of deep blues and greens that contrasted with his black fur. They were held up by a wide belt, the buckle of which was a chunk of gold moulded to look like two ibex crashing into one another. That buckle alone was more than Kiakra had earned this whole season. His boots were rich, heavy leather, and he wore only a single bracelet of twisted silver on each arm. Like other Bavagai, his chest was left bare to show the scars of past battles.

"It has been too long," she said, swallowing, with more than a little trepidation.

The man extended a meaty palm out toward Kiakra, and she mirrored his action. When he grasped her hand to shake it she lost sight of most her forearm, but despite this he was extremely gentle, being a man keenly aware of his own strength.

"I wasn't expecting you back so soon," he rumbled, letting go of her hand and leaning back in his chair. He pulled a striker beetle from his pocket and squeezed it, creating a spark which he used it to relight a pipe he'd left on the table.

"We're fast workers," Kiakra smiled. He was a powerful man, and she did fear him, but he was also good company.

"Will you drink with us?" she said, gesturing at the horn on the table. Manners were important when dealing with a man like Tovum. He nodded slowly.

"As long as you haven't poisoned it?" he winked, picking up the horn and taking a deep swig. It wasn't as brave as it seemed, for Bavagai were immune to almost all poisons.

The huge man leant back in his chair again, taking a pull from his pipe.

"Hello Lax," he drawled, turning his head slowly to face the man standing next to Aldrid. "Aldrid, have a seat," Tovum said apologetically, gesturing to a chair next to Kiakra.

"Thank you," Aldrid replied, sitting and raising his own horn of mead in thanks. Tovum seemed not to hear him.

"You've caused a lot of trouble Lax," he said, turning back to the man, who was now visibly shaking with fear. "You can take those ropes off him now Aldrid."

Aldrid leant over and removed the bindings. Kiakra knew they were pointless at this stage, the man wouldn't be dumb enough to try and run.

"I hear you killed a man Lax, is that true?" Tovum said, taking another pull of his deathweed, letting the smoke drift lazily out his nostrils to hang around his face.

Lax shifted his weight, "It wasn't me, sir," he said, very slowly. The nervous shaking increased.

"Are you suggesting my brother committed the crime?" Tovum said frowning.

His brother?

Suddenly Kiakra felt nervous. She glanced at Aldrid, and his expression told her that was news to him as well.

She began to sweat.

"Well," Lax said, his voice a squeak, which did not suit his heavy, bald frame. "We tried to take the…" he paused, searching for the right words.

"When you were stealing from me, yes, go on," Tovum said, impatiently, which was strange considering how slowly he himself spoke.

"Well, one of your men caught us," Lax said. "And yes, Jutai, killed him."

Tovum's small eyes seemed to linger on Lax for a moment, and then he sighed, turning to Kiakra, "I assume, because he isn't here, that you didn't manage to bring my brother back alive?"

She swallowed, "I-I'm sorry Tovum. We buried him down south on the plains. If we'd have known he was your brother then we-"

Tovum raised his hand, "Don't apologise, it is what it is. You did your job."

Kiakra nodded, calmed by his words, but feeling renewed guilt for the Jutai's death.

"I'm sorry," she repeated, unsure of what else to say and desperately hoping Aldrid wouldn't choose this time to bring up payment.

"What to do with you then?" Tovum said, looking at Lax.

That was when the man tried to run.

He had barely shifted his weight to move before Tovum stood, the illusion of clumsy bulk dissolving as the Bavagai caught him by the shoulder and threw him, sending him twisting through the air and crashing into the corner of the room. All before Lax had even taken his second step.

Kiakra and Aldrid flinched simultaneously.

The force of the throw was perfect, for Tovum could have killed him simply in that action, but as it was, he merely broke ribs. Lax was left writhing on the floor trying to regain his breath.

"That was your own fault," Tovum grumbled,"I don't like people being rude."

It was a mistake to think his mind or body were as slow as his words, and Kiakra was reminded what a ball of power the man was. In here he had to stoop, but his body was immense, even for the Bavagai. At full height his head must have stood at least eight and a half feet above the ground.

He walked over to Lax slowly, the floorboards creaking as he did so.

"See what happens if you try to run from me?" he said.

Kiakra was gripping her chair with white knuckles, her body tense, her breathing fast. All her attention was on this colossus.

"Now what happens if you steal from me," he growled, and picked Lax up by the forearm.

For a moment it looked as though he was helping the thief up, but then he raised the arm higher, holding it above Lax's head. The smaller man began to plead with him, but Tovum was deaf to his words. Panic set in on Lax's face and he tried to prize open Tovums grip, yelling now, white eyes full of terror.

Kiakra was stuck, unable to move, unable to look away.

Suddenly there was a crack, and Lax screamed. Tovum let go, and the man dropped to the floor again. He stared at his mangled, broken arm like it was a foreign being. It was purple from the great man's grip, and his fingers were twisted horrifically. Without blood magic that was a wound that would never properly heal.

Kiakra looked away.

"My arm," Lax whispered in horror.

"Yes," Tovum said, turning away from him and sitting back down. "Now get out, and be glad I didn't break your legs for running from me."

Lax stood slowly, still mesmerised by his own arm, and ran out through the doors, not looking back.

Kiakra breathed out, and unclenched her hands from her chair, shivering slightly.

Tovum turned to Aldrid, "Go have a chat with the barman, he'll pay you. Make sure to count it though, he's a slimy one."

"Ah I see, well I'm no stranger to a bit of haggling," Aldrid chuckled in a poor attempt to lighten the mood.

Kiakra winced. Aldrid'd laughter died down when he caught the stoic expression on the Bavagai's face.

"Well yes, thank you," he said coughing, and left.

Kiakra followed him over to the bar with her eyes, "Sorry about him."

She was attempting to maintain some level of composure. The Bavagai respected strength, and as a Hunter this was not the sort of event that should bother her.

"He's not bad," Tovum offered, "Just odd."

Kiakra nodded and took a swig from her horn, "You seemed to let Lax off pretty lightly? I assumed he was a dead man walking."

Tovum shook his head, "He just followed what my brother was doing, it was mostly Jutai, the fool," then he snorted, an amused sound but one that made Kiakra flinch for the second time during their encounter, "He'll still be able to steal with his other arm no doubt."

Kiakra smiled weakly, and then took another big swig from her horn. They sat there for a while before she spoke again.

"I am truly sorry for your brother," she said, looking Tovum dead in the eye. It wasn't an apology to the trader, the landLord, nor the warrior. It was an apology to the man who had lost his kin.

Tovum looked at her, and it seemed as though he knew that. He nodded once.

"It was a difficult call, to put a price on Jutai. I doubted he could be taken alive, but I still did it. Had my own brother killed."

There was another pause, and then he spoke again.

"Can I offer some advice?"

Kiakra was taken a little off guard, but she nodded.

"There are Hunters I can call upon who wouldn't have blinked at what I just did to that man, some might have laughed even," he said, turning and looking at her. There was an expression on his face she couldn't read.

"I'm still here aren't I?" she replied, quick to defend herself and a little annoyed her emotion had been noticed. If his implication was her weakness, then she would show him otherwise. She'd fought hard for her reputation, and she wasn't going to let it go because of a momentary lapse in her demeanour.

The giant laughed, "I mean no offence, Kiakra of the Weasel Pack." She shot him a questioning look, and he continued.

"I don't respect most Hunters. I don't care if they live or die," he shrugged, very matter of fact. "They've lost the parts of themselves that feel, and they'll do whatever things I ask them without a second thought, long as their pockets are filled. They know this business is messy, and dangerous."

Kiakra felt her hackles go up, "I know the business I am in *very* well. I've been doing this for many seasons, and I can deal with the dangers." There was a sharpness to her voice that she would have checked if she was thinking more clearly. As it was her words were aggressive, not a usual tone anyone took with Tovum, but she had to make him believe her.

The big man seemed not to notice, or else did not care. His eyes were glazed, his thoughts somewhere else.

He sighed, "You misunderstand me. Those others will not be missed when they meet their ends, but you will be. I know that the Kaz man cares for you, as does the fool over there," he said, gesturing to Aldrid at the bar, "And your healer? I know she cares for you more than most care for their kin. Your heart is still gentle enough that you can care back. I would think on that."

She bit her tongue. Her heart was not *gentle.* It was made of iron, how else could she compete with other Hunters in this trade if it was anything but? And she was like that precisely because of those she cared about, that was always how she had looked after Cypher. Hardening her heart. What did he think she was doing this for?

All of that she left unsaid, though only just.

"What is your suggestion?" she said instead, flatly.

Tovum smiled, a tired expression from a man who'd been on top for a long time, "I don't know exactly, maybe you'll understand when you've had to kill your own. Hopefully before that though."

There was a wink in his eye, but she could see it was a cover for pain. She was surprised he'd let her recognise it. Or maybe he thought so little of her that he didn't care if she saw.

The big man shrugged and spoke again, "If you want work other than this, then I have fishing boats."

The thought angered her. She was a warrior, that offer was an insult. She shook her head, fighting the urge to laugh at him, "I am saving for land upriver. On that wage it would take me ten seasons or more to be able to afford it. As a Hunter I will have it by next season, that's how I look after my own."

Tovum nodded, "I understand."

She wanted to continue their talk, so she could vent, and explain to him, but the right words would not come to her, and he stayed infuriatingly quiet. They sat there silently until Aldrid returned. He began saying something about the barkeeps manners but Kiakra cut him off.

"We have your brother's goats Tovum, I assume you'll be wanting to take them off our hands?" she said before standing up and draining her horn.

Tovum chuckled, a low, heavy noise that hit her in the ribs, and suddenly his eyes were a little more playful.

"No, you can keep them," he said, standing as well.

Kiakra laughed and began to decline but Tovum went on, "They are our companions out in the mountains, and very important to us. They'll help to keep your spirit calm, and they produce good milk. Considering how much time you spend out on the steppe, they'll cost next to nothing to feed."

"Oh, thank you very much," Aldrid said beaming, as good as accepting the offer. Kiakra was forced to smile back at him when she wanted nothing more than to slap the man.

"I'll see you later on for a drink I imagine," Tovum said, clapping Kiakra gently on the shoulder with his heavy hand, before walking away.

The whole encounter had drained her.

"What are we going to do with all those animals?" she muttered to Aldrid.

"Keep them," he said smiling and looking a little confused. "Tovum just gave them to us? I think they'd be good for you, you need something to keep you calm, quite often you get very angry."

She was about to punch him when a voice called out her name.

"Kiakra?"

It was the barkeep.

She shouldered past Aldrid, "Yeah that's me?"

The barkeep yawned and pointed over to the other side of the room with a pudgy red finger. "There's a man over there, been asking for the Weasel Pack."

Kiakra nodded and thanked him, then walked over to see this other man. He was in another corner, in front of a much smaller fireplace. He was wearing a thick coat, with a hood over his head that hid his face. One leg was resting on a stool in front of him, and he massaged the thigh with his knuckles. Other than that, no part of him moved, even when Kiakra was only feet behind him.

Gloom clung to all the crevices of his lair.

"Hello," she said, lowering herself down in a chair opposite him. His face was shrouded in shadow, and the hairs on the back of her arm rose.

"Are you Kiakra?" the man said, still not moving. His voice was scratchy from lack of use, but strong despite that.

For a moment she wasn't sure she wanted to tell him any details of herself, but curiosity got the better of her. "I am yes, and who's asking?"

He turned, showing her sunken, tired eyes, and a face covered by a thick beard. He held out his fist, and opened it, revealing enough Olvir's to

172

buy the tavern they were sat in.

"Does it matter?"

Chapter 16

Fin opened his eyes for a brief moment.

Gatty was stood opposite him, eyes shut, humming gently to herself.

He blinked and turned his head. Around him were tall meadows of wildflower, broken on one side by Gatty's house, and by the stream on the other. He watched the water bubbling gently alongside him. A kingfisher was a little way off scanning the water for prey from atop a gnarled, dead, beech tree, its feathers bright in the sun.

"Keep your damn eyes closed," Gatty growled, her own eyes still closed.

Fin's eyes snapped shut.

They'd been stood like this for hours, in the hot sun, arms down by their sides, swaying with the gentle breeze and soaking up the energy of the world. Fin was still unsure what that meant, but apparently it was a good thing.

In the few days he had been with the old woman he had learnt little about her. Despite the strange form she could take on, he knew that she wasn't a Demon, though she'd done little to explain her unusual powers. She'd fed him, and given him space to mourn his brother, and done little more besides that. More than once he had thought of leaving her and returning to Gulbrand's camp, but something had kept him there.

He heard Gatty sigh, "I can tell you've stopped concentrating, so there's no point carrying on."

Fin opened one eye, then, realising it was safe to do so, the other.

"I'm sorry," he said. "But I really would rather you just tell me how you… change."

"And what I keep telling you," Gatty said, raising her voice, "Is that you need to connect with your environment. Otherwise what I say won't matter."

Something he had quickly learnt about Gatty was that the woman had a temper. Along with that there was an aura of mystery around her, and the aimlessness he had been feeling since Herleif's death had slowly been replaced with an odd curiosity toward the old woman. Without asking him almost any questions she seemed to know much about him, like his ability to communicate with his horse, and the pull he had felt toward the great Oak. Both things she had mentioned casually, and then refused to explain further.

Fascination had finally won him over this morning, and he'd begun to ask questions. She had answered none. Instead she took him outside to "listen," insisting that would be more productive for him.

"You cannot become a Recast if you don't listen," she hissed.

Fin scratched his head, "What is a Recast?"

He knew listening would be easier if he understood why he was meant to be doing it. Gatty might be an elder, and a Nomad, but so far she'd been an awful teacher.

Gatty looked as though she was about to spit out an insult, but then she paused, rubbing her eyes in frustration.

"Alright," she said finally. "Sit down and I'll explain."

Fin was on the floor in an instant, feeling like he'd narrowly avoided a scolding.

The animals that followed Gatty around were here as well, the yak was some way off grazing on the tall grass, and the two boar were sunbathing next to him and the old woman. He leant against the broad back of one of the boar, having found them to be quite tame, and the creature barely acknowledged him. Gatty folded herself down to the ground nimbly before pulling her pipe from the folds of her shawl and stuffing it with deathweed.

"The world we are part of is made up of many places, known and unknown," she said slowly. "Bluewind is the name of the world we know, for it refers to the will of the skies and the heavens above, though few still call it that." She gestured up at the cloudless blue expanse that stretched out overhead in all directions. "What lies in the north, east, south and west, broadly speaking?" she asked, cocking her head to the side.

Fin hid a smile, he knew that.

"The Kingdom of Jern is in the west, the Bavagai come from the mountains which cover the north, the Akalen's lie to the east, and the Kazoec empire is south, though much further away than the others I believe."

Gatty's eyes had glazed over, and she was staring off into the distance as though she could see every place he had just mentioned. Then she shook her head and lit her pipe, "Those are just the people, what actually *are* those places?"

Fin wasn't sure he understood the question, but Gatty had an expression on her face that made it difficult to be wrong.

"Um, well, the Bavar mountains are mountains, aren't they?"

He felt stupid saying it, but the old woman nodded approvingly. "Yes exactly! That's what matters, what the land *is*. For that is where we draw our power from."

Our? Was that an implication that he could do the same things she could. He sat up a little straighter.

"The mountains?" Fin said slowly. "I can draw power from the mountains?"

Gatty exhaled a smoke ring into Fin's face, making him cough violently, "Your stupidity baffles me sometimes. No, we draw our power from the *spirit* of the mountains."

"They are one and the same, aren't they?" Fin said hoarsely, forgetting that would constitute as an argument in Gatty's opinion.

The old woman looked at him narrowly, "If you want to make a cloak out of wool, must you kill the sheep? No. They are distinct from one another. Think before you speak or people will think you simple."

Fin bit his tongue.

Suddenly he had a thought and leant forward, his eyes wide, "Is that not how Demons come to be?" he whispered.

"No," she said quickly, lowering her voice. "Spirits reside in all things, some loud and powerful like the Akvast, others quiet and stoic," she picked up a stone, "Like this."

She tossed it into the stream next to them, and then looked at the bubbling water.

"Demons are damaged souls that come to rest in other living beings," she said quietly, as though speaking too loudly might give the words power. "They cannot be controlled. Their lives are pain and they find solace only in death."

Fin realised he was holding his breath. He leant back against the boar again, scratching its side gently, eager to change the subject.

"How do you control spirits without becoming a Demon then?"

"You do not control them," Gatty snapped. Then she spoke again, more softly, "You borrow from them, by listening. Once you can speak to them, you can draw power from them, and once you can do that, you will become Recast."

Fin nodded. There was a question on his lips, but he was hesitant to speak it, protective of an answer he was afraid she would not give him. But eventually he could contain it no longer.

"Does that mean I could change, like you? If I learnt to draw power from them," he said, his voice catching just a little.

Gatty smiled and gave a quick nod.

Fin took a deep breath.

"So, once I can speak to them, I can change into anything?"

"Ha!" Gatty laughed, smoke pumping from her nostrils, "No, no one has that power, there are only four forms that any Recast can take, representing the four Great Spirits of the World."

Fin didn't enjoy being laughed at, but Gatty seemed to do it so frequently that he was growing numb to it.

"Well what forms can you take then?" he said, frustrated.

Suddenly the old woman quietened, and her face twisted into a more sinister smile. "Let me show you," she said, and suddenly her body began to tremble.

Everything changed at once. Fragile arms became thick and taught with muscle, the slim hands that held her pipe so delicately grew padded and tipped with claws. Her nose widened across her face, and her jawline extended back, the teeth suddenly long and white. Pink lips turned black and mobile, hunched shoulders became broad and muscular. Her body was growing outward, as if absorbing the woman, covering itself with hair until the transformation was finished.

"A bear," Fin whispered, for he had not seen her in the light of day before, and only now realised that was what she was. The form was bigger than any bear he had seen however, taller than him at the shoulder, with those grey human eyes peering out at him. The dreadlocked fur hanging from its body gave it a different feel, it looked like a creature designed for battle more than a bear. Though it had looked like one in the gloom of her house and in the darkness of the night, it was no Demon, he could see that clearly now.

The yak looked up at Gatty's new form, then snorted and lowered its head to continue grazing.

Gatty stayed like that for a few more moments, and then began to turn back, the hair receding, the claws shortening into nails on the tips of pink fingers, and the muscle on her back slithering away to reveal the shawl covering her bony spine.

She should have looked diminished in comparison, but the knowledge that she owned that other form meant that she demanded the space the bear had taken.

"You're sure I can do that?" Fin said, his voice hard. He needed to know.

Gatty nodded resolutely.

Thoughts of the Kala'Tam against Aska came back to him. Memories of how helpless he had felt. If this power had been available to him then, the Akalen chief wouldn't have stood a chance.

Herleif would still be alive.

"That form is the warrior of the forest," Gatty said, picking up her pipe which she had dropped during the change.

"Can you be killed like that?" Fin asked.

Gatty smiled, "Not easily, I have fought many times in that form, and never lost."

He nodded. He had to learn how to acquire that strength. "So, if that form represents the Forest Spirit, then what are the other three forms?"

"What are the other three Great Spirits?" Gatty said.

Fin thought back to what histories his brother had taught him. He was angry at himself for not remembering quicker, "There's the Forest, the Mountain, the Plains, and the Ocean."

"And all of those have their own forms," Gatty added. "Each is strongest in its own territory. Here, by the forest, when I become the bear I am as powerful as that form can be, it is the same with the others." Gatty said.

She began to draw a circle in the earth with her pipe. She drew two lines through it and then assigned a rune to each of the four sections of the circle.

"What animals represent the other three places?" Fin asked.

Gatty sighed, "I thought you might know this?"

"No, I don't know," he muttered, splitting a blade of grass with his nail. There was very little he knew about anything, he had only ever been taught by Herleif, and he'd had precious few lessons from their father.

Gatty seemed to notice his tone, and was polite enough to ignore the gap in his knowledge this one time, "The plain is represented by the horse, the mountain by the eagle, and the ocean by the whale."

"I see," Fin said, thinking of all the uses for each of those creatures. "Do you have a favourite?" he asked.

Gatty leant back and took a deep pull from her pipe. "Every form has its use, like the four stages of the Drakins. Unlike the Drakins all should be equal, but I can't fly brilliantly, and I hate the ocean, so the bear is my most comfortable form."

Fin raised an eyebrow, "Why do you hate the ocean?" He had never seen it, but it sounded terrible. Nothing but water stretching off into forever.

"Because the oceans are ancient, and we do not belong there," Gatty said, in a tone that meant she was done with that conversation. She stood up and stretched, returning her pipe into the fold of her shawl.

"Now you've had a lesson in the *why*, it's time to *do*. Stand up."

Fin had many more questions, but they would have to wait until another time.

He rose to his feet, pushing himself up off the boar's warm back. For a moment he felt a sense of purpose. He would learn from her, and then maybe he would return to Gulbrand, when he was able to do some good.

"Why are you teaching me this?" Fin said, suddenly wondering at the old woman's motivations.

Gatty, smiled sadly, "Because there are so few of us left, and that means we have to look after each other." Then she closed her eyes, took a deep breath and began to hum.

No doubt there was more to it than that. If he had learned one thing about Gatty it was that she was not a simple woman. But he would ask about that another time.

He nodded and looked back over to where the Kingfisher had been hunting. It had caught something.

He watched it for a moment, then closed his eyes.

This time, he listened.

***

The light was low, but it was still warm. A Drakinhawk circled overhead, no doubt waiting to ambush messenger crows. Brynjar wondered if it belonged to the Akalens, or if it was wild. Drakins were hard to tame.

A playful breeze flicked at his face, but he had someone to see.

Though no part of him was worried about a battle, he wore his mail and surcoat, hoping they would make him look more intimidating, though maybe that was something he needn't worry about. Since he had killed the soldier in the forest the other men had been far more formal with him, not joking in his presence, or even smiling.

It was no less than what he deserved, but he was grateful that at least Ojak had continued to treat him the same.

They were taking their time to return, for he had received news that Gulbrand needed scouts in their area, and so they were to stay on watch until their replacements arrived. He'd ordered his men to set up camp on a broad hill that gave them a good view in all directions around, so that an ambush would be impossible. There were not enough trees to build a defensible position, their only options were to fight or flee, and that meant they needed a good view.

He took a final look out at the ocean of grass that surrounded him, and then ducked inside the tent.

It was dark, and smelt strongly of human waste. Brynjar walked further in, slowly, allowing his eyes to grow accustomed to the gloom.

"Please, I've told you, I'll do as you say," someone murmured.

There was a shape on the floor, it was the sergeant.

He was bound with his arms behind his back and his feet tied together. A tattered shirt clung to his sweaty body, and judging by the stains his trousers had not been removed for some time.

No less than he deserves.

Brynjar was ashamed of the thought, but it lingered.

"It's me, who were you expecting?" Brynjar said..

The sergeant turned to face him, suddenly a smile was plastered across his face, as though Brynjar represented some divine salvation.

"Nothing my Lord, I'm sorry, I talk to myself sometimes. Helps keep me from going mad."

He sounded different, not the same individual who had struggled against the other soldiers, and glared at him so fiercely, but something lesser. There was something on his face, but Brynjar did not want to get any closer to the man. He stank.

"It's only us, I want you to tell me who ordered you to release the horses. You won't get in trouble."

Brynjar did his best to smile at the man reassuringly.

"It was my poor judgement, I can't blame anyone else," the sergeant said. That would not have been hard to believe, if not for the tune there was to his words, as if they had been rehearsed.

"There is no one to fear, it's only me here," Brynjar said quietly, trying to sound as gentle as he could.

The wind played with the flaps of the tent.

"No, they're listening," the sergeant snapped. And suddenly he realised it was something he shouldn't have said. "No, no, I don't mean that, it was my poor judgement, I can't blame anyone else." Once again the words danced out of his mouth in the same way, almost like he was singing.

Brynjar was wary. He looked around, making sure no one was behind him as he leaned in closer, braving the putrid smell.

"Has anyone spoken to you since I ordered you to be bound?" he whispered.

It was only then that he realised the man had a black eye, sore and swollen, and there was matted blood around where his moustache had been. Someone had definitely visited him.

"Only one," the sergeant whispered.

"Who?" Brynjar urged.

And then he heard some men talking outside, and the sergeant shrank back as though he had been struck.

"It was my poor judgement," he began, "I can't blame anyone else."

"No please, I have to know, people are dying," Brynjar tried desperately, feeling his answers slipping away. "Who was it?" he whispered, so quiet it almost couldn't be heard.

"It was my poor judgement," the sergeant repeated. "I can't blame anyone else."

Brynjar tried to ask him more, but from then on those were the only words he could get out of the man, and he turned away in frustration.

Someone had beat the sergeant into silence, and that alone confirmed one of Brynjars suspicions. The man had been put up to his actions, and his actions had evidently been important. Why else would anyone go to this much trouble to keep him quiet? Someone didn't want the Akalens to have their voice.

Who had been spending weeks tracking their attacks? Who had seen first-hand the damage done? Who had urged him not to take prisoners?

Egil.

It was then he had an ugly thought. He wouldn't give it too much weight until he had spoken to Ojak however.

It seemed darker now, and the wind warned him as it had done before. He could not understand what it said, but, surrounded by men who were potential traitors to Jern, he would be sleeping with one eye open until he was back in Yilland. He would bide his time.

He left the sergeant to his ramblings, pushing his way out of the tent. In front of him were two soldiers, who almost flinched at his presence. The two men were quick to hide their surprise and bowed at him before moving away.

They hadn't been expecting to see me here.

He hurried back to his own tent, circling it once to make sure no one was lingering outside. Ojak was fiddling with the fire when he entered.

He looked up as Brynjar walked in, reading his expression, "I assume you didn't get the answers you wanted my Lord?"

Brynjar shook his head, "No, but I had a thought," he said, sitting down on his sleeping mat. "Gulbrand told me that he didn't know where or how the Akalens were crossing the border."

Ojak nodded and placed a stick on the fire, angling it inward so that the flames could catch it.

"There have been no Akalen sightings by anyone else, and Egil has been away tracking them during every single raid." Brynjar said.

Abruptly Ojak's attention was away from the flames.

"You don't think that," he lowered his voice and glanced about nervously. "You don't think that Egil was responsible for the raids in Yilland?"

Brynjar stared at the fire, "I don't know."

"Why would he? What does he have to gain?"

Brynjar shook his head, "I don't know that either, but his men were ordered to killed all the Akalens we were tracking. Someone didn't want me talking to them."

Ojak went to speak, and then paused. He took a long glance around the room, and then nodded.

"If that's true, we need to be careful."

Chapter 17

Herleif stared at Tiko from across the table.

Her face was no longer just the face of an Akalen. Now it was the face of those that had taken his brother. Those that had pierced his chest with an arrow, and left him to drown in the cold waters of the Akvast.

Her movements were the same as theirs, as were her clothes, her voice, even the way she held her head, as though she and her kind were better than everyone else. It was the same way in which the Akalens that had taken Fin held themselves, and, slowly, he began to realise that he detested not just her, but perhaps all of them.

Tiko did not meet his eye as she raised a cup of strong alcohol to her lips.

Coward.

She could insult him when no one else was around, pour out her hatred when they were alone, but when the others were with them, when there was the risk of judgement, suddenly her fiery words were absent.

Were the rest of the pack any better? Herleif didn't know, but Tiko's words continued to play on his mind, making him question their kindness again and again.

These past few days of milling around and stocking up on supplies were draining him. He had said almost nothing to the group since Tiko had spoken to him, and only left his room to eat and drink. He did not trust his rage, which now lingered so closely to the surface it threatened to take control of him. Fin needed his brother, and the only way Herleif could give him that was if he stuck with the group.

With her.

"Herleif!" someone said as a hand fell on his shoulder.

He flinched, but it was only Rat.

"You alright?" he said, leaning close and furrowing the patch of leathery skin where his eyebrows should have been. "I asked if you wanted a drink, you've been daydreaming again," Rat laughed, evidently a little drunk.

Herleif shrugged off the hand on his shoulder, staring at the smooth plates on the back of Rat's hand.

"I'm fine," he said flatly.

Rat sighed, and then forced another smile, "Well okay, just don't keep us in the dark if there's something serious on your mind." He turned in his seat and stood up, heading toward the bar. Herleif followed him with his eyes.

He is my friend, as are they all.

Herleif could feel eyes on him and noticed Kiakra was watching his movements from the head of the table. Her eyes flicked away as he met her gaze, but it was not the first time he had noticed her watching him.

Even she who, at first, had seemed more interested in his money, had become someone he cared for. He had come to understand that she was part of a harsh world, and that her tough exterior was, at least partly, for show.

I will not let Tiko poison my trust.

He straightened up and took a deep breath. They were sat in one of the many nooks of The Boars Tongue, where they had come for food and drink at the end of every day. It was full of people this evening, as it was every evening, and Herleif could see why. The place had a warmth to it that probably wasn't achievable in most of the drafty shacks Stemtrad was made up of. Most of the customers were simple fishermen, but there were many exceptions. Northern pirates who had come south to trade their goods, and spend their money, were laughing loudly in the centre of the establishment, whilst merchants and craftsmen seemed to cluster at the larger tables in groups, eagerly discussing politics. A group of poorly skilled musicians played drunkenly next to the door, stopping frequently to harass people for tips as they entered. They had gotten into more than a couple of fights with the pirates and Tovum had almost been called on to keep the peace.

Herleif had never seen a Bavagai before this evening, but judging by the glimpses he had gotten, as well as the size of the man's blustone armour hung up on the wall, the polished round helmet made of a single sculpted block of the stone, they were not a people to be trifled with. At any mention of the great man, the violent arguments were quickly silenced.

There were no other Bavagai in the establishment, Akalens and humans made up most of the visitors, but there were a few other of the Spoken Races from further out who also had come here. The most noticeable were the Kaz.

They were smaller than the other races, and clung to the edges of the tavern, keeping largely to themselves, speaking quietly and playing complicated board games by delicate candlelight. They dressed very differently to Rat, wearing beautiful layered robes that were covered in exotic patterns of bright colours that hid most of their alien skin. Herleif was surprised to note that many of them had what looked like long hair. It was in fact, very fine, long feathers that sprouted from the backs of their heads.

Rat gave them a sideways glance as he returned with his drink and seated himself next to Herleif. He hadn't been able to take his eyes off them for most of the night, and there was jealously in his eyes.

"Hiding at the edges of the light, scared of the locals," Rat muttered. "And they call *me* vermin, HA!" The laugh was forced, and he spoke as though he was not one of them.

Aldrid was sat opposite them, next to Cypher who had fallen asleep.

"Do you get to choose your name when you buy back in, or do you get your old one?" Aldrid said, cheeks red with the alcohol and his eyes struggling to focus on much more than his mug of mead. Herleif had never questioned Rat's name, but now it seemed foolish to think it his real one. No one would willingly call themselves that.

Rat grinned, "Oh I get my true name back, and my feathers. I'll be all pretty again and ready for integ…" he paused. "Integration, into high society." The words were a little slurred and from the way he said it Herleif guessed at sarcasm.

"Why didn't I see any of your people in Yilland?" he put in, attempting to take his mind off of Tiko.

Rat shrugged, "The Kingdom isn't that keen on the Kaz."

"That's not exactly it," Aldrid said, before burping into his fist, "Think about it, what is the point in making the trek into the Kingdom, when they can trade through the Bavagai at settlements like Stemtrad here? All the same goods, half the journey!"

Herleif nodded. It wasn't often he thought about the wider goings on of the world, but maybe he should, at least then perhaps he'd understand why all the wars happened.

Rat looked sideways at the other members of his race on the opposite side of the room, "They don't like travelling too far from home either."

Aldrid burped again quietly, raising a finger to his lips, "I hear they've had another good year of harvest, and there are murmurs of…" he leant over the table to whisper loudly at Rat, "Expansion."

Rat nodded gravely and took a deep swig of his drink. "I wouldn't put it past them," he said, lowering his horn.

"How do they expect to expand though?" Aldrid added, "The only way they can go is north to the steppe, and they can't grow anything out there."

"We wouldn't let them get that far anyway," Tiko said. "Those that come onto our lands tend not to do so well." A smile played across her lips, and Herleif knew the comment was meant for him.

He did his best to ignore her, but his hands curled unconsciously into fists. He could feel Kiakra's gaze on him again.

"Well the fighting across the Akvast sounds like it's coming close to war now," Aldrid said, oblivious to the mood at the table, "Though it still seems as if no one is really sure who wants what."

"As long as Teoma doesn't get soft with the enemy, then we should be fine," Tiko said. She turned and winked at Herleif.

No one else saw, but it that was enough.

He stood abruptly. Everyone at the table stopped speaking and stared at him, but he had eyes only for Tiko. For a few moments she didn't move, and then she took another drink from her cup.

"I'm going to get some air," he muttered eventually, and headed to the door, leaving the Pack behind him in silence.

The musicians harassed him as he walked past, but he ignored them and barged through the heavy studded door, into the cool evening air. He took a deep breath and sat down on one of the benches outside.

It was a clear night. The stars looked as though they had been pinned up in the sky, so clear they almost didn't look real. The harbour was calm, fishing boats sat still on water that was so glassy it mirrored the world almost perfectly.

Herleif let the cool air calm him and focused on his breathing.

He would get to Teoma's camp, she would be holding Fin prisoner, and he would rescue him. Fin would not be dead, maybe a little hungry and uncomfortable, but he would still be alive.

They would be okay.

"Look at this scumbag," someone said, wrenching Herleif from his thoughts.

He turned. A group of five Akalen men were walking over to him. They all looked rough, with twitchy eyes and dull smiles. They didn't look like traders, or fishermen.

"This the soldier?" one snapped, before spitting on the floor.

Herleif felt the calmness of the night leaving him.

"What do you want?" he said, pulling his shoulders back and standing up. How did they know he was a soldier?

The man who had spat was taller than him, and had a meaty jaw, but the rest of his body was slim and lithe. He wore fur lined boots, hide leggings, and a thick cloak that looked very worn.

The rest of the Akalens had made to go inside The Boars Tongue but were now waiting outside for their companion.

The man took a few steps towards Herleif.

"We want your filth to have some respect for the earth you stand on," the Akalen said, his words venomous. "We heard the Weasels had taken on a soldier, but I didn't think it was true. Kiakra must be mad to trust scum like you."

"What, do you want?" Herleif repeated quietly, his eyes full of fire. He was in no mood to be insulted.

The Akalen stepped closer, until he was only inches from Herleifs face. "I want you to leave," he whispered.

His breath stank of drink.

Herleif felt himself going taught, winding himself up for a blow. Deep within him something voiced caution, but he wasn't listening for it.

"Get any closer to me and I'll break your fingers," he said, his breathing fast.

The Akalen stepped back, and for a moment Herleif thought he was about to walk away. But the man sized him up and then readjusted himself, his dark eyes searching for weakness.

He had eyes like Tiko.

He licked his lips and leaned in close again, "Teoma, won't kill your brother," he said, taking Herleif completely off guard.

"No, she'll do worse than that," the Akalen continued, "He'll wish he was dead when she's done with him. You won't see him alive again that's for sure, and if you do find his corpse, I doubt you'll even recognise him."

Herleif froze.

"That's enough, leave him be," one of the other Akalens laughed. This one was taller and thinner, with bad burn scars across his temple.

The man in front of Herleif laughed. "He's a soldier, I'm sure he can take it."

It was a monumental effort for Herleif not to attack him there and then. Using the last of his rational mind, he spoke.

"I challenge you to a Kala'Tam," he hissed through gritted teeth.

For a moment the Akalen let his defences down, and surprise flashed across his face, but then it was gone, quickly replaced by an unsure smile, "I accept."

Herleif was lucky, for it was only then he noticed the knife in the Akalen's belt. Had he attacked him without the protection of the Kala'Tam, Herleif would have likely been killed. As it was, the two combatants would now fight on equal terms, which in the town, meant fists.

Herleif turned and pulled his shirt over his head so aggressively that it ripped below the armpit, before throwing the garment to the floor and walking several paces away.

The Akalen's companions were interested now and stepped away from the light of the tavern to watch the imminent fight out on the harbourside.

"You're in trouble now," the scarred one said, shaking his head with a smile. "My brother's going to throw your body in the harbour when he's done with you."

Herleif did his best to ignore the talk, but he could barely contain his anger, pacing left and right, staring the man down.

The Akalen removed his cloak slowly, folding it up and then handing it to his scarred brother before stepping forward.

Herleif was almost dizzy with rage and had to keep repeating the ceremonial words, so he didn't forget them.

In contrast the Akalen looked relaxed to the point of drowsy.

"Let the Sky hold up the honoured," the Akalen drawled, rolling his shoulders.

"And let the Earth pull down the wretched," Herleif finished, his heart pounding in his ears.

"The Sky watches," yelled another Akalen.

Herleif let his anger take over.

He rushed the Akalen, not giving him a single moment to measure their encounter. His opponent had obviously been expecting a more cautious approach, and the action caught him by surprise as Herleif crashed into the man, knocking him to the floor where he began to furiously rain down blows.

The Akalen twisted desperately, already bloodied, managing to buck Herleif off and scramble to his feet. Herleif fell back, and rolled onto his own feet, immediately rushing the Akalen again with bared teeth. Completely misjudging Herleif's strength the Akalen tried to back up, looking for an opportunity to counter as the enraged boy crashed into him again.

As Herleif grappled with him, he felt arms snaking their way around his neck. He picked him up before the Akalen could tighten his grip, holding his opponent high over his head. For a moment he felt the man panic in his arms, but before he could do anything Herleif dumped him back down onto the cobbled ground.

He heard something crack in the man's body.

The Akalen opened his mouth to grunt in pain, and as he did so Herleif's fist smashed into his jaw, bloodying his own knuckle and sending a tooth flying from the Akalens mouth. He was beyond feeling his own pain now, and continued the attack relentlessly, slamming his fists into any target that presented itself. His rage made him feel invincible.

The Akalen tried to force him away, pushing a palm into his face, but Herleif grabbed the hand and wrenched the wrist forward into itself, feeling the bones pop as the Akalen screamed in agony.

Herleif recognised the look in his opponent's face. It was a look of fear.

He almost had a moment of mercy, but then he remembered those words, *'If you do find his corpse, I doubt you'll even recognise him.'*

Herleif powered his fist into the Akalen's ribcage.

The warning in his head had been utterly silenced, his body was working off instinct now. Sight, sound, touch, none were considered alone, they were merely experiences that melted together as he continued to attack.

The Akalen's broken wrist was raised up again defensively. Herleif grabbed it, twisting a finger off to the side and feeling it crack. The Akalen screamed again.

"I told you I'd break your fingers!" Herleif yelled into his opponent's face, spittle flying from his mouth as he raised his fist up for another blow.

Abruptly he was aware of the Akalen's other hand, which was scrabbling around in his belt, almost behind him. Herleif paused, just for a second, and in that moment his opponent pulled the knife from his belt.

The Akalen's expression had changed now. There was desperate savagery there, like a cornered dog who can see his escape. His face was bloodied but full of concentration, his injured hand curled up into a useless claw while his other hand clutched the knife.

Herleif snarled and drove an elbow down into the man's face, before winding up for another blow, unable to recognise how much danger he was in.

There was shouting around him now, but he couldn't hear.

The Akalen swiped at Herleif's face and he closed his eyes instinctually, feeling the blade slice into the skin on his cheek, stopping only when it hit bone. He winced, but it didn't stop him, and he dropped another fist into his opponent's ribs. He heard the expulsion of breath from the Akalens mouth as the blow connected.

It almost sounded like a laugh.

Then he felt the knife sink deep into the meat of his thigh.

Herleif should have wailed in pain, but it was little more than a dull ache, and he used the time to pin his opponents shoulder, isolating the remaining good hand and twisting it away from the knife that was still embedded in his leg. Breaking the wrist was automatic, easy. He was like a child snapping sticks.

Below him the Akalen winced and drew up his other hand, both of them useless and twisted, his face a swollen mess of blood. The man was completely helpless now, but Herleif wasn't thinking about that.

He straightened up, using his good knee to keep his weight on top of the Akalen, as he slowly retrieved the knife from his own flesh. The blade tugged from deep in his muscle as he pulled it from his body, grunting as it slid free.

His opponent coughed blood.

"I- I yield," he said, his voice only a whisper, his eyes bright.

Herleif barely heard the words as he drove the knife into the Akalen's chest, feeling it punch through bone.

He pulled it free as the Akalen gasped at the air, like a fish out of water, his face open in shock. Herleif raised the knife up again and drove it down another time.

Blank eyes were all that stared back at him now, as he continued to drive the blade home, again and again.

He didn't realise he was screaming until his arms began to tire.

Finally, the pain in his face became sharp, and he was aware of the blood leaking from his thigh in torrents. His arms ached, and he lowered them for the last time, falling away onto his side, leaving the blade stuck in the ruined body of his enemy.

There was a stench of blood and sweat, and he was soaked in both.

Around him were many people, come to watch the fight. Many were joking and laughing despite the bloodshed, but they were not the ones Herleif cared about. Kiakra was the leader of the Pack, and she wore a face of iron alongside Rat. But Cypher was staring at him as though he was on fire.

He tore his eyes from the Weasel Pack. In front of him was a sight that only now could he truly comprehend. The battered, ruined corpse of his foe. The smooth fur that covered him was soaked in blood, the expression of shock still clear on his face.

He looked up at Cypher again, and she looked down on him as though he was a stranger, her expression one of confusion as much as sadness.

Tears began to collect in his eyes.

The consequences of victory.

The Akalen who had announced the Kala'Tam was standing in stunned silence, whilst several others were snarling. The one with the scarred face was pinned to the spot, unable to take his eyes from the body of his brother.

A massive creature stepped forward.

He needed no announcement, it was Tovum. The great Bavagai leant down and picked Herleif up off the floor as if he were a toddler.

"It is over, this one is victorious," Tovum said, once Herleif had found his feet. The massive man had stated the obvious, but beneath his words the message was clear. *No more, or I'll get involved.* He stared at the Akalen's for a moment, and then gestured to the tavern.

"Are you coming inside for a drink? Or clearing up this mess?" he said calmly.

Herleif watched in anticipation as the Akalens stared back at the huge man.

"We will have justice for this," said the one with the scarred face, ignoring his question.

"Not here," Tovum replied flatly.

Herleif swayed, having to hold Tovum's side to stop himself from falling. His breath was ragged and with every passing moment a new pain blossomed from his body. He squeezed the wound on his leg as hard as he could, trying to stem the bleeding, but blood still poured through his fingers.

Nodding at Tovum, the Akalen gestured to one of his companions, and together, wordlessly, they picked up their fallen comrade and carried him away from the light of the tavern and into the night.

It was then that Herleif collapsed.

***

Kiakra watched as Cypher began to make the incisions on Herleif's body. She shouldn't have been doing it, this was the third time the girl had undertaken a severe healing job in only a matter of weeks, her body wouldn't be able to take much more.

"I'll be fine, go, talk to Tiko," Cypher said, as if reading her mind.

Kiakra sighed, "Don't do any more than you have to."

Cypher nodded, but it was unconvincing. Herleifs actions had shaken her, and Kiakra wasn't sure where her head was at.

She looked down at the boy. Ever since Kiakra had spoken to the cripple in The Boars Tongue she had been watching him, trying to figure out if he was capable of the deeds she had been warned of. Every day since then she had believed more and more that they were lies, Herleif had been kind, mild mannered, had even saved Cypher. But after tonight…

He was a different creature in that fight.

She shook her head. It didn't matter, she didn't break contracts.

Kiakra sighed again and walked out of the room, closing the thin wooden door behind her. To leave Cypher alone seemed wrong, the girl needed her company, but Kiakra knew there were more pressing issues at hand. She waited for a few moments, until the faint red glow shone through the cracks in the frame, then made her way downstairs.

The tavern she had chosen to stay in was small and airy, located on the edge of town, where buildings became sparser, and were replaced by the fertile floodplains. It was cheap here, and simple. Rooms upstairs with clean beds, and downstairs, a fire and a few rickety chairs next to a fireplace. The Weasel Pack were the only ones staying here which had been the case almost every time they had come to Stemtrad.

The stairs groaned as Kiakra made her way down, alerting Tiko and Rat to her presence. Aldrid was asleep by the fire.

"Finally, you've come down," Tiko almost yelled, before hushing her voice. She was pacing the room with a fiery look on her face. "Why have we taken-" she gestured upstairs "Him, back with us? He killed an-"

"I don't break contracts," Kiakra interrupted. "That's why he's still with us."

Tiko's jaw dropped, "He killed one of *my* people," she said, digging a thumb into her chest. "You're lucky I haven't taken his head!"

Rat had been leant on one of the chairs, holding his head in his hands, but he looked up now. "It was a fair kill. They were looking for trouble and he accepted the challenge. The Akalen was the one who pulled the knife, that boy isn't in the wrong here. He's nuts, but not wrong."

Tiko turned on Rat, "Didn't do anything wrong? Did you see what he did to that man!"

He tilted his head to the side, "It was pretty bad I'll admit, but no less than what they were planning to do to him," Rat said calmly. "They baited him, and got more than they were expecting, that's all."

Tiko stared at him with disgust, but she had no rebuttal.

"He's right," Kiakra said, bringing out the authority in her voice. "Technically he did nothing wrong." As she said that she thought about the ferocity of his attack. She had seen anger like that before, and it never ended well.

Tiko lowered her tone, pleading now, "Please, Ki, just take the other contract, we have an easy out here!"

Rat shot Kiakra a puzzled look, but said nothing.

Kiakra didn't need reminding of the contract. She silently swore at Aldrid and his big mouth.

"I told you, I'm not taking it," she said.

Tiko stared at her for a long while, her jaws clenched tightly.

"If you don't take that contract, I'm leaving," she said finally. There was a long pause.

Kiakra shook her head, "I'll not be manipulated like that."

"Just, take the deal," Tiko said slowly, spitting out each word.

Kiakra was not one to give in to threats. She liked Tiko, the Akalen woman was fierce, but she had saved her more times than Kiakra could remember. However she would not allow herself to be bullied out of her decision because of some street brawl. She had a reputation to keep, both as a leader and a Hunter, and she would not be dictated to.

"I've made my decision," Kiakra said hardening her voice. "Do what you will."

She only realised how much the words stung until she spoke them. Abruptly Tiko was defeated, all her bravado revealed in that confused, hurt expression. In a moment she had composed herself, and she nodded once, her eyes turning red as she collected up her saddlebag and headed for the door.

Don't do this you damn fool.

The door opened with the wail, and wind rushed in making the fire low and the embers bright.

Kiakra wanted to urge her back in, but she said nothing. There was no room for that sort of weakness here.

Tiko turned back as if expecting protest or apology, but when none came her face darkened, and she walked out, slamming the door behind her.

For a while after, the room was deathly quiet. No one moved. There was a feeling of tremendous absence.

"You made the right decision," Rat said finally. "I know that wasn't easy, but Tiko isn't our leader, you are."

Kiakra nodded. She wasn't feeling like a leader, but at least her reputation was intact.

Rat paused, waiting for her to speak, and when she didn't he continued. "Tiko spoke about another contract?" he said raising an eyebrow.

Kiakra sat down in a big cushioned chair. She closed her eyes and scratched her head, "After me and Aldrid saw Tovum, another man wanted to pay us to bring him Herleif."

Rat sat up, paying full attention to her, "Why would anyone want him?"

"Well, not to give him a hug and a warm meal," Kiakra said quietly, glancing upstairs, "Apparently Herleif killed his son."

Rat paused, but she knew his next question.

"A lot," she said, "He offered a lot."

Rat nodded, looking very thoughtful. The cogs were whirring in his head, weighing up Herleif's life with the chance to get back into his homeland. She could guess at the result and didn't want to know how the conversation with Tiko would have played out had Rat known about this earlier.

"I see," Rat said stretching. "Well, I suppose it's a good thing we don't break contracts, because I like Herleif, but I like the south more." He grinned at her mischievously. Though his words were playful there was an offer there; *If you change your mind...*

"Who was he anyway?" he asked.

"Some guy from the Outskirts," she said quietly.

"What was his name?" Rat asked.

Kiakra glanced upstairs again, aware of how thin the walls were.

"Dagtok," she whispered.

Chapter 18

"Listen," Gatty whispered to Fin.

He was in the river, naked, sat up against the roots of an old willow tree which stretched out into the water around him. Cold water flowed past his skin, oddly more refreshing than uncomfortable.

Power gathered in the place where the forest met the river, at least according to Gatty it did, and so here he was forced to sit. This was in reaction to Fin having a complete inability to "master his body" as Gatty kept putting it.

"I can hear them," Fin said frustrated. "But that's all. I can't draw from them, they keep… twisting away."

Spirits had more of a feeling than an actual noise, a subtle presence on the mind when Fin emptied himself. The feeling was beautiful and harmonious, but there was a duality to it, an undercurrent of struggle on which it was based. Fin would have been content to simply feel, for as soon as he reached out with his thoughts, the spirits ceased, shying away from him or pushing him back into himself. He felt like oil in water, in the middle of the current, bound to its course but unable to join with it.

Reaching out again he felt the tree against which he leant. It was old and powerful, humming deeply with a wisdom from the ages. He let himself go, like Gatty had told him, forgetting where his body was in space to focus on exploring with his own spirit. The feeling that had terrified him at first now brought him a deep sense of calm.

He observed from a distance, sensing a patrol of ants along the bark and some woodlice taking shelter in an old wound where a branch had snapped away. Eggs lay dormant in the crevices of its skin, the tree enduring the energy they stole with each passing day. Then he moved a little closer, almost able to pick out the webs that connected this tree to all the others, responsible for its knowledge of so many things it had not seen.

Finally, he reached out. As soon as he touched the tree he felt its song change, and was thrust away from it forcefully, gasping as he was shoved back into his lungs.

He opened his eyes.

"Keep them closed!" Gatty snapped, slapping him on the arm from her perch on top of a particularly large root which bobbed with her every movement. It was a miracle she hadn't joined him in the river.

Fin stood up, shivering as he felt the air steal warmth from his skin. "I'm done, the tree keeps rejecting me."

Gatty looked at him as if he were a dog that had just bit her. "You are done when I say-" she began, stopping as her face became thoughtful. "Rejecting you?" she whispered, her brows furrowing. Then she turned and scuttled along her root back to the riverbank.

He shook his head as he watched her.

Fin was sick of his training, he'd been doing so much and had made so little progress. Every day for the past week he had been in another seemingly random location, trying to connect with the spirits. Today was the second time he'd been able to reach out with himself, and it had been nothing but disappointing. Every encounter that failed seemed to drain him that little bit more.

"Come with me," Gatty said, walking purposefully back toward the house.

Fin waded over to the riverbank awkwardly, slipping a few times as his numb feet struggled to discern which rocks were safe to stand on, and which were slimy with algae. He collected up his clothes, pulling on his shirt and leggings before following his mentor back to the house. He left his boots off; his toes enjoyed the freedom.

As he walked back to the house, he felt eyes on his back.

He looked up.

Perched high in the branches of a beach tree across the river was a Drakinhawk watching him. He'd never seen one come so close, they were usually only seen drifting on the wind, high in the air.

It was the size of a large fox, but had the shape of eagle in the way it stood. The feathered reptilian head was ever present, as it was in all Drakins, and was covered in shimmering blue plumage. It had vicious black talons at the end of its thin toes, and Fin knew the two front limbs would have those claws as well, but they were hidden under its dappled grey plumage. Its massive wings were folded neatly by its side.

What are you doing here?

Large, amber eyes stared back.

Fin looked up at it, taking in every detail of its build, but eventually it's gaze forced his eyes down. The Drakin had a powerful stare and he felt it watching him long after he had turned away.

Outside the house the two boar were snuffling around in the dirt looking for roots, their strong necks easily brushing away the hard earth. The yak was less occupied with food, and nuzzled at Fin's shoulder as he walked past.

He only realised how cold he had been once he got back inside and the warmth of the fire hit him. He sat down next to the flames on a rug made from shaggy bison fur, and pulled a blanket around his shoulders.

Gatty was above him on the second floor where she kept her books. The cursing and swearing that accompanied the creaking floorboards were oddly reassuring to Fin, and he smiled as he listened to her search for the specific tome she was after. With a heavy heart he realised he wished Herleif was here.

Just as his eyes were growing heavy she hurried back down the stairs holding several massive leather-bound volumes.

She threw them down onto one of the benches and took a seat, quickly flicking through one of them.

"What are you looking for?" said Fin, stretching as he stood up to join her.

Gatty continued to flick through her books. "You said you were rejected, not that the spirits didn't hear you, or you couldn't communicate with them, but that they rejected you?" she said, pausing to look up at him through her eyebrows.

"Yes, it felt like I was being pushed away," Fin said.

Gatty nodded and returned to her books, "That's a sign of something."

"A sign of what?" Fin said, taking a seat opposite her.

"If I knew then I wouldn't be looking through these books," she replied calmly. "But it's important, I know that much, you won't be able to Recast until we work out what it means."

She left it at that and continued rifling through her books. Fin sat in silence for a little while, watching the pages turn. He was little use here, he could only just read, and it was a time consuming practice for him.

"Gatty?" he said after some time.

She looked up expectantly.

"Can anyone become Recast?" he said, wary of a scolding. Gatty wasn't always the most understanding when it came to questions she deemed stupid. Luckily, she smiled.

"No, you are born Recast. Our souls are loose within our bodies, there is nothing that can change that, and if you do not have our power then there is nothing that can be done," she said.

Fin nodded, stifling a yawn "Is that why there are so few of us?"

Gatty nodded, pulling her pipe out from within the folds of her shawl. "Ours is the least common of abilities, it seems the Recast are only born into the Nomads, and there are so few of us left now."

Fin only knew of blood magic, but her tone suggested there were other abilities. She guessed his question and chuckled.

"I'm sure you have heard of blood magic, but there are other types of magic as well." Gatty fumbled for her pipe as she always seemed to do when she had something to say. Fin was beginning to associate the smell of deathweed with the feeling of confusion.

She lit her pipe with a striker and leant back, keeping the tiny glowing ember well away from her books.

"The Sight is an ability unique to Drakins, they can bestow it upon anyone, and no one knows why or how they do it. It heightens the senses, letting the chosen person see and react differently. Many great warriors have been gifted it, and the Akalens respect that power over any other," she said.

"Why that over the Recast, or blood magic?" he said.

"Because they are strange," she said grinning with her yellow teeth, "But also because the Drakin represents the four stages of life, humility, knowledge, strength, and finally, death. And the Khutaen is the only creature to willingly walk the steppe alone."

Fin remembered the touch he had with the Khutaen Drakin, and what he had seen during those brief moments. He remembered the feeling vividly, though he had experienced nothing since then. If that was the power she was referring to, then he could understand it's uses and the respect you would have toward its giver.

Gatty didn't notice Fin's reaction and continued, "Soul Voyaging is another type of magic, where people were able to transport themselves hundreds of miles in a matter of moments, but I know of no users still alive today, for that power was tied to a race that has passed."

As he was processing that she paused, as though there was a sour taste in her mouth.

"Are there any more?" Fin asked, noticing the change in her demeanour.

"Yes," Gatty replied, though her voice was quiet now. "The Vaag used to call it God's Hand, but for everyone else it was known as the Confliction."

Fin did not know who the Vaag were, and had no knowledge of what the power was, but he sensed trepidation on her part, which was unusual for the old woman. She didn't speak for a long time, and then abruptly continued, as if she'd finally gathered her thoughts.

"Recast ask for energy from the spirits. The Confliction is different. It is the wilful binding of a spirit into the body of one of the Spoken Races."

Fin narrowed his eyes, "That is how Demons are made, two souls in one body?"

Gatty nodded, her grey eyes shining out at him, "And in most it has the same effect, driving the user mad, distorting their body into terrible forms," she paused again.

Fin wrapped his deer hide around his shoulders tighter, suddenly feeling a chill.

"In others, the effect makes them stronger. Much stronger," she said, slowly.

A being stronger than the Recast was difficult to imagine, but Fin had become accustomed to her type of humour, and this was not it.

She smiled suddenly, "But that is not something you need worry about, and anyway you're tired. Get some rest."

Fin was about to protest, but was interrupted by a yawn, "Alright," he said, realising how exhausted he was.

Gatty chuckled, smoke falling from her nostrils as she took a pull from her pipe. "Today will have tired you out, I suggest you get some sleep whilst I try and work out how to get you..." she paused, making a face "Functional. I can explain magic some other time."

Fin nodded, now barely able to keep his eyes open.

He wandered over to the fire and curled up in front of it, pulling another thick hide over his shoulders as he closed his eyes.

"That Drakin is still out there," Gatty remarked to herself. "They usually never come here."

There was a curiosity in her voice, but Fin was past noticing as he drifted into sleep.

***

He awoke suddenly, a few moments before they knocked. Something had warned him of their arrival.

It was dark now and raining heavily outside. The fire burned low, light drifting across the embers. Fin could smell a stew that was still warming over it.

Gatty stared at the door, she sensed it as well.

Two figures burst in, slamming the door behind them.

Gatty was on her feet in an instant. Fin scrambled to his own feet to defend the old woman, the sleep gone from his eyes in an instant. Then he remembered the great bear was only a moment away for her. If the two figures posed any threat, Fin was not the one to fight them off.

But seeing them in the dim light of the fire, Fin didn't think they were a threat.

Both were wearing long sodden cloaks that stretched to the floor with the weight of the rain. One was a man, tall and slim with a dark widow's peak and a narrow face full of terror, the other was very round, barely coming up to the man's waist and barely able to walk. The smaller figure was hooded, but a tiny hand had emerged from an oversized sleeve and was clinging to the man's fingers.

"Please, we mean no harm," the man said. His voice was weak and throaty. He sounded sick.

"Why have you come into my house without so much as a knock at the door?" Gatty hissed with a dark look. She was still standing tall against them, the firelight enhancing her wrinkled face, making her look even more fearsome.

Fin could tell she was angry.

"I'm sorry, we wouldn't if we didn't have to, but we had no choice, they are still chasing us," the man said, taking a sideways glance at the closed door behind him. "W-we, are the only survivors," he said, stopping to cough.

As he was coughing Fin became aware of the sound of horses thundering outside the house. A dog barked and men shouted it encouragingly.

What is going on?

"Please, they will kill us," the man whispered through his coughing.

Gatty snarled and pointed to the stairs, "Don't touch anything."

The man's face brightened into a smile and he dragged the little figure up the stairs with him.

Just as he disappeared there was a banging on the door.

"Open up," someone yelled.

Gatty looked at Fin, "Don't say anything."

Fin nodded quickly.

She advanced on the door, took a deep breath, and opened it. Fin followed her, watching over her shoulder.

The air was damp and cold, and it seemed to stick to Fin's face as he peered outside. Outside were three men, all wearing dark clothes, and darker expressions. They all had weapons of some sort strapped to their hips, and three black horses were stood solemnly in the downpour behind them. One of the men was holding the lead to a slim dog with wiry hair and a wagging tail. It was extremely interested in the house.

"Hello," one of the men said, long black hair plastered against his pale face. A warm smile appeared between his cheeks, and had his companions not been looking so angry, it might have looked genuine. "We are looking for a criminal, he has abducted a child."

The man wore shining black boots, a thin gambeson and a long cloak collared with otter fur. He was too well dressed to be a farmer or a bandit, but he was no Lord either.

"A tall man without much hair, accompanied by the child he took.

Have you seen anyone like that?" His tone was reasonable, and his face was open.

Gatty looked up in mock ponder, putting a hand on her hip and biting the inside of her mouth. Then she shook her head, "Sorry but no. There were a couple of loggers come past this morning, but nothing since then I'm afraid."

She then stared at the dog, who became less and less interested in the house, until it began to back away whining.

"Ah I see, that is a shame," the man said smiling apologetically. He let his hand rest on the pommel of his sword in a motion that was well rehearsed. "You're really sure you haven't seen anyone?" He raised his eyebrows as rain dripped off the end of his nose.

Gatty shook her head, ignoring his gesture, "I hope you catch him soon, got no patience for criminals," she grumbled.

The man's smile disappeared.

Herleif could feel the tension in the air, Gatty taught and ready to twist her body into that of a beast, the man's grip becoming tighter on his sword, unaware of the fight he would be getting himself into.

Suddenly the man noticed the dog which was now begging to go in the opposite direction of the house. He did a little half bow with his head and walked briskly over to his horse. One of the other men shot a questioning look his way, but no one said anything.

Once the dog was let off its lead it bolted away from the house, and the men kicked their horses on to follow.

Gatty watched them disappear down the road before slamming the door.

"Flashing me his sword as if he were anything other than an annoyance. Bastard, I should have flashed him my claws," she muttered to herself as she returned to her bench.

Fin paused, "Why didn't you tell them-"

"Oh, they were lying!" Gatty said exasperated. Obviously, her patience from earlier had faded. "The man we have upstairs did not steal that child, did you see the way it was squeezing his hand?"

Fin nodded, gesturing to the men who had ridden away, "I did think they seemed a little… off."

"Yes, I scared the hell out of that dog, so they shouldn't be bothering us again," Gatty said. "However, I still don't know where these two *have* come from," she turned, looking up the stairs. "Get down here you two, you've some explaining to do."

Upstairs Fin heard a creak of floorboards, then the man appeared, the child still grasping his hand. The child's hood was down now, revealing a girl's face with pale freckled cheeks and dark brown hair.

"Have they gone?" the man said, looking cautiously around the room to make sure they were alone.

Gatty waved him down, "I sent them away, they won't be bothering us again, though they seemed to think that little girl with you is not your own?"

The man walked down the stairs holding the girls hand tightly. It was him using her as reassurance now. "Of course, they would say that, none of them have an honest bone in their body," he said. He was shaking slightly, but to Fin it looked like anger rather than cold.

"Where are you from?" Fin put in.

"Just a village in Yilland, nowhere you'd have heard of, and not that it matters," he muttered, his words dropping away.

"Have some stew, then I want answers," Gatty said, obviously content that he wasn't a criminal by her definition.

The man gave her a grateful look and took a seat on the bench opposite, hefting the little girl up next to him. He removed her tiny cloak, and Fin realised the reason she had looked so round was because of all the layers she was bundled up in. She was actually very skinny and shivering violently.

Gatty had moved over to the fire and was crouched down ladling stew into wooden bowls. Fin served them out to their guests and together they sat down to eat. It was wholesome food, and the small girl ate ravenously.

"She yours then?" Gatty said, smiling warmly at the girl and then looking back to the man with comparative venom.

Fin watched his eyes go empty.

"In a way. She's my granddaughter," he said, spooning a tiny morsel of carrot into his mouth.

"Why aren't her mother and father looking after her?" Gatty questioned.

The man clenched his jaw and stared into his stew, "Because, they're dead."

There was a silence.

"What happened?" Fin said gently.

As he spoke the little girl reached out to the man, hugging his side as she shivered. He picked up an elk skin and wrapped her up in it, before putting an arm around her protectively.

"I was out with this one fishing in the river, my daughter asked me to bring her with me see, I was meant to start teaching her how to swim," he rubbed a hand over his face, screwing his eyes shut.

Shadows danced over the lines in his face.

"End of the day I got my damn fishing lines tangled, had to spend an age sorting them out and by the time I was done it was dark. I rushed to get this one back home, knowing that her parents would be worrying," his voice was husky now, and he paused again, his eyes still closed tight, hands shaking.

"But when we got back to our village, the whole place was on fire. Bodies piled up, people lying dead in the road…" His eyes were still shut but a tear managed to escape, rolling down his cheek and falling off his chin to land on the little girl's head.

Fin's hairs stood on end.

The Akalen raids.

This man was a survivor.

"You were attacked?" Fin said quickly.

The man nodded and opened his eyes, which were bloodshot and teary. "Yes, we'd heard about the raiding, but we never thought…" he broke off again.

Suddenly Fin had a thought, "Then who were the men that were following you?"

The man looked puzzled, "They were the raiders? They killed *everyone*."

It finally hit him, he was an idiot for not understanding sooner. Air caught in his chest.

The Akalens hadn't been carrying out the raids, humans had.

A hundred thoughts spilled into his mind at once, but one was more clear and painful than all the rest.

Herleif died fighting a people that were not our enemy.

He died for nothing.

Fin stood.

"I have to leave."

Chapter 19

Fin was lost.

Despite all the time he had spent at Gatty's house, he had never known exactly where it was, only that Gulbrands camp was north of there. Perhaps he should have spoken to the old woman more before he left, but he did not trust her to let him go if he had hesitated.

He was walking across a grassy meadow, flanked on one side by a forested ridge which blocked the evening sunlight. Dusk was becoming night that much sooner.

Idiot, why didn't you bring anything with you? he thought. With nowhere to sleep, nothing to start a fire with and no food, he had only his current energy with which to get to Gulbrand. Until he came across some people, he had no way of knowing how far that was. His stomach groaned, already nervous. He ignored his hunger, Nomads were survivors. He was tied to the land, and he knew it would provide for him.

The night brought silence with it.

A bright moon lit up the land, and so he continued to walk on, listening to his footsteps, concentrating on the good he could do. He would go back to Gatty eventually, once he had spoken to Gulbrand or Brynjar and let them know who the real enemy was, or at least who the enemy wasn't. That action alone could stop a war, and perhaps that deed would free him from the grief of his brother's death.

The old woman could wait.

He marched on through the grey light, watching his feet rhythmically moving one after the other, almost in a trance.

After some time, he became aware of a sound other than his own tread. Looking around there was nothing to be seen, but it was hard to tell which way the noise was coming from, especially with the noise of his movements muddying the air.

He stopped, and for a while he wondered if perhaps he had imagined it, but then, as he was about to resume his march, he heard it again. A heavier tread, clumsy shuffling as though something big had been injured.

Though the moon made the landscape bright enough to walk through, Fin still could not see the source of the noise. He walked on, quickening his pace a little from what it had been, feeling very vulnerable out in the open. Heading for the safety of the trees he imagined it was a wolf pack, perhaps they had injured an elk, or a boar. Even if not they wouldn't be interested in him, wolves had learnt a long time ago that hunting the Spoken Races came with a price.

Wolves don't make that much noise, he thought, critical of his optimism.

As he got closer to the treeline his courage found him, and he stopped to take another look around.

That was when he saw it, a great shambling shape, right out in the open. How it had got there so fast he did not know. It was of a size with Gatty's bear, but moving in a twitching, conflicted way that she did not. For a moment his legs betrayed him, locking him to the spot as he wondered if maybe it had not caught his scent yet.

Its own stench was clear to him though, a heavy smell of rot that forced its way into his mouth and made him gag.

The creature stopped suddenly, its head turning toward him.

Fin saw two pits of darkness where its eyes would have been, spots that were blacker than the absence of light.

A Demon.

It screamed, a pitiful, human noise, and then rushed at him. The movement was abrupt, jerky and uncoordinated, as though it were fighting its own body. But even so it was fast.

Fin turned and sprinted. Outrunning it was impossible, but if he could get to one of the trees maybe he would find safety in its branches. He flew past a few pines that were no good for climbing, thin branches sprouted from wide trunks and he knew from experience they were all too keen to throw climbers from their crowns. Instead he opted for an old maple, launching himself up into its lower branches.

As he began to climb he heard the Demon come sliding to a halt beneath him. It shook the trunk, and he dared not look down in case its eyes took him. He climbed higher, face covered in sweat, his hands sticky with sap. Then there was a crack, like the snap of lighting, but drawn out so that it had more time to pierce his ears.

Fin looked down.

The Demon was massive, but somehow its body was still obscured by shadow, as if the light of the moon would not touch it. He could see its eyes though, and up close they were even worse to look upon. Pain swam in those pools of darkness, eager for company.

It had snapped off one of the lower branches and was trying to reach up for him in the tree.

A withered claw swiped at him, snagging on the material of his leggings. He felt them mercifully tear away, but hot blood ran down into his boots.

Fin pulled himself higher, the branches thinning in his hands and beneath his feet.

The Demon swiped at him again, pulling itself higher into the tree. He could see its ruined flesh now, hanging in strips from its forelegs, smearing its own gore on the bark with every angry swipe.

So much pain.

Its hot breath rose in a claggy mist, the stench of decay clinging to Fins clothes and face, making him choke.

Abruptly there was a more familiar sound, a roar, and the Demon had fallen. Something below had pulled it down and was now worrying at its throat. The Demon screamed again, scrabbling at its attacker with those dead, hooked limbs, desperately trying to fight back.

There was a snap, and the sound of flesh tearing from bone, and then the Demon was still.

Fin dared not move from his perch in the branches. He stayed there as the shape below him receded away, until all that remained was a frail old woman.

"Get your bony arse out of that tree and help me build a fire," she yelled up at him, wheezing.

Fin laughed until the sweat cooled on his brow.

***

They built a fire quickly, Gatty showing him exactly how to stack the wood to make it catch better, so as to burn away the body of the Demon. It took a little while for the flames to catch, for the wood was a little damp from the rains the day before, but once they did the rotten body of the monster burned as fast as oil. It smelt terrible, but the warmth trumped the smell, and he huddled close to it.

"Now its spirits are free, its torment is over," Gatty mumbled, watching the Demon burn. She had three thin cuts visible on her neck, running up and onto her chin. Fin guessed that the hide of her bear was thicker than her human skin.

"I didn't think there were Demons in these parts?" he said, looking over at the old woman.

Gatty sighed, "There didn't used to be."

Fin nodded, "You think this," he gestured at the huge form in the centre of the flames, "Was caused by the raids in Yilland? The man did say the raiders just left the dead in the streets."

Gatty nodded.

There was a long pause, "I didn't want you to go. And you were a fool to run off as fast as you did." she snapped. "But whoever is responsible for this slaughter needs to be stopped, and that can't very well be done by Yilland if they're busy fighting the wrong people. Otherwise this place will end up like the Outskirts, crawling with Demons and devoid of life."

Fin processed what she was saying.

"So, you're letting me leave?"

Her eyes flicked over to him, "You were never my prisoner, boy," she spat.

Fin nodded, "I know, I'm sorry."

The flames hissed and fizzed.

"This needs to be done though," she said, "And Gulbrand's lot know you better than they know an old woman. They might actually listen to what you have to say."

Fin had a hope, just for a moment, "Did you bring the man and his daughter with you?" They were both witnesses to what had happened, if they were lurking nearby their word could be invaluable in convincing Gulbrand and Brynjar of what was going on.

Gatty was shaking her head though, "I didn't. They're back home, getting some rest before they move on. You'll have to convince those Lords yourself."

Fin felt somewhat defeated by that, but he was glad the old woman was there to give him her blessing.

"I don't know the way to Gulbrands camp," he admitted, eyes downcast. The question was there though, *will you show me the way?*

Gatty grinned her yellow grin, "That's because you're a fool. Lucky you've got me eh?"

***

Drizzle fell, muddying the road under an iron grey sky. It was the kind of weather that soaks you slowly, constantly eating away at any reserves of energy, trying to sneak the cold into your bones.

Kiakra's toes had long since gone numb in her boots. She would have adjusted her position in the saddle to help the blood flow to her legs, but she was sat on the only patch of leather that was still dry.

She pulled the hood of her cloak over her head, and then pushed it off again. The inside was damp.

She cursed quietly.

They had been on the road for over a week, heading north again. For most of that time Kiakra had been thinking about Tiko. The Akalen was a good friend, and she worried for her. Hopefully she had fallen in with another group of Hunters, or maybe returned to her kin. Kiakra knew that she wanted to be a part of the conflict in the north, so maybe she would see her again up there.

The track in front of her was narrow and muddy. To her left was a cliff face, ancient granite covered by moss and dirt. Eyes shone out at her knowingly, the pupils made from sharp crystals entombed in the rock. It was an eerie place.

To her right was the Lowland forest. It was the largest forest on the steppe, and situated in a bog. Trees were ancient here, and each one seemed to have twisted itself perfectly into the space it was given, growing in endlessly varied formations between the pools and boulders that were littered throughout the place. Moss covered every available surface, but the low light warned the Spoken Races away.

No birds sang, and no wolves howled, the only sounds were the footfalls of the horses.

This was a place for the spirits, and the living were not welcome.

Kiakra peered at the trees, but a few hundred feet in her view was obscured by a thick fog that had clouded the forest. Dark shapes drifted through the trees at the edges of the mist, travelling without moving. It was not a sight meant for her eyes.

She looked away with a shiver, and then instinctually checked behind her for Cypher.

That was her other worry. The girl had healed Herleif too much and was now barely able to walk unassisted.

Time had not made her condition better, and with every passing day she looked weaker. She was currently slumped over her horse, even just the act of sitting upright was too much for her. They'd fed her as much as they could gather, but no amount of food seemed to help the girl, another poor sign.

Kiakra was happy to lay blame at the feet of Herleif, who was traipsing along at the back of the group with the goats, who were still determined to follow the Pack. If he could have controlled himself then Cypher wouldn't be in this state.

And Tiko wouldn't have left.

Damn fool, he's crippled us, she thought, knowing there was nothing to be done about it now.

Dagtok's offer still played in the back of her mind. Herleif was a murderer according to him, and what she had seen only backed that up. Would anyone really blame her for changing her loyalties? Loyalty to evil men was surely worse than no loyalty at all, and it *would* fix all her problems. The Pack would get a bigger payout, they wouldn't have to worry about the boys temper and Tiko would rejoin them.

She pushed those thoughts away, she had a reputation to uphold, for all their sake. There was little work for dishonest Hunters.

Abruptly Kiakra caught sight of something up ahead.

It was a figure, blocking the slim path between the Lowland forest and the wall of rock. The figure was hooded and tall, holding a strung bow easily down by their side. It looked like a man. Kiakra pulled her horse to a stop and saw him raise a hand up above his head. For a moment she was puzzled, only recognising what he was doing when it was too late.

It was a signal.

An arrow whizzed through the air and hit Kiakra in the calf, pinning her right leg to her horse. Pain shot up her leg, so intense her eyes blurred.

She winced, trying to stay calm as her dappled mare reared up, threatening to buck her off. She gripped the reigns and pulled them hard toward herself, exercising her control over the beast.

"Ambush!" she yelled as another arrow fizzed past her head. Behind her she heard the distinct twang of Aldrid's crossbow, followed by a yell from within the forest. Looking back, she saw the sleek blue blur of Rat's deer as he chased someone into the trees, whilst Aldrid wound up his crossbow beside the two yaks.

How many are there?

She reached for her own bow and realised with dismay that it wasn't strung. Another arrow thudded into the ground at the horse's feet, panicking it so it almost bucked her off again. It took huge effort not to scream every time the animal moved, for it created friction against the arrow in her leg.

She could see two figures in the forest, both hiding behind large twisted beech trees, about fifty feet apart. They were wearing cloaks, but their tall frames helped identify them as Akalens. Both had bows but only one was looking at her.

Kicking her horse hard with her left foot, and, pulling a shortsword from her scabbard, Kiakra rushed the attacker. Galloping made the pain in her leg almost unbearable, and cold sweat dripped from her brow into her eyes, making them sting.

Despite all that she was grinning wildly. The fight had taken her, and all she could think about now, was them, and her.

The man loosed another arrow her way, but stupidly aimed at her head instead of her horse. She ducked under the shot and closed on him.

At the last moment he tried to take cover, his dark face disappearing behind the tree. But he'd turned too late, and Kiakra hacked at him as he presented his back.

He yelled out as her blade connected, slicing so deep into his shoulder that the weapon stuck there and was wrenched from Kiakra's grip.

She left him writhing on the floor, for his companion had noticed her now, and was knocking an arrow to his bow.

Side on to him and at such close range, she had few moves other than to hope his aim was awful, and wheel her horse around as fast as possible. The Akalen took advantage of the easy target and an arrow leapt from his bow, sinking into the flesh at her hip.

Kiakra screamed and her whole right leg went numb. Her horse panicked and bolted towards the Akalen as he threw down his bow and began to draw his sword.

Kiakra reached for her knife, and with the last of her strength, lunged off her horse as it flew past the Akalen. For a long moment she was weightless, and then she crashed into him, the force of the impact winding her as they both slammed into the ground. The knife was torn from her grasp and she closed her eyes as the earth rushed up into her face.

She tasted dirt and for a moment she couldn't breathe, rolling blindly on the floor trying to get her lungs to work.

Eventually she gasped, taking a massive breath. It was then that she felt the stickiness in her hands, and noticed the absence of her knife.

Opening her eyes, she saw the Akalen led next to her, the blade embedded in his chest up to the handle. His blood was all over her hands. Despite his wide eyed and unmoving stare, he looked somehow familiar. She heard the other Akalen groaning some way off. Still alive for now, but she knew he would not be getting back up.

Laughter churned up from her stomach. It was the same maniacal feeling that always took her after coming so close to death. It faded fast, and she knew that, so she enjoyed the moment.

And then the pain kicked in, as it always did.

She winced, silently gritting her teeth through her smile as she rolled onto her side. The arrow embedded in her calf had snapped off cleanly, but the one in her hip had been pushed further in when she fell. Part of it had broken off, but it was so deep in her leg she couldn't see any of what remained. A steady flow of blood leaking from the wound mesmerised her.

Her head wheeled.

The muffled cracking of damp twigs alerted her to a figure off to her side, nearer the path and stalking through the trees like a wolf. It must have been the Akalen who'd been blocking her way.

He glanced over at her and saw his fallen companions. Pain etched itself into his face as he took the scene in, tiny droplets of water gathering in his fur. He looked away and continued moving towards where the others were. Where Cypher was. His bow was knocked and ready for use.

Kiakra stopped smiling. She thought of Cypher in her weakened state. The girl was already close to death, and that was without any added injury from this man.

She had to draw him away.

"Oi," she croaked, her voice much weaker than she'd expected. "I killed your friends."

Her head was spinning but she used all her effort to keep her eyes on him, trying to bait him over with her words. What she would do with him if she could draw him over was something she'd worry about later.

The Akalen turned and pulled his hood down, revealing harsh burn marks that covered his head. Kiakra recognised him immediately as the Akalen from Stemtrad.

"I know," he muttered. "Now I'll kill yours."

Kiakra's smile faded, along with her vision. She blinked but saw nothing.

Herleif, this is his fault. All of it.

Then her head dropped.

***

Herleif watched Kiakra's horse canter back onto the path. She herself was nowhere to be seen.

"That isn't good," Aldrid muttered, finally reloading his crossbow, before levelling it at the trees warily. "You can go help Rat now lad, I'll look after Cypher."

She had managed to sit up but could do little more than that.

Herleif nodded and kicked his horse after Rat. Ducking under low branches that were draped in wispy lichen, he followed his companion's tracks. It wasn't long before he found him.

He heard them before he saw them, mostly yelling from Rat, clear calls for help interspersed with curses.

Herleif burst into a waterlogged clearing and was met with the sight of Rat desperately fending off a cloaked Akalen, who was swinging at him wildly with a club. They were in thick black water that came up to the Akalens hips and was midway up Rat's torso, both struggling to keep their footing as they fought. Rat's feathered mount was circling the water, obviously distressed but unable to help.

Herleif jumped off his horse and pulled his sword from its scabbard, rushing forward into the water. It was freezing cold and had the consistency of porridge, much more difficult to wade through than the Akalen made it look. Warmth left his bones as he waded toward the Akalen, his breath catching as he struggled with the temperature.

Rat slipped in the sludge, and in that moment the Akalen turned to face Herleif, backing up so as not to get sandwiched between the two. He took a half-hearted swipe at Rat as he tried to regain his footing, but missed, and Herleif forced the Akalens attention on himself by rushing him.

He feigned low, and then flicked his elbow inwards at the last moment to bring his sword in from the outside. The Akalen blocked the move but Herleif's blade slid up his club and nicked his finger, making him grimace, but not disarming him. In an instant he'd switched the club to his other hand and stepped forward with a big overhand swing aimed at Herleif's head.

At that moment Herleif suddenly recognised him as one of the men from The Boars Tongue.

They've come for me, he thought, a pang of guilt jolting through his chest. The realisation made him stumble as he sidestepped. Water weighed heavy on his clothes and he barely avoided the deadly strike from his opponent, managing to get his sword in the way just enough to redirect the blow onto his arm. It hurt but he knew it wasn't an injury that he needed to worry about. He tried to counter but his foot slipped on something under the water, something soft that wriggled out from under his boot and sent him crashing into the water.

Cold stung his face and he was reminded of Hok and his gang, pushing his head into that freezing mud until he had passed out. That had been his fault too.

His foot found solid ground and he pushed hard on it, bringing his head clear of the water once again. The Akalen had brought his arm back for another blow, and it surely would have killed Herleif had it connected.

But then Rat was there, looking like something from a nightmare, his bare, scaled skin covered with thick black mud, and mixing with the blood from an arrow wound in his shoulder that Herleif only now noticed.

The Akalen tried to turn, but his heavy cloak made the steps awkward, and Rat grabbed his clubbing arm as he drove a blade into his opponents side. Gasping the Akalen tried to struggle, even with his wound, but Rat forced him down into the dark water, holding him there with thick arms until the struggle was over. Only then did he remove his blade.

"I'm glad you got here when you did," he said, chest heaving.

"Me too. You alright?" Herleif said, gesturing at the broken haft of arrow only just visible from Rat's shoulder.

"Ah, it's a pain, but I'll live," Rat replied, wading out of the putrid water to his deer. She lowered her ears in greeting as he leant on her, his softly spoken apologies still audible to Herleif as he regained his breath.

He waded out on the other side of the water, looking around for his own mount.

"I'm going to check on others, meet me back on the path?" Rat yelled over to him as he jumped up onto his sleek mount.

Herleif nodded and waved, before turning and heading further into the forest.

He found his horse standing under the branches of a long limbed yew tree, sheltering under the pines.

The ground was soft and mossy, and Herleif took a step towards her.

"Don't move," a voice from behind him said.

Herleif recognised it.

He turned to see the burned Akalen from Stemtrad.

"Don't you dare move," he said again. He was about thirty feet away, holding his bow down by his side with an arrow knocked. At this range he couldn't miss, but if Herleif tried to rush him then he'd have enough time to shoot.

The sound of Rat trotting back to the path echoed through the trees. There was nothing he could do, and no one was here to save him.

"What do you want?" Herleif said, holding his sword by his side.

The Akalen shifted his weight awkwardly, and it was then that Herleif noticed he had a bolt sticking out of the top of his thigh, close to the groin. There was a heavy flow of blood coming from the wound.

"I want justice, for my brother," the Akalen said.

His voice was shaky.

"It was a Kala'Tam," Herleif replied stiffly. "He accepted. There is no justice to be had."

The Akalen raised his bow to Herleif, his fingers twitching on the string.

"There was no need for what you did to him. He was drunk, you could see that, and he yielded to you!"

The bow was shaking.

"What sort of monster kills a beaten man?" he said breaking into a sob. Blood pooled at his feet. Even the hungry moss couldn't soak it up fast enough.

This sort of monster, Herleif thought, but he had no reply for him.

"Now all of us are dead apart from me," the Akalen said. Abruptly he swayed sideways, splaying out his legs so he didn't fall. Then he dropped to one knee, his bow going down with him.

Herleif took a step forward.

"Don't move!" the Akalen screamed, raising his bow up again. He tried to pull back on the string, but his strength had seeped out with his blood. "No, no, please," he muttered, pulling back with all his might.

The bow barely flexed with his efforts.

For a moment Herleif saw the face of Hok once again, that same fear, that same anger etched onto his face.

The Akalen's eyes went dull and he fell backwards, supporting himself on a hand. Herleif wanted to turn away, to leave him, to turn from his mistakes and hope they would vanish when he could no longer see them.

Pity welled up from inside him as he watched the wretched man weep.

You caused this, no one else but you.

He turned away, mounted his horse, and left the man to die.

***

Herleif rode back to the path. This place could take care of the Akalen's spirit without the aid of a burial.

It was the only comfort he had.

The misty forest was disorientating and when he got back to the path he thought the others had left, but they were simply further away than he had anticipated. As they came into view Herleif saw that all of them had dismounted, which was not a good sign.

As he got closer he realised what he had taken to be a saddlebag was actually Kiakra, slung over the back of one of the yaks and wrapped up in several hides. She was very pale, and not moving. They had left her face uncovered though, so he assumed she wasn't dead.

Rat was knelt on the ground holding Cypher whilst Aldrid wrapped a cloth around her neck. She was just as pale, but her eyes were open and glassy. She looked drunk, and a lot like the Akalen had moments ago.

Don't think like that.

"Don't do it up… too tight Aldrid," Cypher mumbled through ragged breaths.

"I won't, don't worry," Aldrid said with more confidence than Herleif was expecting.

"Let me… Kiakra is…" Cypher struggled to get the words out.

Aldrid continued his wrapping and spoke softly, "Kiakra is fine, just rest."

"What happened? Can't she heal herself?" Herleif whispered as he swung a leg off his horse.

Aldrid tied off the bandage and then turned to him.

"One of those Akalens nicked Cypher in the neck with an arrow, and she's too weak to use her powers," he said in a hushed tone. Herleif couldn't meet his eye when he said it. They both knew the reason for her weakness was the same reason for Herleif's strength.

Aldrid shook his head, "Bastard should've been aiming for me though, I was the one with the crossbow. I was meant to be looking after her." Guilt was written across his face.

Herleif put a hand on his shoulder in an attempt to reassure him, "Well at least it was just a graze."

Aldrid nodded, flashing a nervous smile at Herleif, "Exactly, and I got the bugger in the thigh, bastard's probably gone off to die in the woods."

His hope was all too evident.

"Probably," Herleif muttered. Thinking about his encounter with the scarred Akalen made him feel sick.

He paused, "What happened to Kiakra?"

Rat hefted Cypher back up onto her horse, she had fallen asleep again.

"I found Kiakra off in the woods lying face down in the mud. Two arrows in her leg," he said bluntly. "The arrows were in there pretty deep, but they've stemmed the bleeding somewhat, so she might still make it."

He didn't sound confident, and he was still bleeding himself from the wound in his shoulder.

Herleif stared at Kiakra. She looked like a corpse, and so did Cypher. This was all his fault.

Herleif nodded, "Where is the nearest place to find a healer?"

"Yotan, it's close actually," Aldrid said, brightening up a little. "Only a few miles past the forest, it's a permanent Akalen camp, They're fishermen mostly."

"Good," Herleif said reluctantly. He wasn't keen on more Akalen encounters, but if either of these two died because of his actions, there would be no forgiving himself.

"We need to get moving. And keep an eye on the trees, there were five of them at the Boar's Tongue."

Rat tried climbing up onto his deer. He failed, wincing as he held a hand over his injured shoulder, "Don't have to be too careful, Kiakra was lying next to two others, pretty sure we got them all."

Herleif nodded, watching Rat's strained movements. He didn't want to insult him by offering help, but even Aldrid was quicker getting up onto his yak.

When finally Rat did manage to get up onto his deer, he looked exhausted. Herleif looked from him to Kiakra, and then to Cypher.

"Let's go," he said, kicking his horse forward through the rain.

Time was not their ally.

Chapter 20

A warm wind was blowing in from the south, driving away the cold that had swept down from the great northern ocean. Songbirds which had been so absent in the winter months were finally beginning to return, chattering amongst the now blooming wildflowers.

Brynjar sat outside his tent, eyes closed, enjoying the sun on his face and the faint smell of lavender blowing in from the fields around him. He was grateful for Ojak setting up his tent on the fringes of the camp. Here at least he had some measure of peace.

He was happy to be back in Yilland. The nights out on the steppe with Egil had become sleepless, and when he did manage to rest, the battered face of the sergeant haunted his dreams. The man had not lasted his captivity, being found dead in his tent the day after Brynjar had visited him. Apparently illness had taken him, but Brynjar wasn't that stupid, he suspected he had been killed to hide Egil's secrets.

Yesterday they had finally been relieved from the outpost, Gulbrands men had arrived in the morning and sent them on their way, hurrying them back to the safety of the camp in Yilland. It was a good thing too, Brynjar was exhausted, and last night had been his first good sleep in weeks.

Footsteps brought his thoughts back to the present.

"My Lord, Gulbrand has requested your presence," came Ojak's voice from behind him.

Brynjar opened his eyes and turned to face the boy, "Thank you Ojak."

"Shall I fetch your horse?" he said expectantly.

Brynjar shook his head smiling, "No I'll walk, I'll do enough sitting once I'm there," he said walking past Ojak and clapping him on the shoulder as he did. The boy nodded, and then stepped after him.

It was a hot day and he wore only his boots, leggings and a loose red tunic that was tied at the waist with a simple leather belt. His sword was at his hip as always, and he rested a rough hand on the pommel as he walked through the camp alongside Ojak, a content silence between them.

The place had almost doubled in size since he had left. Displaced villagers had begun to get used to life here, and the ones who found work had been allowed to set up temporary homes. They'd had to expand outward to accommodate these new builds, and now the place was an odd mixture of military activity and domestic work. Men training for battle were now watched by confident young women and children played in the roads once reserved for carts and warhorses. It was as if the whole of Yilland had been concentrated into this one strange camp.

I suppose it has, which is alright until we run out of food.

Though Gulbrand's stores were full, there was heavy rationing and Brynjar knew the farmers needed to return to their fields if anyone was going to survive the following year. Hiding from their enemies was not a long term strategy.

He walked past a couple of young girls carrying heavy buckets of water, and then a broad chested man pulling a cart filled with grain. Two soldiers flanked him, no doubt with orders to protect the food he was carting.

He carried on, down the main road through the camp which the sun had now baked into hard earth, preferable to the knee high mud he had last experienced. The gates out of the camp were already open for several returning scouts who were exchanging jokes with the guards, and they stopped as Brynjar passed by, each man nodding his head solemnly and giving a nervous smile.

Perhaps his reputation had not been tarnished forever.

As he made his way over the wooden bridge and the gates closed behind him, he noticed a commotion on the fields around the Great Oak.

A good hundred or so horsemen were gathered in front of a small, neat camp, full of grey tents that were all flying the flags of their houses. In the centre of the camp stood a large white pavilion, and from it, sailing on the wind, was a banner depicting a Rotstag holding its antlered head high as it battled with a bear.

The purple cloaks of the horsemen also flowed in the wind as they performed various synchronised riding feats, turning like a shoal of fish, one way and the next, moving as one unit to demonstrate their skilled horsemanship.

Brynjar cracked a smile. He recognised them.

He walked briskly, followed closely by Ojak who was momentarily confused by the display. Then the boy recognised the banner flying from the pavilion.

"Those are men from Rukland my Lord!" he said looking eagerly at Brynjar.

He nodded, "I see them, I had no idea they were coming."

Brynjar increased his walking pace to something near a jog, and Ojak had to skip every few steps just to keep pace with him. He could tell the camp was a temporary fixture, for as he drew nearer there were no unpleasant smells to greet his nose, and all the soldiers looked clean and well rested. Not men who had spent weeks under their canvases.

Nobody tried to stop him as he made his way to the central pavilion. Brynjar noticed a Rotstag with gilded antlers grazing on the grass outside the ornate tent. Even now he found the creatures enchanting, and he stopped for a moment to watch it.

It was half as big again as a horse, with sharp shining antlers and a body that was not as heavy set as a bison, yet not as delicate as a deer. But it's great size was not the only thing that fascinated him; where the lower jaw should have been was a thick mass of root like tendrils which, when lowered to the ground, would probe the ground and seek out plants and water. At a distance the Rotstag looked like it had a huge, twisted beard, but this was in fact, how it fed itself.

Brynjar turned to say something to Ojak, but the boy was wide eyed. He smiled at let him watch a moment longer, then smacked him on the back, "Come on, we need to talk to Gulbrand."

Ojak snapped out of his trance, "Sorry, yes my Lord," he mumbled.

Two guards stationed outside the pavilion had obviously been told about Brynjar, for they didn't say a word as he entered. Inside, the pavilion was cool and open, filled only with some cushions and a long low table, around which, several men were stood in full mail armour.

They all looked up as the young Lord entered.

Brynjar's eyes were fixed on one man in particular.

He was tall and broad, though his stomach had widened even more since Brynjar had last seen him. His head was shaved and covered with runes that marched up from the back of his neck, ending somewhere around where his hairline would have been. His face had been handsome, but now his cheeks were pinking, and his eyes were narrow and weary, looking out from above a short thick beard that rounded out his jaw. A surcoat of deep purple fell to the man's feet, it was fraying at the edges from long years of use and covered most of the mail in which he was clad, though not the heavy pauldron's on his shoulders. A sword of the same design as Brynjar's was strapped at his hip, and he was grinning broadly.

Brynjar returned the expression and bowed.

"Lord Alvard," he said.

The man laughed and stepped over to him, pulling Brynjar into a hug.

"It is good to see you my son," Alvard said in a deep voice.

Brynjar hadn't seen his father in months, seeing him here had taken him by surprise. He would have liked to ask him how his friends back home were, if his mother was still in good health and whether the old temple was close to completion. But he said none of that, this was not the time or place for indulging the curiosity he had for his home.

He noticed Egil was here as well, standing next to Gulbrand in his mail. That was who he really needed to speak to his father about, but the conversation would have to wait.

"Why did you wait so long to come? I heard you've been hanging around the border for months?" Brynjar said as he broke the embrace with his father.

Alvard's smile lost some of its charm, and his eyes shifted down, "King's orders, Olvaldr did not want me to cross the border in case I escalated the situation," he shrugged and forced a laugh, "And so there my forces wait."

That made little sense to Brynjar, surely a show of strength would have been exactly what was needed to keep the Akalens from starting a fight?

If it is even them, he thought, glancing at Egil.

"Brynjar, good to see you again," Gulbrand said. He was also wearing his mail, though the surcoat that covered it was the dark green of Yilland. "Come take a seat, we have things to discuss."

Gulbrand kept glancing over to Alvard, and Brynjar did not miss it. He wondered why he had been summoned here.

Bowing his head, he took a seat at the table next to where his father was stood. Ojak had stayed by the door, and stood like a statue by the entrance.

There were four other men here, two of which he recognised as his father's generals. The other three he assumed belonged to the Lord of Yilland.

"I hope you're feeling well rested?" Gulbrand said to Brynjar as they all sat down.

"It's was nice to spend a night a little further from the enemy," Brynjar replied, deciding against a glance at Egil. The man needed no warning about his suspicions.

"Good to hear," Gulbrand said, before taking a deep breath. "I'll get straight to the point, your father has been allowed to come here to decide whether or not extra forces are required in this conflict."

Brynjar's palms began to sweat.

This was too soon.

Gulbrand continued, "I believe that they are not only necessary but crucial, however, I wish to hear from you, after all you have just returned from enemy territory?"

Alvard cut in then, he was used to holding power and he knew he had it here, "He's all but decided to bring my army across the border, but the Lord of Yilland needs to give me some further reassurance."

Gulbrand ignored the obvious insult, but Brynjar was watching Egil. The man stared at him with those cool green eyes, and Brynjar could not tell what it was he wanted him to say.

If the Pale Wolf did have her eyes set on Yilland, then a show of strength would be exactly what was needed to deter her.

But is it her? a voice cautioned in Brynjars head.

If they had got it wrong somehow, and she was not behind the raids, then bringing an army to the border might exacerbate the situation, and end up causing the exact conflict they wished to avoid.

He remembered the words of the dying warrior, *No Akalen has set foot in your lands*, that's what he had said. Why would a dying man lie about such a basic fact?

He looked at the Captain. Accusing Egil of treachery without evidence would be pointless, all he had now were suspicions, he needed more time to investigate. But that was exactly what his decision revolved around, that man's innocence, or lack thereof.

All eyes were on him, and he realised he knew nothing.

"I am-" he began, not knowing where his words would take him. But abruptly Brynjar was cut off as several soldiers piled into the room. They were holding a scrawny looking boy by the scruff of his neck.

***

"He came up to one of our men earlier asking to speak with Brynjar," the guard said. "Claims he's a soldier."

As the man spoke, his hand on Fin's neck did not ease up even a little. His grip was like iron, and as the boy was forced to stare at his feet, he wondered whether he had made the right decision coming here.

"Show me his face," a familiar voice said.

His hair was yanked back as he was forced to look up.

"Fin," said the voice again in a whisper. It was Brynjar, looking like he'd seen a ghost.

The man stood up slowly, eyes never leaving Fin.

"Let him go," he said quietly, and the guards hesitantly loosened their grip.

Fin rubbed the back of his neck, it was sore. Then he remembered where he was and tried to hide his rudeness with a low bow.

Brynjar grabbed him by the shoulder and stood him upright. There was a smile beginning to form on the young Lord's face.

"My Lord," Fin said as confidently as he could.

Brynjar pulled him into a hug. It felt more for his own benefit than for Fin's.

"Where have you been?" Brynjar said, breaking the embrace and staring at him. "We searched for you…" His words failed him, and his gaze lost its focus.

Fin wasn't ready to give Gatty up, and he paused for a moment.

"I stole a horse and managed to escape onto the steppe," he lied, shaking slightly under the gaze of the Lords and generals around him. "I spent a few days on the run, and when I finally got away I realised I was lost. I've only just managed to find my way back."

He noticed a man with green eyes looking at him differently than the others.

"An Akalen told us you had been killed by a Demon?" Brynjar said, looking troubled.

Fin shrugged, "I'm sorry, I don't know."

"So, they have told us even more lies then," Gulbrand muttered. Fin remembered this was the man he had come to convince.

"Maybe those ones have my Lord," he interjected, looking past Brynjar. "But others may be telling the truth."

A large bald Lord with a tattooed head gave Fin a narrow look, "What do you mean by that?" He paused, "And why did you ask to speak to my son?"

Fin looked from the man, back to Brynjar. Noticed that despite the paunch on the man's belly, and the lack of hair, he had the same eyes, and face as the young Lord Brynjar.

Lord Alvard.

He took a deep breath, and chose his words carefully.

"I have new information about this conflict," he began. He told them of how the strangers had come to him in Gatty's home, though he had changed her name and the location, painting her as a kind old woman who had sheltered him for a few days.

It was a surprisingly difficult change to make.

He told them about the old man who had seen human men burn his village, not Akalens. He told them how the men who had visited had been dressed, how they had acted, and from which direction they had come.

When he had finished speaking the room was silent.

The man with the green eyes had not moved since his story began. Not even a blink.

"When did this happen?" Brynjar said carefully.

"A few days ago, the raid must have happened a little while before that."

He saw Brynjar glance at the man with green eyes, and then drop his head in thought.

Then Alvard spoke, "Ha! A lie, surely?" he said, turning to look at Gulbrand across the table. He wasn't sure of himself though, Fin could tell.

The Lord of Yilland said nothing, but one of the generals spoke up.

Fin did not know his name, but he was a weathered man with a white widow's peak, "It would make sense. All the locations were deep in our territory, and there have been no survivors from the villages that were attacked," he said, looking around the pavilion with a cautious hope.

Gulbrand was staring off into nothing.

"Why have the Akalens not tried to contact us then, if the raids were not their doing?" the man with the green eyes said. It was the first time Fin had heard him speak.

Gulbrand suddenly snapped out of his trance, "No, there could be something in this, however I cannot take only your word for it Fin."

Fin was surprised the he had even remembered his name, but Gulbrand smiled apologetically, as though his mistrust was some great offence.

The Lord looked at Brynjar, "I would ask that you, the boy, and Captain Egil go to track down these men, if they exist, and capture them if they are indeed real," he paused. "If you cannot bring them to a trial here, then destroy them."

Fin felt a restlessness begin within himself, some morbid excitement for justice.

"My Lord," Brynjar said, removing his hand from Fin's shoulder and addressing his father. "What will you do?"

The great man scratched the back of his neck and scowled, "I will stay here, this sounds like a fool's errand to me but go if you must. We know who the real enemy is."

Brynjar looked a little taken aback by his fathers words, but there was no reply from him.

"It is decided then," Gulbrand said, doing his best to ignore Alvard's words. "Lord Brynjar and Captain Egil will lead a group of my men to track down these bandits in our homeland."

"I have tried to track them before," Egil muttered.

"And you will do so again," Gulbrand said, cutting him off before he had a chance to mutter any more protests.

He stood from his chair, Alvard and the rest of the generals following suit.

Though it seemed to Fin that the meeting was over, Gulbrand stayed and spoke with his generals, unfurling great maps, deciding which men would be best to bring and how many days the mission should take.

Brynjar had not left his side since he had entered the pavilion, and he now patted him on the shoulder, "We'll leave them to their plans," he said, leading Fin outside.

As they walked out Ojak joined them, though he was not smiling. Brynjar seemed to catch his look and turned to Fin once they were back outside under the great branches of the Yilland Oak.

"I wanted to ask you something Fin," Brynjar said slowly, staring at the Rotstag which had stirred from its grazing and was looking over intently, the tendrils from its mouth probing through the air as it held its head high.

"Anything my Lord," Fin replied, though he had already guessed at the question.

"Your brother, does he live also?" Brynjar said, not meeting his eye.

In his chest Fin felt the great hollow that had been torn out with Herleif's life. The feeling threatened to bring on tears, but here was no place to shed them and he breathed deeply, calming his mind.

"He fell, injured in the raid we conducted together," Fin said clearly.

You failed him, and he died for nothing, were the words he left unspoken, but judging by his face Brynjar had heard them all the same.

"That raid was a mistake I have paid for in many ways. That was my failing, and I am sorry," he said, and it sounded as though he meant it.

Watching this great man mourn for his brother brought back a jealousy that Fin hated himself for. If their positions were reversed, would they have mourned for him, or would he simply have been forgotten?

"So, the Akalen's have killed our own then," Ojak said suddenly. There was unmistakable anger in his voice. "Why are we rushing to find proof of their innocence when we have proof of their guilt?" he said, louder this time, his hands balled up into fists.

Brynjar looked down from the Rotstag, "That's enough," he muttered, and though the words were only quiet and held no malice, Ojak flinched as though he had been struck.

Fin waited for Brynjar to say more, but he didn't.

The Lord raised his eyes and went back to watching the stag, though it wasn't looking at him. It was looking at Fin.

Chapter 21

Yotan was a grim place.

When they'd arrived in the afternoon Aldrid and Herleif had been the only two conscious members of the Pack, Rat having passed out only moments before the settlement came into view.

It was lighter here than in the Lowland forest. Trees had begun to give way to choppy grassland dotted with boulders, and birds had returned to the landscape, brightening it with their song. Between the boulders, and short, windblown trees, tents and ovook sat on the outskirts of the place, silently watching the land. Past the ovook, Yotan was made up of tall, narrow, wooden houses, that hung over muddy streets. The eerie forest was long behind them, but an ill feeling still hung in the air.

Locals stared with tired, hungry eyes, and Herleif had been worried at first, having so many of his companion's in such a helpless state. But no one bothered them, and as they pushed further into the settlement, he saw more familiar sights. Human traders were peddling wares, their dull voices thugging through the air as they absently pointed at various clothes, foods and tools. He'd spotted filthy Akalen children, sprinting through the gloomy streets with wide smiles and loud laughs, whilst barkeeps smoked deathweed outside their taverns, waiting for the profits that would accompany the night.

The more Herleif looked, the more he had noticed the bustle the place had about it. It was nothing like the village where he and Fin had grown up, but somehow it still reminded him of that place. The sooner they were gone, the better.

"The locals might not yet have a part in the conflict up north, but they will sympathise with Teoma's ranks," Aldrid had whispered as they'd trotted down a narrow alley, drawing the eyes of more than a few stoic locals. "Best not to mention that you're with Gulbrand eh?"

Herleif had nodded, he had no intention of speaking with anyone, other than a healer needed for his friends.

Guides, not friends.

He had to keep reminding himself; they just wanted his money.

He'd helped carry Kiakra and Cypher in, but Rat had woken up long enough to stumble into the establishment himself, before promptly passing out again. The wound in his shoulder had begun to smell, even though it was less than half a day old. That muddy slick they'd been submerged in hadn't done the wound any good.

Inside it had been dark, the rooms had low ceilings, with candles that cast inky shadows about the place. Pungent smells came from burning sticks, which mixed the shadows with smoke and burned the eyes.

The healer there was a shorter Akalen woman, broad, with dark red fur and a heavy face. Despite her being an Akalen, she seemed trustworthy enough, though she had a weariness about her and kept glancing at Herleif. Two younger looking Akalen girls accompanied her, tall and proud despite their age. They looked unsurprised when presented with the corpse-like bodies, and merely waited for instruction from their mistress while she examined each of them carefully.

Kiakra was taken first, as her wounds were the most severe and there was no heat to her body. Cypher was better, but not by much, and Rat was able to hold a conversation if you slapped him hard enough.

Aldrid decided to stay with the others whilst they were being seen to, but Herleif wandered outside under the pretence of keeping an eye on their supplies. He knew that the cost for such a service as this would be high, and if they were set upon by thieves out here then they might well find themselves starving. He'd also been glad to get out of the house, the air smelt too close to death for him and the smoke was starting to make him drowsy.

Now he was sat on a dry patch of ground, with his back against a solid wooden wall, waiting outside the healing house. The yaks, horses and Rat's deer were lying next to him unceremoniously, their heavy packs still strapped to their backs. It was a miracle they fit, for the street was narrow enough to be blocked by two men standing abreast, and it let in such little light that Herleif could barely read the poster that was pinned up opposite him.

Peering forward like an old seer, he managed to read a few words: "Wanted: For desertion of the Pale Wolf"

Below the words were two portraits of Akalen men. The drawings were detailed, capturing not just the physical traits of the men, but some element of who they were. Herleif could imagine them speaking and moving, and he wondered why such a good picture would be pinned up in such a dingy place where so few would see it.

A goat began to nibble at his ear with its lips, and he pushed it away before it had a chance to bite him. The herd was still following them even now, and were crowding the alley he was sat in, irritating the yaks as much as him.

He smiled as one nipped Rat's deer on its tail, and was gifted a swift kick to the side that sent it bleating over to its companions.

Leaning his head back against the wooden wall he looked up at the overhanging eaves, and the sky beyond. His brother would be out in that world, far away and alone. And the only people who would help Herleif find him were lying in pools of their own blood, battling with death.

Too tired for self-loathing he closed his eyes, and sleep took him.

***

Herleif woke to the sound of someone moving beside him. Immediately he knew it wasn't one of the animals, though they were still with him. He could smell them, and hear their breathing.

The noise next to him was the sound of someone moving as though they didn't want to be heard, little slow, shuffling noises, broken by long silences.

Herleif had ended up lying down during his nap, and now he rolled over, feigning sleep.

The shuffling stopped.

After a long pause whoever it was began to move again. Herleif waited a moment longer and then peered through the slit of his eyelids.

A few feet away was a lanky Akalen boy stroking the nose of a yak, he was handling it well and the animal seemed at ease around him. His fur looked mostly clean, though it was hard to tell, being a shade of light brown that wasn't dissimilar to dirt. Narrow arms linked to skinny shoulders which had yet to grow out, and his face was thin and nervous.

Herleif watched him. The boy looked to be a couple of years younger than himself, certainly not a man, but not a child either. His movements were almost smooth, but he had that clumsiness that accompanied early youth, as if he didn't quite trust his body to do what he told it.

The boy moved his hand into one of the pouches of a supply bag that was strapped to the side of Aldrids yak. When he brought his hand out Herleif saw what he'd taken. It was money, the money reserved for paying the healers.

A thief.

Jumping to his feet Herleif knew his sword was too far away to threaten with, so he palmed the knife strapped to his belt. The Akalen boy jumped with him, dropping the money bag and smiling in terror.

"S-sorry sir you scared me," he mumbled, backing away slowly.

It was then that Herleif noticed the other bags slung through the boy's belt.

How much had he stolen?

"What are in those bags?" Herleif growled. Thieves wouldn't usually get a warm welcome from him, but the boy had taken money reserved for the welfare of his friends, and that added another level to his anger. There was also a fair amount of guilt at play, he'd caused Tiko to leave the Pack, and been responsible for their wounds. He couldn't let them get robbed as well.

"Just herbs I've picked," the boy said quickly. The he frowned and looked over Herleifs shoulder, "Is that your friend?"

He followed the boys gaze, and, just as he realised no one was behind him, he heard the boy bolt. Herleif spun back around and darted after him, kicking himself for his stupidity.

Vaulting over a goat and pushing another one aside, he pursued the boy down the narrow alley like a fox down a rabbit hole. The boy was nimble, and faster through the winding jumbled streets that made up Yotan. He swerved left before he got to the main road, disappearing down another street that was narrow enough to be blocked by a single man.

Herleif tried to follow, turning, but he slid on the mud and crashed into the wall. Swearing, he pushed off it hard, continuing his chase.

The ground was as slippery as ice down here, and so dark it was almost a tunnel, the only sky blocked by hanging clothes and buckets of filth.

Herleif was glad he couldn't see what he was running through.

Here the boy made ground, his arms and legs swinging more freely than Herleif's own limbs, so that by the time Herleif got to the end of the street and it opened out into a wider road, he'd almost lost him.

Abruptly he heard a grumble and spotted the boy again. He'd just knocked a man struggling with two pails of water, and was ducking through a crowd, not looking back.

Herleif resumed his chase, relieved, but no less irritated.

Sprinting full out his only obstacles were people, and he pushed past them easily. He made up ground, getting almost close enough to grab the boy's shoulder, but at the last moment the Akalen swerved right down another alley. It only took Herleif a moment to right himself but that was enough for the boy to regain some distance, slipping in and out of vendors and food stands, whose owners recoiled at his sight as though he were a rabid dog.

Herleif followed, losing ground again but keeping his eye on the boy. He could see him tiring now as he rounded a corner and tried to disappear down another alley.

It was a poor choice. The street was clear, and wide enough for Herleif to open up, with no people to get in his way. Mud sprayed up from his boots, soaking his leggings and misting on his cheeks as he ran the boy down, gritting his teeth with rage.

The boy tried to jink and double back, but he slipped, and Herleif caught him with one meaty arm and tackled him into the thick mud.

Once on the floor the Akalen boy struggled wildly, kicking and swearing, but Herleif flipped him onto his back and pinned him with a knee.

"Let me go!" the boy hissed through gritted teeth, but Herleif ignored him.

"You realise how much trouble we'd be in if you took that!" he shouted, pulling the pouches of money the boy had tied to his belt. He'd taken almost all the bags Herleif knew of.

Though the boy was younger than him, Herleif could see in his angered face the same fire that had been in Tiko. He could see the same cold lack of empathy in those who'd taken Fin. And the same fury that was present in the men who'd attacked the Pack in the forest. Those eyes were full of hatred, burning and icy, all at once.

The boy spat in Herleif's face, and he recoiled, wiping his eyes with his sleeve. When he looked back down there was a knife in the boy's hand.

It was his own knife, the boy had drawn it from his belt.

Herleif pinned the boy's arm before he could thrust with it, grazing his wrist on the back edge of the cold steel.

"Get off me!" the boy screamed as Herleif tried to prize the weapon away.

The boy managed to twist the blade into Herleif's wrist, cutting him. In response, he dropped a fist into the Akalen's face. Immediately the knife came away in his hand. The boy's head lolled, momentarily stunned.

Herlief hit him again.

You took Fin.

Another strike, opening a deep cut on his brow.

You injured my friends.

His breathing was quick now, and he raised his fist for another blow.

"Let him go," came a small voice off to the side.

Herleif turned. On his right was another alley, one that he hadn't noticed until now. It was so narrow he himself would have to turn sideways to walk down it. In the entrance was a tiny Akalen boy, one that couldn't have seen more than five or six winters. His pudgy hands were wrapped around a stick that he held out like it was a sword, and even though he was bound up in rags, trembling, his face was full of defiance.

"Shiah, get out of here," said the boy under Herleif's knee, suddenly changing his tone to one of calm. He'd tried to keep his voice firm, but it trembled just a little, and that was enough for the child to ignore him.

"No, I'm helping you," snapped the smaller one. He coughed and then staggered his stance clumsily. "Let him go," he said quietly, almost shying away from Herleif, afraid of the consequence of his bravery.

"Shiah, mother wouldn't want you here, now get away from him. He'll hurt you," the older boy said reasonably, but his voice cracked with desperation. He had gone utterly still under Herleif's knee.

Herleif looked down at the thief, and then back at the child.

Brothers.

The bright eyes of the little Akalen boy stared into Herleif's own, full of fear. He was terrified, and yet he did not move.

"No," the little one said again, breathing heavily. He was trying not to cry.

"Just go!" his brother screamed from under Herleif's knee as tears flooded from his face. The little one flinched at the words, but stayed put.

All of this Herleif experienced from somewhere far off, as though he were watching himself, puppeteering his own limbs. His fist was still raised, but as he looked down now he saw only himself, crying and terrified, all the fight gone from him. He couldn't feel the cold mud, nor the still, damp air, nor the fast breathing of the Akalen beneath him. There was nothing but the world shaking him back to his senses.

Abruptly he stood, eyes avoiding the boy's gaze. The one in the mud didn't move, and the smaller one had screwed his eyes shut in anticipation of a beating.

They are at your mercy he realised.

There was a long pause, silent and weighty.

"Next time don't get caught," Herleif mumbled finally, having no other words.

Covered in filth, the thief scrambled up and grabbed his brother. The Akalen gave him a narrow look, and then faster than wind, they fled.

The pouches of money were left at Herleif's feet.

He shook, and tears fell unbidden from his eyes. He stooped to pick up one of the pouches, but found that he could not rise, and crouched in the mud sobbing.

So much anger was inside him, and for what? It had always been his motivator, the force that kept his brother safe, that scared the evils away. He'd fought fire with fire for so long that he hadn't noticed he burned everything he touched. Nothing but sorrow had ever come from his rage, he realised that now. Before he had told himself that he had fought only to defend his brother, but now the truth was laid bare. Hatred and pain, bitterness and fear. Those were his motivators, nothing noble.

For a long while he crouched, his head roaring with self-loathing. All the bad he'd experienced was his own doing, and that realisation threatened to tear him apart. But something deep within held him together. To break now would cost him not only the safety of his brother, but the redemption that might come with saving him.

They are my mistakes, it is my responsibility to fix them. Anything else is selfishness.

Slowly he stood, and that action alone took more effort than chasing a hundred thieves. He tied the pouches to his own belt and limped through the streets, following his route back to the alley at the healing house. His rage was gone, and for the first time in a long while, he felt clear eyed, ready to take on the world. But the great weight that had been lifted from him seemed also to have taken his strength. Tears washed the mud from his cheeks.

When he finally arrived back at the house, he checked the supplies and found that, luckily, nothing else had been stolen.

Standing outside looking worried was Alvard, and he seemed even less happy when he saw Herleif.

"What's happened?" Herleif asked.

Alvard shook his head, asking no questions as to where he had been, "Come on in lad."

Herleif suddenly felt himself go weak again. If one of the Pack hadn't made it...

Don't think about that.

He stepped inside, and was relieved to see Rat, who was stoic faced. There was no sign of Kiakra and Cypher.

Please let them be okay.

Rat didn't meet his eye, but dipped his head to the side, "In there," he muttered, gesturing to a small curtained room, from which smoke drifted ominously.

Cautiously Herleif pushed the curtains aside.

The room was gloomy, lit by a single candle in a corner. Something hissed, and he spotted a caged Pixie Drakin hanging from the ceiling as it snorted tiny puffs of flame and smoke.

A figure moved in the gloom, just out of the candles light, and a floorboard creaked under Herleif's foot.

Cyphers voice cried out, "Herleif don't!" but it sounded like she was in another room.

"Hello?" he tried, loudly.

As soon as the word escaped his lips something jabbed him in the chest and suddenly Kiakra's face was inches from his own. He flinched, but

247

there was a sharp pain when he moved. He felt his legs immediately begin to buckle. Kiakra held him up, she was stronger than she looked, for he was dead weight in her arms.

Something wet trickled down his stomach and soaked into the material of his shirt and leggings. There was a knife poking out from between his ribs, just above his right nipple.

"Rat, some help," Kiakra shouted over Herleif's shoulder, there was a tinge of frustration to her words, "I've gone a little high, closer to his heart than I meant to."

The room was dark enough that he couldn't tell if his vision was blurring, but he felt strong hands pull his arms back, not that he had any strength in his arms. Rough rope was pulled tight against his numb wrists and then another person was holding him up.

"Oh, what a bloody mess," he heard Rat mutter from behind him.

"What, what's happening..." Herleif tried, his words were barely audible in the quiet struggle, his voice was nearly gone, and he realised, with a strange absence of panic, that he couldn't really breathe. But Kiakra heard him, or else felt he deserved some explanation.

"I'm sorry, but... you've cost us too much already," she said, her voice hard, avoiding his eyes. "This way at least we won't be at a loss. Are his hands bound?"

"Yes," came Rat's voice from behind him.

"Good, then get the healer in here quickly. The client wants him alive, but there's no need to overdo it," Kiakra said, holding Herleif like some precious creature she didn't want to hurt. "Damn, I've cut him deeper than I meant to."

"If he dies now..." Rat said, leaving a threat unspoken.

"He won't!" Kiakra snapped. She sounded almost worried, but it was hard to tell, her voice was very quiet now. Very far away.

Instead, Tiko's words came to him in the dark, mocking him.

None here are your friends.

It was the last thing he heard before he slipped into the black.

Chapter 22

For all the days they had been travelling he had thought. He had wondered. He had sat quiet at the fires, and only spoken softly when his words were needed, the other men avoiding him and his strange silence.

Brynjar had been around the point a hundred different ways, and he didn't like the conclusion he'd come to.

The Akalen's swore they hadn't crossed the border.

Egil, the man he'd thought might have been responsible for the raids, had been alongside him during the last attack. Initially he had assumed that the Akalen he had spoken to was lying, and that would have been the simple answer, but then Fin had arrived and muddied everything up with his reports that the raiders were human.

Then slowly, a third possibility had entered his mind, one that at first he had tried to ignore. He'd succeeded for a while, but the more he tried not to think about it the more it had played on his mind.

There was another man it could be, one who had spoken out against their current mission, which was to track down the raiders. He had seemed the most sceptical and least willing to believe it could be anything other than the doing of the Pale Wolf, and perhaps he had reason to make them believe that.

What if it had been his father, Alvard? That man who had left an entire army waiting on the border of Yilland.

But what if not all his men had waited, what if some had been allowed to roam under his command?

The thought forced its way into his mind, pushed everything else out, until, finally he had put pen to paper and sent Ojak, reluctantly, back to the camp. His instructions were to keep the letter to himself, that was unless Brynjar didn't return, if that happened then Ojak would give the message to Lord Gulbrand. Nearly many of their number were made up of soldiers from his father's army, soldiers his father had insisted they bring. Brynjar doubted they would try to kill him even if they were working with the enemy, but if he was taken prisoner then he would not be around to warn Gulbrand of the betrayal.

He couldn't pretend to know his father's motives, Alvard had never particularly liked Gulbrand, always mentioning that the borders were protected by the commander of grass, but to kill his people...

No part of him wanted to believe it, but he would not let his personal feelings get in the way of his duty to the Kingdom.

"Lord Brynjar!" came a cry from up ahead. It was Egil, waving at him to come forward.

Slipping past the veterans of Gulbrand's elite, he made his way to the front of the column. He felt somewhat inadequate leading such experienced fighting men as these, their faces were weathered and scarred from past campaigns, many had been involved in the last war against the Akalens. Proud green surcoats covered their worn mail, and they held themselves tall atop their mounts, eyes quick and alert, still ready at any moment for a fight.

When he reached the front, he saw Egil speaking with a red faced scout. They both stopped when they saw Brynjar and dipped their heads respectfully.

"The lad says he's seen a column of men moving through the trees on the other side of the village," Egil said, his expression one of concern.

"Human?" Brynjar hung on Egil's reply.

The Captain nodded slowly, "Apparently my Lord."

Egil had not believed men to be the culprits of such evil acts, and Brynjar could see the confliction on his face, a doubt beneath the surface.

"These are evil times Captain," he muttered to Egil in an attempt at sympathy. Then he turned to the scout, "How many did you see boy?"

The scout was a young man with open eyes and a small mouth, and he glanced at Egil nervously before replying, obviously not accustomed to addressing Lords of the Kingdom.

"M-my Lord, I reckoned around sixty or so, m-maybe more, it's hard to tell through the trees you see, and they're h-headed this way it seems," he stumbled over his words and finished speaking very abruptly.

Brynjar nodded, ignoring the boy's nerves, "That's a lot less than us," he muttered, looking ahead.

Egil thanked the scout and told him to keep an eye on the enemy. The boy nodded quickly and kicked his horse back off the road and into the trees around them.

"This could be an opportunity to end this here, today," Egil said, staring at where the scout had been.

"Why are they still so close to their last raid though? Surely they'd want to have moved on by now?" Brynjar said puzzled. There was no reason he could think of for sticking around by an abandoned village, unless they were waiting for further orders...

He glanced behind him at the men his father had contributed to their force. Every one of them was big, and most were younger than Gulbrand's elite. Fighting men in their prime. Alone, they would not be enough to defeat all of Egil's men, and especially not while they were backed by Gulbrands elite, but with the help of that many raiders there might be a chance.

"Probably celebrating, enjoying the spoils of terror," Egil snorted derisively, and then abruptly he turned to face Brynjar, "I don't want to let them get away with this, not if they're so close."

Brynjar could see the desperation the Captain was trying so hard to hide, he was trying to stay calm but there was a rage burning in the brilliant green eyes. He had been hunting them for a long time.

Brynjar nodded, whirling his horse around, "I agree, we move up closer to their position and lay an ambush."

"Yes, my Lord," Egil said, a tentative smile spreading across his face.

Brynjar turned away and rode back down the great column of men, searching for an individual. As he looked, he picked out a member of Gulbrand's elite and asked the man to join him.

He found the boy Fin near the back of the column, riding quietly and rubbing his horse's neck. There was a tired look on his face, but when he saw Brynjar it vanished.

"My Lord," he said grinning.

Brynjar rode up alongside the boy and gestured to the man behind him.

"This man is here to guard you when the fighting begins," he said.

He saw Fin's eyes flick from them to him and then he stood up in his stirrups and looked ahead over the column of soldiers.

"Have we found the raiders?" he said, his eyes bright.

Brynjar nodded, "But you will not join the conflict, you are my eyes and ears. If anything goes wrong I need you to report back to my father and Lord Gulbrand."

Two messengers will be better than one if anything goes wrong, he thought.

For a moment the boy looked exasperated, then he seemed to remember who he was addressing. He lowered his eyes and spoke quietly, "My Lord I'm sure I could be of some use in the battle if-"

"No," Brynjar cut in. Then he smiled, "I know you want to help, but the battlefield is not a place for you, you are far more useful in other ways."

"But my Lord," Fin said his breath catching in his throat. "These men caused all this… If they hadn't..." Fin paused, looking straight ahead as if he could see the enemy. "If they hadn't done this then perhaps Herleif would still be here."

Brynjar winced. He understood the boy's motivations.

"I promise you," he said reaching across and grabbing Fin's shoulder. "I will avenge your brother, and all the others they have taken. But I need you safe."

Something flicked across the boy's face for a moment, anger, defiance, he wasn't sure. And then it was gone, replaced with resignation.

"Yes, my Lord," he muttered.

Brynjar let go of the boy's shoulder and turned to the tall, heavy man who was next to him, "Defend this one, at any cost."

"Yes m'Lord," he grunted. He looked lethal, and as Brynjar rode away he decided he was far less concerned about Fin's safety than his own.

After that he rode up front with Egil, and a little while later, when the sun was nearing the end of its climb into the sky, they reached the village.

Brynjar held up his hand at the treeline, signalling the column to stop.

They had approached from the north, and until now the path had been flanked on both sides by patchy, open forest. Here it opened out into a large flat plain of short yellow grass. The road led toward a cluster of cottages and shacks that were arranged seemingly randomly, with dirt tracks connecting them together and low coppiced hedgerows dividing the small gardens visible even at this distance. Past the homes was another stretch of plain that ended at a thick treeline about a mile away. To the west there was forest, and to the east the plain stretched on into the horizon.

It would have looked beautiful, golden grass and clear blue skies, the apple trees that Brynjar could make out from here, their branches already thick with blossom. But the beauty was spoiled by blackened rock, the skeletons of homes, and the lack of movement the place had about it. It seemed frozen.

Brynjar waited for a moment, on the treeline, at the edge of the large plain on which the village sat, listening to the birds sing in the forest around him.

"My Lord, I suggest we get out of view," Egil said gently. The rest of the soldiers had gone quiet.

"I agree, we'll set ourselves up here, just off the path where the trees are a little thicker," Brynjar said, leading his horse to his right, west of the path and up into the forest. The soldiers followed him, purple and green riders eerily picking their way through the trees as the birds now changed their calls to ones of warning.

They set up only a hundred or so feet from the path, facing the village so Brynjar could see the enemy approaching. If the enemy were indeed heading north, they would move down the main road, and there Brynjar would have his ambush.

They will come like sheep, and we will strike like lions from the grass.

His own men were positioned in a loose formation, so they could still find cover, with the purple clad soldiers of Ruklund in front of Yilland's elite. He reasoned that, were Rukland to turn against them, then it would be better to have them in front, that way at least he and Egil wouldn't be surrounded. He hoped that his worries were misplaced, but he would take no chances.

Brynjar wasn't worried about being seen, the sun was bright enough that anything in the shade was difficult to make out, and the contrast in light from the trees gave them a multitude of shadows in which to hide.

Once the men were settled into position, they waited.

It seemed like an age, listening to the coming and going of the now single scout, as he reported on the movements of the enemy, who still seemed to be heading back to the village. The air was hot and dry, and soon Brynjar was soaked in sweat under the weight of his mail, any loose stands of hair from his braid now plastered to his brow.

Tension hung in the air like mist. He could feel the nerves of the men around him, and he wondered if they could feel his. Even the horses were silent.

After a while his legs and back began to ache from sitting, but he didn't move, he kept still, listening to the birds, which had grown accustomed to his men and so started up their songs. There was contradiction in their chorus, and in the land. Such a beautiful place for such terrible acts.

It reminded him of the calm before his previous storms.

Maybe this will be the last one for a while, he hoped, glancing behind him and searching the forest for Fin, who had been with him in his very first. The boy was behind the Yilland elite, barely visible under the low shade of a bushy yew. On one side of him was the beast of a man Brynjar had charged with protecting the boy, sitting tall in his saddle, red faced from the heat, but no less alert. Fin was not his worry this time.

Brynjar turned his gaze back toward the village and in his mind spoke a short prayer to the spirits around him.

Let me end this.

The silent trees were unreadable, utterly quiet under the calm, midday sun. Only the birds spoke, and their worries were not the same as his. Their songs were beautiful, but useless.

And then finally, it happened.

Brynjar spotted movement on the other side of the plain, at the treeline. Immediately he was upright, his eyes wide.

Like a rotting snake their line slithered from the forest, heading out from the trees and toward the village. Some were mounted, some were on foot, but they moved as one. It was a long time before Brynjar could make out more details, but it was clear as soon as he saw them, that they were warriors. It was also clear, they were indeed, human.

Brynjar glanced at Egil. The Captain was sat on his horse next to a small boulder, nervously squeezing his reins as he watched the men moving forward. He noticed Brynjar's gaze, and glanced over at him, shaking his head.

Now he had to believe.

The Captain cocked his head at Brynjar and moved back behind the purple lines of Ruklund so he was at the head of his own force. Brynjar got the message, two leaders were better than one, and when the fighting began, they'd need all the help they could get.

Either the nerves of the scout had got the better of him or the raiders had been well hidden in the forest, because there were far more than sixty warriors. There were near on double that number, and they were well armed. Brynjar could make out the tops of spears, and he could see weapons of varying kinds on the hips of the men as they paced easily along the road. He'd expected them to slink across the land like disloyal dogs, ashamed and paranoid, but instead they moved with an easy confidence, almost swaggering. They wore no coats of arms, flew no banners, and their pale skin was bright against their dark clothes, marking them out as men of the Kingdom. Brynjar would indeed be fighting his own. If they were his father's men as he suspected, they might even be his countrymen. He glanced to the Rukland men at his sides, and though they gave him no cause, and watched the enemy with the same distaste, his suspicion was renewed.

Around him the air grew tight. He heard murmurs and whispers from his men, barely audible above the birdsong, but there nonetheless.

The raiders slipped into the village, and just as easily passed through, not slowing for a moment as they headed along the road toward his position.

A drakinhawk screamed overhead and abruptly the birds fell silent as they too waited, trying to remain unseen. Unlike the birds however, Brynjar was the hunter, and he was ready to spring the trap.

He could make out clearer shapes now, and the colour of the men's cheeks as they drew ever closer. Sweat stung his eyes and dripped from his brow off the tip of his nose. His throat was dry and parched but he dared not move to drink.

Closer they came, and now he could hear them talking with one another, joking and singing. His hand slid over the pommel of his sword, grasping the hilt tightly. Now he was barely breathing, and the quiet of the forest was heavy on his shoulders. Around him his men were poised, ready for battle, ready to spring their trap. He could *feel* them, more than hear them, an unshakable presence, ready to deliver justice.

Brynjar could make out faces now, they were only a few hundred feet away, not quite at the treeline yet. He stared at a single raider, a man with long black hair, a hooked nose and dark eyes. The man was riding a large brown destrier and wore a dark quilted gambeson, which, in this heat, must have been boiling him from the inside out. His hand rested easy on the pommel of his sword as he rode, and though Brynjar had no idea who the man was, he tried to get some measure of him.

Slowly, the man's head swung round, and met Brynjar's eyes through the trees. The young Lord stayed stock still, unable to move under the man's gaze, heart hammering in his chest.

Just as he thought his cover was blown, and was readying to move, the man turned away, as though nothing had happened.

What?

How had he not seen him? Brynjar let out a shallow breath.

Thunder rumbled in from the west ominously, the battle was nearing. It was then that he should have noticed it, but he didn't, for his eyes were still glued to the raiders.

Why had that man not alerted his comrades?

It registered far too late. He looked sideways at where the thunder was coming from, it still hadn't stopped. There were no clouds in the sky, and he glanced around puzzled.

Then another thought.

Where is the scout?

He heard it then, finally.

What he'd heard wasn't thunder, but a charge of cavalry.

Horses coming in from the west. Brynjar quickly glanced at the raiders to his east, who were now turning to face the forest and drawing weapons.

They were not the hunters after all.

Brynjar tried to speak but the words would not come. He gripped his sword so hard his knuckles went white, but he couldn't draw it.

How?

One of his men behind him shouted something and still he could not speak.

The thunder was coming, closer now.

Someone grabbed his shoulder, a tall man, with the Rotstag on his breast, pulling the reigns of his horse tight so that its head was against its chest. The man screamed something to Brynjar, but the blood was pounding in his ears, and he heard nothing.

How had they known?

He stared at the soldier. The man's face was red and panicked as he yelled at Brynjar, pointing all around them. Suddenly an arrow burst through the man's throat, cutting off his speech and spraying Brynjar's face with blood. He fell from his horse and writhed on the ground, tearing at the coif around his neck as blood flowed from the wound.

The trees to Brynjar's right exploded, horses tearing through the forest as their dark clad riders bellowed a war cry. An arrow fizzed past the young Lord, and suddenly his voice was back.

He tore his eyes from the dying man and shouted out.

"Charge!" was all he could think of, as he rushed to meet the attackers to the west. He glanced behind him and saw a flash of battle, purple and green and black all tangled together in a viscous melee.

He couldn't work out what was happening, the how or why were beyond him now, but if Egil could hold the line to the east, and his own troops could hold the west, perhaps they would survive.

As he turned back toward the western attack another arrow flew past his shoulder. He drew his sword just as he and his men collided with the attackers, several horses going down in the initial collision.

Brynjar leant back as a raider flew at him, dodging the man's attack as his own swing caught the man in the jaw. Bone turned to pulp under the weight of his blade and the raider crumpled from his horse, hitting the ground like a sack of meat.

Brynjar paid little attention, more were flooding in from the forest, threatening to overwhelm his force. One of his men cut down a raider before his horse was killed under him with an arrow. He fell and hit the dirt, and Brynjar lost sight of him as horses trampled the ground where he had fell.

In front of Brynjar was another raider waving a longsword at him menacingly. He caught the man's eyes and simultaneously they rode at each other, Brynjar catching the man in the ear as he passed, sending him screaming into the dirt holding his head. The raiders sword had hit him in the chest but his mail had held, and he shrugged off the strike easily.

Brynjar turned from his charge to rally his own men, they were outnumbered and had to regroup, for yet more men were swarming in from the trees. In doing so, he finally saw what was happening.

Breath caught in his throat.

Behind him, the dark forms of the raiders were mixed with the green men of Yilland. But instead of fighting, they were shoulder to shoulder, facing the men of Rukland.

Brynjar stopped dead as he saw Egil hack down a soldier clad in purple and silver. The Captain's face was covered with blood, his green eyes wild with the rage and terror of battle.

Traitor.

Bodies of men and horses were strewn across the forest floor like dead leaves, most were men of Rukland. The ones still standing fought like wounded lions, hacking at the crowds of killers around them, surely knowing the end was near.

Brynjar couldn't move. His horse tried to run but he held the reigns tight, keeping it still amongst the slaughter.

An arrow punched into his ribs through his mail, making him gasp and numbing him further. His arm fell uselessly to his side.

Run.

The raiders closed in on him, supported by the green men of Yilland. The elite. His own men were utterly overwhelmed, hopelessly outnumbered, and now the battle was finished, the slaughter had begun. He tried to raise his sword, but the limb ignored him, hanging limp at his side. Though his hand would not release the blade from its grasp.

Run.

He watched one of his men crawling desperately for safety, one of his legs a broken, crooked, mess. A nameless man in a black gambeson stamped on the poor man's back, and ran him through with barely a second glance. The sting of the spear shot through Brynjar's own bones, and he flinched as though he himself had been struck.

His horse snorted and whinnied as a Yilland soldier and several raiders moved toward him with deadly intent. The old grizzled face of the veteran was brightened by fearful, but excited eyes.

Run.

Sweat fell from Brynjar's cheeks. He kicked the side of his horse and fled.

He flew between both forces, running down the few men on foot that tried to block him, hacking at them savagely, sending them spinning into the dirt, whilst desperately searching for any survivors from Rukland.

But there were none.

He made it past the trees and out onto the open fields.

The sun was hot and he was slick with sweat as he rode, breathing so fast his head spun. He'd sent Ojak off with a letter condemning his father, when it was Egil who had betrayed them.

Fin, he remembered. *But I guarded him with my enemy.*

He had to make it back to Gulbrand, had to let him know what had happened.

The village was some way off but his horse was fast. He would make it to the buildings, and then lose any who pursued him in the forest beyond. It would be difficult to track him if he followed the messy trail left by Egil's raiders, and once he had done that he could turn west, loop around north and get back to camp. He, moving alone, would be faster than Egil's men.

Another arrow glanced off his shoulder blade making him wince, and then another hit him in the centre of the back, piercing his surcoat and slipping through the chainmail links to sink itself into flesh and bone.

His horse was fast, the village was close. But not close enough.

Pain tore at his vision and he toppled from the horse, his foot catching in the stirrup as he crashed into the ground. Something cracked in his knee, but the horse continued its flight, dragging him through the dirt as dust choked him. His mount turned sharply, and he rolled onto his front. Pushing his free hand into the dirt he tried to right himself, but he was too weak, and the earth pulled his shoulder back, tearing at the exposed skin of his face.

Eventually the creature came to a stop, and Brynjar, with the last of his strength, pulled his foot from the stirrup with a cry of pain. His body, broken.

His horse *was* fast, and it bolted, leaving its master under the scorching midday sun.

***

Any time she slowed he kicked her harder, willing himself away, the sun burning his neck as he fled.

Fin had no idea who had survived and who had not, he'd only barely managed to slip from the grasp of his protector, the man being too large to chase him.

Now he didn't know who to trust as he flew up the road they had walked down, his horse kicking up plumes of dust behind him. Only this morning they had been together, friends, comrades, joking and laughing.

There had been something in the air before the battle, but he hadn't been able to place it. It was only now he realised that what he had sensed was treachery.

He reached a crossroad, saw a tall dead pine that leant over to one side, held up by the other trees, like a skeleton propped up in a crowd. For a moment he didn't know which way to go and his horse clattered to a halt.

His head was spinning.

Egil had betrayed them.

It was easy to assume he had been behind the raids from the beginning, carrying them out instead of stopping them. It was easy enough to send false reports, and obviously the men Egil led were more loyal to him than they were to their own Lord. He would have led them into battle, fought and bled with them, of course they would respect him more.

Fin suddenly remembered the way and kicked his horse on again, ignoring its heavy breathing and the sweat dripping from its sides. He glanced behind him but there was nothing except trees and dust.

Tearing through the woods he startled a gang of weasel like skiven that were bathing themselves in dust under an ash tree, but he was gone before they had a chance to see him off. Their chatter could be heard in the distance, but he was fast, faster than anyone in Egil's host. He was smaller, had no armour, and his horse was better suited to the long road ahead, for it would take him at least a couple of days to get back to Gulbrand's camp, even riding as fast as this.

Warm wind buffeted his eyes, and he told himself that was why they'd begun to water.

You led them into a trap, he thought, chastising himself for again making mistakes that had cost other people their lives.

He would set this right. Egil would find justice when he returned, or else he would not return, and this time Fin would do his part. Brynjar had made him wait. Hadn't let him help, protecting him like Fin was a child.

And he kept you alive, just the same as Herleif did.

He hoped Brynjar would be alright. He hoped with everything he had left to hope with. The man was a Lord, and surely worth more alive than dead.

All through the hot day he would ride, and when night fell, he would continue on, but for now, the sun continued to burn his neck.

***

The grass crackled under his boots as he walked, the ground hard and dry beneath it. It was unbearably hot, and his throat was dry. He stopped and pulled a waterskin from his belt, upending it, drinking deeply.

He kept it in his hand as he walked over to the body.

He'd followed his quarry from the forest on horseback, all the while watching the heaving frame of the man as he lay in the dirt. He hadn't moved, but there was a steady rise and fall of his back that he could see even from this distance. The fall had looked bad, and left alone he was sure the young Lord would be dead before nightfall, but the man did not take chances like that.

From behind the treeline his men were be piling up the bodies of the Ruklund soldiers and counting their own dead. He knew they had taken casualties, and he knew the men would be in low spirits because of it. In the coming days caution and kindness would be his friend, he could only push them so far before they broke. Despite their loyalty he knew they did not enjoy their work, and that their conscience was often their own worst enemy.

But they too understood the bigger picture.

He himself figured the losses on his own side were a good thing, too suspicious if his own men had taken no casualties, questions would be asked, difficult ones.

The blade must be double edged, that was a necessary evil.

Onward he walked.

He was about twenty feet away when he heard the wheezing. Shallow, laboured breaths that reminded him of a wounded animal, something from a hunt that was not long for the world.

The young Lord was still led on his face, and as the man drew closer he saw the long hair, now tangled and dirty, twisted about his shoulders and neck.

The lion grows old before his prime.

The man walked a full circle around Brynjar, making sure he was no longer a threat. Both his arms were crumpled up under his body, whilst his right leg was twisted at an angle away from his hip. The arrows that had downed him had snapped off into splintered brushes that poked out from his back and ribs.

Satisfied the young Lord would not put up a fight, the man moved in close, and, with a heavy boot, pushed him onto his back. Brynjar groaned as he was twisted into the sun, before coughing blood onto his chin.

His face was a mess, but nothing that the man hadn't seen before. The fall had skinned one side of it, and the dust had dirtied the wound so that now it was a large oozing sore. One of his eyes had closed completely into a black swollen mess, whilst the other roamed around desperately, receiving no help from his body. It looked to be the only part of him left undamaged.

The one eye stared up at him.

"Why?" Brynjar snarled, though it was quiet enough to be a whisper. His teeth showed through a thin sliver of skin on his cheek.

Anger? That would get him nowhere in this state.

His voice sounded like rust.

"Because I had to," said the man as he drew his sword.

It was true, though that did not mean he didn't enjoy it.

Putting such a young man in a position of power above himself, a competent commander, had been a massive insult to his own competence. He had fought in wars, he had known battle, and all his years of experience had been trumped by blood. He would certainly not miss Brynjar, and he would make his legacy one of terror.

"I will not burn your body, nor will I bury you." he said calmly, "Your soul shall wander, and you will become a Demon. Walking blind and deaf and afraid, until someone decides to kill you again. And only then, when you have known torment beyond imagining, and the second touch of death is welcomed, will you finally rest."

Let the child know how beaten he truly is, how utterly he has failed.

The young Lord looked up, and for a moment his one good eye was full of rage.

"I hope..." he began, spitting the words out with that ruined voice.

The man smiled in anticipation. Which curse would he receive this time? He'd have to add it to the list.

But Brynjar paused. His eye glazed over, and he looked directly into the sun.

When he spoke again it was with tenderness.

"You are a lost man, and I hope… I hope you find your way," Brynjar said gently.

The man scowled. Inadequacy flushed through him and he felt like a child, patronised and belittled by a dying fool.

Quickly he raised the blade up, a little higher than necessary, but if any of his men were watching he didn't want to seem hesitant. He searched Brynjars face for fear, for a plea, but there was none.

He brought the sword down, feeling mail and flesh part before his steel, the bone scraping against the blade, hearing the lungs of the young Lord deflate like a pigskin. Brynjar winced for a moment, and then his broken face relaxed into death.

It should have felt good, but somehow, at the last moment the boy had stolen his victory.

He pulled his weapon from Brynjar's corpse and turned away.

Let the flies have him.

Chapter 23

Kiakra picked up another stick and balanced it on the pile she already held under her arm. At the edge of the trees she could look out over the vast steppe and watch the sun begin to set, the light low and red, glowing through the long grass so it appeared as fire over the hills. A gentle breeze made the meadows whisper. She had heard that was what the ocean sounded like, though she had never seen it. There were still many things she had never seen.

"How much you got?" came a call from next to her.

It was Rat, wrapped in a thick reindeer hide like the northern Nomads wore. Kiakra smiled at him, for she was barefoot, wearing only her tunic and leggings.

"I forget how foreign you are sometimes," she mumbled.

Rat nodded dismissively, "It's warmer down south, I'll be glad to get home."

He turned and moved through the open forest of oak and birch, up the hill to where they had decided to camp. Kiakra watched him move away. He hadn't been the same after what they had done to the boy.

Nothing less than what he deserved, she told herself.

She followed the small Kazoec man up the hill, slowly, placing her feet as quietly as she could, like children do when they play at being beasts, not letting a twig snap, nor letting her feet touch heavily on the ground. She was still weak after her recovery, and it felt good to use her muscles again, to feel them building and working.

At the top of the hill was a large grey oak, long dead and split down its centre by lightning. At its roots a spring had bubbled up, and now, down one side of the hill ran water, and with it, life. The bare branches watched over the spring, and over the hills and valleys of the northern steppe, and it was under these silver branches that they had set up their camp.

Kiakra stepped over a sleeping yak, rubbing its side gently as she did so. They were beginning to settle down together outside Cypher's little ovook, having been unpacked and given time to graze and drink from the spring. They lived hard lives, their beasts of burden, but Kiakra couldn't help but wonder sometimes how nice it must be, having no moral code to navigate. Their days were difficult, but simple, and to her that sounded refreshing.

They'd set up in a circle around a firepit as they did most nights, but it was quieter now than usual. Aldrid was sat up against a huge saddlebag, reading a book on the path of the Akvast river by the light of a little lantern. He was silent as she walked by, though she caught him glance away from his book for a moment, staring at the ground. Rat was blowing into some embers by the firepit, and she dropped the gathered wood down next to him, before sitting down.

"How many jobs will you do after this one, you know, before you leave us?" she said, watching him.

He didn't meet her eye, "If he pays us what he promised, none. I'll have enough to head south then and there."

Kiakra felt a tinge of sadness, she knew he was close to buying back in, but she didn't realise how close. She wasn't sure if she was ready to give him up.

"Surely you'll need money to set yourself up? The life of a street urchin in the empire is still the life of a street urchin."

He looked around at her, and she saw the conflict in him then, "I want to get home more than anything else, but it's my life for his," he said, ignoring her question. She knew exactly to who he was referring. He continued, "I'd pay that price a thousand times over, but I know the shame of it, and I will do no more after this." His voice was like iron, and in that moment, she caught a glimpse of what was driving him on. That drive ruled him, but she could see the man that opposed it.

She nodded and stood up, "The boy endangered us all, he's just another criminal with a bounty on his head. Don't let this one action spoil everything you've worked for."

The words were as much for herself as they were for him, and with them, she walked away from the growing flames.

The sun was gone from the land now, but it lingered in the sky, caught on the edges of the clouds. Kiakra grabbed her bearskin cloak and moved down the hill to a young oak. It was not yet twenty feet tall but had an impressive crown of green that darkened everything beneath it. In the gloom under the tree she could make out Herleif, sat awkwardly with his head down, chin resting on his chest, long hair messy on his shoulders. His hands were bound behind his back, and then tied to the tree so he could barely move. Maybe this was as comfortable as he could get.

He would be weak after his treatment, the same as she was, and that was why she had injured him so severely, to pay the price for his healing once he had been bound and tied. It was a costly method, but safer than trying to take him by force when he was conscious, and the amount Dagtok was giving them made the healers fee a nominal loss.

Slowly he began to sense her presence and looked up at her. She avoided his eyes and carried on down the hill to find Cypher.

The girl was sat on a huge, low branch of an old thick tree. Her legs dangled like a toddler's would in an oversized chair. She was facing east, where they were heading, and there the sky was darker, the stars almost visible in the deep blue before the night.

"Rat's just got the fire going," Kiakra said, easily scrambling onto the branch next to Cypher. It wasn't yet cold, but the girl shivered.

Kiakra noticed, "You should come sit in the warm."

She draped her cloak over the girl's shoulder, but Cypher pushed it away and turned to face her, eyes deep, and full of sorrow.

"You had one rule, "I don't break contracts" that's what you used to say, and you broke that rule," Cypher said quietly.

Kiakra furrowed her brow, she had known this conversation was going to happen, but that didn't make her any more keen to have it.

"That rule is there for business, but he put our lives in danger, he put *your* life in danger."

When Kiakra had woken from her wounds and found Cypher cold and corpse like, she had felt helpless, knowing she could do nothing to fix the girl but wait and let the healers try to work their magic. She would not let it happen again. Taking the boy out of the equation would keep Cypher safe.

It would keep them all safe.

Cypher seemed not to care, "You betrayed a friend. I thought that went against everything you are," Cypher's eyes bored into her, questioning Kiakra's being, and judging her more a stranger than a friend. "What stops you making exceptions for anyone else?"

The implication didn't need to be spoken.

Would you do that to me?

Kiakra opened her mouth to speak but no words came out. She tried again, "You know I wouldn't ever do anything to hurt you?" she said quietly, and though she meant it as a statement, it came out as a question. "You're why I made that decision, because I care about you so-"

"I don't worry about me!" Cypher cut in. "I worry about Rat? What if he puts me in danger? What if Aldrid accidentally insults the wrong person, and they offer a reward for his head, would you turn him in? Let him die, for *my* safety?" Cypher was angry now, her eyes red and mistrustful.

Kiakra shook, "Herleif wasn't part of the group, he was a job-"

"We were doing a job *for* him!" cried Cypher.

"But he wasn't family."

"He saved my life?" Cypher yelled, confusion in her face.

"We saved him first," Kiakra growled, trying to put an end to the dispute. "He was repaying a debt, nothing more. And he almost got you killed, those Akalen's wouldn't have attacked us if he hadn't provoked them. That's all without mentioning the money from this job!" Her voice had risen as she spoke, and now she paused, getting her breath back, "When we have enough, then we can wash our hands of this work. We can settle on the shores of the Stem, and we'll be done. For good. That's where I'm trying to get us, don't make it more difficult than it already has been."

Cypher stared at her as if she were a stranger. "That is all you care about isn't it?"

"Yes!" Kiakra snapped. "Being with you, and staying safe. Nothing else matters."

"Well you aren't there yet," Cypher said, very quietly, "And he trusted you."

Kiakra sighed, "I know it's difficult letting him go, but it has to be done, he's a killer."

Cypher shook her head, "You believe the word of a man you met once, over the word of a friend who saved my life?"

"I believe my eyes," Kiakra hissed, turning and facing the girl next to her. "You saw what he did in Stemtrad, he is capable of violence, we know that."

"And you aren't?" Cypher said, quick as a viper. "You've killed before, same as him."

Kiakra didn't reply.

"Do you remember when you first met me?" Cypher said "I was flawed, I put you in danger, and yet you protected me because it was the right thing to do."

Kiakra was angry now, and she ignored the comparison, "You're a child, you don't understand."

There was a long pause.

The two of them sat looking up into the sky until the stars shone brightly over the land. Cypher continued to shiver in the cold night breeze, and Kiakra found that her own cloak would not keep her warm.

"That man, Dagtok?" Cypher said finally, turning to look deep into

Kiakra's eyes. "What do you think he'll do to Herleif?"

Kiakra shook her head, "I don't care, but better he suffers than any of us. He made his own decisions. This is the cost."

"What about Herleif's brother?" Cypher murmured. "Will he have to pay as well?"

Kiakra glanced at her, searching for a rebuttal, but couldn't find one.

"He cares about Fin the same way you care for me," the girl continued, all the while staring into Kiakra's eyes. "And what wouldn't you do for me?"

Kiakra'd had enough, "Sometimes as a leader you have to make difficult decisions for the good of the group. He isn't safe. I won't hear any more about it."

"This time you made the wrong decision," Cypher said after a pause. Despite the words her voice was gentle. "We aren't meant for this work. No one is. No one should have to know the price of their friends. I know it's difficult, and I know you try and do the best for your own, but don't let your care for me blind you to evil, or excuse you from it."

The girl leant over and kissed Kiakra lightly on the forehead, and before Kiakra could speak again Cypher had jumped off the branch and walked away up the hill.

She wanted to follow her, to ask her what she meant, to grab her and wrap her up in a cloak of mail and fur so that she was safe from the world. But she knew she could not, she knew that cloak would be a tomb. So she just sat.

Why can't she understand?

The boy was flawed deeply, he had already driven away Tiko, Kiakra would not lose any more. Cypher was just a girl, a child, she couldn't understand. Hard decisions had to be made, it was just her healers heart getting in the way of reason, if blood magic did not flow through her veins she would understand.

Kiakra thought all this, and told herself this, and yet she knew it was a lie.

Anger welled up inside her.

She stepped down from her branch and marched uphill to the young oak.

Beneath it her prisoner was awake, staring off into the distance. He was barely visible now in the dark.

She hated him, and yet she pitied him too. His kin had been taken from him, and the anger from that had driven him to stupidity and rage. If she were in his situation, and Cypher was at risk, would she really act that differently?

His pained eyes turned and met her own.

But he was the risk to Cypher. His own deeds had validated Kiakra's actions, for in her situation he would have killed anyone between him and his brother.

She couldn't bear to look at him.

"You did this to yourself!" she screamed at him. "I'm just looking out for my own!"

She was breathing so fast the words came out shaky and weak, and that made her even more angry. She kicked a stone at him as hard as she could. It hit him in the shoulder, and he winced painfully.

Get angry, show me why I've done this. She begged in her head.

"I'm protecting my family the same as you are yours!" she shouted. Tears threatened her eyes, but she was stronger than that.

"And I'm better at protecting my own than you are, look where you're sat," she said gesturing at the ground under the tree, mocking him. "This is all on you."

She wanted him to strain against his bonds, to yell back and threaten her. She wanted to see that anger there again, to be reminded of the fire she had been forced to put out.

She needed an excuse to let him die.

Herleif spoke no words though. He lowered his head and stared at the ground, utterly defeated.

Kiakra's body relaxed in confusion, and she stumbled back to the fire, leaving her prisoner in the dark.

***

Sleep had not come to him.

Kiakra had been right. His woes were the fault of no one but himself, and though the ropes about his wrists were foreign, he could blame no one else for their presence.

The cold breeze from earlier had yet to die, and it routinely drew the heat from his body. Grass murmured at him from time to time, and the expanse of the sky hung heavy over his head. Though he stayed hidden under his tree, he felt exposed, it was as if the bad within him had moved on and left very little behind.

"It's a beautiful night don't you think?" came Cyphers voice from close by.

He opened his eyes and blinked at her. The girl was crouched in front of him, close enough to touch, her eyes glinting brightly even in the faintest light from the stars.

He said nothing.

"I'm here to apologise," she said clearly.

Herleif had to swallow before he spoke, his mouth was very dry, and he was very tired, "You tried to warn me, I heard your call in the healing house. There is nothing to apologise for."

She smiled then, a sad smile, "I am leaving."

He noticed then that she was dressed for the weather, her hair tied up neatly, her face showing no signs of fatigue.

"Why?" he said, sitting up a little straighter.

She twisted away from him, so she was resting on one knee, looking out from under the branches of his den. "Because it's the only thing Kiakra will listen to. I love her, but she has gotten lost in her work."

Herleif could see her eyes, and he knew she did not question herself.

"Are you taking me with you?" he said. It wasn't a plea, he was just curious.

She shook her head, "I'm not."

He nodded, unfazed and unsurprised. There was almost a sense of relief.

"Then why have you come?"

She smiled at him again, "To let you know that I am not abandoning you. You will be okay, Ki will come to her senses, but not with me around."

He nodded, and smiled back at her, "You better go before you're missed then."

Quickly she twisted toward him, pulling him into a hug. It was an awkward movement and his arms were tied behind him, so he could not hug back, but she was warm and smelt of earth and woodsmoke. He only realised how cold he had been when she let him go.

And then she was gone, leaving him to the night.

***

He waited in the grass, watching the soldiers move by him, close enough to hear their tired breath. Fin should have known them as friends, but he wasn't sure how many were loyal to Egil, and did not want to test his luck.

Once they were past him, he scrambled up off his belly and into a crouch, keeping low so his frame would not show up against the night sky. It was late, and ahead of him the Great Oak spilled out into the above, its branches mingling with the stars. Off to his side he could make out fires in the main camp and hear the songs of lonely men as they waited for their watches to end.

How many were traitors though? Fin had spent time with the men, and most of them were honest and simple, defensive of their fellow countrymen. Their enemy was Teoma, not the people on their own soil, Egil couldn't have turned that many. Could he?

He moved like a shadow, creeping ever closer to Gulbrands pavilion. Several other sentries moved past him, but they weren't expecting anything and were easily avoided. Once he was under the tree it became much darker. Here the ground and canopy seemed to eat up sound, creating a damp silence which was close and ready. He found himself checking behind him every few steps, his breathing becoming more and more shallow.

The pavilion glowed a dull white in the darkness, and in front of it Fin could make out two silhouettes, undoubtedly Gulbrand's guard. He knew that were he to approach from the front they would stop him, and no matter how good his excuses he would not get an audience with the Lord. So he instead moved to the back of the pavilion where the material was almost pressed up against one of the huge roots of the Oak.

Then he ducked under the heavy canvas.

Inside was brighter, several candles were lit, sending soft shadows creeping across the interior. Gulbrand was sat at the head of a large table, shuffling through papers and maps, with quill in hand. He was dressed plainly, and looked tired.

Only when Fin stood did he look over.

His face was unreadable.

"My Lord," Fin said, bowing, "I am sorry to sneak into your quarters like this."

Gulbrand smiled then, and looked back down at his work, "Well I'm hoping there's a good reason for it?"

"I couldn't be seen by the other men," Fin said, relaxing a little at the big man's smile.

"And why would that be?" Gulbrand said, pushing himself back in his chair and looking over at Fin through thick eyebrows. His arms were bare, and several long scars were visible, the smooth skin catching the light from the candles.

"You have been betrayed," Fin said, trying to keep his composure.

The big man furrowed his brow, "Go on."

Fin did his best to explain the exact events as they had happened. Sighting the enemy, then that long wait in the trees followed by the ambush, the battle, and then his own flight as his bodyguard had attacked him. He had to stop now and again, but Gulbrand was patient, and did not interrupt him.

When he was done Gulbrand leant forward and put his head in his hands.

"Brynjar is dead then, along with the men from Rukland?" he mumbled.

"Yes, my Lord," Fin mumbled. "Egil betrayed you, and I don't know how many men stand with him."

Gulbrand shook his head, "No, Egil has done what I asked of him, but that does little to numb the wound."

Fin's breath caught in his throat. He hadn't heard him properly.

"My Lord?"

The big man stood up and poured himself some wine from a bottle that had been sat on the table. It had already been opened, for the cork popped off easily, and it smelled as though it had soured a little.

Gulbrand took a long drink, and when he was done he turned back to Fin, "Egil is not to blame for those deaths, that is on me." His eyes were red as he stroked his beard, a habit of men trying to hide their faces from shame.

"He is a tool, my hunting dog. He does the things I ask of him," it was then that his eyes dropped, staring into nothing, "The things I cannot bear to do myself, but which need to be done."

Fin paused. This wasn't right.

"But, why would you? There's no reason to? Brynjar was helping you." His words were little more than a whisper, as gentle as the waves of light that flickered from the candles.

"He was, I know, but he was suspicious of Egil, and the men. When you showed up and told everyone about the raiders being human, I knew he was lost. He'd follow that thread and unravel everything I've tried to do, and then all that death would have been for nothing."

Fin felt his arms go weak, the blood draining from them.

"The Akalen's were never attacking the villages. You were," he said, hoping he was wrong.

Gulbrand nodded slowly, "Egil destroyed them, but yes, I gave the orders."

There was a long silence.

Fin couldn't process what he was hearing. There were a thousand questions on the tip of his tongue, but he couldn't rid himself of a single one.

Then the big man spoke, "The Akalens brought war to your home, and do you know who pushed them back into their own lands?"

Fin shook his head, his mind too crowded to think clearly.

"The Kingdom did. I did. And our mistake was not driving them back until they reached the eastern mountains and every single one was destroyed."

He looked at Fin, catching his eye and not letting it go, "You come from the north, the Outskirts?"

Fin nodded.

"And what is up there?" the big man continued. "A handful of people from Jern, eking out an existence in a Demon infested forest. Not a single clan of the Nomads remains. They destroyed your land, and if we hadn't of stopped them, they would have done the same to Yilland. And then Rukland, and Heimland until there was nothing left but ruin. The Kingdom of Jern is expanding, and though we aren't on Akalen lands, they fear that."

Anger welled up from inside Fin, lending him confidence.

"But *you're* the one killing your people, not them," he spat, his hands shaking. The words stung Gulbrand, Fin could see it on his face. He guessed, from that reaction, that very sentiment had kept the big man awake more than one night.

The Lord of Yilland broke eye contact, and looked at the ground, "I have no great armies, my country is still young, and weak because of it. We barely have as many people as Brunland, and that place is little more than a wasteland. The power lies with King Olvaldr, and with Lord Alvard."

Fin watched as Gulbrand's hands curled into fists, and his jaw tightened, "I asked them again and again to take their armies onto the steppe and destroy the enemy before they regained their strength, but neither would listen. They said the Akalens were no longer a threat," he turned then to Fin, a desperate look in his eye, "But they are a threat. The Pale Wolf will unite them, and in a decade or so, when their children are grown, they will be strong enough to attack us again, and this time they will know us. They will destroy this country."

"How does killing your people, and Alvard's son, help you gain his support?" Fin whispered. His voice trembled with every word, but he needed to know.

Gulbrand sat back down in his chair, taking the wine with him and pouring himself another cup.

"To make them listen, to make them understand how serious this threat is." He sighed and leant back. Fin was listening to this man's confession, and Gulbrand was eager to give it, to be rid of these terrible secrets.

"The Pale Wolf set herself up across the border at the beginning of winter." He continued, "While she was there I would allow Egil to destroy a village close to the river, there would be no survivors, and we would blame it on her. It would be an act of war, and Olvaldr and Alvard would muster their armies to wipe her out."

His mouth twisted awkwardly, and a tear made its way down his cheek. He looked nightmarish in the gentle light that played over his features. "That action I regretted enough, but neither of them sent help. They said I could deal with it alone, that it was the work of only a few. So Egil destroyed another village, and then another. Still Olvaldr will not treat it as a threat to the Kingdom, but now Lord Alvard *is* listening."

Fin followed the trail of logic, "And now Brynjar is dead you will blame that too on the Akalens, and Alvard will bring his armies to avenge his son."

Gulbrand nodded, and then suddenly his posture broke and he dropped his head into his hands, his chest heaving as he sobbed.

"I love this land with everything that I am, and that lad was good, to the bone he was good. But it had to be done, it *had* to be done."

There was almost a question there, as though he wanted to Fin to agree with him, to justify the decisions he had made. Fin watched the man weep, and almost felt sorry for him. It seemed that Gulbrand's actions truly did hurt him, and he knew the shame of them. Conflict had ruined him.

A pit grew in Fins stomach as he had another thought.

"That day, when you sent Brynjar out to raid the Akalens, did you know they weren't warriors?"

Gulbrand rubbed his eyes.

"Yes, I did." He sat up straight, keen to explain himself even though Fin did not ask, "No one was sending help, I thought perhaps I could get Teoma to attack Yilland prematurely. That would be an act of war, and Olvaldr would be forced to respond. But it seems as though she is not that easy to bait, so the Captain destroyed another village instead."

Fin stared at the man and tried to convey as much pain as he could through his words whilst keeping his voice steady, "My brother died in that raid. Because of you trying to kill the innocent, to start a war with the innocent."

Gulbrand nodded again, "I am sorry, I truly am. But if we destroy the Akalens, we could be safe. There would be lasting peace in the Kingdom, and I have a duty to pay any price for that ideal."

How this man could be so naïve Fin could only guess at. His mind seemed rotted from hate, carrying only remnants of the conscience from the man he used to be. Fin didn't care anymore though, he needed to get away, to warn Alvard. Only one thing kept him there.

"Why have you told me all this?" he said.

Gulbrand gave him a puzzled look.

"Why not kill me?" Fin said bluntly. "You've killed many others."

"Because I couldn't," Gulbrand said, his voice going very soft. The big man looked around the pavilion for a moment, and then his eyes rested on Fin again. "I know what you are, I couldn't even if I wanted to?"

Fin must have given something away in his expression, because suddenly Gulbrand's face opened up, his eyes wide like a dog that has just spotted a hare. The man stood up and stepped toward him slowly.

"You don't know *what* you are, do you?"

Fin was pinned for a moment, whatever defence had been keeping Gulbrand from killing him had been turned to mist, and now he knew there was no reason to keep him alive.

Gulbrand took another step forward.

Fin ran, ducking under the heavy canvas and sprinting out into the dark.

But he was less measured in his flight, less cautious, and he heard footsteps behind him. There was a shout and abruptly someone crashed into his legs throwing him to the ground. Struggling earned him only a bloody nose, then his hands were bound, and he was gagged with rope, big men keeping him pinned as they tied him. His legs were tied together so he could barely move, and the ropes were so tight he felt his hands and feet beginning to tingle with numbness.

Panic consumed him. He tried to make noise, but someone hit him again, stuffed a gag in his mouth. Then he was being lifted up onto a horse.

Low voices muttered around him, and despite the quiet he couldn't make out what they said.

Then he heard a familiar voice speak over the others, and that he heard clearly, for it was Gulbrand.

"Take him outside the camp, if anyone asks, he's a thief. When you're far enough out not to be heard, take him down and slit his throat."

Fin went cold.

He tried again to kick and struggle, but against all his strength the bonds held fast.

Gulbrand must have noticed, for he stepped close, so Fin could just about make him out in the light of the stars.

"I am sorry lad," he muttered.

Then he moved away, and a blindfold was tied around Fin's head.

"Burn the body when you're done."

Chapter 24

Struggling brought no reward.

Every time he moved he was struck by one of the soldiers. He managed to wriggle off the horse once whilst they were at a trot, the bouncing of the creatures back helping to dislodge him. But he just winded himself, and then was tied to the back of the saddle so he could move even less. He wasn't entirely sure what he'd been expecting, and the pain of the fall was a reminder of his stupidity.

And my failure, he thought, as they moved across the plain, though he could see next to nothing through his blindfold, only light, or dark.

There was only one trick he had left to try, but that would have to wait until they stopped, he wouldn't be able to focus whilst they were moving. Both of his hands had gone numb despite him trying to keep them flexed, but the blood was cut off by the rope at his wrists. Another obstacle in the way of his escape.

His vision grew darker, and he assumed they were in the forest now, for the men began to speak amongst themselves. They were strangely kind to Fin, speaking soothingly to him as though he were a frightened animal. It puzzled him, it wasn't nearly enough to redeem them, but they certainly were not the agents of evil he had expected.

Much like his conversation with Gulbrand their words confused him, as much as worried him.

Eventually they stopped, and Fin felt those same strong hands lifting him off the horse and placing him gently down onto solid ground once again, in a kneel.

It was then that he put his plan into action, the last effort to save himself.

He focused on the world around him, dark yet alive, and reached out with his mind.

In this world he could see, but it was an obscured sight, like sunlight through linen. Here he had no ropes or shackles binding him, and the quiet world was awake.

Birds roosted where he would not think to look, their little bodies warm against the cold of night. Pixie drakins hummed up above the trees, whilst others lurked in the dark recesses of the forest, under rocks and roots, waiting for the morning sun. Further out he could feel the battle of wolves as they set upon a young stag, their struggle bright against the world as they fought together, locked in a combat Fin would not know the outcome of.

He could even see a Drakinhawk, somewhere far off, high up in the starlit sky, though he dared not go near it, for its thoughts were sharp and warned him away.

Something bright murmured in the distance, but like the Drakinhawk Fin was fearful of approaching it, for the sounds were ominous and full of power.

For a moment he was lost in the freedom, but then he remembered his purpose. Approaching a great dead tree, he reached out, feeling its spirit, just as strong as it had been in life but not yet ready to leave its body.

Please, this time, he begged silently.

Then he touched it. Just lightly, but that was enough.

It crashed into him, hard, flinging him back into his body. He winced and was physically knocked onto his back from the force of the encounter.

"He isn't even strong enough to kneel," someone snorted sadly.

I will escape. This is not my end.

He repeated the words in his head over and over, making himself believe them, forcing himself not to accept anything other than survival. But he knew at heart he was not a survivor, his life was owed to others, time and again. Herleif protected him right up to his own death, Gatty after that, and Brynjar kept him out of the battle that had ended his own life.

Fin had squandered that care, dishonouring those who had given so much for him.

Now he had run out of friends.

I failed, and I deserve this.

"Leave it," one of the other soldiers said from much closer as they helped him back up onto his knees. "He's got his punishment, no need to add more pain to his passing."

Fin was grateful for the help, that was all he could be grateful for now. Though being spoken about, rather than spoken to, was the most worrying thing.

"He's gonna be dead in a minute anyway, I don't think we have to worry too much how we treat him," said the other voice.

Fin felt the blindfold being untied from his head, and suddenly he could see again.

Despite it still being dark, Fin was almost overwhelmed at the light there was, for it was beautiful compared to the near pitch black he had been experiencing. Stars shone above the silent trees, and the sky was not black, but a deep blue. It was how he imagined the great depths of ocean to look, and in that ocean he could see the drakins he had felt, whirring slowly about on their tiny wings, dancing in the night. Far above them, illuminated against the moon was the outline of their kin, the Drakinhawk, the great predator of the sky.

As he looked down from the sky, the bright moon was burned into his vision. It made it appear as though the whole forest was alive with shadows.

Fin breathed a ragged breath through the rope between his cracked lips. He was not destined to become a Drakinhawk, nor from there the hunter Khutaen, or the immense Agu Khalim that ruled the vast oceans. That great beast that no creature alive could match in size or strength. His story would end here, in the shallows of the world, as nothing more than promise and wasted potential.

He drank in the beauty of the place, oddly calm.

"Looks like he doesn't mind his grave," said one of the men, a large, ratty haired man with a big scar on his neck. He stepped over and kicked Fin in the chest.

He fell into the earth, it wasn't hard ground, and dead leaves softened it further, but tied as he was the action jarred his shoulders awkwardly. There were six men around him, all of middling years. He imagined most would have been with Gulbrand on campaign in the first Akalen war, which might have explained their loyalty to such a cause. Maybe they had been driven mad by the same things which had driven Gulbrand mad.

He caught a flash of movement, something in the corner of his vision moving through the trees. When he blinked to try and sort his eyes out, and it had vanished again.

Another man stepped forward from behind Fin, his mail shimmering weakly in the starlight. He had short black hair and a friendly face that suited his age.

"I said leave it! He doesn't deserve any more than what he's getting," then he turned to Fin, helping him up and undoing the gag in his mouth. "I'm sorry we have to do this lad, do you have anything you'd like to say before it's done?"

The man spoke softly, and Fin saw the same resolved regret in his eyes that he had noticed in Gulbrand. It was the type of regret that precedes the action which causes it.

Fin smacked his lips. His mouth felt horrible.

"I don't have anything to say, but could I have some water?"

Again, Fin saw something move out in the darkness, it was not his eyes betraying him, there was something out there.

"I'm sure-" began the short haired man, before the other one cut him off.

"Just kill the bastard, don't waste water on him if he's about to die," he said loudly with an annoyed expression on his face. "You don't water dead weeds, do you?"

"Kaval stop. The boy's done nothing wrong, let him die with at least his thirst quenched," another man said. The rest of the soldiers obviously did not take to their task quite as readily as this man Kaval did.

The shadow moved, much closer now. One of the other men noticed, turning to face the trees.

Fin began to sweat.

"Let the boy drink so he can pass on in peace, he's not a criminal," the short haired man said, but Fin could feel his resolve waning, he could hear it in his voice.

He looked behind him, then back over to the man who was looking out into the forest.

"Exactly, let him pass already," the scarred man said, stepping over to Fin and drawing a wicked, curved knife from his belt.

The short haired man gave Fin an apologetic look and stepped back from him.

"You forget," the scarred man said, stooping down behind Fin, and pulling his head back by his long hair as he put the knife against his throat. "We still have to build a fire-"

He was cut off by a yell.

Turning suddenly the scarred man cut Fin's neck, and then there was carnage.

The shadow was suddenly among them, close enough to smell. It swiped at one of the men, sending him flying. He hit a tree with a crack and fell to the floor unmoving. Another man was flung off to the side. He was wounded badly and crawled through leaves, leaving them shining with his blood.

The scarred man let go of Fin's hair and rushed forward, drawing his sword and cutting at the shadow. But it was faster than him, and his blade met nothing but air as the beast danced in the night.

As he raised his weapon for another swing, it darted in and closed its teeth around his sword arm, picking the soldier up and shaking him in its jaws as he yelled out. The short haired man had drawn his own weapon but was hesitant to move, but the yelling from his companion seemed to drive him to action.

He rushed at the beast, shouting at the top of his lungs. The shadow paused for a moment, and then threw the scarred man at him. He twisted in the air for a moment, and then collided with his comrade with such force that Fin heard their bones snap. One went still, the other groaned, speaking in earnest to the man beside him, quick panicked words.

The shadow was in no hurry to end them though, and turned its attention back to the other wounded man, who had managed to get some way off from the action crawling as he had been, leaving the trail of his blood. Lumbering over, the beast pinned him with one massive foot, and then closed its jaws around his head, ripping it from his shoulders in one swift movement.

Only one soldier remained, and Fin could not see him from here, but he knew it was the one who had tried to give him water. As he watched, the creature turned back toward the man, who was still babbling to his comrade.

Part of him thought about speaking up, trying to do something, but he hesitated. In that moment he heard a rending of flesh, and the man went quiet.

Fin shivered on the ground. His neck was dripping blood, though he barely noticed.

The shadow turned and began to make its way toward him. For a moment there was no change, and Fin began to tense up, but then, gradually the shadow began to shrink. It kept shrinking until, by the time it got to Fin, it was smaller than him, crooked and shambling.

It was then he saw, illuminated by the light of the moon, his friend.

"You look awful," said the old woman, as she began to untie his bonds.

***

The old woman spat into his face.

"Pfftt, be more careful," Fin said as he picked bits of chewed herb from his lips, somehow even more disgusted than he had been.

Gatty had mixed together wild garlic and nettles, along with some foul tasting roots, then chewed it into a paste, which she now dribbled from her mouth into the wound on Fin's neck.

She loomed over him with a hideous scowl, then spat out the rest of her concoction onto his stinging cut. The wound wasn't deep, but the old woman had warned of infection.

"You're an ungrateful child, all you do is complain," she muttered as she shuffled away from him and over to the fire. She moved on her hands and knees, stiff and awkward.

Fin had to stay on his back until the paste had dried, she'd insisted.

A blue sky had begun to prevail in the east now, the stars beginning to fade. It was nearly dawn and soon the birds would start their morning chorus. Fin could hear the roar of the Akvast somewhere behind him, as the great river tumbled down south, hurrying along on its eternal journey into the sea.

Gatty had walked here with him to get some distance from the men she had killed. Fin wasn't worried about their burials, he knew they would be missed soon and hopefully picked up by a patrol.

Together the boy and the old woman had walked through the night, saying very little to one another, perhaps stopping now and again to listen out for men or beasts. They had come to a stop up against the western bank of the Akvast where the river was split for a long stretch by a large rocky island, reconnecting a little further down. Here there were few trees, and the steppe could be seen clearly on the other side, stretching out into vast sweeping hills for hundreds of miles. It was also here Fin had explained what Gulbrand had told him. She had said nothing, and simply tended to his wounds.

For now, Fin was content listening to the water, and he closed his eyes in rest. Gatty had built a low wall around her fire with rocks, to keep the wind off, and she huddled behind it as she cooked some fish and smoked her pipe. Fin couldn't have moved anyway, but he was enjoying the chill of the wind on his face, the feeling of light moss beneath his body.

He was alive, and that felt good.

For a moment he thought of the man who had tried to give him water, the kind eyes were vivid in his mind, and part of him felt guilty about not speaking up. A word from Fin and Gatty might have spared the man. He was mad, but he had believed he was doing good.

Fin scowled even with his eyes shut.

He had still planned on killing me though, he thought, and maybe that went to show how much faith Gulbrands men had in him.

"Can I move yet?" he said, taking his mind off the dead men and putting it back on the fish, which smelt delicious.

"No," Gatty snapped, not looking away from the fire.

He looked sideways at her, keeping his head still, "I want to come back and learn from you."

Her eyes flicked over to him then, suspicious, "You have work to do first."

"What work?" he mumbled, knowing her answer.

Her head cocked to one side and her face curled up in disgust, "You have learnt of Gulbrand's intentions, and now you will leave? Watch the war happen as you grow soft and fat at my house? I thought you better than *that* boy."

Fin stared up, his jaw clenched so the skin at the wound on his neck pulled taught. It stung, but he didn't care.

"You thought wrong," he muttered.

"You're a failure," the old woman hissed. "Too used to relying on the people around you to take care of you. And now you realise how useless you are, you're happy to just accept that?"

Fin scowled, and nodded, keeping his eyes fixed on the sky, "I cause more trouble than I'm worth. I've gotten good people killed."

The old woman cackled, and that drew his eye. He saw smoke pouring from her nose as she snorted with laughter, and that made his cheeks flush with anger. If he'd been able to stand, he would have walked away, but he was stuck there, being mocked by this ancient woman.

"So have I! Oh you are so self-obsessed, and yet you have no faith in yourself?" Gatty finally managed after she'd finished laughing at him. Abrupty her voice turned to iron, "It would be easy for you to lounge in your pity, to hide away and learn from me. But people have died believing in you. How about you honour them by living up to their expectations, instead of shaming them with failure?"

The wind seemed to scratch at the warmth in his cheeks, turning anger to shame. Tears began to well up in his eyes. She was right, he knew that, but it hurt to hear it.

She smiled then, a little playful thing, "You're not as useless as you think lad."

"I don't know what to do," he managed, his voice weak. "Even if I could help, I wouldn't know how."

Gatty had obviously exhausted her sympathy for him and she sighed, exasperated, "What does Gulbrand want?" she said.

Fin glanced her way, "To start a war?"

"Yes, but there are two sides to every conflict, aren't there?" she said slowly, trying to lead him to a conclusion he was a long way off finding.

"Yes?" he replied sheepishly.

"I'm ten times your age and my mind is still faster than yours. Perhaps the young are getting more stupid," she said plainly, looking into the flames in front of her. "Go and speak with Teoma."

Fin paused.

When she failed to speak again, he realised she was being serious, "Teoma? I-I can't, she'll kill me on sight."

Gatty shrugged her shoulders, "Then don't speak with her. You grew up in the shadow of war, it's not that bad is it?"

He could hear the mocking in her voice, and knew the intent of her words, but it worked. Fin thought back to those cold nights in a land that was not his own, constantly hungry, living amongst people that despised him. If he had not had Herleif, he would have died a long time ago.

Fin stayed quiet for a while, the smell of cooked fish getting better every moment that passed. He turned his head just a little to get a better look at her, wincing as the paste on his neck seeped into another part of his wound, making it burn.

"Did you lose anyone in that war?" he asked suddenly.

He saw her start, just a tiny movement, but he knew he had caught her by surprise. Often, he'd wondered if she had fought in those forests, but he'd never dared ask. Speaking about her past was not a common occurrence for the old woman, and when she did talk, it was through the eyes of history, not her own.

This time she nodded.

"Aye," she muttered, "My man. A quiet soul, not a Recast and nothing to look at, but I did enjoy his company." There was a sparkle in her eyes as some pleasant thought passed through her mind, and then it was gone, replaced with the hard stare that was her norm.

"I'm sorry," Fin said as gently as he had before.

"Don't be, wasn't you that killed him," she twisted her neck and it made a satisfying crack. "Some Akalen did that."

There was another long pause, Fin watching Gatty, afraid of moving his head again, and Gatty watching the fire, now and then taking a long draw on her pipe. If this bitter old woman was selfless enough to try and help the Akalens who, in living memory, had killed her kin, perhaps Fin was capable of more than he thought.

"I will talk to Teoma," he said. "Will you come with me?"

She shook her head and reached over to a fish that was dangling above the flames. She plucked it from the fire and held out her hand to Fin.

"You can eat now."

Hesitantly he sat up, and found that the pain in his throat was already mostly gone. He moved over to her and took it gently from her tiny wrinkled hands. It tasted delicious, he had barely eaten in two days and when he was done he licked the oil from his fingers.

"I can't help you," Gatty said, after she'd eaten, leaning back and closing her eyes. "I can tell you what to do, but I am known from the war. You will be one your own in her camp."

"Thank you," Fin said, and he meant it. Kind words weren't always what he needed to hear, and though sometimes he begrudged her, she was his friend.

Another thought popped into his head.

"Did you know Gulbrand?" he asked quietly. It was common knowledge that the Nomads had worked together with the Kingdom, and there was a good chance their paths might have crossed.

"I did," she said. "He was a good commander, cunning on the field with a fierce care for his men. He lost his son in that war, early on I think, before I met him, but I think that's why he cared about them so much." She smacked her lips, "Soldiers are a pitiful replacement for your children, but I think it was the only one he had."

She spoke with knowing.

"Maybe that's why he's doing all of this," Fin said quietly. "He said that I didn't know what I was? Do you know what that means?"

Gatty began to repack her pipe with deathweed, "Did he tell you what he thought you were?"

Fin shook his head as he looked into the flames, "No, he thought you might have told me."

"Good," Gatty said, not looking at him. "You don't need to know yet."

Fin sensed she would not tell him any more, and he knew he could not change her mind. He was about to ask again, but then he stopped and smiled at her stubbornness. Perhaps this time he would accept what she said.

He curled up next to the fire and shut his eyes.

Gatty stayed awake next to Fin, silently watching over the boy in the predawn gloom.

Chapter 25

Kiakra found it hard to concentrate.

She watched the valley path from her perch up in the tree, waiting for the deserters to arrive. Her concentration was elsewhere though, Cypher was still what her mind lingered on, stealing away her sleep in the night. Burning a hole in her chest.

Don't think about her, she told herself, forcing focus into her surroundings.

She was twenty feet up, standing on the thick branch of a heavy pine tree. Her hands were sticky with sap from the climb up here, tiny wounds in the bark bleeding resin.

Below her, down in the bottom of the valley, was a thin snaking river that had cut through the steppe over the years, leaving a rocky scar in the landscape. The sides of the valley were steep, and many of the beach and ash trees were angled and crooked, but no matter how steep the slopes, the pines stood straight, as they always did.

Stubborn, and unchanged by the world around them.

A little dusty path wound its way under the trees, down to one of the few good crossing points of the river, before twisting up the other side of the valley where the trees petered out and gave way once again to the grasslands of the steppe. It was a track well used, a haven for both people and animals, for it was one of the few water sources out in these barren lands.

"Kiakra," Rat hissed from below, she hadn't noticed him approach.

She glanced over at the trees on the other side of the valley. She still couldn't see anyone.

"Yes?" she said, finally looking down at him.

"Any sign of them yet?" Rat said.

Idiot, I wouldn't be speaking to you if there was.

"No," she said quickly. "Is the *he* secure?"

She wouldn't call him by name any more, not after what he'd done, after all the strife he'd caused, almost getting her killed and driving her friends away. Driving her Cypher apart. The boy didn't deserve his name.

"Yes," Rat said in his loud whisper. "*He* is, Aldrid has left him further up the path with his hands tied. He's just securing the yaks and then he'll be with us."

The Weasel Pack was down to just three now, Kiakra, Rat and Aldrid. She missed Tiko a little, but Cypher... That was still being processed. The girl had been her sister in everything but blood.

She's gone now.

It was no matter, Kiakra could manage on her own if she needed to. People had left the Pack without notice before and she had slept soundly. This should be no different.

"You bind the boy's legs?" she asked, a little louder now. The deserters they were hunting were likely still a long way out, and the wind was strong enough to cover their voices.

Rat shook his head.

Kiakra's free hand curled into a fist, "I told you to bind him so that he couldn't move? What if he runs?"

Rat looked around and raised his glittering arms, "Where is he going to go? This river goes on for another fifty miles before it reaches the Akvast, and there's nothing but grass ahead and behind. Even if he takes a horse, he's looking for his brother, he's going the same way as us. This isn't where he's planning to escape."

Kiakra sighed through her teeth, she was tired, she didn't often argue with Rat but lately they had clashed as frequently as mealtimes.

"Alright, but if he does decide to run, you will be tracking him back down. And don't forget how dangerous that boy is when he's angry," she said.

Visions of him beating the Akalen to a bloody pulp burned vividly on her mind. His brutality in that fight was consolation to her. He was a criminal, like all the rest had been. He'd just done a better job of hiding it.

No teeth until the bite, like a snake.

She could see by the look on Rat's face that he was remembering it too.

"Alright," he said quietly.

As he spoke, Aldrid appeared on the path, stumbling awkwardly down toward them. Rat looked from Aldrid to Kiakra with a questioning look.

"Get it done," she said, looking back over to the valley path.

For a moment it was the same as it had been, quiet and empty, then abruptly three men appeared from the trees, making their way down to the crossing.

"Wait, wait!" she whispered loudly, looking back down at the two. "They're coming, close, just about to reach the crossing. Leave the boy and get off the path!"

Rat darted into the dry brush uphill of the path, just below Kiakra's tree, whilst Aldrid went downhill of it. That way if it came to a fight, they would have a few different angles of attack.

Kiakra reached for her little recurve bow which she'd hung on a branch next to her, and then led down on her perch, legs hanging either side of the big branch on which she'd stood.

For a little while they were still, Kiakra watching the deserters, and the other two waiting patiently for her signal.

After a while she heard a whisper from Rat.

"Are you sure you want to do this?" he said. She couldn't see where he was hidden, but she imagined he had just caught sight of their targets, who looked formidable to say the least.

They were three Akalens that had killed a chief in Teoma's Warband before deserting. She'd seen a poster for them outside the healing house in

Yotan. The reward wasn't massive, but it was not to be scoffed at either. They were going to Teoma's camp anyway, it made sense to make the journey more worth their while, even if there was a little bit of risk involved.

They'd spotted three riders across the valley as they came over the skyline, and had set up a watch after that, waiting for them to reappear from the trees further down the valley.

"Yes, I'm sure I want to do this," Kiakra hissed. Now was not time to be having this conversation.

"But there are three of them, and we have no healer, we can still back out if-"

"I know we have no healer, you don't have to remind me. We're still doing this," she said in an iron voice.

Rat stayed silent after that.

She'd been so focused on losing a friend she had barely time to realise they were without a healer. Wounds that Kiakra was used to shrugging off, could easily prove fatal.

"We're still doing this," she muttered under her breath, speaking only to herself.

The deserters were slow coming up the trail, and it was a while before they came back into view. Now they were committed, it was all or nothing.

The men rode easily, chatting as they moved toward the Pack. Two were side by side whilst the third trailed closely behind. The two up front were not much to look at, both average height for Akalens, one thin with red fur, the other slightly stockier with a sandy brown coat. The one riding behind had black fur and was taller by half a head than the other two. Kiakra knew he would be too strong to take alive if there was a struggle.

She pressed her face against the bark. Though she was high up, and well hidden, there was always the chance one would look up and see her before the trap was sprung. She slowly knocked an arrow to her bow, holding it loosely in one hand, her index finger pinching the arrow against the grip, while her other arm hugged the tree.

Rough bark dug into her arms, and her breathing became quiet as she prepared to move.

She waited until the Akalens were almost directly below her, then sat up, crossing her legs so she would not fall, and aimed an arrow at one of them.

"Oi, you there, stop!" she said.

All of them started, their heads snapping up to look at her, their horses shying.

"Who are you?" the Akalen with the red fur called out, slowly raising up his hands to show he was not armed. Kiakra could see the blustone club at his hip, if he kept his hands up, she'd be happy.

"The Weasel Pack," Rat answered from the brush.

Then red one's horse bucked as Rat spoke, obviously startled at another noise so close. The Akalen grabbed the reigns and Kiakra, her shoulders twitching, loosed an arrow at him. Just before it leapt from her bow she realised her mistake and aimed high, turning it into a warning shot, but Aldrid mistook it as a signal to attack, for an arrow flew out from his side of the path and thudded into the flank of the sandy Akalen's horse.

"Wait no!" Kiakra yelled, but it was too late.

The horse reared in pain, and threw its rider into the dirt before sprinting away, whilst the red haired Akalen pulled out his club and wheeled around looking for the other attackers. The taller one took a moment to yell out something to his companion who was writhing on the ground winded, and then drew his own weapon.

Rat suddenly leaped at the red Akalen from his hiding place on the bank, knocking him from his mount so that both were rolling in the earth, twisted up as Rat tried to restrain, and his opponent tried to kill.

Kiakra watched helplessly from above as her advantage was squandered.

No, no, no.

The big Akalen was stepping out of his stirrups watching Rat wrestling on the floor with his companion, club in hand. There was no way she could take him alive now, he was too big, too dangerous. Nimble fingers fitted an arrow to her bow and a moment later it was whipping through the air. The large Akalen was halfway off his horse when the steel bit into the meat of his thigh, and as his leg gave way he fell from his horse with a wail.

By this time the sandy coloured Akalen had gotten his breath and managed to stumble back to his feet. Kiakra saw him glance at his companions, one screaming in the dirt and the other pinned on his belly by Rat.

He ran.

Aldrid emerged from his hiding spot and tried to tackle the deserter, but the Akalen kicked him hard in the gut, throwing him backwards.

"Aldrid," Kiakra yelled, helpless as she watched him flee up the path, past them and toward where the boy and their supplies were. "He's getting away!"

But Aldrid was curled up on his knees, not moving.

Kiakra watched as the man sprinted up the path. If he got hold of one of their horse's then he'd be gone.

She scrambled down the tree as fast as she could, cursing as she did.

"Old fool," she muttered, stepping down onto a thin branch.

It was rotten and snapped under her foot.

She dropped through the air, branches whipping up into her face, forcing her eyes closed. They ripped the fabric of her tunic up, raking across her bare stomach and breaking off as she hit them. She landed well, falling sideways and rolling onto the path, but she was covered in cuts and her eyes were blinded by bits of twig and bark.

She stood up spitting and blinking, but as she put weight on her ankle it gave way, and she fell back down again.

She cursed and stayed down, rubbing the debris from her eyes until she could see again.

The Akalen had gone.

Next to her Rat had finally subdued the red Akalen, who now had a badly broken arm and was lying on his stomach gritting his teeth in anger as rat held his arms pinned against his back. Aldrid was still curled up in a ball groaning next to the wounded Akalen, who was trying to claw his way away from the fight.

She stood up again, tears in her eyes from all the blinking she'd done.

Her ankle was bad, she could put almost no weight on it without agonising pain, and it was already beginning to swell.

Rat looked up at her with a grimace.

She stared at him for a second, "Why did you speak?" she hissed.

"I thought they'd-"

"No!" she yelled at him, her chest heaving, "You didn't think! That's the problem!"

He recoiled from her.

She heard Aldrid's voice from behind, "It wasn't his fault."

She turned to face him as he continued, her jaw tight.

"I'm sorry, I shouldn't have shot at them until your signal, but I thought you had begun-"

Kiakra cut him off by blasting a kick into his face with her bad foot, sending his head snapping back. She cried out as she did it, for her ankle erupted in agony and once again she toppled to the floor. She landed in the dirt with tears on her face, howling in pain.

It took her a moment for the pain to subside and for her to realise what she'd done. Aldrid's face was covered in blood, eyes wide in disbelief. For an instant she felt guilt threaten her, but why should she care? They were all using each other, Rat for entry back into his precious homeland, and Aldrid for a stake in land on the banks of the Stem. Caring wasn't ever a part of it, Kiakra had been a fool for ever thinking it was.

"Don't give me that look," she mumbled, pushing herself back up to her one good foot. "Get that one tied up." She gestured at the red Akalen under Rat.

"What are we going to do with that one?" Rat said, nodding at the dark haired man that was crawling through the dirt, trying to whistle to his horse. "He's hurt pretty bad."

"Cypher isn't here to heal him," Kiakra said, and began to hobble over to him.

"We can't leave him like that," came Aldrid's voice, quiet and nasally.

She wondered if his nose was broken as she moved over to the Akalen in the dirt. Kneeling, she pushed him onto his back, his lazy eyes meeting her own.

"Get off me," he said levelly, his voice more powerful than his body would have led her to believe. Wounded though he might be, his mind was still that of a man who had not known many physical equals, and that confidence showed through.

Kiakra pulled out her knife and shoved it into his chest.

His eyes went wide with panic, and he grasped at her hand, the nails on his fingers scratching shallow cuts into her wrist. Kiakra paid him no mind and twisted the blade as she ripped it out, watching his blood seep into fur.

It was the sensible thing to do, it would cost them more to try and keep him alive than he was worth. Part of her wondered what Cypher would think.

No sense debating it now, the deed is done.

She turned back to the others and Rat glanced up, nodded once, neither in support nor disdain, simply in acknowledgement, and then continued binding the Akalen on the floor.

His captive was not so quiet though.

"What have you done? He was your prisoner!" he yelled.

Rat grabbed him by the back of the head and smashed his face into the ground, "Shut up."

As she walked past them, she caught sight of Aldrid's face, pale in disbelief, watching her like a sheep watches a wolf.

"Get your eyes off me," she hissed. "Blame Cypher for that," she gestured at the corpse behind her on the trail, "If she was here then he wouldn't have had to die."

And it's his fault that she left, she thought, as she marched up the trail towards her prisoner.

***

It took her a long way to get back up to where the boy was.

As she hobbled, she barely thought about the Akalen who had fled, instead her thoughts went to *him*. This whole thing had been a disaster, this entire trip they had embarked upon in the north, and they had done it because of that boy. Why had she not left him by the river to die that day?

That is what empathy gets you in this world, I was weak, and I paid for it. I should have been sterner with the girl, made her leave him to die. It would have been better in the long run. That was her fault for letting him live, but she wanted to hurt him, to make him understand how she felt. To make him know what he had done to her pack. To her family.

She rounded the corner and stopped.

Under the tree was the boy, and he was clinging to the brown furred Akalen man. The rope that tied his hands was pulled tight across the Akalen's throat, his eyes were closed and he didn't move.

Her heart jumped. If only Cypher had been there to see, to understand what he really was, the person he had been hiding from them all that time. How had the girl not seen it?

In that moment Kiakra broke.

She would kill him.

If she killed him she would not be paid, and all of this would have been for nothing. She would have lost her friend for nothing.

She didn't care any more.

Cypher wasn't coming back.

The boys hatred had spread into Kiakra like poison, making her sour to those she loved. She had watched him kill with such evil intent, such anger, and that anger had seeped into her bones, forcing her family apart.

There was no good in him. The pain she had inflicted on Aldrid was this boy's fault, he had made her into this. So had Cypher, she had done this to her by leaving.

She had betrayed Kiakra, because of him.

She advanced on him with her knife drawn, shuffling toward him with the same awkward gait as a Demon.

Who cared if the boy died before his time? As a hunter Kiakra upheld justice, what did it matter if she inflicted that justice instead of Dagtok. She would kill him, and be done with it, be done with all of this.

Will that make anything better? Something inside her voiced, making her pause.

Then the Akalen coughed.

It was a small noise, and at first Kiakra thought she had misheard it. But then it happened again, and he began to struggle. As he did so she watched the boy pulled the rope tight across the Akalens neck again until he stopped, and once again went limp.

The boy caught sight of her then.

"Kiakra!" he shouted, relief in his voice, as if she were a friend, perhaps forgetting he was her prisoner. There was a dark welt under one of his eyes, and blood on his lip. He had kept the Akalen alive despite the struggle.

She hobbled over and put her knife up against the Akalen's throat.

"Don't move or I will kill you," she growled, though he still looked unconscious.

She stood and pulled some rope from a saddlebag to tie him up with.

"He was trying to take one of the horses," the boy said.

She didn't reply, and bent down to tie the Akalen's hands, then his feet.

She couldn't look *him* in the eye.

***

Kiakra stared into the flames, Rat opposite her.

The wind was strong, and there was a gentle drizzle that would soak them through in a few hours. Neither seemed to care though, both had thick hides covering them, decent enough protection from the elements. The boy would be having a long night.

"I'll leave at dawn," Aldrid said again, as if she hadn't heard exactly what he had said the first time.

Don't do this.

"I understand," she said, not looking at him. She would have left as well, considering the way she'd treated him, but then again, she wasn't a fool, and that was the only reason she treated him as such.

The man took a deep breath, "I have enjoyed our years of travelling together, and it's a shame it's come to this. But I can't overlook your recent actions, and I don't think you are, currently at least, in a good state of mind for leading the Pack."

The Pack. Without you there are only two of us left. What a pitiful "Pack" we have become.

"You can think whatever you want. If you leave you forfeit your share of both the boy and the deserters," she said, still not looking at him. It wasn't what she wanted to say, but what she did want to say was weak, and weakness was no longer an option, not with only two of them left. Her heart had to harden more for every friend she lost.

He swallowed loudly and nodded once, "I know."

Kiakra felt Rat's eyes on her, but she wouldn't look away from the fire.

I'm sorry.

"Goodnight then," was all she could manage, trying to dismiss her old friend.

Aldrid nodded again and made to walk away. Just as he was leaving, he turned, "I'll be in Stemtrad, if you need me."

"I won't," she said curtly, hating herself for the choppy reply. But her face was blank, and did a good job of hiding her feelings.

Please, please don't go, not now.

The man paused, and then was gone. Kiakra pulled her face tight against her cloak, hiding her frustrated tears from Rat.

In the morning the goats had disappeared, and there was no sign of Aldrid, except for the tracks that led back to the south.

Chapter 26

An eagle soared overhead, its vantage point unmatched in this open, flat terrain. It would have spotted them before him, but even Fin, low on the ground, saw the group long before they reached him.

A dozen Akalens, galloping towards him, kicking up dust in their wake. They didn't rush and were not panicked. And why would they be? He was only one boy.

Once he saw them approaching he dismounted from his horse and waited on their arrival, trying to look as unthreatening and well intentioned as possible, which wasn't difficult considering his stature. Akalens killed any messengers sent to bargain with them, that's what he'd been told, but now he assumed that was just part of Gulbrand's deception. A lie, in attempt to further vilify this group in the eyes of his people.

Still, seeing them ride at him, spears held high and their face paint visible even from here, Fin did begin to doubt his assumptions, which was a little worrying, as he'd bet his life on them.

Calm down.

He looked to his side for the old woman out of habit, but she was not there.

You don't need her.

Glancing up he caught sight of the monstrous eagle, hanging lazily on the gentle wind. Even absent from his side, it was nice to know that she was at least watching over him.

He breathed deeply and turned his gaze back to the Akalen's approach.

Unlike his experience with Herleif in the village, which felt like a lifetime ago, these men were all clearly dressed like warriors. Their spears were wrapped with colourful cloth which snapped in the wind as they rode, and even their horses were painted with zigzags and swirls on their head and sides. They were not the most subtle scouts Fin had encountered, but they hardly needed to be. There was no cover out here in which to hide, so why try?

They closed quickly, and surrounded him at a distance, some riders breaking away to position themselves behind him and cut off his escape, whilst a few others hung back ahead of him. He found their caution remarkably amusing.

There were ten men and two women. All seemed keen eyed and uneasy, but he did notice that the women, despite being almost identical in stature to the men, were carrying small recurve bows instead of spears, and seemed far more relaxed. The only difference Fin noticed physically, was that the necks of the women were slightly longer, and they wore patches of bejewelled armour on their upper arms and thighs.

One man dismounted and turned to two of his companions, "Look to the north and the west, if this is somehow a trap, that'll be where they come from," he said quickly.

The two nodded and kicked their horses away.

The Akalen turned to Fin, planted his great spear into the ground, and then strode toward him.

He was a stocky build for an Akalen, heavy arms hung from broad shoulders, and a thick neck held his head steady as he walked. He wore trousers of dark silvery grey which contrasted with the light brown of his fur, and, like the others, he wore large gold bands on both wrists. But by far the most distinguishing item he wore was his headdress, a large tuft of black mane that framed his face, and on either side were two buffalo horns, polished so smooth they glinted like jewels.

Undoubtedly, he was a chieftain.

"Greetings boy," he said to Fin as he approached, never taking his brown eyes off Fin's own. "What brings you here, so far into our country and so far away from your own lands?"

Fin held his gaze, "Greetings, I wish to speak with Warlord Teoma."

The Akalen smiled knowingly, "Ah, you are an assassin from the Lord of Yilland? I do not think the Pale Wolf will speak with you."

Fin swallowed, "I'm no longer under the command of Lord Gulbrand, and I bring a warning to Teoma, it's important that I speak to her." He shook his head, "I am no assassin."

He could feel the gaze of the other Akalens, and shifted nervously. They were not on his side, and he could tell that none would argue if this man decided to kill him.

"What is the message?" the man said coyly, but Fin knew that was his lifeline. He'd heard Teoma herself was a good leader, but the clans and chiefs she had called upon largely ruled themselves.

"My message is for Teoma," he said, and bowed low, trying to be as respectful as he could.

The Akalen gritted his teeth, "You are a spy or an assassin, there is no message, no humans have spoken to us before," he said, grabbing the handle of the knife in his belt.

The sun beat down on Fin's neck, and he felt himself begin to sweat.

"I am unarmed," he said loudly, looking around. "You can check my things, and bind me, I will go wherever you take me, but please, let me speak with your leader."

"You lie," the Akalen said, pulling the knife from his belt. It was a long greenstone thing, straight and wickedly sharp.

The eagle screeched overhead.

Fin could sense everyone's attention on their leader. He stood there for a moment, but did not advance on Fin any further, something was holding him back.

"I am unarmed," Fin said again, for he guessed that was what stayed this man's hand.

The Akalen said nothing for a while, and then turned on his heel, walking back over to his horse and pulling a regular steel knife from one of the small saddlebags on its side. He returned to Fin and threw it at the boy's feet.

"There is a weapon for you, I challenge you to a Kala'tam," he said clearly.

Some of the Akalens around them laughed. Fin would have in their position. He was more than a head shorter than the man, and probably only a little more than half his weight. There was no way Fin could defeat him.

Above him the eagle was flying much lower now. If it came to a fight, he would not be the one participating.

"I do not want to fight," he said slowly, unfamiliar with the conditions of turning down such a challenge.

"No, you want to sneak off in the night to report back to your Lord, or stab our leader in the throat whilst she sleeps. I know what you want, and your youth will not save you. Once again, I challenge you," the Akalen said impatiently.

They cannot kill me outright, that is not their way.

Fin thought for a long while. He looked at the Akalen's around him. Their confidence was superficial, he could see that now, they were afraid of even him, a boy. That was what Gulbrand's raids had done to them.

"I do not accept your challenge," he said clearly, "So kill me here, a boy trying to help those he has wronged. Then you will be no better than your enemy, and if Gulbrand has convinced you that *we* are enemies, he has already won."

The Akalen, scowled and clenched his jaw, "If you tell me what your message is then you will be free to return."

Fin shook his head resolutely, "I am not under his command any more, as I have said, and I need to give Teoma the message myself. It will mean nothing coming from one of her own."

The chief was about to argue when one of the others spoke up.

"Yakal, can we not bind the boy and bring him before her this way?

310

We have had no messengers from the humans, he could be useful."

He looked over to the woman who had spoken, and paused.

Fin jumped in again, "You are fighting people you do not understand, I understand them, and I could help Teoma bring an end this conflict. No more fighting. No war."

The Akalen looked at Fin, then at his warriors around him. He shook his head and spat at the ground.

"Fine, I will not kill as the humans do. Bind him."

Fin breathed a sigh of relief.

The chieftain turned and three other Akalen's dismounted to tie Fin. They bound his hands behind his back, then checked him for weapons and put him up on his horse, which they tethered to one of their own.

Fin watched the eagle as it drifted away on the wind, heading back into the west. He took a deep breath to calm his nerves. He was really on his own now.

He smiled then.

Once again he was a prisoner, but at least this time it hadn't been an accident.

***

Ojak ducked under the low thatch roof and into the large wooden pavilion. The structure was open on all sides and usually served to keep the elements away from the handiwork of the many craftsmen that were needed in a military camp. Today it sheltered Lord Gulbrand and a small group of youngsters from the drizzle that was misting its way down from the clouds, dampening the camp.

There were low worktables set up, made from thick slabs of oiled pine. Standing around them the children watched Gulbrand as he shaped a thick stick of yew down into something that might one day resemble a bow. Some watched him intently, barely speaking, others held their own sticks and tried to imitate what he was doing, tongues stuck out in concentration, or heads cocked in confusion. In the centre of the work space was a small fire that was kicking out as much smoke as it was heat, though it still was warmer than outside.

"Right, now I'm trying to even it out so there's no point of weakness," Gulbrand said in a grumble to no one in particular.

It was strange to see him like this, wearing a dirty linen tunic, working like one of the peasants. Ojak watched him much like the children did, with fascination, for the man seemed so different here. Gone was the air of worry that always hung about him, the anticipation of bad things to come. Here he seemed somehow well placed, at home getting lost in the labour of his work.

Perhaps he would have been a better carpenter than a leader.

Ojak scorned himself for the thought, stowing it away like some evil secret. But he did not mean it as insult, it was just that for the first time since he had met the man, he looked content.

It was the same look Lord Brynjar had when he used to spar with sword and shield, a moments respite from a world of responsibility and heritage that was always waiting for him. Ojak leant against one of the large wooden beams the supported the thatch roof and grit his teeth. He missed Brynjar.

He had dreamed of one day seeing him become the Lord of Rukland, and had hoped that he himself would live out his days serving as a general or advisor to that man. Those dreams were dust now though, as Brynjar's body was.

At first there had been pain, and grief for his fallen friend, but now he felt only aimlessness. A great absence in himself where once his purpose had been. Now he was about to give the last of that purpose away, and perhaps that was why he had been putting it off.

He patted his breast pocket and felt the paper crinkle.

Still there.

Abruptly Gulbrand looked up and caught the boy's eye.

He smiled warmly and set his bow down, wiping sweat from his forehead with one big callused hand.

"Alright, I have work to do," he said softly, but immediately the children were paying attention. "Keep working at your bows, and remember you can always cut them smaller but you can't cut them bigger, so be careful how much you shave off."

The children then began to scramble away chattering and giggling, though all of them held their shaped pieces of wood carefully, and with a little pride.

Gulbrand rose from his seat, a simple wooden stool, and placed his own creation on one of the tables.

"My boy, how are you?" Gulbrand said, his smile turning a little empathetic.

Ojak dipped his head a little and lowered his eyes, a movement that was automatic.

"My Lord, I've come to you because I have only now remembered an order that Lord Brynjar gave me before he died."

Gulbrand nodded, no doubt noting how Ojak had dodged his question, "What order was it that Brynjar gave you?"

He said the words so softly that Ojak felt a fool for even coming to him, however when he pulled the piece of paper from his pocket the man's expression seemed to harden somewhat.

"I was told," Ojak said carefully. "That in the event Lord Brynjar did not return from his expedition, that I was to give this letter to you, as he had not had the time to do so himself. And that, should he return, there would be no need for the letter anyway."

He did not remember the encounter well, he'd been too annoyed about being sent away to concentrate fully on Brynjar's words. This fact annoyed him greatly, for it was the last time he had ever seen his master.

Before he had been killed by those beasts.

Gulbrand raised one eyebrow, "You *forgot* to give it to me?"

"I'm sorry," Ojak said, though he could tell Gulbrand saw through him.

Then the great man surprised him.

"Have you read it?" he said plainly.

Ojak was taken aback.

Suddenly the letter in his hand felt very feeble, holding much less of the power he had given it.

He glanced sideways at Gulbrand, gauging if this was some sort of test.

"No, my Lord, I haven't. It is not my place."

"There's no seal," Gulbrand pointed out gently. "If he'd been so worried about you reading it, surely he would have put a seal on there?"

That logic stumped Ojak for a moment, why hadn't Brynjar put a seal on this letter? He knew it was important, perhaps he did want Ojak to read it, or at least he didn't mind if he did.

Or maybe it was because he trusted you.

Ojak stood for a moment, unable to say anything. He had no answer, and he didn't want to offend Lord Gulbrand.

The man smiled reassuringly, "This isn't a test lad, I'm just curious as to what the letter says, and why he would want only me to know."

Ojak stayed quiet.

"All I'm saying," Gulbrand continued, "Is this- I know Brynjar had doubts about the causes of this conflict, and I don't blame him, I've had my doubts as well. But he was killed, along with many of my men, by Akalens. Surely his dated opinions are not worth sharing?"

Gulbrand leaned in close. Ojak smelt pine sap and woodsmoke.

"You want justice for him, and we are now, more than ever, ready to deal out that justice, alongside my troops. Let me do so with a clear head, free of guilt or doubt."

He moved back and sat down heavily in his stool, going back to his work on the bow and giving Ojak some room to think.

Ojak looked down at the letter, he had crinkled the edge of the thick paper because he had been holding it so tight. He wanted to serve Brynjar, but he also wanted justice for him.

"Read it before you choose what to do with it, don't let ignorance be your shield. That is all I ask," Gulbrand said, not looking up from his work.

Ojak pulled out a stool and sat down, opening the letter as he did so.

Lord Gulbrand,

It troubles me that this letter should come to you. I would rather speak openly about a topic so complex, however the nature of this letter should explain why I cannot speak openly.

This conflict is not as it seems. I have met with the enemy, if that is what we must call them, though they do not act as such. They fight us yes, and commit the same atrocities that we also commit, that is simply the nature of battle. But they do not push us, they do not attack. They are like a wounded wolf who has been cornered- snarling and biting, but out of fear.

I have spoken to the wounded, and I have plundered the innocent, and the enemy have not initiated battle once. The targets they attack within Yilland do not seem strategic, and they do not push their advantage, for they both outnumber and outmatch us. All I have seen on their part is display, and the rightful seeking of vengeance for wrongs done against them, and even in that they have been mild compared with our treatment of them.

It pains me to say it, but there are several factors which lead me to believe my father may have had a part in the raids on your lands. I know coming from his son that must sound strange, but my father is a rash man, and has many rash men at his disposal. I would not be surprised if he had orchestrated these attacks in preparation for some larger plan. The purpose of these attacks I am still unsure of, but political advantage is not unlikely. With your lands weakened he may have sought to gain rule over Yilland, and perhaps use that as a platform to wage war against the Akalens, whom he has despised since the first war. That is only a theory, and my word should not be taken as fact, but merely used to direct your suspicions.

If this letter comes to you then I have likely been taken prisoner by my own father, and it is therefore likely too that I am being treated well, for, despite his shortcomings, he cares deeply for me.

I am but one man, and I do not think the war should be judged by myself alone, however I have seen more than many, and what I have seen is not the aggressive enemy I was told we fought, but a proud people unwilling to die without opposition.

All I beg of you is caution Gulbrand.

Your friend,

Brynjar.

Ojak was shaking as he closed the letter.

Brynjar had been too cautious, put too much faith in their enemy, and now they had made him pay for his hesitation.

A lack of aggression?

Now he was dead in the mud, killed by their hand. These views, though written by he himself, were surely no longer relevant. He would not ask for forgiveness for those that had taken his life, and the life of his men.

And his father to blame, of all people. These are the words of a delusional man.

Gulbrand looked over.

"Was I correct lad?"

In the great man's face there was pity and understanding.

Ojak stood, and walked over to the fire, dropping the letter into its writhing yellow jaws and staring into the flames as the words were consumed. Ojak would preserve his memory. No one else would read that letter, and Brynjar would not be remembered as a mad fool, but as a good man. A man of bravery, and honour, and country.

Gulbrand nodded as he too watched the flames, a sad smile on his lips.

Chapter 27

The road to the Teoma's camp was not a long one, but neither was it enjoyable. As they tracked further east Fin had been blindfolded with an old bag made of sheepskin, though this puzzled him, as the location of Teoma's camp could hardly be a secret. It was situated out on barren plains of the steppe. Anyone could see it and find it.

At first his only indicator of their arrival had been the smell of livestock, which was strong, but not unpleasant. Then he had heard voices, and felt the path change from straight and purposeful to winding and confused. He assumed they were moving through the camp then, for he felt the hot sun flicking over his shoulders, it's warmth there one moment and then absent the next as he passed under whatever structures made up this place.

Voices turned to touch, and he felt people grab at his clothes, pat his shoulders from below, and at one point try to pull him gently from the saddle. Despite these touches he did not feel threatened, for though he could not make out much of what was being said through the thick bag and heavy accents, the tones did not sound aggressive.

Then the chief, the man named Yakal, had leaned in close to him and spoke.

"Stay here, make no noise," he had whispered, with no emotion in his voice.

That had been some time ago, but Fin did not move. He could not move even if he wanted to, for the bindings were tight around his wrists and pinned his arms to his back, but that didn't worry him. Trust, and an audience with the Pale Wolf were not going to be won by Fin undermining the decisions

317

of Teoma's cheifs. He was where he needed to be. There was nothing for him to escape from.

So he waited.

He rolled his shoulders, and stretched out his neck, yawning as he did and listening to the camp more closely. The place sounded joyous, despite the fact they had been continually raided by Gulbrand. It was strange, the atmosphere was excitable almost, a bustle of preparation and confidence as he heard people move past him.

Someone patted his leg and muttered something he couldn't hear. It made him jump but the touch was instant, and then gone.

Again, there was a long wait, then finally he heard voices approaching. One he recognised one as Yakal, but the other he didn't know. They must have stopped very close to him, because he could make out a lot of what they said.

"Wouldn't she be angry?" that was Yakal, sounding nervous now.

"No, not if she doesn't know," said another voice.

A pause. Enough time for Fin to become nervous.

"I'm not sure, I told him-" Yakal started, but he was cut off.

"It doesn't mean anything, he's one of Gulbrands lot, they aren't to be trusted."

There was a pause. Fin began to worry.

"What if he's telling the truth though? There were no soldiers with him and my people scouted the area."

The other Akalen sighed, "Let me have a look at him first."

Suddenly the sheepskin bag was ripped off his head. Fin was blinded for a moment in the evening sun, and he blinked furiously.

In front of him was a tall Akalen woman, dark haired, covered in jewels, and staring at him with a knowing gaze. He watched her eyes flitting over his features, before a broad smile came onto her face.

This took place in an instant, and then the bag was pulled back down over his head.

"It's him, I'm almost certain. The boy spoke a lot about what his brother looked like on our trip, and if it isn't him then the cripple won't want him, will he?" she said.

Fin had no idea what they were talking about, but a sense of unease was growing in his stomach. This was not part of the plan, and who was this cripple?

"I'm here to speak with Teo-" he started, before being struck hard across the face. His eyes streamed with tears under the hood.

This was not good.

"Take him to the cripple, we have no need of him," said the woman. There was a pause.

"Tiko I know you don't agree-" said Yakal, but something cut him off. He started up again a few moments later. "I will take him," he said, and then Fin was moving again.

"Where am I going?" he whispered once he reckoned he was further away from the Akalen woman.

"Shut up," someone said, not Yakal, but one of the warriors who had been riding with them. It seemed as though Yakal was no longer with them.

The air grew cold as they moved along further. Time was difficult to judge in the dark, but the sun must now have been setting. The voices and bustle died down with the temperature, and after a while Fin found himself shivering slightly.

It went from quiet to near silent, the only sounds coming from the horses. It felt like there was nothing around them, any noise vanished into the night and was lost to a great space around him.

Finally, they stopped, and he was heaved down from his horse. The relief of company and touch quickly faded as he realised, he must have reached his destination.

Someone pushed him forward. His legs felt weak from lack of use, and his head spun, making it an effort to even stay upright. His head was pushed down as he ducked into what he assumed was a ovook, feeling the hide and fur brush past his shoulders as he entered.

Then the hands let him go. It was warm in here, but he found no comfort in it. It was like the sickly warmth of a fever, close and dirty. He felt itchy just standing there.

There was some muttering, and then he heard, and partially felt, the Akalen's leave him.

"Yakal?" he whispered.

No answer.

It was utterly still around him, he was alone.

Where had they left him? He guessed this was not the warchief's residence, but he had no idea where else it could be.

Then he heard shuffling. Something was in here with him.

He stiffened up, sweating now in the heat of this place. Alone, bound and blind he felt his breath begin to quicken. What was in here with him?

He heard wheezing, and the shuffling again, coming closer now.

Something touched his arm and he flinched.

It was a hand.

"I was looking for your brother, but I'm glad I've found you," someone whispered, right in his ear. It was a man, and his voice was harsh in his throat, rough from disuse.

The words coiled around Fin's neck, and it made him squirm. It sounded oddly familiar.

"My brother is dead," Fin said, trying to ward off fear with his voice.

Something grabbed the bottom of the sheepskin bag and pulled it up off his head.

Fin was inside an ovook, though it was bare, nothing was here except a traveller's bag and a fire that glowed bright in the centre.

A man stood close in front of him.

Old eyes stared into Fin's own, and each of them recognised the other.

Dread seeped into his limbs and his face.

How?

"No he isn't. Not yet," Dagtok said, with an empty smile.

***

Few humans had seen a full Warband of Akalens on their native steppe. Kiakra knew of many humans that had fought them, but only whilst on the defensive in the lands of the Kingdom. There the people of the steppe were not equipped for the terrain, or the style of fighting that came with it.

As Kiakra looked out over the camp of Teoma she could understand why. It stretched out for what looked like miles across the great grass sea, thousands of ovook and animals and people, all mingled together, living symbiotically as one entity. They were like moss on a landscape of stone. It was a far cry from the rolling hills and forests of the empire.

She knew humans had the forgery, the ability to make armour and weapons from iron, as well as the inclination to mine for it. Out here they had little means of making metal, and so used it sparingly, it was reserved mainly for ancestral jewellery and spearheads. Blustone was a staple, though that too was not easy to acquire, and most weapons of that material were passed down from parent to child. It was stronger than iron, but heavy, and difficult to craft.

Still, despite their lack of weapons, and traditional means of warfare, this host looked formidable, and crucially, it could move.

They were set up on a large flat plain, at the centre of which was a small spring. That spring turned into a stream which spread out into a mossy plain in the northwest. Other than that, and some old weathered mountains on the horizon, there was nothing but gentle slopes, for the Akalens did not rely on heavily fortified positions as the Kingdom did. If they were attacked, Teoma would simply withdraw into the hundreds of miles of open ground until she felt better suited for combat.

Here, defence was awareness and mobility, both things she possessed.

It didn't surprise Kiakra then, that they had been spotted from such a long way out. She was currently riding alongside a young warrior, tall, with a

321

thin face and a nervous authority about him.

A group of twenty or so Akalens had met her several miles away from the camp, and upon seeing the deserters she was transporting, had decided to escort her and Rat to Teoma themselves. At first, when they had set eyes on the criminals, she was worried they were might kill them and rob her of the reward, but they only spat and hissed, before setting themselves up in a close formation behind her yaks. They had paid little attention to Herleif.

A good thing too, Kiakra decided. Having to explain him, might be more difficult.

"You see the power of the Pale Wolf," the young Akalen said to her with pride, interrupting her thoughts as a little smile crept onto his face. She ignored him, if he wanted his ego stroked he could go elsewhere. After a moment of silence he flashed her an awkward grin, before resetting his posture and sitting up tall on his huge horse.

Part of her felt rude, but she did not possess the energy for that sort of talk right now. The last few nights getting here had been long and sleepless, and once her anger at Cypher had been spent, she had exhausted herself worrying about the girl. Where had she gone? How would she feed herself? Would she find other people to take her in?

That last thought worried Kiakra in a different way.

Understanding why Cypher had left had taken longer than she was comfortable admitting. Now it was about accepting it, and hoping that she would return. Life seemed very lacking without her. The sharpness of the world had been taken, life had been dulled in her absence, and Kiakra couldn't help but wonder- how much did anything matter any more?

Behind her she heard Herleif cough.

She glanced back at the boy. Behind him the sky was a brilliant sapphire against the golden hills of the steppe, but that same dullness was in his eyes. He too had been numbed in much the same way she had.

He's a fool as well, just like I am, she thought.

Behind him were the deserters, whose blatant terror heavily contrasted against the boy's calm depression. The Akalens were moving closer to their judgement. Their fate was no longer in their hands.

Together the group made their way down the gentle hill and into the camp. Goats and sheep wandered under the shadows of cattle, and under the watchful gaze of older warriors who made sure the food supplies didn't wander too far.

The camp itself was a hive of activity, Akalens walked purposefully down the wide lanes between the ovook, some carrying water, others leading horses or cattle. Young men stood around watching a lot of the work take place, wrestling with each other harder than they worked, trying to make names for themselves in the brief time they had gathered together. A Warchief's call to arms was mainly directed at the men, and so those who didn't have families yet often turned up together, forming big groups of mischievous youths that were obsessed with looking for fights they didn't really want, but that their egos forced them to seek.

Kiakra watched them with a healthy amount of caution.

The ovook she moved between had a good amount of space surrounding them, and outside each there were more Akalen's working. Kiakra saw men mending arrows and crafting spears, whilst others prepared food on wooden boards they lay across their knees, for there was little seating out here. All manner of animals guarded the ovook, dogs on long leather leads paced excitedly around the comparatively slow torku's, leathery, toad like creatures, which mostly just wallowed in the sun, occasionally nipping at their more active companions with huge tusked jaws.

Many homes also had pixie drakins buzzing around them, tied up to long thin pieces of material near the entrances to ward off the mosquitoes. They would do little to stop human or Akalen thieves, but they were very good at keeping the steppes biggest pest at bay.

Kiakra looked down at her bare forearm and flicked away a bloodsucker just before it established itself. She could do with her own pixies.

Perhaps I could braid them into my hair.

The thought made her smile. It was the sort of thing she would have mentioned to Cypher, but Rat was her only companion now, and recently he didn't ever seem to be in the mood for jokes.

Most of the work in this camp was based around the animals these people kept. There were a host of them, all with different roles, and all of which needed feeding and watering. The excrement wasn't too much of a problem, for it went into fuelling fires, though this meant the camp could be smelt almost before it could be seen. The biggest plume of smoke came from a great structure that they were led up to.

Kiakra thought it looked a little like a longhouse, but it wasn't solid. It was made from leather stretched between massive curved wooden stakes, and was open at the bottom so that you could duck inside. Surely that was an effort to transport?

The tall Akalen that had been leading them dismounted. Some of his men followed suit, bundling the deserters off their horses and leading them into the curious structure.

"Wait here please," he said with a little nod, not waiting for Kiakra to answer as he turned away.

She jumped off her horse to stretch her legs. Rat stayed atop his deer, rubbing her neck lazily with a thousand mile stare as the camp moved like wind around him.

My last friend, and after today he will be gone too.

She shivered, and suddenly felt very heavy.

Just then the young warrior ducked out from under the leather house, this time led by a fierce looking woman, who was only a little shorter than him, but twice as thick. Dark red fur covered her body, and two thick bands of blustone hung around her meaty forearms.

All Akalens were warriors in times of war, and though the men made up the bulk of a Warband, many young men brought their wives, leaving children to be watched over by elders. Some women were simply there to transport their homes and to look after livestock, but others took up roles on the battlefield, often used for scouting or raiding.

Looking at her build however, Kiakra guessed this woman was more used to the melee.

"You are Kiakra?" the woman asked quickly.

Her tone wasn't rude, but she wasn't wasting time on niceties.

"I am, yes."

"Good work," the woman said, her face opening up so it was marginally more friendly. She gestured behind her at where the deserters had disappeared, "These ones have caused a lot of trouble, Teoma will be glad to see them found."

The Akalen then untied a small pouch from the silver studded belt around her waist, handing it to Kiakra. She was wise enough not to check it in front of the woman, questioning her honour so openly would likely lead to a fight, and besides, it felt heavy enough.

"The reward is in Ivors," the woman said, referring to the currency of the plains, small ivory coins banded with gold. The message was clear- *Don't expect* their *money.*

"I'm glad my Pack could help," Kiakra said, unbothered and already tired with the small amount of talking she'd had to do today.

"Teoma will speak with you tomorrow, to thank you, but she is busy today," the woman said, unable to apologise for her chief. "You can stay in one of my homes this evening."

Kiakra was taken aback.

"I was not expecting to speak directly to Teoma?" she said carefully as to avoid insult. Though obviously considered a high honour, all she wanted was to be paid and allowed to leave. This was as good as imprisonment for the evening.

"They caused a lot of trouble," the woman repeated, clenching her thick jaw. "They killed people that Teoma cared for, she would like to honour you herself," the woman smiled briefly, flashing bright white teeth. "I have work to attend to, but if you come back here before sundown I will take you in for the night, you'll be alright until then?"

Kiakra was irritated at this turn of events, but there was little she could do. She glanced back over to Herleif, who was watching her speak with the attention of a hovering kestrel.

"Thank you for your hospitality, and yes we'll be fine," she said slowly. "We have our own business to take care of."

***

This was the place he wanted to be in, with the people he wanted to be here with, but the circumstance couldn't be any worse. It seemed whatever choices he made they were always wrong. Anger had lost him his brother, but acceptance had given him a death sentence. He'd tried to turn himself around, and been punished for it.

One moment of clarity cannot undo my wrongs, he thought.

Now that he was here he could count cowardice as another of his flaws, death was scaring him. He knew who he was being taken to. Dagtok would not treat him kindly.

Not for the first time he tried to untie the knots that bound him. When he realised, they were too tight he pulled against them, almost relishing the pain as the rope cut into his forearms. It made him feel as if he were at least trying.

Sat between two ovook on the edge of the camp, he watched the sheep and horses graze under the deep blue of the sky, leaning back against the unmoving wooden post he had been tied to. He could hear the yaks breathing behind him, comfortable now they were no longer bothered by the goats.

He closed his eyes.

He understood why Kiakra had done what she had, he was a danger to her group, he had proved that time and again. There was no blame to be laid at her feet, even though she was walking him to his death. Even Rat, who he had considered one of his closer friends within the group, had not argued with his entrapment. The Kaz had spoken fondly of his home, and Herleif took some comfort from the fact that perhaps his death might provide the little man some lasting happiness.

Even looking on his situation in the best way he could, Tiko's words still haunted him.

Remember, they are only after your coin.

He felt like an idiot, but he could understand it.

During his time as a captive he had taken a step back, and tried to see himself as they had. He'd pulled apart the lies he told himself and looked to the person beneath his rage. The rage that ignored all commands, an anger without a master, that recognised neither friend nor foe, and excused itself as pride.

And under that he had found fear.

Fear of losing those last slithers of love left to him in this world. Now there was nothing more he could do, those embers of care were gone. Fin's fate was up to the Akalens, and his own fate was now sealed by those he had once called his friends.

Amidst failure and pain, he had found calm.

When his eyes opened again the sky was darker, and someone was tapping him on the shoulder. He must have slept.

"You need to eat," said Kiakra, placing a bowl of cold meats and vegetables down next to him.

Herleif tried to ignore his aching stomach, "I wouldn't be wasting food on me anymore," he said, unable to take his eyes off the meal.

Kiakra sat down opposite him, folding her legs up neatly. She moved awkwardly, discomfort in her motion. She leant over to him and pulled at the ropes behind his back. She smelt of smoke and sweat, powerful, not to be embraced.

Herleif felt the ropes go lax behind him. He thought briefly about running, but he knew she could've put a knife in his leg before he made it to his feet. The strength advantage would be his, but she was faster.

Kiakra moved back, sitting up straight.

He didn't move for a moment.

"Eat," she said, acting as though she had done nothing unusual by untying him.

He picked up the bowl and stuffed some salted meat into his mouth, the flavour electrifying his tongue. Only then did he realise how hungry he was. Kiakra waited until he was almost finished and had slowed down the consumption of his food.

"You are free to go," she said quietly.

He turned, hesitant to believe her.

"Why?"

She took a deep breath, "The deserters have paid more than I expected, and apparently Teoma wishes to gift us even more tomorrow. I don't need to keep you."

Coming to terms with his death, and then finding himself free was... strangely anticlimactic. He didn't say anything for a while, and neither did she. She would not speak first, he knew that much, for under her pride was a layer of regret he could sense even from here.

"What did Rat think?" he said finally.

Kiakra shook her head, "I haven't told him yet," she said.

There was a rift between them, and he could tell she was as wary of him as he was of her. She wasn't trying to mend that rift, only to communicate from the other side.

"I would have done the same," Herleif said, looking down at his food, "And I probably wouldn't have let you go."

Kiakra snorted, a little smile lighting up her face, "Don't make me regret my decision."

Herleif returned her smile.

She stood up to leave.

"Was it really just the money?" Herleif said, knowing it wasn't but needing to understand her logic. His own thoughts didn't feel reliable.

The smile slipped from Kiakra's face, and she looked up at the sky, staring at nothing.

"Cypher," she said, and glanced down at her feet, her eyes blank, focusing on somewhere he could not see. "She was right, as usual. I'm not tough enough for this work, and I don't think I want to be."

Herleif had only seen her lose her temper once, and here she was the picture of wisdom, a young woman in a large, bloody world. In his own brief time beyond the village he had fared far worse, with far better odds, and in that moment he realised why her Pack had followed her.

"It's sometimes hard to understand how good intentions can have such bad consequences," he said after a long pause.

She looked him in the eye then, only briefly. Then smiled quickly and walked away.

Herleif went back to his meal, his wrists cold without the burn of the rope.

Chapter 28

Her smile alone was almost enough to rouse his anger, but not quite.

Leave that in the past, don't give her the satisfaction of knowing you are so easily controlled.

Tiko was on the other side of the ovook, head poking through the heavy hide entrance, confident even though she was on her own. He would have enjoyed accusing her of cowardice but, though she had many flaws, he knew that was not one of them.

It was evening, and they had been drinking the strong alcohol of the plains people by the warmth of the fire, a luxury in comparison to Herleifs recent sleeping situation. Lounging in the ovook, he and Kiakra had been listening to the stories of their host, the big woman who had paid Kiakra for the deserters, whilst they waited for Rat to return. Their host was a widow named Lettan who had so far been generous with her space, though Tiko's interruption had blatantly not been appreciated. The big woman was staring at her fellow Akalen with disgust.

Tiko had pretended not to notice the look of loathing, but Herleif was sure it was what had kept her from entering.

Despite her smile he could see the hurt in her eyes when she noticed the scene; her old friend, now lounging with him on the floor, whilst she was barely permitted entry. Though he was attempting to rise above his old failings, he had to force himself not to smile. Her discomfort was a little amusing to him.

"Is it safe, with his restraints off?" she drawled to Kiakra from the entrance, not quite ready to cross that threshold of the ovook.

"What do you want?" Herleif said, standing from his meal.

"Sorry, I didn't mean to let the heat out," she said, ignoring him but sounding quite genuine as she stepped just inside the structure. Lettan bristled from her seat.

"I'd like to speak with your captive," she said, still ignoring Herleif, acting as though he hadn't spoken.

He shifted but Kiakra replied quickly, "He is no longer our prisoner Tiko, you know that. What do you want of Herleif?"

It was unusual having her speak for him, and though he appreciated it, this was between him and Tiko.

"I'll come outside with you," he said before the Akalen had a chance to answer, trying to sound as unthreatening as possible. If there was business between the two of them, he didn't want to bring Kiakra into it.

Tiko stopped then, caught slightly off guard. She dipped her head, and led the way out. Herleif followed, not looking back at the others.

The sun had gone but the dark hadn't quite taken over, and the grey sky promised a starless night. It was cold outside, especially in contrast to the warmth of the ovook, but he did his best not to let his discomfort show.

"I wasn't wrong, was I?" Tiko said, her smile gone as she turned to him. He had forgotten how big the woman was, and the squat ovook to her sides seemed to exaggerate her form further, making her seem taller and darker than she was.

Herleif knew exactly what she meant, "Kiakra released me, I am grateful for that, and it's what I will remember."

"They were happy to bring you to your death, not sure I would forget that," Tiko said plainly, as if talking to friend.

"And they cast you out, yet you're still happy to speak with Kiakra," Herleif replied coolly.

Tiko's mouth twitched into a half snarl, and she regained her composure a moment too late. That had cut deep for her. "I was not cast out, I left, because of you and your stupidity. They just saw it a little later than me.

The only thing that saved you was that brat Cypher leaving."

"What did you want?" Herleif snapped. They could insult each other any time.

Tiko's smile returned at that, and she rested a hand on the blustone club at her belt.

"Kiakra was planning to bring you to Dagtok wasn't she? To be killed?"

Herleif breathed deep again.

"I thought we'd finished with the insults?" he said, but part of him suspected this was the only way she knew how to speak with him. To her, he would never be anything other than the enemy.

"Interesting that stating facts to you is considered insulting," she said, cocking her head to the side with a smug look. "But I have news for you, concerning your brother."

Herleif felt himself suddenly lose his composure. Her friendly expression did not promise good things.

"What news?" he said quickly. There was no point in feigning indifference, Tiko knew his brother was a weakness, no point in trying to hide that fact.

"Well, he arrived in camp a some time ago, turned himself in for some reason, not sure why if I'm honest." She spoke as though she were telling a children's story, "Anyway, I wanted to make sure he wasn't going to feel unwelcome here, he obviously isn't used to our ways."

Herleif didn't understand, how had Fin gotten away from the Akalens in the first place, and why would he hand himself back in if he'd managed to escape?

"You're lying," he said, a statement, but meant as a question.

Tiko shook her head, holding up her long hands.

"No, no, all true," she said innocently. "But I thought it would be best to take your brother to Dagtok, then at least he'd have some human company, and turns out Dagtok appreciated that as well."

Herleif's felt his blood rise.

"When Kiakra turned up with you as her prisoner." Tiko continued, obviously enjoying her talk. "I thought you two might get reunited, but she's messed that up by letting you go free. All I'm doing now is ensuring you find your brother, I'm helping you. You should thank me."

Herleif balled his hands up into such tight fists his nails cut into the skin of his palm.

"Where is he?" he said, shaking.

"Where are *they*," Tiko corrected. "And if you thank me then I'll take you to them."

Herleif looked her dead in the eye. There was no point thinking about what he wanted to do to her, it would do him no good, he might lose, and either way he'd lose any chance of finding Fin.

He glanced behind him at the ovook.

"If you get Kiakra involved then you'll never see him again," Tiko said, all playfulness gone from her voice.

Just after she spoke, he noticed Rat standing in the shadows between the ovook and a cart. Once he saw that he'd been noticed, he stepped forward.

Herleif looked at him with a smile, then turned to Tiko, "Rat has heard everything already, if you don't tell me where my brother is…"

The sentence fizzled out as he noticed Tiko smiling back. Worry began to eat him up as he noticed her smile grow. She'd held all the card's, she just hadn't played them yet. Finally, when she had soaked in all of Herleif's despair, she spoke.

"Who do you think I bumped into earlier? Rat was happy to tell me what had happened, though he seemed disgruntled at the money Kiakra had let go. Half of this was his idea," she said gesturing to the Kaz man.

There was a grim look on Rat's face as she said it, as though he could scarcely own up to his own wrongdoings.

"You'd want to go and see Dagtok anyway, to get your brother back," he said slowly, "It's just this way, I'll still get paid." His voice was hoarse, eyes downcast.

It took a moment for Herleif to believe it, but Rat looked too ashamed for it to be anything other than the truth.

"The Kaz wants to get home!" Tiko laughed, "You can't begrudge him that."

He'd been so close. Eventually he shrugged, consigned to his fate.

"Take me to my brother," Herleif said.

Tiko raised her eyebrows at him, or the patches of skin where her eyebrows would have been, it was hard to differentiate from the rest of her hair. "You've missed something," she said sweetly, "You need to thank me for helping you out."

In that moment Herleif hated her more than he had hated anyone, even Rat seemed like he was about to cut in, before he was silenced by a glance from Tiko.

Herleif took a deep breath.

"Thank you," he said. "Now take me to him."

Her face once again turned dark.

"Follow me."

***

Tiko walked swiftly through the camp, disturbing torku and guard hounds from their restless sleep, and ignoring the drunken warriors that wandered through the darkness. Now was a time to be inside, in the warm, not braving the night. Warriors on watch followed Herleif only with their eyes, for it seem none wanted to bother his guide.

The outskirts of the camp felt oddly exposed when they arrived, Herleif felt vulnerable, as if he was standing on the edge of a great cliff ready to step out onto the air. The animals were mostly rounded up in small pens, a practice only usually carried out in wartime, normally they would be left to roam. This made the edge of the camp that much more barren, and when Tiko stepped out from the shelter of the ovook and into the darkness, Herleif felt a twinge of unease.

He could see what they were headed toward, the only structure out here, hard to see at night because it did not sit on the horizon and therefore was not illuminated by the sky. It looked abandoned from a distance but as they moved further from the camp Herleif noticed a faint glow of light from between gaps in the material.

It was a long walk across the plain, and for a while it seemed as though they had made no progress toward the structure. Rat said nothing as he trailed behind him, and Tiko was similarly quiet up ahead, adding to the coldness of the night.

This might be my final march, thought Herleif, expecting the idea to scare him. Instead he felt nothing, only tired.

When they got nearer he caught the smell of faeces and rotting food. He tried to watch his feet so he didn't step in anything, but it was too dark to see.

Tiko stopped outside the entrance to the ovook, her long cloak fidgeting slightly on the gentle wind as she waited for him and Rat to catch up. Upon first glance the ovook looked much the same as any of the others, but there were slight differences. The canvas covering the outside was different to those in camp, of a lesser quality with obvious damp patches and holes through which the light shone, and the roof was slightly bowed on one side giving it the appearance of an injured beast.

Tiko seemed to be looking at it as well.

"Humans shouldn't live out here," she said, snorting. The build was obviously not up to her standards.

"When I've got Fin back, I'll be happy to leave," Herleif said, not quite managing to decide whether he wanted to say it with venom, or whether he was trying to console her.

She glanced at him, her face a pool of darkness. "I don't think you will," she said.

Before he could answer she called out.

"Cripple! You have guests, will you let us in?" she yelled.

The wind was that much louder when her voice was gone.

"Come in," came the faint call from inside.

Tiko stepped through the opening in one fluid stride, leaving Herleif outside with Rat. The man was shrouded in a thick grey fur cloak, which he was holding closed with one hand.

"I'm sorry," he said, so quietly that Herleif wondered if he had even meant him to hear.

Tiko appeared from the inside of the ovook.

"Come on little soldier," she said, light from inside spilling into the night where it was diluted to blackness.

Herleif followed her in.

Inside, the ovook was bright, and offered respite from the cold night in which Rat waited. Despite that fact, it felt very different to the ovook he had shared with the Kiakra. Back in Lettan's ovook it was a comfortable warmth, and reassuring light. Here the heat of the place clung to him like sweat. It chilled his insides like a sickness, and the light was no more of a comfort, harsh and sinister it promised to illuminate only the things which should be confined to the dark.

There were tattered carpets on the ground, and the skeleton of a pixie drakin was hanging from the ceiling, tied by its neck. A fire was crackling in the centre of the ovook.

In front of the fire was a man. He was sat in a wicker chair covered in blankets, his face bearded and rough, eyes bright and quick, and pinned to Herleif's own.

It was Dagtok, a man he had not seen in months, and whose presence had never brought him joy. Age seemed to have followed him more than evil had, he looked ten years older than he had when Herleif last saw him, and empty somehow, the fire exaggerating his faults.

His face was unreadable.

"The weasel girl failed then?" he said, his voice like gravel.

Herleif had told himself that here he would show no weakness, no fear, but as soon as that voice reached him he once again felt like a child.

"Kiakra has turned soft yes," Tiko replied. "But the last present I delivered you has brought this one here willingly, so there was no need for her."

Dagtok nodded at Tiko, his eyes never leaving Herleif. He reached into his pocket and held out a large leather bag toward Tiko. She snatched it from his hand and opened the contents out into her hand. It was Olvir's, more than Herleif had ever seen.

By present, she had of course meant Fin, and suddenly Herleif caught movement from the corner of his eye.

In the shadows of the ovook, a thin figure, damp with sweat, was lying curled up on his side. He was far too thin to be his brother, and he had no hair. He was just about to speak up when the figure turned, and he caught his brothers face in the firelight, shiny with perspiration. Dull eyes looked at Herleif with no recognition, and his cheeks bones looked ready to cut through the thin skin of his face.

It was indeed his brother.

Herleif was rooted to the spot, he wanted to embrace his brother and take him away from here, back to the warmth of Lettan's hut. But something was stopping him. Some cruel fear that kept him pinned to the spot.

Never should he have seen his brother like this.

His eyes, bloodshot with exhaustion, turned to Dagtok.

The man was still watching him with a face that could not be read. Dagtok glanced at Fin, just for a moment, and Herleif felt a wave of fear crawl through his spine as he did so, wanting to shield his brother from whatever else this man would do. He knew he could not rush however, for if he did Tiko would relish killing him.

And then Dagtok smiled. It was such a small expression, but with it the old man stripped away Herleif's power, and he felt that helpless anger rise in him once again. His hands balled into fists and his jaw clenched.

"What have you done to my brother?" Herleif said, his voice shaking.

Dagtok's smile vanished. "What did you do to my son?" he said.

Suddenly he was back in the forests, in the outskirts, turning away from Hok and trying to ignore that scream.

"I didn't do anything, he tried to kill me," Herleif said.

"And I haven't done anything to your brother," Dagtok replied. "Not speak to him, not feed him, nor water him. I have disciplined him once or twice for trying to steal food, but nothing a boy his age can't handle."

Herleif glanced at Fin again. He looked close to death, and dangerously thin. How long had he been here? How much time did he have left?

"He's coming with me now," Herleif said, a threat more than implied, he was hoping for resistance. He would kill this man. He would *burn* him.

"I don't think she will allow that," he said, gesturing to Tiko who was obliviously counting out her money.

"All there," she muttered when she'd finished. She raised her head and looked side to side at the two humans squaring off against one another. A look of amusement crept onto her face.

"Ah this *is* a treat," she said, revelling in the conflict she was watching.

And in that smile, strangely, Herleif's anger vanished.

He saw clearly in that moment how little his own rage served him, how it only fuelled his enemies.

Looking at Dagtok he saw suddenly a grieving father, past his prime who had travelled across the great Akvast river and into the Akalen steppe in search for revenge. He was no longer the powerful villain Herleif had known as a child, but a pitiful man chasing a peace that he would never find, even if he killed both Herleif and his brother.

His rage abruptly dissipated into nothing, and all he was left with was the concern for his brother, and pity for the man who had hurt him.

His hands relaxed. His jaw unclenched.

"Pain breeds pain," Herleif said slowly. "I challenge you to a Kala'Tam."

"Ha! Ever the angry child, I can see you really have mastered your temper," Tiko laughed, the sarcasm in her words thin, and meant to be cutting. "He has your brother, you are in no position to issue a challenge."

But Herleif wasn't talking to Tiko. He stared at Dagtok and saw anger there, saw that weakness that Herleif knew so well. That weakness that promised strength, the great driver of conflict.

The power Dagtok had over Herleif was gone, and the boy stood tall, feeling the height he now had over this man.

"The challenge is there," Herleif said. "What is your answer?"

Tiko looked unsure now as well, and she looked over at the silent man with confusion on her face. But Herleif knew that rage well enough, and Dagtok's answer was clear even before he spoke.

"I accept," he said slowly, standing. He was a large man, taller than Herleif by half a foot, but his acceptance was a victory.

At least now there is a chance, he thought.

"I will make you *bleed,*" the cripple said.

***

They lit a fire out on the plains some way off from Dagtok's ovook, using dried cow dung for fuel. It took quickly, and, helped by the gentle breeze, it soon became a beacon of flame out in the vast nothingness.

No other torches were lit, but Tiko and Rat stood silently on the edges of where the light fell, watching with dark eyes. Tiko would initiate the combat, but other than that, this was not their business. She'd relish seeing him fall to the other man, but he knew even she was not fool enough to dishonour herself by interfering.

Before him, beyond the flames, stood Dagtok, the last obstacle between him and his brother. The man's leg was crippled yes, but he was monstrous. His torso a twisted mass of muscle and sinew, his arms thick like gnarled branches, as if all the strength lost from his broken limb had been transferred to the rest of his body. Every line in his frame was given depth from the shadows cast by the fire, making it appear as though he was covered in tattoos that would not settle upon his skin.

Herleif breathed deeply, embracing the chill of the night.

I've got one chance, that's it. All or nothing.

They were using knives in this Kala'Tam, a risky thing. He had a thin, reliable steel tool which he held down at his side, whilst Dagtok was brandishing a fat blustone blade the shape of a beech leaf.

Knives meant bloodshed. It was a fast, vicious style of combat, one that was almost guaranteed to injure both fighters, that was if they weren't both killed. Knife fights often ended with dual fatalities, and Herleif knew that, win or lose, he would bleed. To try and avoid that fact might get him killed.

"Let the Sky hold up the honoured," Dagtok said from the other side of the fire, malice in his voice, eager to start the fight.

How long has he been waiting for this?

"And let the earth pull down the wretched," Herleif replied, taking another breath.

One simple plan, and one chance, that was all he had. If he failed, both he and Fin would be dead.

"The Sky watches!" Tiko yelled, some of her enthusiasm spilling out into her words.

Dagtok immediately moved toward Herleif. His hobble was as close as he could get to rushing him, and as unsettling as it was, Herleif followed his plan.

He circled, moving away from the cripple as his opponent tried to get into range, staying away, keeping the fire between them.

"Fight me boy," Dagtok said as he advanced, "Or are you a coward as well as a murderer?"

Herleif felt the old flame in him ignite, a voice that would not tolerate that insult. But he suppressed it, saying nothing as he moved away.

Dagtok stared him in the eyes, "I can see your face boy, you might not admit it, but I know my words are true and so do you."

"It is not true," Herleif muttered, immediately regretting his reply. Now the man knew he had a foothold in his head.

Dagtok smiled then, a sickness on his face, "You killed my boy, I will kill yours."

Control yourself, Herleif thought, focusing on the hard earth beneath his feet and the chill on his back. *You've become better than this.*

"I will speak to you no more," he said quietly, ridding himself of his emotions as he spoke. There was nothing left for him to say to Dagtok.

The older man grit his teeth, almost snarling as again he hobbled toward the boy, "I will kill you, and then wait until your spirit wanders and you become a Demon. Then I will leave your brother out here to be devoured by you, then you will not need to run because he will always be with you!"

It is nought but words, and will never become truth.

Herleif's breath misted in front of him, the warmth of his anger spilling from his lungs and misting harmlessly into the night.

"Fight me you coward!" Dagtok shouted, spittle flying from his mouth.

Herleif didn't reply, moving over the short brown grass away from him.

He didn't know how long the man had been hunting him, but it must have been months. Months of waiting had led to this encounter, months of brewing hate and plotting, and now, so close to his goal, Herleif was denying him the opportunity for his revenge.

As he paced away from the man he stumbled on a rock. For a moment it seemed as though Dagtok would catch up, but at the last moment Herleif hopped away, staying once again out of the range of the knife.

The frustration on Dagtok's face was palpable now. His eyes were hungry and his teeth were bared. He needed combat, but Herleif was not giving it to him.

Not yet at least.

"Fight me!" Dagtok shouted again, and Herleif saw Tiko shift out the corner of his eye. She wanted to see blood as well but to interfere with this would be unthinkable. He forced himself to ignore her and concentrate on the enemy in front of him.

Again, and again Dagtok came at him, and every time Herleif moved away, letting him get closer sometimes, just to feed the man's fury, before twisting off to the side and moving the fire back between them. Always he stayed a healthy distance from Dagok's knife.

The darkness deepened, until those two were the only figures that existed, dancing in the jaws of the night. The moon broke into the sky as the fire died, bringing an eerie grey light through the clouds, which made the world seem like a dream. And still Herleif moved away, listening the insults of the old man, but never replying. Dagtok followed like a starving dog, unable to leave his chase, screaming threats every once in a while, shouting about what he would do to Fin once Herleif was dead, promising all the tortures he could imagine.

Herleif heard every vivid detail, and still would not engage. The threats only made him pity the man.

Dullness became fatigue, fatigue became exhaustion, but still Herleif would not settle.

When the sky began to lighten in the east, the black turning purple for the coming dawn, finally, he made his move.

He stopped, letting Dagtok catch up with him as he had done a hundred times before. The man's anger drove him forward, as it had done a hundred times before, the hope of vengeance too sweet a lure, and like a hundred other times, Herleif sprung back just as he neared.

In that moment the Dagtok's face fell, the same as it always did. He

342

lowered his head to chase again. But Herleif was not running any more. Unlike every other time, he moved forward, putting everything into his attack just as Dagtok lowered his defences.

The big man barely had time to react before Herleif drove his knife into the shoulder of his weapon arm, grabbing the older man's hand as he did so.

There was a look of shock on Dagtok's face, and then in one smooth movement Herleif twisted, dropped his hips, and threw him to the ground. There was a heavy thud as he landed, and the wind was forced from his lungs. His knife was lost during the throw, and so he had no weapon to use when Herleif dropped a knee down onto his chest.

Herleif's blade was embedded in Dagtok's shoulder, right in the dip where the arm meets the collarbone.

"You are beaten," Herleif said, his voice wavering.

The fight had lasted all night, but it was over in an instant.

"I can't feel my arm," Dagtok said calmly, the madness from earlier lost in the shock of the throw. Herleif was shaking, electrified by his own actions, but this wasn't over yet.

"Submit now," he said, his voice quieter than he meant it. "I have won."

"It was a fight to the death," came Tiko's voice from beyond the smoking remains of the fire. She had stood, and in doing so reminded Herleif that she existed. Rat sat by her with a hopeful smile cutting his cheeks, but when he caught Herleif's eye it vanished, and the look of sheepish regret returned.

"If he submits, there does not need to be any death," Herleif said sternly.

She scowled, knowing he was right. Beside her he saw Rat's shape adjust slightly.

Herleif turned away from them and knelt down by Dagtok. His breathing was fast and shallow.

"I can't feel my arm," he said again, his eyes flicking around wildly, but seeing nothing. His voice was still calm.

"Submit," Herleif said quietly, though the words were difficult to speak. Dagtok's threats were still in his head, and though he gave them no weight now, the intent of this man had been made clear many times. Glancing down he saw that the blade had cut deeper than he intended, he himself was covered in the man's blood.

"I will not," Dagtok said between breaths.

Herleif nodded.

"We will both die, the two of us," Dagtok whispered, looking up into the sky with his blank eyes.

Herleif ignored him, waiting until all the blood had run from Dagtok's veins, and he finally ceased to move.

Eventually he stood up and turned back toward Tiko and Rat. She was smiling at him again, and Rat looked like he had seen a ghost, but Herleif didn't care. He walked past them, and the fire, which was long dead.

"Unless you want a demon out on your steppe, I'd burn him," Herleif said, not looking behind him.

His back ached from the fight as he walked, and he was utterly spent from the night's activities, but he was victorious, and that gave him strength.

When he arrived back at the ovook, he went straight in. It was dim inside, but the morning was turning the gloom yellow, opening it up. Fin was asleep, and when Herleif bent down to pick him up, he didn't wake.

He hauled him up onto a shoulder with more ease than he remembered, feeling his brothers bones dig into his shoulders, for Fin was very skinny. He left the ovook without a backwards glance, making his way back toward the camp. As he walked away from the lonely structure Fin began to slip a little on his back, and he tried to readjust his grip. But his left hand had no strength left, and he had to let Fin down onto the grass.

Looking at him now in the light he could see just how close the boy was to death, his face was pale, and his cheeks were sunken. He looked more like a corpse than Dagtok had.

Herleif placed a hand on his chest, and then recoiled. It was damp, there was blood soaked into the tattered jerkin Fin was wearing.

Herleif panicked, checking his brother all over for wounds.

Please no, not now that I have you back.

But there were no wounds, none open anyway.

It was only then that Herleif began to feel an ache in his hand, he turned it palm up and stared at the huge gash that went from the base of his finger to his wrist, blood steadily dripping from the cut and soaking into the earth. What he'd taken to be Dagtok's blood was his own, an injury he must have received during his throw. How had he only now noticed?

"Your, back," said a weak voice next to him.

He looked down and smiled, his eyes tearing. Exhaustion had caught up with him, and this was a moment he had been waiting on for some time.

"I am, yes, and don't worry we'll get you some food," he said, placing a hand on his brother's shoulder. There was no muscle there, just thin bone.

"No… your back," Fin said, with as much force as it seemed he could muster.

Herleif furrowed his brow and twisted his good hand behind his back. There was a sharp pain and his hand came away bloody, and once the pain was noticed, it seemed to grow.

"It's not that bad, come on," he said, trying to pull Fin back onto his shoulders.

But now he couldn't stand up himself, and that pain spread from his back into his core. Dropping to a knee next to his brother he tried to straighten, and found he couldn't. He realised his leggings were soaked with blood at the waist.

He stared up. The sun was almost up now, and the sky was a soft pink. It was quiet, except for the sound of horses galloping in the distance.

He closed his eyes, feeling quite cold.

He'd gotten so far, why now?

"I need a rest," he said finally, finding that breathing deeply now elicited even more pain. "We can go soon, just let me get my breath back." He dropped to his side closing his eyes, and despite the pain, he felt sleep was very close to him.

Eventually a half sleep did take him, his only focus the sound of hooves pounding against the earth. Every step vibrated within him, shaking him.

You did it.

Warmth spread through his bones, from the morning sun, his hand reached out and felt Fin's. It was warm too. He felt himself smile.

And then abruptly the sun was gone.

How long has there been sun?

He cracked his eyes open into a squint and saw a figure leaning over him, silhouetted against the sky, which was now blue.

"Found your brother then?" Kiakra said.

Herleif managed a laugh, and it was worth it, even despite the pain.

Chapter 29

Fin was tense, and for good reason.

The girl, Kiakra, had finally managed to get him a meeting with Teoma, and though his words were true, he couldn't help but feel nervous. She was one of the most powerful Warlords out on the plains, and he had to try and convince her to be meek.

Herleif patted his shoulder as they waited outside her ovook, a sensation he was still getting used to.

"Don't worry," his brother said awkwardly, sensing his unease. It had been a long time since they had spoken, and there were changes in both of them that were still not quite visible.

Fin studied his brothers face with scrutiny, the same way he had done so many times since he had awoken. After being dead for so long, this was taking some getting used to, as would his own lack of hair. He felt naked without it.

"I'm not too bad," he replied, though he knew Herleif could feel him shaking like a leaf. He had always hated seeming weak in front of his brother, that was no different now, except he was forced to accept his help. Despite that, he'd be lying if he said the hand on his shoulder was not a comfort to him.

Dagtok had beaten him often with sticks during his many fitful outbursts of rage, where he had cursed Herleif and mourned the death of his son. During the entirety of his captivity, which had lasted nearly twenty days, Dagtok had also denied him food, and let him drink only a handful of times. When he had finally been given food by the weasel pair, he had thrown most of it back up. He thought he was going to die then and there, but he hadn't been that lucky.

Sores covered his body from long days of lying in the dark, and his eyesight was still a little blurry, but according to the Kazoec man known as Rat, he was recovering well, though it would take some time before he fully regained his strength. Until then he needed help even walking.

He felt like an old man, without any of the wisdom, walking through a heavy surreal world in which the ground swayed, and the dead did not die.

Herleif squeezed his shoulder. "Stay awake," he said with a smile.

Fin nodded, and forced himself to take in his surroundings. He'd had trouble concentrating on anything since he'd woken up, another side effect of starvation.

Teoma's ovook presented itself as something worth staying awake to study. It was three times the size of any he had seen before, with pictures sewn in intricate detail on the outside, depicting some of the histories of the people of the steppe. Creatures he had never seen before were ridden by the Akalens as they battled against strange, dark shapes, some of which looked human, others of which did not. In other pictures there were celebrations where people cheered around isolated wrestlers, and Fin couldn't tell whether they were meant to be friends or foes. Still more showed great gatherings in tall halls, structures Fin did not know the Akalens even knew how to build, whilst outside small people played games on horseback. Almost all the pictures had livestock featured in them. They weren't a people that would forget to honour their way of life.

"Look there," said Herleif, noticing Fin's eye and pointing at a picture showing a tiny Akalen cutting the throat of some huge creature. "Aldrid told me about this, that's Gera the giant, and the man cutting his throat is Toman. They say that when Gera fell, his body created the world, his hairy arms created the mountains in the north and south, his feet stuck up making up the mountains in the east, and his massive stomach became the steppe."

Surprisingly, despite being on the outside of the grand ovook and open to the harsh elements of the steppe, many of the colours still looked vivid and bright. Fin suspected they were regularly repaired.

"I suppose his head became the Kingdom then?" he said, taken in by the tale.

Herleif nodded, "Yes, and they say the Akvast is the blood from his throat, which still runs to this day. Meaning he is yet to die…" His words trailed off and he gave Fin a look of mock terror.

Fin smiled, but it didn't quite reach his eyes. He hadn't expected to ever hear another of his brother's stories.

In front of a large battle depiction that seemed to have the door to the ovook as its centre, stood two real Akalen guards, holding long spears tipped with blustone heads. Both were huge, even for their kind, towering over Herleif by more than a head, and Fin by even more than that.

Neither were wearing any bands of silver, or any other type of jewellery. This was significant because every other Akalen Fin had seen wore at least some item designed to indicate their level of wealth, be it necklaces, bands around the arm, or studded belts. But these two were bare chested and wore only plain leather belts over long, plain trousers.

As Fin was studying these men, the door swung open and another Akalen pushed his way out of the ovook. Fin hadn't seen his face in a long time, but he recognised it immediately, even without the antlered headdress he had worn when they last met.

It was Chief Aska, the man who had ordered Herleif killed all that time ago.

Fin tensed up, but Herleif's hand on his shoulder stayed heavy, the message clear.

Leave it.

Aska stared at Fin with furrowed brows, and then at Herleif with a similar expression. He was blocking the entrance to the ovook.

"I remember you two," he said, plainly, and then with some infliction in his voice, "You're alive?" He sounded neither relieved nor disappointed.

"Yes, we are," Fin snapped before Herleif had a chance to speak.
No thanks to you.

Aska's expression did not change, "You have information for Teoma?"

"Yes," Fin said again, trying his best not to look as weak as he felt, though he could feel the loose skin around his cheeks.

Aska nodded, "Good, this conflict has taken too many." With that he walked away, his long cloak swaying behind him, leaving Fin even more confused, though slightly less angry.

"Strange," was all Herleif contributed, and then he gave him a gentle push in the back. "Time to go."

One of the warriors was holding open the entrance for Fin. He straightened his back, kept his head up, and walked inside.

Smell hit him first, and then smoke burned at his eyes. This was nothing new, for most ovook were smoky, the difference here was that the smoke came from long sticks of incense which smelt strongly of substances Fin had trouble placing. None were unpleasant scents, far nicer than the aroma of cow dung which the Akalens usually used to make their fires. No, this was soothing, albeit strange.

The inside of the ovook was similar to the outside, covered in tapestried stories to hide the latticework. There was a little fire in the corner, many candles, and a huge wooden bed against the edge of one wall, sheeted with silk. Thick patterned carpets covered the floor, and huge cushions on top of those surrounded a low table that had a map of all the known world spread out over it. At the head of the table was a large low seat, made of heavy, bare oak.

Fin saw all this in his peripheral, and it barely registered. His focus was taken up completely by the massive creature lying to the side of the chair.

He felt his brother stop behind him, frozen.

"Is that…" Herleif whispered, unable to quite get the word out.

"A Khutaen," Fin breathed, for its deep blue eyes were fixed on him, and speaking was more than a little difficult.

Its feathers were a dark mottled grey, a colour that it would shed in winter once again for its white coat. It looked to be slightly bigger than the one Fin had seen at the end of winter, and seeing a creature like this inside only seemed to exaggerate its massive size.

"Almost as interested in you as I am," came a voice from the creature, and for a moment Fin thought it was speaking to him. Then he noticed the Akalen woman who had been standing just off to the side of the Khutaen, in the shadows, watching him with the same intense gaze.

"I assume you're Fin?" she continued. Her voice was rough with age, but she spoke softer than silk. The Khutaen seemed not to bother her in the slightest.

Fin nodded quickly, and it made his head hurt.

She inclined her head very slightly, gesturing to Herleif, "Then he needs to go, I was to be speaking with Fin."

There was no question in her voice.

Herleif glanced at her, then at him.

"I'll be okay," Fin said, trying to believe it.

His brother nodded, "I'll be just outside."

Again, he glanced at the woman, and then slowly made his way out of the ovook.

Without Herleif it was very quiet, only the crackling fire and the massive breaths of the Khutaen Drakin.

The woman stepped out from the shadows, but to call her movement walking would have been an insult. She moved like a leopard, soft and calculated, fully aware of every minute movement in her limbs, as she prowled into a lighter part of the ovook.

Her fur was white like broken waves, not dirty, but not quite pure either. Her face was strong and open, with a cutting jaw, and her bright eyes betrayed a fierce intelligence behind them. They were a grey blue that shone out at Fin, changing hue with the light as she turned her head. The only items of clothing she wore were patterned turquoise trousers and a gilded cloth that fell from her groin to her knees. Her feet were bare, and, like the warriors that guarded her home, she wore no jewellery of any kind.

But even without riches draped over her body, there was no doubt in Fin's mind that this was the Warlord Teoma, the Pale Wolf who patrolled the great Akalen steppe.

"Come into the light," she said. The tone was friendly, but it was a command.

Fin took a few paces forward, feeling even more stupid and clumsy than usual after seeing her graceful actions.

"I heard what happened to you," she said, looking him up and down. "I would like to apologise to you for that treatment, of which I was not aware. Please, sit."

She sounded sincere, and angry, and she didn't try to hide it.

Fin mumbled a thanks and lowered himself onto one of the cushions with some difficulty, leaning on his arms heavily like an old man. Teoma effortlessly folded herself down onto a cushion opposite him, leaving the chair at the end free. There was no need for it anyway, her power was obvious, she did not need a throne to prove it.

She stared at him for a long time with her bright eyes, which were grey in this light, mirroring the Khutaen that was led in the corner.

"I hear you killed some of my people," she said finally.

Fin paused, and then nodded, keeping his eyes down. His raid with brother and Brynjar had seemed so long ago, and surely she wouldn't have invited him here if she just planned to kill him? No, she was getting his measure.

"Innocents among my people," she said, her tone neither hostile nor familiar.

"I did, yes," Fin said. "But at the time I believed you were my enemy, and I believed them to be warriors."

"And now?" Her tone was the same.

"Now I understand that you are not my enemy."

She cocked her head to one side, a deliberate motion, "And how did you come to that conclusion?"

Fin breathed deeply and then told her of the battle he had seen with Brynjar, of his encounter with Gulbrand, how the troops had been manipulated and what the Lord of Yilland planned to do. All the time he was talking she waited patiently, interrupting only to make confirmations of things Fin had said too quickly, or mumbled through. It took a lot of effort on his part to stay on track, his story was long, and a few times he forgot what he was saying or why he had mentioned certain details, but Teoma seemed to understand his condition and possessed almost an endless amount of patience.

"He has blamed you for crimes he himself has committed against his own people, to make them hate you," said Fin, trying to summarise. "And when the other Lords listen to that hate then they will march on you."

Teoma nodded gently, taking it all in.

"I would usually be hesitant to believe you, and I still am," she said. "But what you say…" she paused, "It makes sense."

She paused again, and Fin understood that this was not the time to speak.

"So, my next question is, why tell me this?"

Fin had been expecting this question, and had his words ready. "Because your people are innocent. And because the soldiers on the other side of the river are innocent. No one deserves to die, and there is no reason to fight."

The Pale Wolf laughed quietly to herself and leant back on her cushion, the picture of confidence. She exuded control in everything she did. Nothing was an accident.

"Maybe my people would enjoy a fight? You say all are innocent and yet *my* people have been attacked by *your* people. Have been killed by *your* people. We are the only innocent party here."

Fin swallowed, "Would you convict your people of crimes they didn't know they had committed? I was part of one of those attacks, because Gulbrand told me you were my enemy, he is the only guilty one here."

Teoma smiled into her cheek, "You speak well, I can understand your motivations. But what would you have me do?"

"Continue to do nothing," Fin said, confidence finding him finally. "Take you people away from the border, demonstrate that you are not a threat, then they cannot start a war. Gulbrand will not cross the river if he has no target, and he cannot blame you for the attacks in his lands if you are a hundred miles away."

The Warchief's face turned hard and she leant forward, pulling him away from his body with those blue eyes.

"I have gathered all my warriors to me. It has taken a long time, but finally they are all here. We are powerful enough to attack Yilland in the next few days, and your suggestion is meekness? To surrender my lands and hope they do not continue to terrorize my people?"

Attack in the next few days? Fin had no idea that they were on the verge of assault, this war was even closer than he had realised.

"You think my warriors would follow me if that was my course of action?" Teoma said, peering at the boy.

Fin unconsciously moved back, worried that he had overstepped, and nervous now that he had made himself the only obstacle in the way of Teoma's plans.

"Well y-yes," he stammered, "In a way. Only for a few months or so, that way they won't cross into your lands, I promise you that. Gulbrand's only support comes from fear. If there is no fear, then there is no conflict."

The Warlord said nothing.

"Disengage," Fin said, trying to sound as sincere as he could, "This fight is avoidable."

Teoma looked at him for a while and said nothing.

Instead the Khutaen in the corner began to move. It stood, slowly, demonstrating its size and weight as it did, the muscle in its shoulders rippling under the feathers. Its eyes stayed on Fin, seemingly fixed in place as it slunk over.

He had been this close to a Khutaen before, but he'd forgotten how humbling it was.

It towered over him, completely filling his space, darkening the ovook with its size until Fin could only make out its piercing eyes. Eyes that were remnants of something ancient. Fin was acutely aware of the multitude of ways the creature could kill him as he tried to keep himself composed.

Abruptly it pushed him back with one huge paw, splaying his bony form onto the ground and putting a small amount of its weight onto Fin's chest. Even using only a fraction of its mass, the paw was heavy enough that he couldn't breathe.

He couldn't even cough.

For some reason he looked to Teoma for help, but she was not watching him. She stared at the Khutaen like a child staring into the eddies of a river, searching obsessively for some meaning in its actions. There was no worry in her face. If it killed Fin, then it was meant to be.

Moisture from the creature's breath soaked his cheeks, vapour turning to beads of water that clung to his skin, but he could barely feel it. His vision was spotting, white flecks swam across his eyes. Something sharp cut into his cheek.

He tried to speak but no sound came.

And then it was gone. All at once the weight lifted and he was free, coughing violently on the floor and shivering as the moisture from its breath cooled on his face.

When his vision returned the creature was lying back where it had been, now with its eyes closed as though nothing had happened.

Fin sat up and felt his chest. No ribs were cracked, and he could move okay, his vision was also undamaged. He put a hand up to his face and found he was bleeding from his cheek. The cut stung, but it was so shallow, he couldn't believe a Khutaen could have made such a delicate incision.

Teoma was watching him from her pillow like a snake watches a mouse. She still hadn't moved.

"What," Fin said, struggling to form any words. "What was that?"

Teoma looked away, over toward her massive companion.

"Khutaen are sacred to us," she said quietly. "This one came to me of its own will, and when it did, I became the Pale Wolf. They speak to us in ways we understand, but that we do not *know*."

She looked back over at Fin, and there was the slightest hint of vulnerability in her eyes, the first he had seen.

"They are the only creatures that can draw power from their own spirit, for they are powerful beyond knowing. To ignore the Khutaen is to ignore storms and wildfire."

Fin didn't know exactly what she meant, but he felt as though somehow the creature had helped him.

"What will you do?" he said slowly.

The Pale Wolf lifted her chin, "I will remain here. My people are returning from the border anyway. I would like to attack Yilland, but it seems as though he trusts you," she gestured at the Khutaen. "And we must listen when he speaks. That will be good enough reason for even the keenest of my warriors."

"That's good to hear," Fin said, smiling weakly.

"You promised me that no army would cross the Akvast," she said with a voice of iron. "I will trust you and hold off my attack. However, if anything other than messengers cross that river, innocent or not, the sky will blacken from the smoke of their corpses."

Fin looked into her eyes and once again saw the power there, both as a warrior, and as a leader. He did not doubt her words for a moment.

***

Summer was here in full force.

356

Ojak studied the valleys of Yilland with worried eyes. Fields of crop stretched over the hills, light cutting through the vegetation, injecting the leaves with colour. The land was scarred with stone walls and hedgerows, forests filling the spaces that were not taken up with growing grain or grazing livestock. In his time stationed here Ojak had come to love this land, and he felt uneasy leaving it.

Exploration was their mandate. To try and work out what the enemy wanted, what their goals were, how many exactly were willing to fight against them. Ojak was smart enough to understand this was a lie told to the troops. They were looking for a fight, and he knew that Alvard, and perhaps Gulbrand, wanted one.

It would have been a lie to say he didn't want one as well, but he was sensible enough to realise that they would be outmatched in a battle taking place in a land they did not know, especially with a smaller, inexperienced force such as theirs.

Gulbrand had tried to convince Alvard to call his banners, the force in Rukland would have amounted to almost twenty thousand men, but the great Lord would not exercise patience after the death of his son. To get words to his bannermen would take days, and then days again after that for them to muster.

It might be a month before they arrived, and he needed vengeance sooner than that. This was not time that Alvard was willing to waste, he would bring the several hundred he had come here with, and no more.

Ojak had watched this conversation and had expected Gulbrand to refuse.

Moving out into enemy territory with a force of only a couple of thousand men would be suicide. Last he'd heard the Pale Wolf had more than eight thousand warriors. More were flooding to join her cause, and that was before even considering the terrain, or the experience of her fighters. Out there on the lonely steppe, she would know the land, as well as having the advantage of mobility and numbers.

At first Ojak had been correct, and Gulbrand had refused to move out, telling Alvard that they would be destroyed by the Warband, trying to make him reconsider.

But after only a little persuasion, Gulbrand gave in.

Ojak thought again on that, for the tenth time today. Why had he agreed? Alvard was blinded by grief, he was in no position to lead an attack on the Akalens. None of them were, and yet, today the camp which had been their home for so many months, had been nearly abandoned. Gulbrand had ceded his own men for a reason Ojak still could not understand.

He knew Brynjar deserved justice, and he was, after Alvard, probably the most eager to deal out that justice.

But at what cost?

He turned away from the valleys of Yilland, and instead watched the marching of the soldiers, their bright banners of green and purple snapping in the wind. Colourful gambesons reflecting their excitement at the prospect of battle, contrasting with the barren plains they were advancing across.

That same excitement coursed through him, but he did not ignore the worry that accompanied it.

Chapter 30

Herleif woke before the others. In the dim morning light, he was barely able to tell the bodies of Kiakra and Fin from the bags of supplies they kept in the ovook. Only tufts of unruly hair indicated that people were sleeping. Lettan the widow, knowing that their stay had been prolonged, had provided them with their own ovook, one that her children had once used. It was small, and a little musty, but they had been grateful for it nonetheless.

He shivered and pulled his leggings and a tunic on, looking over at his brother, whose face was so alien to him still. The little cut on his cheek showed up vividly against the pale skin of his face, but it wasn't that, nor was it the sunken cheeks and dulled eyes that made his brother seem so different.

Standing, he adjusted his belt, and then made his way outside, finding a seat on the edge of an empty cart. His back was stiff, and he was still awkward on his feet. Wounds received from Dagtok had cut him deep, and would take some time to heal.

The morning was beautiful, clouds high in the sky seemed to catch the sunlight before the sun even showed itself, and that gentle light seemed to reflect off the dewy spiderwebs that had been spun in the grass.

But Herleif didn't really *feel* it. He felt aimless, and out in this vast place, that lack of direction was inescapable.

Fin looked different because he was no longer the boy Herleif had grown up with. Life had caught up with him, and in Herleif's absence he had grown in confidence, so much that now, Herleif felt useless. Despite his fight with Dagtok to free his brother, Herleif no longer felt like the protector he once was. He had lost his anger, and his reason for it, and he found himself wondering what was left.

Is that all I was? All I am?

Kiakra emerged from the ovook then, hair frizzed by the night and her eyes puffy from sleep. It was strange not seeing her hair neatly on top of her head.

"You're up early," she croaked, her voice harsh from sleep.

"I wanted to see the sun rise," Herleif said, gesturing to the fist ray of golden light breaking over the sweeping hills.

She wandered over, glared at him, then hopped up next to him on the cart.

Her presence was oddly comforting, her leg touched his gently and that small contact he was grateful for.

"I know that look," she said, rubbing her eyes.

She looked at him for a while, while he avoided her eyes.

Eventually she spoke up, "You know a while back it was just me, Aldrid and Cypher in the Pack? Anyway few years ago, we tracked this young Kazoec man down, accused of murder he was. I was on my own for jobs back then, Cypher was our healer, Aldrid found us jobs, made sure we didn't get ripped off, but I was the one actually taking our targets down. Took us weeks to find him, but when we did he tried to run. I shot him, and usually my aim's pretty good. Wasn't that time though. Didn't mean to, but I killed him outright."

She shook her head, snorting, "We went back to Stemtrad, got our reward anyway. Then a few days later and we got another contract, for the actual killer. Apparently, the guy I'd killed had been wrongly accused." Kiakra looked down, "Cypher wanted to talk about it, but I never did. I always avoided that conversation."

Herleif had no idea what this had to do with anything, but he'd never heard her speak so openly. He looked sideways at her, "Any idea why?"

She shrugged, "I didn't want to think about it, I just kept moving. On to the next job, and on and on, long as I had Cypher with me and a job to do, I was fine. I think maybe that was why she left, to get me to stop and actually think about what I was doing for once."

She yawned deeply, and then continued, "I've stopped. And I'm thinking about what my place in the world is." She grinned at him then, "And I think you have as well."

Herleif nodded slowly. He was aware that Cypher filled the same space for Kiakra that Fin had done for him. Perhaps by filling that empty space with a person, they had been treating merely the symptom of a larger problem.

"Maybe you're right," he muttered, and then, feeling guilty that he hadn't offered his own thoughts said, "She will come back, but maybe you need to know how to survive without her first?"

Kiakra snorted again, "Maybe. Or maybe she just went to sulk because she was worried I was gonna let you get axed."

She winked at him, and despite feeling a little foolish, Herleif smirked.

"Far too soon for jokes like that…" he said, his voice trailing off as Kiakra's face dropped.

He turned to follow her gaze, and saw a large group of warriors approaching, all in full battle dress.

"What do these lot want," she muttered.

A big man with copper brown fur and a lion's pelt slung across his shoulders addressed Herleif.

"The human, Fin, is he here?" the man said quickly.

Herleif stood up and glanced at the ovook, "What do you want with him?"

The big man pointed at Herleif and two warriors set upon him, pinning his arms behind his back and holding him tight, locking his elbows so he was forced to stand on tiptoe. Herleif put up little resistance, he didn't want to get Fin into any more trouble than he was already in. Whatever that trouble was.

The big man stepped easily into the ovook and emerged a moment later dragging Fin by the arm. He had only managed to get his leggings on and he looked very small next to the large warrior.

"I'm coming with you," Fin was saying over and over, trying to placate the big man.

"What are you doing?" Herleif interrupted, keeping his voice as level as he could, trying not to argue in case he made the situation worse. Something was very wrong.

The big man held Fin as another tied his hands behind his back.

"The boy assured the Pale Wolf there would be no aggression from the humans," the Akalen said, aggressively pushing Fin up onto a horse. "There are men marching on camp as we speak, this one is a liar."

Herleif began to struggle a little more, "Please where is he going?"

Not again.

The big man sighed as if it was obvious, "To the Pale Wolf. She will decide what to do with him."

***

Fin had never seen so many bodies.

Horses and men, stretched out over the landscape, covering it like a plague, throwing up dust wherever they went. There was seemingly no order to it, only a chaos of warriors screaming and chanting, holding their spears and colours high. This was a Warband, and it was a terrifying sight.

And at the head of it all was this woman.

Teoma looked very different to how she had yesterday. Atop a huge white horse, her face was painted with solid black lines, two running from her eyes to her cheeks and one running from the lip to the chin. *Two tears for the dead and saliva down the chin in hunger for the enemy.*

The Nomads did something similar for battle.

She wore a cloak of wolf pelts, and bands of gold and silver ran from her wrist up to her elbows, with two isolated bands of blustone on the upper arm. A necklace of boar tusks, some longer than Fin's hand, hung on her chest alongside a necklace of seashells and ivory figures. In her hand was a seven foot long spear that she wielded as if it had no weight, and at her belt was a short sword of blustone, something Fin had never seen.

But by far the most distinguishing feature was her headdress. White feathers had been braided into the hair on her head, and fell down past her shoulders like hair, and on the back of her head, framing her stern face, was a plume of peacock feathers that stuck straight up and out.

She would be unmissable on the battlefield.

As Fin was led up to her he felt the contrast couldn't be greater. He was short, pale and weak, bones sticking out of him like a leather bag full of sticks.

She was watching the horizon when Fin was thrown down in front of her horse, and her eyes didn't move as she spoke to him.

"Two days ago, you made me a promise," she said quietly, and somehow softening her voice made it all the more terrible. "I withdrew my people, and you told me no one would cross that river."

He fumbled for words, "I didn't think they could. H-he doesn't have the men… I told you the truth, I *promise*. He doesn't have the men..." he trailed off, as suddenly an answer presented itself.

He almost recoiled as the realisation hit him. He spent a few moments searching for alternatives, but none came to him. There could be no other reason why Gulbrand had ventured out here with so few men.

He was going to lose.

He would throw his petty army into the jaws of the Pale Wolf. Such a loss would destroy him as a Lord, but he had made sacrifices before. It would be too great a loss for King Olvadr to ignore, but not so crippling that he would risk the fate of the Kingdom as a whole. Olvaldr would be forced into calling his banners against the Akalens, or else risk looking weak.

Fin kept hoping he was wrong, but there was no other explanation he could think of. And even if he was wrong, and Gulbrand genuinely thought he could win this fight, the outcome would be the same.

Teoma's only counter would be to flee, and betting against that was as close to a sure thing as there could be.

"You see that dust over there?" Teoma said finally, holding her spear perfectly level and using it to point at the horizon.

Fin nodded, he could see a cloud that had been kicked up by movement, though he couldn't see any actual troops.

"My scouts tell me behind that cloud is a host of nearly two thousand soldiers. They are carrying banners and sounding trumpets, on the lands of *my* people," she said beating her chest with her free hand. There was nothing but contempt in her voice.

"And you told me," she went on, "That they would not cross. You *promised* it."

She turned and looked at him for the first time. Her eyes were depthless, unforgiving.

Fin shivered, thinking hard on what to say. He knew what it was, but he couldn't bring himself to say it.

The Pale Wolf stared down at him, "Perhaps you are a spy, like my Chiefs say."

Fin breathed in against the cold that squeezed his chest. He was freezing, even in the morning sun.

"I am no spy, and I know why they have crossed," he said, sounding as confident as he could.

Teoma bared her teeth at him, "Why?" she hissed.

"He does not plan to win," Fin said, and he caught the subtle intrigue on her face. He had her attention, if only for a moment.

"If you destroy his army here today, he will have proved you are the threat he has made you out to be. King Olvaldr will call his banners, and instead of fighting two thousand men you will be at war with the entire Kingdom."

She returned her eyes to the horizon, "If that is true, then what would you have me do?"

Fin knew this would be the hard part. He glanced left and right at the warriors surrounding her, other Chiefs and elders, all ready for battle and eager for blood.

He took a deep breath.

"Run," he said. "If you run, they cannot catch you. There will be no fight. You will have proved that you are not a threat and Olvaldr will not call his banners. Leave now and you will rob Gulbrand of his war."

"If you lose," Fin said, trying to sound as sincere as he could, "Then Gulbrand has proved himself a competent commander worthy of support, and if you win, then he has proved that you are a serious threat that needs to be dealt with. Either way he gets his war."

Fin paused for a moment, for there had been no reaction from Teoma, but her Chiefs were almost snarling with rage.

Ignore them, she is your target, they will listen to her.

"If you attack him now, then even in victory he will defeat you," Fin said, putting as much weight on the words as he could.

Teoma kept her eyes high, fixed on the hills of her land.

"Run from the border," she said quietly. "Run from your camp. Run from the steppe. Run from the land and swim out into the ocean. Maybe there we will find peace." She turned and looked at him, "If I run now, where will it end?"

Fin winced, closing his eyes.

"Put him on a horse," Teoma said, looking away. "We will send him home."

***

It was midday before Gulbrand's force arrived. Fin watched them from up on the smooth ridge, only a few hundred feet from Teoma herself.

The host was large, and would have seemed impressive had he not seen the Akalen Warband that stretched out behind him, hidden by the hill he was looking out from. He knew that most of Gulbrands host had never seen action, but the Akalen army was made up of many seasoned warriors, and even the more fresh among them were eager to prove themselves.

He glanced behind him. Earlier they had been a hive of activity, rushing around the land outside the camp in a random, hurried fashion, but now the warriors were deathly still. Each one was dressed as extravagantly as a king or queen, and they seemed to hold themselves as such.

Over the next hill Fin could hear soldiers murmuring and moving even from here, but Teoma's army was silent. Poised like a snake.

If it came to a fight, he did not think it would last long.

He squinted over at the Warlord. She had barely moved since their talk, watching the approaching army with a stoic confidence that was indicative of nearly all good leaders in a time of crisis. Despite his frustration with her, Fin couldn't help but respect the woman, and he could see why so many others did as well.

He shivered, grateful for the summer sun and the cloudless sky. The morning had been freezing for him, and it was still cold now, especially as he was still without a shirt, but the sun had at least kept his fingers from going numb. If he somehow survived this, his first priority was to put some fat on.

Turning his gaze back to the crest of the hill across from them, Fin waited. As he watched, a line of men on foot began to appear over the brow, and then another.

And another.

It wasn't long until the entire army was in view, moving down the hill and crossing the flat plain toward the Akalen position. Fin could see that, in contrast to the hugely mobile Akalen Warband, the force Gulbrand had brought to the field was mostly foot soldiers. He could see cavalry on the flanks of the army, wearing the purple colours of Rukland, but there were far too few of them to make a difference. The vast majority of the army was made up of skinny, disorganised young men, representing their homeland in the

Yilland green.

Green boys in green coats.

He hoped they would flee the field before there were too many losses. In that moment, watching the shabby, rough lines of young lads, Fin discovered a new hatred for Gulbrand. These men were doomed. This was not his sacrifice to make.

They gradually came to a stop in the middle of the plain, different parts of the lines stopping at different times so that the by the time they finally had halted, most were out of position. Fin heard yells, and the lines began to straighten up a little, tweaking here and there until they resembled lines again. During this time Teoma did not move, the Pale Wolf sat atop her horse and waited, unreadable.

After some time, he saw a small group of figures on horseback ride out from the enemy army, stopping midway between where they had come from, and the hill where Teoma and her chiefs were sat.

Abruptly an Akalen man grabbed the reigns of Fin's horse and began walking him over to Teoma. She didn't look at him as he was approaching, and when he got to her, the man who had been leading his horse handed the reigns over to one of her chiefs.

It was Aska, his stag horn headdress standing tall on his head.

Fin stared at him for a moment, but Aska would not meet his gaze. The man looked ready for battle, but still wore that same woeful expression on his face.

In front of them Teoma muttered something to an impressive looking man wearing a lion's pelt and they began to trot down the hill.

Aska followed, leading Fin's horse.

He suddenly felt very exposed. As a prisoner amongst strangers he had only been bothered about the cold, but now he was going to be in the presence of familiar faces. He wished he had a shirt, or cloak, or anything to hide himself in.

The hill was steep, and Fin had to lean back so far on his horse that his lower back touched its flank, it would be a difficult fight up there for Gulbrands men.

When they reached the other group, Fin recognised three of them instantly.

His heart began to quicken.

In front was Gulbrand, and flanking him were Lord Alvard and Captain Egil. All were staring at Fin, two of them with utter hatred. There were two generals behind them, and several Rukland soldiers to the sides of the men. They looked extremely agitated, and Fin guessed this was their first time seeing Akalens face to face.

Trust that fear, retreat.

Teoma stopped a few feet away from Gulbrand. Her group of chiefs was slightly smaller, but utterly outmatched the other group with its confidence.

"You have brought an army to my lands," she said, breaking the silence. "Go home and I might not destroy it."

They were aggressive words, but she was giving them a way out, something Fin had not expected. Alvard looked expectantly at Gulbrand, a little nervousness showing, perhaps worried that the other Lord might take the offer.

But Gulbrand's bearded face was dark.

"I think not, you have too much to answer for. Too much of my people's blood on your hands," he said slowly.

Teoma raised her chin, looking down on the men, "We have nothing to answer for, and no blood on our hands that was not caused by you."

"Liar," growled Alvard. "You let your warriors run wild in Yilland. You killed my son… I don't even have his body to mourn!"

His eyes were red and pained, and he looked half mad from grief.

"This is a false accusation," Teoma spat. "I do not lie. None of us have passed into your lands."

She then addressed Gulbrand, "What else do you have to say? Or will your last words be gibberish and lies?"

Alvard's hand went to the pommel of his sword but Gulbrand stopped him with a little motion of his hand. Fin was amazed how much the power dynamic had changed. Last time he had seen these two, Gulbrand had been almost grovelling at the feet of Alvard, asking for troops. Now he was acting like the other man's commander.

"We came to accept your terms of surrender," Gulbrand said. "If you come with us now, and accept your execution, we will take only the land this far east of the river."

Teoma outright laughed. Even Fin knew how ridiculous that sounded, but it wasn't an offer Gulbrand wanted her to take, and so it served its purpose.

"I am done speaking to you," the Pale Wolf said smiling. "Take your spy and think of the home you left behind, because you'll never see it again."

Then she gestured to Fin, "This one is yours. He will die with you."

Inwardly Fin was screaming at her to retreat, and at Alvard to use his head. But he knew that now their honour had been put on the line.

With those words she turned and rode away, back up the slope to her army. Her chiefs all followed, Aska dropping the reigns of Fin's horse, leaving him to the Lords of the Kingdom.

Egil kicked his horse toward Fin, and Alvard watched him, shaking his head.

He knew he had to try and talk to the Lord, there was nothing else he could do. Gulbrand would have filled his head with lies, but even so, he had to try.

"Please my Lord," Fin begged, staring at Alvard, "Gulbrand wants this, he has set this up. He means for you all to die. His men killed your son! The Akalens have never crossed the Akva-"

Egil got alongside him and interrupted his words with a smack across the face with his mailed glove. The force of the blow knocked Fin from his horse, and with his arms tied he had no way to break the fall, landing heavily on his back. He coughed and squirmed, trying to catch the breath which had been knocked out of him.

"How is it you survived the attack that killed his son? I know you helped them somehow, you were working with them!" Egil shouted. "My men died in that fight!"

For a moment he was puzzled, but then he realised what Egil was trying to do, he just hoped Alvard was smart enough to see through it.

"No… I wasn't," Fin groaned. He felt something hard and sharp dig into his ribs underneath him. He was about to roll over before he realised what it was. Awkwardly he squirmed his way up so that his hands could grab it.

He heard a blade being pulled from its scabbard and looked up. Egil was on foot now, holding his sword down by his side, looking over Fin.

"Brynjar trusted you and you let him die," Egil hissed, his act believable enough to make Fin question himself.

The Captain looked down at Fin but addressed Alvard, "It would be my pleasure to end his life now for you my Lord."

Fin caught Gulbrands eager expression.

Please no, just a little longer, he begged Alvard silently.

"Not now," Alvard said with something other than hate on his face. He looked weary,

perhaps Fin had managed to make him doubt Gulbrand just enough.

"We need some solidarity the men right now. We will execute him formally on our return, after a trial. Anyway, I'd like to hear how he defends himself," he muttered.

Fin could see Egil grit his teeth, and over on his horse Gulbrand took a deep breath.

"As you wish," Egil said carefully, the words struggling to get past his teeth.

He hauled Fin up onto his horse. Alvard turned away from him, his eyes not meeting anyone else's.

"Let's get back into formation, we don't want to be out here when they attack," Gulbrand said, as he wheeled his horse around.

Then Fin was moving, heading back into the arms of his enemies.

He could still stop this battle. There was a chance, a flicker of doubt he had seen on Alvard's face, and that was all he needed. Gulbrand wouldn't let him speak to the Lord of Rukland, but maybe Fin wouldn't need his permission. He had only one chance, and he held it tightly in his hand.

A little flint rock digging into the rope at his wrists.

Chapter 31

"I need to get to Fin," Herleif muttered.

Kiakra looked sideways at him. This was the third time he'd said that, and it was becoming irritating.

"Well you can't," she said, attempting a reassuring tone, and failing. Reassurance had never been her strong suit. "That's a battlefield now, anything that goes toward either of those armies is going to get destroyed."

Herleif shifted uncomfortably, worry written across his face. She sighed and looked behind her at their escort, three young Akalens. Two men and one woman, all looking equally as annoyed at having to stay behind and keep an eye on these humans whilst their companions readied for battle.

"And don't forget, these lot won't let you go either," she whispered to him.

They were standing on the same ridge as Teoma and her army, except they were much further north, far from any action. Despite their distance from the two armies, they had a near perfect view of what was going on. They'd watched the exchange between the leaders, noting the human that the Pale Wolf had left behind, concluding that it must have been Fin.

"If what he's told me is true," Herleif had said, "Then he is in more danger with them, than he ever was here."

Kiakra hadn't known what to say.

Now everything was still. As if the sky itself had turned its eyes down to watch what was to come.

Gradually a drum began to sound from the ranks of the Pale Wolf. It was quiet at first, but grew steadily in volume, more joining its call until it became so loud that the earth seemed to shake. Yells began to rise up with the drums, a great wall of screams and whoops, unintelligible at this distance, but no less fierce because of it.

Suddenly Kiakra felt just as worried about Fin as Herleif was.

She placed a hand gently on his shoulder. He was solid, so taught with stress that Kiakra feared he would snap.

The drums continued to sound.

"We can't go out there, but you've told me he's clever. He'll be okay." She spoke softly, more hope than belief.

For a while he said nothing. Then gradually he relaxed. His shoulders lowered, and he nodded his head solidly. Worry seemed replaced by determination.

"Yes, he will."

Kiakra wasn't sure how much he believed himself, but she hoped he was right.

***

The fear in the air was tangible.

When Fin had been paraded past the ranks of soldiers there had been that childish confidence, the sort borne of ignorance. They had sung and jeered, some spitting at him as he was led past on his horse to the middle of the formation, where the higher ranked officers were waiting. Even they had been watching him smugly, eager to witness his execution as soon as their victory had been secured.

Once the drums had started that confidence had evaporated like mist.

The men went silent. The Rukland cavalry began to grow restless, horses neighing and bucking on either side of the infantry, as if they too knew that this was not a battle to be won. Even the sergeants who had been yelling orders, all rough, experienced men, were now less enthused than they had been.

Fin needed to be quick if any measure of peace could be salvaged, and he'd begun to cut through his bonds as soon as he'd come to a stop. There were two Yilland veterans beside him acting as guards, but their concentration was consumed by the drums, and neither noticed him straining at the ropes behind his back. And anyway, he only needed to get to Alvard.

"Look there," one of the guards said quietly, gesturing with a nod to his companion.

Fin froze, but the man had been referring to a line figures coming up onto the ridge. This was their first look at the enemy.

"How many are there?" the other one said. He was a big man, but he was fidgety, hands playing with the leather wrapped around the hilt of his sword.

Egil spun around on his horse from in front of them, he was a line forward but not deaf.

"No more than we can handle," he said confidently, "So shut it."

Luckily only the Captain was close, Gulbrand had moved to the back of the army to oversee the action. And, Fin imagined, so that he could retreat quickly when they were overrun.

Fin continued cutting through his bonds, trying desperately to ignore the figures coming into view over the ridge, more showing themselves every second from a line that was three times the length of the one Fin was in.

Come on.

The rope was thick and fibrous, and cutting through it was far from easy. He was freezing cold but sweating from the stress. At one point he almost dropped his little flint stone and had to stifle a cry by biting his lip.

"Cavalry, spread out!" Alvard yelled from some place up ahead, only just audible over the sounds of drums. Fin couldn't quite see him, but from that shout he had a good idea where he would be.

Alvard's order was repeated by several officers, and the cavalry slowly began to spread out, probably in an effort to try and combat the much wider line of warriors that Teoma had set up. But it was clear to see that even if they had spread out so that they were in a line only one man deep, they would still be engulfed by her force. Akalens covered the ridge opposite them, and on the higher ground they seemed to loom over Gulbrands army like a cat over a mouse.

The drums continued to sound.

Still more warriors poured over the ridge ahead of them, spreading out across the landscape. Now Fin could see heads turning from within the lines of infantry around him, men looking behind them at their own ranks. They were beginning to realise that they didn't stand a chance. But they were penned in by their own comrades.

Abruptly the rope holding Fin's wrists together gave way.

He took a shaky breath, still holding them together behind his back. Speed would be of massive importance, but he had to pick his time. If he moved to try and get to Alvard now, he would be recaptured and retied immediately.

Ahead, Teoma's warriors continued to move forward, making their way down the hill.

You're running out of time.

Suddenly the drums stopped, and there was a piercing scream.

The signal to attack.

All the Akalens took up the cry, loud enough to make him flinch, and then there was the thunder of horses charging. Thousands of warriors kicked their horses together, churning up the earth behind them, choking the sky with dust as they began to tear down the ridge toward Gulbrands army.

They'd begun the charge.

Fin saw a couple of soldiers turn, only to be grabbed by their friends or officers and shoved back into line, and it was then that he made his move.

He slipped off his horse, losing all sight of the approaching horde as he did. The guards either side of him were late to react and could only shout after him as he pushed his way through groups of soldiers whose last concern was a thin, pale boy running through their ranks.

Fin heard Captain Egil shout from behind him, but most of the men were deaf to his orders, and the rest couldn't hear what he was saying over the sound of thousands of horses tearing apart the earth underfoot.

There is still time to retreat.

Fin kept repeating it in his head, over and over.

One man tried to grab him, but he twisted away easily, continuing on to where he had heard Alvard yelling his orders from. He pushed through another line of men, and finally saw him.

The Lord of Rukland looked like he was born to be on the battleifield. He was still yelling orders, his sword drawn and raised in an attempt to rally the men around him. It obviously worked, because it was only here that Fin was finally stopped, by a couple of soldiers only a few years older than himself. They grabbed his arms with heavy hands, and Fin's struggling amounted to nothing in their strong grip.

"My Lord!" Fin yelled, and by some miracle Alvard heard him.

The man turned, cutting a gap through the lines of men around him with his horse, and making toward Fin with look of severe concern.

"Let him go," he shouted at the two men holding Fin's arms, and they did so immediately, stepping quickly back into the safety of their line.

"You shouldn't be here!" he bellowed over the roar of the approaching enemy, as though it was merely an inconvenience. But the fact he hadn't immediately ordered Fin killed spoke volumes. He was curious, and Fin could see it on his face.

Maybe there was still a chance.

"My Lord!" Fin repeated, yelling at the top of his lungs, "Retreat, I beg of you! Gulbrand wants this. If your forces are destroyed today, then he can start a war! He was the one who ordered your son killed, I saw it! I was there!"

Fin rushed the words out as fast as he could, his throat sore from shouting so loud.

There's still time.

Alvard glanced behind him and then back at Fin, saying nothing, but the look on his face showed that he had lost his conviction.

Fin pointed behind him, "He's at the back of the army because he knows you'll be destroyed! Why would I lie?"

Alvard stared at the back of the army, maybe he could see Gulbrand from there.

There's still time.

Fin shouted once more, "Please! It has to be now!"

Alvard nodded once, curtly, and then sat up straight and opened his mouth.

"Cavalry! Cover the infantry! Cover our retre-"

An arrow ripped through his throat, catching him just above his mail. He coughed once, and a hand grasped at his throat. Then slowly, he slipped from his horse, crumpling onto the ground where he lay still, eyes wide with shock.

Fin stood still, stunned, staring at the Lord's lifeless body as arrows poured down around him.

That had been his last chance.

More arrows rained down, thudding mostly into the shields of the soldiers around him, who were huddled together in an attempt to weather the storm.

When the arrows finally stopped, somehow Fin was still standing unhurt. He'd done better than Alvard's horse, which was lying lifeless next to its master.

A yell from up front brought him out of his trance.

The charge had finally arrived.

Chapter 32

The Akalens crashed into the front lines like a river of death, splitting their formation apart like an axe splitting flesh. Soldiers were cut down in droves, skewered on spears or bludgeoned by heavy clubs of blustone. Horses fell and were trampled, but did little to hold back the weight of the warriors that followed. Men disappeared under the sheer bulk of the Akalen Warband, broken down by the crush of flesh and bone that ripped through their formation, their momentum seemingly endless.

Fin couldn't move. There was nothing left for him to do, except watch the slaughter.

I failed.

The sound of battle was everywhere, inescapable and huge. It was the sound of bone cracking, shields splitting, steel scraping against rock. Screams filled the air, both sides taking casualties as more fell every second.

And at the head of it all was the Pale Wolf.

Teoma moved even better than Fin had imagined. Having leaped from her horse she was now using her spear with the precision of quill, dancing between her enemies like fire, and so fast that her opponents looked as though they were fighting in mud. They shrank from her, some even running, but again, and again they fell to her spear.

When she fought, battle was made an art.

Fin was frozen to the spot. He was a several lines back from the front, but the action was getting closer with every passing moment. The soldiers around him were shifting uncomfortably, all confidence lost and ready to do whatever it took to stay away from the approaching enemy.

Fin was mesmerised by the fighting, but there was one dominant though in his head.

You failed.

Someone grabbed him.

He turned to see the Captain. Egil had a wound on his cheek, a deep messy cut probably caused by an arrow, and his face drooped to that side, oozing blood.

Suddenly energy surged back into his bones and Fin could move again. He kicked Egil as hard as he could in the knee, pulling away and running through the soldiers.

Don't die, stay alive.

Arrows began to fall again, and he could see riders out on the flanks fighting for their lives. The men of Rukland were doing better than the infantry, holding back the enemy and managing to keep up with the fast pace of the Akalens. But they were still impossibly outnumbered. Fin knew they couldn't keep up their work for long. He had to keep moving to stay alive. He had to get out of this crush.

A hand swiped at his shoulder and Fin turned again to see Egil pursuing him, seemingly not caring about the battle as he pushed his soldiers aside. His attention was so focused on Fin that he didn't notice the state of his men, and what effect his wild pursuit was having on them. They had looked nervous. Now they were terrified, and as Egil ran past, some were turning and pushing their way out of line.

Already they were beginning to route.

Fin ducked between two men, and then was knocked over by a smaller boy, even younger than him by the looks of it, who had dropped his gear completely and was sprinting through the formation, horror, and blood, plastered across his face. Fin tried to scramble up from the ground, but he was knocked over again by more men running from the front. The dribble of despair had become a flood. The battle had barely begun but already it was lost, Gulbrands army was fleeing.

He finally managed to get to his feet when the Captain barrelled into him.

Fin struggled to get away again but this time Egil was not letting go.

"You almost ruined everything," he yelled over the battle. The drums had begun to sound again, a great ominous booming that threatened total destruction.

Fin hit the Captain in the face with all the strength he could muster, aiming right for the open wound on his cheek. As Fin's fist smashed into the exposed flesh, Egil roared in pain and threw Fin to the ground.

He hit the earth so hard that his vision blurred. He couldn't hear. Shapes swam past him, becoming soldiers as his sight returned, their panicked yells once again audible. They were running from the enemy, and the Akalens were cutting them down as they fled.

Over Fin stood Egil, the real enemy. His sword was drawn, held lazily in his right hand. Fin shifted up onto his elbows but Egil flattened him with a boot to the chest, putting his full weight on him, crushing the air from his lungs.

"We've won," he said, and somehow Fin could hear him, even though he spoke so quietly. A smile flickered across the Captains face, and he pressed his sword gently against Fin's throat.

Fin closed his eyes, and silence took him.

***

There was nothing now, the battle was gone, the screams had stopped.

He moved, without substance or restraint, searching for something. He realised he wasn't actually alone, there were things all around him, burrowing through the dirt, drifting in the currents of the sky, waiting deep below the earth, unmoving but full of power. He could feel the beings around him, full of pain and fear, covering the ground in every place he could see. The souls of the warriors from both sides.

He reached out to one, and it buzzed and hissed, warning him away before he touched it. Another spirit of a great mountain below the earth he tried to touch, but that also forced him back, burning the edge of his being. Silently he asked why they would not accept him. He had tried so many times before, but now he needed them more than ever.

There was no answer, so he reached out a final time, now looking skyward. It was vast and unending, a pool of power so great that it scared him.

Surely, he could not draw his power from there, the spirit of the sky?

It hummed deeply, and in that song was a warning like the others. But this being was so vast he understood the undertones. It did not keep him away out of hate, but of respect. It challenged him to look inward, and so he did, retreating into the depths of his being.

Down he went, until he could see nothing but himself. Darkness enveloped him, until it became light, and there he found the well of power that was his own soul.

***

Suddenly the world was shaking, screaming, louder than anything he had ever heard.

Fin opened his eyes.

Egil was still poised above him, still looking down, but now his face was full of terror.

Fin rose, brushing away the Captain's boot like it was a feather. The man stumbled back but still Fin rose, until he was level with him, staring into bloodshot desperate eyes.

Power rippled through Fin's body. He felt immense.

He struck the Captain once, with a heavy hand of daggers, and once was all it took.

Egils body was thrown backwards by the force of Fins strike, armour melting away against the power in Fin's claws. He was dead long before he hit the ground, and when he did he lay motionless in a crumpled mess of split mail and ragged cloth. He smelt of old sweat and rot, so strong it forced Fin to look away.

Behind him the Akalens were still coming forward. Fin needed them to stop, but he didn't know how to get their attention.

A yell was formed in his chest, a final desperate cry, but instead it turned to a roar in his throat.

Slowly, the screams began to fade. The pounding of hooves slowed. The battlefield became quiet.

Fin turned his now massive head, and saw the Pale Wolf watching him.

Her eyes were calm, levelled at his own. Behind her the wall of warriors had stopped their advance, nervously waiting for their leader as the few Yilland soldiers still tangled in the melee took the time to flee. Teoma's hand was held high, the message clear.

Stop.

Such power she had, to stop an entire army with the smallest gesture. Fin envied her, but why now? He swung his head around to look behind him and saw the bulk of Gulbrand's forces fleeing across the plains, bloodied, but mostly intact.

He looked back at the Pale Wolf.

Why had she halted her advance? Her forces had been unstoppable. Was it only for his benefit?

She walked toward him, graceful as always, so controlled that her headdress barely moved. As she drew closer he realised that she did not look down on him as she had once done, instead her long neck was tall, her eyes forward to meet his own.

She stood before him and raised her hand, touching his face gently. He recoiled at the motion, and she flinched slightly, before resting her hand on his face. It felt hot and light.

Fin tried to speak, but words did not come to him. His heavy breath was for fuelling power, not for talking.

"Khutaen," she breathed.

Fin cocked his head, and then looked down at the fine feathers, covering the thick limbs where his arms had been. He flexed his hands into the earth, finding that his fingers were gone, replaced by tough skin and claws.

How?

An eagle screamed overhead. Fin knew those ragged wings, and knew that it was no ordinary eagle. And then the Pale Wolf spoke again, so softly that human ears would not have been able to hear.

"I should have listened."

Chapter 33

Ojak watched Gulbrand yelling at his troops, trying to convince them to turn around.

But he knew they wouldn't.

The gates had opened, they had seen their enemy, and they had been far more powerful than any of them. None were stupid enough, or loyal enough to face death for him. Even the men of Rukland had turned around once they had seen their Lord was dead. Their second in command, a young general named Yagrit, had taken over, and was likely taking them back to Rukland. He had no allegiance to Gulbrand, and would send a report to Olvaldr about the battle.

After the Khutaen had appeared the enemy backed off, leaving the army to flee without harassment. Ojak didn't understand what had happened, and he was still wary of a follow up, but for the moment he was just grateful that the Akalens had ceased. He didn't think there would have been an army left had the Akalens decided to pursue them.

Gulbrand was still shouting at the men, riding around desperately going from one patch of men to the other. His words fell on deaf ears though, even the officers were done.

Ojak wondered for the final time why he had made the decision to ride out against the Pale Wolf, despite being heavily outnumbered, and with such green men.

"When we come back here you will curse yourselves for fleeing! Deserters will hang!" Gulbrand yelled, trying to hold on to a measure of authority.

Ojak shook his head.

They would not be returning, and certainly not under the leadership of the man who had been so soundly beaten. He'd proven his incompetence, and the Akalens had, strangely, demonstrated mercy. There was neither the reason, nor the will to return here, and Gulbrand must surely know it.

Ojak watched him for a few moments longer, then kicked his horse on, following the troops that were streaming back into the west.

***

"Perhaps it was best that you stopped us little Khutaen," Teoma said, as she walked alongside Fin.

The rest of her Warband was busy collecting their own dead, of which there were relatively few, and building pyres of dried grass on which to burn them. Many were already wrapped in blankets of turquoise and gold, ready to be burned.

"Gulbrand will leave you alone now," Fin said solemnly, for he was back in the form of a scrawny young boy, and once again had the power of speech. "I'm sure of it."

"I think you are right," Teoma said, her voice reserved still as she placed a hand on his shoulder. It felt heavier now that he was a boy.

"And I hope we never meet as enemies," she said, with a smile, and enough edge in her voice that Fin knew she was serious. After seeing her in battle he wasn't sure who would be more hesitant to fight.

He nodded, "Me too."

She jumped up onto her horse, "I must go and speak with my chieftains, but tonight we will celebrate the dead. Join us little Khutaen, but your friend is *not* invited," she said sternly, before riding away.

My friend?

Abruptly there was a rush of wings and the old woman was beside him, standing in her tattered old shawl with a grin on her face, "Well done."

Fin smiled broadly and went to give the old woman a hug, "Gatty, its good to see you."

She recoiled, holding him at arm's length, "Get away from me lad, you stink."

Fin hesitated, a little offended, but Gatty seemed to sense that and backtrack.

"The day is won, you should be pleased," she said, smiling at Fin as she began to walk alongside him. The bodies that littered the field behind them made that hard to accept, but he reasoned that there were a lot fewer dead than there could have been.

"I suppose it is," he muttered.

Fin stopped, changing the subject, "What was that? Why did I not become one of the creatures of the Recast? And why didn't you tell me how to draw on my power, you said you knew my power?" He was ready for an argument then, if he'd known to draw power from his own spirit then he could have done so a long time ago, and potentially avoided many poor situations.

Gatty scowled, sensing his mood change, "I think perhaps you had an encounter with a Drakin, one that you didn't tell me about?"

He blushed, bright pink, "A while back yes."

Gatty nodded slowly, "Hmm, well, I think that would have been helpful to know."

"Do you kno-"

She interrupted him with a cuff to the back of the head, "Stupid boy! Taking that tone with me, its your own damn fault I didn't know sooner!"

Fin nodded quickly, "Yes, I'm sorry, but, what was the reason?"

Gatty pulled her pipe from her shawl as she had done so many times before. It was comforting to Fin, she didn't look right without her pipe.

"Best I can tell, I think that is what happens when a Drakin gives The Sight to a Recast, it alters your power. I didn't tell you because... I didn't know how you could access it, it's not something I've ever done. We'll do some research together soon, get you fully in control." She lit her pipe then, taking a deep pull as her eyes dulled in satisfaction. Fin stifled a laugh, forgetting she was not all knowing.

As she blew smoke in his face, he gave a wistful look over to the west, "Why would it give me The Sight? And I suppose now I can only become a Khutaen. He was a little sad he wouldn't ever be able to fly.

"Ah," Gatty said, her eyes lighting back up, "I think actually the Drakin has four stages, like the Recast."

Fin turned his head to her, and her little grey eyes were bright.

"As for why it chose you," Gatty said, gesturing upward to the sky, "Everyone is happy. Teoma has her victory, her people have their justice, and Gulbrand has lost the trust of his people."

She paused, "You did well boy."

***

Kiakra had been given permission to leave by Tiko, and now she watched Rat as he packed up his things, putting them onto his deer whilst around him the camp bustled with energy at their victory. He had only a few possessions, and they fit onto the small saddlebags, which were the only ones the creature could carry.

He'd understandably avoided them since taking Herleif to Dagtok, only engaging with them to offer his knowledge on healing for Fin, which was more limited than Cyphers, but better than Kiakra's by far. She'd hated him for a few days, but there was some reason to what he'd done.

"You will go home now?" Kiakra said, hoping somehow that he wouldn't. He'd also been waiting on Teoma's permission to leave the camp.

Rat turned to her, his leathery face showing little emotion as he walked forward and placed a bag of Olvirs in her hand, "These are for you and the lad, tell him I am sorry for what I did."

Kiakra gave him a quizzical look, "How are you going to get back into your empire without your money?"

"I'm not," he said. "But I can't stay with you after my actions, and I wouldn't enjoy going home, knowing I had done such things to get there."

Another friend lost, her last one.

No.

Kiakra stepped forward and grabbed him, "We've both made mistakes, there's no need to punish yourself any more."

Rat's shoulders went stiff and he looked down, "I can't..." his voice trailed off.

Kiakra squeezed his shoulder, "I was the one who betrayed that boy, I was the one that drove Cypher and Aldrid away, not you. None of that was you," she said, handing the money back to him. "Take your coin and *go home.*"

She smiled at him then, a pleading expression.

The Kaz man put his own hand over one of hers, on top of his shoulder, "I will not let this be the way I get myself home. I love my empire, but when I get there, I want to live without regret and shame gnawing at my back."

Kiakra's face dropped, and her hands fell from his shoulders.

Rat smiled then, his mischievous grin, "Let me help you find Cypher."

***

Herleif stared at the boy he had known as his brother.

He looked similar to Fin, but he was changed, and it wasn't just the weight he had lost. He had returned with a strange glint in his eye, and bigger somehow, not physically, but perhaps his confidence had grown. He stood straighter, his eyes didn't dart about quite so much as they had used to. The Akalens had certainly sensed it as well, for he had returned walking alongside the Pale Wolf herself, and she seemed to speak with him as her equal.

He had done more than just survive that battle, he had grown in it. Herleif felt a twinge of guilt for worrying so much for him.

"I need to go and speak to him," Herleif said to the Weasel Pack.

Kiakra and Rat were waiting some way off from where Fin was, holding the reigns to their animals. He'd spoken with Rat too, and whilst it would take a little while for him to forgive the man fully, the Kaz had given back the coin he'd taken for Herleif.

"He's welcome to join us, let him know that much," Rat said, patting Herleif on the shoulder awkwardly and gesturing to Fin.

Kiakra nodded, "Need to get our numbers back up."

She was fidgety, eager to head off and begin tracking down Cypher. Truthfully, Herleif was too.

He nodded to them and walked over to his brother.

Fin was dressed and warmed up again, and Herleif approached him at a quick pace.

He was sat up on the ridge where Teoma had been before the battle, but now he was looking east. The sky was deep blue, and a gentle wind was playing with Fins sleeve.

"How are you feeling?" Herleif tried, sitting down next to his brother and looking out at the sky with him.

"I don't really know," Fin said. "I showed my face at Teoma's celebrations, but I didn't stay."

He had more to say but was hesitant.

"Go on," Herleif said gently.

Fin sighed, looking away from the sky and at Herleif. His eyes seemed different too, they were darker, had seen more.

"I know you went to a lot of effort to find me, and I am truly grateful to you for getting me away from Dagtok. But…" he paused, searching for the right words, and not quite finding them.

Herleif knew what he was trying to say.

"It's funny, I spent so long trying to find you, and now that I have, it seems you don't really need me any more," he said smiling. Fin began to speak but Herleif cut him off, "I'm proud of you, and you'll always be welcome at my side, but I understand if that's not what you want," he smiled again, warmly.

His brother looked at him, "Thank you. I will remember that, I'll see you again, but for now there are… other things I need to do."

"What will you do?" Herleif said.

Fin sighed and ran a hand through his prickly hair, which had only just begun to grow back, "Gatty, the woman who helped me, she wants to help me master my different states. Once I'm better at controlling myself she wants to clear out Yilland of the Demons that Captain Egil caused with his raids, and then maybe the both of us will try and clear up the Outskirts…"

Herleif had wide eyes, "You have grown," he said.

Fin ignored the compliment and glanced at Kiakra and Rat, who were still a way off waiting, "What about you?"

Herleif laughed, "Nothing nearly as impressive as ridding the world of Demons. But I have a debt to pay Kiakra, and I need to help her find a friend."

"They look eager to go," said Fin, and suddenly there were tears in his eyes.

Herleif nodded, "I think they are."

He grabbed his brother and pulled him into a hug. It was long, but neither were hesitant to separate. When they did finally break the embrace Fin's tears were gone, and he was smiling too.

Herleif stood slowly, gave his brother a nudge, and walked away.

The End

Printed in Great Britain
by Amazon

24380333R00223